In t

MAUREEN CHILD
KATHERINE GARBERA
BARBARA DUNLOP

MILLS
BOON

Published in Great Britain 2015
by Mills & Boon, an imprint of Harlequin (UK) Limited,
Eton House, 18-24 Paradise Road, Richmond, Surrey, TW9 1SR

IN THE TYCOON'S BED © 2015 Harlequin Books S. A.

One Night, Two Heirs, The Rebel Tycoon Returns, An After-Hours Affair were first published in Great Britain by Harlequin (UK) Limited.

One Night, Two Heirs © 2011 Harlequin Books S. A.
The Rebel Tycoon Returns © 2011 Harlequin Books S. A.
An After-Hours Affair © 2011 Harlequin Books S. A.

Special thanks and acknowledgement to Maureen Child and Barbara Dunlop for their contributions to The Millionaire's Club series.

ISBN: 978-0-263-25238-5

05-1115

Harlequin (UK) Limited's policy is to use papers that are natural, renewable and recyclable products and made from wood grown in sustainable forests. The logging and manufacturing processes conform to the legal environmental regulations of the country of origin.

Printed and bound in Spain
by CPI, Barcelona

ONE NIGHT, TWO HEIRS

BY
MAUREEN CHILD

Maureen Child is a California native who loves to travel. Every chance they get, she and her husband are taking off on another research trip. The author of more than sixty books, Maureen loves a happy ending and still swears that she has the best job in the world. She lives in Southern California with her husband, two children and a golden retriever with delusions of grandeur. Visit Maureen's website at www.maureenchild.com.

To Charles Griemsman, a world class editor.
Thanks for making working on this continuity such a
pleasure, Charles!

One

Marine First Sergeant Rick Pruitt had thirty days' leave to decide the rest of his life.

"But no pressure," he muttered and loped across Main Street. He lifted a hand to wave at Joe Davis. His boyhood buddy was still driving that battered, dusty red truck. Rick paused on the sidewalk when his friend pulled to the curb to talk to him. Joe rolled the passenger-side window down and grinned. "Look what the east Texas wind blew home. When'd you get here, Rick?"

"Yesterday." Rick tipped the brim of his hat back a bit, leaned his forearms on the window frame and only winced a little at the red-hot feel of the metal against his arms. If there was one thing a Texas boy learned to deal with at an early age, it was the summer heat.

Right now, the sun was blazing down from a brassy sky and there wasn't so much as a hint of a cloud in sight. July in Texas was good training, weather wise, for a marine who spent his time deployed to the Middle East.

"You home to stay?" Joe asked.

"That's a good question," Rick replied.

"And not much of an answer."

Truth was, Rick didn't have an answer yet. He had spent a lot of years in the Corps and he had enjoyed them all. He loved serving his country. He was damn proud to wear the uniform of a U.S. Marine. But, he thought, glancing at his surroundings, he'd missed a hell of a lot, too. He hadn't been here when either of his parents died. Hadn't been around to run the family ranch, instead trusting in their longtime foreman to do the heavy lifting. And, since the Pruitt ranch was one of the biggest in Texas, that was some serious duty to push off on someone else.

Funny, all those years in the Corps and not one of his buddies had ever known that he was one of the richest men in Texas. He had always been just another marine—and that's how he had wanted it.

He'd been around the world and back. Had seen more, done more than most men ever would. But, he thought, his heart had always been here. In Royal.

Rick smiled and shrugged. "It's the only answer I've got. For right now, I've got thirty days' leave and decisions to make."

"Well," Joe told him, "if you want any help deciding, you give me a call."

"I will." Rick looked at his old friend. They'd grown up together, had their first beers—and hangovers—together. They'd played side by side on the high school football team. Joe had stayed put in Royal, married Tina, his high school sweetheart, had two kids now and was in charge of the family garage. Rick had gone to college, joined the Corps and had come close to love only once.

For a second or two, he allowed himself to remember the girl he'd once thought unattainable. The woman whose memory had kept him going through some ugly days in the last few years. There were some women, he figured, just designed to get into a man's soul. And this one surely had.

"While you're in town, we should do some fishing," Joe said, drawing Rick up out of his thoughts.

Grateful, he said, "Sounds like a plan. You get Tina to make us some of her famous fried chicken for lunch and we'll make a day of it at the ranch lake."

"That's a deal." Joe stretched out his right hand. "It really is good to see you home, Rick. And if you want my opinion, maybe it's time you stayed home."

"Thanks, Joe." Rick shook his friend's hand and blew out a breath. "It's good to be back."

Nodding, Joe said, "I've got to get back to the shop. Mrs. Donley's old sedan had another breakdown and that woman hasn't let up on me for days about it."

Rick actually shivered. Mrs. Marianne Donley, the high school math teacher, could bring a cold chill to the spine of anybody in Royal who had survived her geometry class.

Joe saw the shudder and nodded grimly. "Exactly. I'll call you about the fishing."

"Do that." Rick slapped his hands against the truck, then stepped back as Joe pulled away.

He stood there for a long minute, just soaking up the feeling of being home again. Only three days ago, he'd been with his men in the middle of a firefight. Today, he was on a street corner of a quiet little town, watching traffic roll by.

And he wasn't sure which of those two places he most belonged.

Rick had always wanted to be a marine. And the truth was, since his parents were both gone now, there wasn't much to hold him in Royal. Yeah, there was the duty he felt to the Pruitt dynasty. The ranch had been in the family for more than a hundred and fifty years. But there were caretakers out there, a foreman and his wife, the housekeeper who lived in and saw to it that the Pruitt ranch went on without him. Just as Royal had.

He narrowed his gaze to cut the glare of the summer sun and quickly scanned his surroundings. Things didn't change in small-town America, he told himself and was inwardly glad of it. He liked knowing that he could go away for a couple years and come home to find the place just as he'd left it.

The only thing that had changed, he admitted silently, was him.

Tugging the brim of his Stetson lower over his eyes, Rick shook his head and turned back toward the Texas Cattleman's Club. If there was one place for a man to go to catch up on the news about town, it was the TCC. Besides, he was looking forward to the cool quiet. The chance to do a little thinking—not to mention the appeal of a cold glass of beer and a steak sandwich in the dining room.

"Bradford Price, you're living in the Stone Age." Sadie Price glared up at her older brother and wasn't the slightest bit surprised to notice he wasn't denying her accusation. In fact, he looked proud.

"If that's your roundabout way of telling me that I'm a man of tradition, then I'm all right with that." Brad leaned down and kept his voice low. "And I don't appreciate my baby sister coming in here to read me the riot act because I don't agree with her."

Sadie silently counted to ten. Then twenty. Then she gave up. Her temper wouldn't be cooled by counting, or the multiplication tables or even with thoughts of her twin daughters' smiling faces. She had been pushed too far and, like a true Price, she was fighting mad.

The main room of the Texas Cattleman's Club might not have been the perfect spot for a throw-down, she thought, but it was too late to back off now. Even if she had wanted to.

"I didn't move back to Royal from Houston just to sit at home and do nothing, Brad."

In fact, now that she was home again, she intended to make a name for herself. To get involved. And the TCC was just the place to make a start. She had been thinking about this all night and the fact that her older brother was making things hard on her wouldn't change her mind.

"Fine," he said, throwing both hands high. "Do something. Anything. Just not here."

"Women are a part of the club's world now, Brad," she insisted, glancing over at the two elderly men sitting in brown leather club chairs. At her quick look, they both lifted the newspapers they were hiding behind and pretended they hadn't been watching.

Typical, Sadie thought. The men in this once-exclusive club were determined to ignore progress of any kind. Heck, they'd had to be hog-tied to get them to allow women in the club at all. And they still weren't happy about it.

"You don't need to remind me of that," Brad said tightly. "Haven't I got Abigail Langley riding me like a bull in the rodeo? That woman's about to drive me out of my mind and I'm damned if I'm going to take it from you, too."

She hissed in a breath. "You are the most hardheaded, ornery…"

"I'm going to be in charge around here, little sister," he told her. "And you'd best remember that."

Here being the Texas Cattleman's Club, of course. Brad was planning on running for club president and if he won, Sadie knew darn well that the TCC would stay in the dark ages.

Sadie bit down on her bottom lip to keep the furious words that wanted to spill from her locked inside. Honestly, the TCC had been the bulwark of stubborn men for more than a hundred years.

Even the decor in the place reeked of testosterone. Paneled walls, dark brown leather furniture, hunting prints on the walls and a big-screen TV, the better to watch every single Texas sporting event. Until recently, women had only been allowed in the dining room or on the tennis courts. But now, thanks to Abby Langley being an honorary member—with full club privileges—due to her late husband Richard's name and history with the club, all of that was changing. And the women in Royal were counting on the fact that now that Pandora's box had been opened, the men in town wouldn't be able to close it again.

But if dealing with her brother was a sign of how difficult change was going to be, Sadie knew she and the other females in town were in for a whale of a fight.

"Look," she said, trying for her most reasonable tone—which wasn't easy when faced with a head as hard as her brother's—"the club is looking to build a new headquarters. I'm a landscape designer. I can help.

I've got the name of a great architect. And I did some sketches for the new grounds that—"

"Sadie..." Brad sighed and shook his head. "Nothing's been decided. We don't need an architect. Or a landscape designer. Or a damn interior decorator."

"You could at least listen to me," she argued.

"I may have to put up with Abby Langley giving me grief, but I don't have to listen to my baby sister," Brad said. "Now go on home, Sadie."

He walked away.

Just turned his back and walked off as if she didn't matter at all. Fuming silently, Sadie thought briefly about chasing him down and giving him another piece of her mind. But that would only give the old coots like Buck Johnson and Henry Tate even more to gossip about.

Her gaze shifted to those two men, still hiding behind their newspapers as if they were completely oblivious to what was going on. Well, Sadie knew better. Those two had heard every word of her argument with her brother and by tonight, she expected that they would have repeated it dozens of times. And men said *women* were gossips.

Grumbling under her breath, she tucked her cream-colored leather bag beneath her arm, got a hard grip on the folder of sketches she'd brought along with her and stormed for the front door. The sound of her needle-thin heels clicked against the wood floor like a frantic heartbeat.

Disappointment and anger warred inside her. She'd really hoped that she would be able to at least count on her brother's support. But she should have known better. Brad was like a throwback to an earlier generation. He liked his women to be pretty pieces of arm candy and he liked the club just as it was—a male bastion against the ever-encroaching idea of equality of the sexes.

"He's a caveman," Sadie muttered, rushing out of the dark interior of the club into the bright sunlight of a July morning in Texas.

She was still running on pure temper and her eyes were so dazzled by the brilliant light, she didn't see the man until she crashed right into him.

One day back in his hometown and Rick Pruitt ran smack into a tornado. A tall, sleek, blond tornado with eyes as blue as the Texas sky and legs that went on forever. He'd been thinking about her only a minute or two before and now here she was. She stormed out of the Texas Cattleman's Club in such a fury, she'd run right into him only to bounce off like a pebble skipping across the surface of a lake.

He reached out to grab her shoulders and steady her. Then she lifted those big blue eyes up to him and the look on her face said clearly that he was the last person on earth she had expected to see.

"Mornin', Sadie," he said softly, letting his gaze sweep over the patrician features he remembered so well. "If you're really looking to run me over, you should maybe try it in a car. You're not nearly big enough to do it on foot."

She blinked at him. Her face paled and her eyes were wide and shining with shock. "Rick? What are you doing here?"

A long, humming second or two passed between them and that was all it took to get Rick's blood rushing and his body tightening. But Sadie swayed unsteadily.

"Hey," he asked. "Are you okay?"

"Fine," she murmured, though she didn't look it. "I'm

just surprised to see you, that's all. I didn't know you were home."

"Only arrived yesterday," he told her. "Guess the town gossip chain needs a little time to get up and running."

"I suppose so."

Her cheeks got even paler and she looked uneasy. Rick wondered why.

She shook her head. "I'm sorry about running into you. Coming out of the gloom of that man-cave into the bright daylight, I couldn't see and I was just so darn mad at Brad.…"

Good to know, he told himself. He'd much rather she be furious with her brother than him. The one night they'd spent together had been haunting him for three long years. He'd spent a lot of time in the desert, remembering her taste, her touch. She was the kind of woman who slipped up on a man. Got under his defenses. Which was why he'd been glad to be leaving for his tour of duty right after their night together. He hadn't been looking for permanent back then, and Sadie Price was not the kind of woman to settle for a one-night stand.

He took a breath, inhaling her scent—that soft swirl of summer rain and flowers that always seemed to cling to her skin. That scent had stayed with him while he was deployed. And it didn't seem to matter where he was stationed or the misery that surrounded him…if he closed his eyes, she was there.

Thoughts of her had pulled him through some dark times. Looking down into her blue eyes, he could only think, *Damn, it's good to be home*.

"How about you?" he asked. "Last I heard you were living in Houston." Which was why he'd planned to drive into the city to look her up in a day or two. Much handier this way—having her right here in Royal.

"I was," she said and chewed at her bottom lip. Her gaze shifted from him. "I, um, moved back a few weeks ago."

"You okay?" he asked, noticing just how nervous she really was. Shaken, really, and he didn't like how pale she was, either. In fact, she looked small and fragile and every protective instinct he had rose to the surface, temporarily, at least burying his physical reaction to her.

"You know what? Let's just go back inside and sit in the cool for a minute. You don't look too steady on your feet."

She shook her head and said, "Oh, I'm fine, really. I just…"

"You're not fine. You look like you're going to pass out. This heat'll kill you if you're not careful. Come on." He took her elbow in a firm grip and steered her right back into the clubhouse.

"Really, Rick. I don't need to rest, I just need to go home."

"And you can, as soon as you've cooled off a little." He drew her to the bench seat beneath the legendary plaque that read Leadership, Justice and Peace.

She took a breath and Rick watched her gather herself. Her fingers clutched at her purse until her knuckles whitened and he had to wonder what the hell had her so upset? Was it seeing him again? Was she embarrassed by the memory of their night together?

"What's going on, Sadie?" he whispered and shook his head as one of the club attendants stepped up to see if he could help.

She laughed shortly, but there was no humor in it. Her

gaze lifted to his and he read worry and trepidation in her eyes. Now he was really confused. "Just talk to me."

For most of his life, Sadie Price had been the dream girl for him. She was beautiful, popular and even as kids, out of his league. Rick ran with a crowd that didn't appreciate the country-club parties that Sadie and her friends attended. He'd always thought of her as pretty much perfect, except for the prim and proper attitude. He used to dream about getting past all of her barriers to find out who she really was.

Then he'd joined the Corps and Sadie married a rat bastard who'd ended up cheating on her and making her miserable. Three years ago though, Sadie had been divorced and Rick was about to ship out for Afghanistan when they ran into each other at Claire's restaurant. They'd shared a drink, then dinner...then a hell of a lot more.

Just remembering that night had his body stirring to life again with a kind of hunger he'd never known before. After three long years, she was close enough to touch again. And damned if he was going to waste any time.

"You're just as beautiful as I remember," he said, lifting one hand to smooth her silky blond hair back from her cheek. His fingertips skimmed along her skin and he felt a jolt of heat hit him hard.

She sucked in a breath of air at his touch and he smiled to know that she felt the same sizzle he had.

"You know, why don't we head over to Claire's?" He leaned in closer. "We could get some lunch and catch up. Tell me everything you've been up to the last few years."

"What I've been up to," she repeated, then huffed out

a sigh and looked up into his eyes. "That's going to take some time. Oh, God. Rick…we really have to talk."

"That's what I'm saying," he told her, a smile curving his mouth.

"No," she said, "I mean we have to *talk*." She looked around and seemed relieved that no one was close by before she turned back to him and added, "But not here."

"All right," he said, a little wary now. What the hell was going on with her? At first she'd just seemed shocked to see him. Now she was a little jumpy. Not exactly the welcome-home response he would have hoped for. "You want to tell me what this is all about?"

"Not really," she admitted.

"Sadie…"

She stood up, tucked her purse under her arm and said, "Just, take me to my parents' house, will you Rick? I'm staying with Dad until I get my own place. Once we're there, I'll explain everything."

Standing, he nodded. Whatever the hell was going on, Rick would deal with it as he did everything else in his life. Head-on. "Right. Then let's get going."

Two

Sitting in Rick Pruitt's black truck brought back a flood of memories. Three years ago, she and Rick had shared one amazingly hot, sexy night that had changed her life forever. The next morning he left, reporting for a tour of duty in the Middle East.

And maybe that was partly why Sadie had given into her impulse to grab at that one night with him. She had known he'd be leaving again right away. But the reality was, Sadie had just needed someone. Back then, she had felt as though she was disappearing. Becoming nothing more than the socialite daughter of a wealthy man. She never did anything for herself. Never stepped out of line from what was expected.

Until that night. Neither of them had made the other any promises. Neither of them had been looking for anything more than exactly what they had found together. A little magic.

But the truth was, that night with Rick had changed Sadie's life forever—and he had no idea.

She looked at him from the corner of her eye and felt a flutter low down in her belly. His square jaw, gorgeous mouth and deep brown eyes were enough to make her body tremble with a need she hadn't felt since that long-ago night. She remembered it all so well. The soft touches, the hungry sighs, the frantic whispers. She could almost feel his hands on her skin again. His hard-muscled body covering hers, his heavy thickness sliding deep inside—

"So," he asked companionably, "how've you been?"

Sadie jolted, called herself an idiot and forced a smile. She wasn't going to have the conversation they needed to have while riding through town in his truck, so she stalled. "Fine, really. No complaints. How about you?"

"You know," he said with a shrug, "I'm good. Nice to be home for a while though."

A while?

"How long are you home for?" she asked.

"Trying to get rid of me already?" He shot her another quick look and steered the truck down Main.

"No," she said and half expected her tongue to fall off due to that whopper. "I was just curious. You haven't been around much the last few years."

"And how would you know that? Weren't you living in Houston?"

"Houston isn't the moon, Rick," she said. "I talk to friends. My brother. They keep me up on hometown news."

"Me, too," he said. "Well, not your brother. He and I never really were friends."

"True," she said and silently added they were even

less likely to be friends now, though Rick didn't know it yet.

"Joe Davis told me when you moved out."

Sadie smiled and nodded. Joe and Rick had always been close. Not surprising that the town's best mechanic had kept Rick up to date on things. She was more glad than ever that she had left Royal when she had. If not, Joe would have told Rick her big secret and heaven knew what might have happened then.

"He, uh, also told me about Michael. I'm sorry."

A twinge of pain rattled through her heart at the mention of her late brother. Michael Price had led a troubled life. Somehow, he had never been able to find happiness, but he'd always looked for it in the bottom of a bottle. Eight months ago, he had been driving drunk and driven off a cliff road in California. She would always miss her brother, but Sadie hoped that he had at least found the peace he had been searching for.

She lifted her chin. "Thanks. It was hard. Losing him like that. But I was grateful that he hadn't killed anyone else in that wreck," she said simply.

"He was a good guy," Rick said softly.

"He was a good brother, too," Sadie said, smiling sadly. Her memories of Michael were mostly good ones and she clung to them.

"And," Rick said, changing the subject, "now you've left Houston to come home again. You're living with your dad?"

"Just temporarily," she said. "Until I find a place of my own. Ever since Mom died several years ago, Dad spends most of his time on fishing trips. He's in the Caribbean now, and Brad doesn't live there anymore, so…"

"You're not lonely in that big place all by yourself?"

She nearly laughed. "No. It's fair to say, I haven't been lonely in a long time."

Rick frowned. "What's his name?"

"His? Who his?"

"The guy you're seeing," he countered. "The I'm-too-busy-to-be-lonely guy."

Sadie snorted. "There's no guy. Too busy for one of those, too." She left it at that, not bothering to explain what he would find out for himself all too soon.

Silence stretched out between them, the only sounds the crunch of the wheels against the asphalt and the soft sighing of the truck's air conditioner. Outside, summer sun beat down on Royal, Texas, making even the trees seem to slump with fatigue.

"You know," he said finally, "I seem to remember you being a hell of a lot friendlier the last time I saw you."

Oh, boy. She remembered, too. In fact, her memory was so clear and so strong, it was all she could do not to squirm in her seat. A flush of heat spread through her body as images rushed through her mind. His body. Hers. Locked together. Desperate kisses, amazing sensations. Didn't seem to matter that she was already so nervous she could hardly swallow. In spite of everything, Sadie knew that if he reached over to touch her right now, she would probably go up in flames.

"You okay?" he asked from beside her and that deep voice of his seemed to roll across her skin.

Oh, she really was *not* okay.

"Sure," she lied. "Fine."

The familiar scenery raced past them as he left town behind and drove along the highway toward the Price family mansion in the exclusive development of Pine Valley. Three years ago, Sadie had walked away from the home where she grew up to live in Houston, losing herself in the hustle and the crowds. At the time, she had definitely needed to get away. To find a fresh start where no one really knew her. Where her private life wouldn't be fodder for local gossips.

Now though, she was back and the past was reaching out to grab her.

She looked at Rick again. Funny, she'd known him most of her life and yet hadn't connected with him at all until that one, memorable night. He'd changed, she thought. He looked older, more serious, more self-confident somehow. And that was saying something, since Rick had never been lacking in confidence.

His brown hair was trimmed military short, his brown eyes locked on the road in front of them. His hands were wrapped around the steering wheel and she watched as the muscles in his arms flexed.

"You sure you're okay?" Rick asked, glancing at her briefly before shifting his gaze back to the road.

That was Rick, she thought. He wasn't the kind to be distracted from what he saw as his duty—which at the moment, was driving. He appreciated rules and order and as far as she knew, always did the "right" thing, whatever that might be at the time.

There was simply no way he would ever accept *her* version of "right." This day wasn't going to end well, yet Sadie couldn't find a way out of it. Now that she was home in Royal, people were going to talk. And the fact that Rick had only been home for a day was probably the only reason he hadn't heard whispers already.

Well, she couldn't let him hear this news secondhand. She owed him the truth. At last.

"Yeah, I'm fine." *Just trapped like a rat,* she added silently. Oh, she had known that this day was going to arrive, sooner or later. She had just been hoping for later.

Much later. Which was ridiculous really, she argued with herself. She had moved back to Royal. She knew that, eventually, Rick would return. And keeping a secret in a small town was just impossible. Wasn't that one of the reasons she had left in the first place?

Frowning, she focused on the road and tried not to think about what would happen when they got to her family home.

"If you say so," he said, his tone telling her he wasn't convinced. "So. Since you're fine and I'm fine and we're not talking about anything else, why don't you tell me what you were doing at the TCC besides making your brother crazy?"

She blew out a disgusted breath at the mention of her brother. "Shoe was on the other foot, actually. Brad is the most stubborn, hardheaded man in the state of Texas."

"This is news to you?" he asked with a chuckle.

Brad Price had long had the reputation in town of being the most hidebound traditionalist in the known universe. His hard head only added to the fun.

"No," Sadie said, grateful to have a safe subject to talk to him about. "But I keep hoping that somehow, someday, Brad will wake up in the twenty-first century. Anyway, I went in to talk to him about being a part of designing the new clubhouse."

"There's going to be a new clubhouse?" Rick whistled, long and low. "Never would have believed that. The club's been the same for more than a hundred years."

Sadie rolled her eyes and shook her head. "So it should always stay the same? Why put in electric lights? Why aren't they still using oil lamps or candles? Why have a telephone? Is tradition so important that no one wants progress?"

"Whoa!" He laughed, then asked, "Is progress so important you just forget about tradition?"

She glared at him, those warm, sexy feelings she'd been experiencing only moments ago dissolving as surely as sugar in hot coffee. "You sound just like Brad. Is this a guy thing? Is it only women who are willing to look at the future?"

"No, but looking to the future doesn't mean forgetting the past."

"Who said anything about forgetting?" Sadie waved her hand in dismissal. "All we're talking about is an up-to-date, comfortable club that *every* member can enjoy."

"Now I know what this is about." He smiled and nodded sagely. "I heard Abby Langley's a member now. I suppose that's what's got the women in town up in arms?"

She just stared at him. "Is it all men or just *Texans?*"

"Huh? What?"

"You have that drawling tone to your voice when you say 'women' like you're describing a child throwing a tantrum."

"Hold on a minute, I wasn't trying to start a fight."

"No, you're just stuck in the same rut every other man in town is in."

"I've been home for a day and suddenly I'm the enemy?"

"No," she said on a sigh. "You just caught me at a bad moment. Sorry."

He shrugged. "No problem. I know what it's like to be up to your eyeballs in something and take it out on someone else."

"Still not much of an excuse. It's just that Brad makes me so furious."

"Isn't that what brothers are for?"

"I suppose so," she acknowledged, then she smiled. "Besides, I think Brad having to deal with Abby is going to be payback enough."

"Who knew you had such a mean streak?" he asked, his grin taking the sting out of his words.

"I'm a Price, too, don't forget."

"Wouldn't dare." He steered into a left turn lane and stopped for the red light. "I've done a lot of thinking about you in the last few years, Sadie."

"You have?" She tensed up again. What was it about this man that could set every nerve in her body to jangling?

His long fingers tapped against the steering wheel. "Sometimes, thoughts of you were all that kept me sane."

"Rick…"

"You don't have to say anything," he said. "I just wanted you to know that the night we had together has stayed with me."

"It stayed with me, too," Sadie said, then turned her head to avoid his gaze.

That single night with him three years ago had changed her life so completely, it was no wonder that she'd thought of him often. But now, knowing that he had been doing the same, made her feel even more of a terrible person than she had been. What could she possibly say to him? How would she ever explain?

She'd spent a lot of time assuring herself that one day, she'd tell him everything. That when he got back she would apologize and do whatever she could to make things right.

Yes, she could have written to him, but she had talked

herself out of that. She'd been…worried about him. A career marine, he had been in harm's way for most of the last few years, and every night, she'd said a prayer for his safety. If she had told him the truth in a letter, it might have distracted him when he could least afford it. Besides, a letter would have been the coward's way out. Face-to-face was the only honorable way. And like she said, Sadie was a Price, too. Her parents had raised their children to be honest, to keep their word and to never break a promise. Honor meant something to the Price family.

But that didn't mean that she had room for him in her life. She wasn't looking for a husband. She didn't need a man, her life was busy enough at the moment, thank you very much. But she did owe him the truth.

And that was something she wasn't looking forward to.

He pulled to a stop at a red light, then turned his head to give her a quick grin. Only one corner of his mouth tipped up, and in that instant, Sadie felt a flash of heat wash over her. Just like it had on their one and only night together three years ago.

"So tell me what you did in Houston."

She eased back into the seat. "I did a lot of charity work. The Price family foundation is based in Houston," she said with a lift of her shoulders. "And I served on the board of my father's art museum."

"You enjoyed that?"

She looked at him. "Yes, but…"

"But?"

"But, I always wanted to go into design. Landscape design, really." She turned to face him. "Planning out gardens, parks, working with the city to fix the roads along the highways…"

When he just stared at her, Sadie stopped talking and shrugged. "It just appeals to me."

"You should do it then," he told her. "Go take classes. Learn. Doing what you love is what makes life worth living."

The light changed and he drove on.

"Is that why you're still a marine?"

He laughed. "There's an old saying—*once a marine, always a marine*."

"Yes, but you're still active duty. Why?" She was watching him closely, so she noticed when his jaw tightened slightly. "You could come back to Royal, run your family ranch. Why stay in the Corps?"

"Duty," he said simply. "It's an old-fashioned word, but I was raised to take it seriously. My father was a marine, you know."

"Yeah, I know."

"We traveled all over the world when I was a kid. Finally settled here when he left the Corps, because my mom had roots here." He glanced at her. "But when you grow up on bases, when you see what people are willing to give to serve their country... Well, it makes you want to do the same. And by doing my duty, serving my country, I help keep everyone I care about safe."

She felt a sting of tears in her eyes and frantically blinked them back. Here he was talking about honor and duty and she had been lying to him for nearly three years. She was a rotten human being. She deserved to be flogged.

They drove down her street and suddenly Sadie had to say something. Try to prepare him for what he was about to find out.

"Rick, before we get to the house, there's something you should know—"

"If it's about the flamingos, I've got to say that maybe you should rethink landscape design."

"What?"

Grinning, he pulled into the driveway and that's when Sadie noticed the flock of pink plastic birds on the front lawn. Thank heaven her father was off on his fishing trip. If Robert Price had seen his elegant lawn covered with the tacky pink birds, he—well, Sadie wasn't sure what he'd have done, but it wouldn't have been pretty.

"Oh, for heaven's sake." As soon as Rick parked the car opposite the front door, Sadie hopped out and walked around the hood. She crossed the front yard until she came to the closest flamingo. The birds were staggered across the expertly trimmed lawn and looked so ridiculously out of place, Sadie couldn't help laughing.

"What's this about? A new trend in decorating?"

She jolted when Rick came up behind her. As hot as the July sun felt on her skin, his nearness made her temperature inch up just that much higher. There had never been another man in her life who had affected her like Rick Pruitt did. Not even her ex-husband-the-lying-cheating-weasel.

She took a breath, steadied herself, then looked up at him, trying not to fall into those dark brown eyes. It wasn't easy. He was tall and muscular and even in his jeans and T-shirt, Rick looked like a man used to giving orders and having them obeyed.

He was the quintessential Texas man. Add the Marine Corps to that and you had an impossible-to-resist combination. As the quickening heat in her body could testify.

Swallowing hard, Sadie fought past the dry mouth to say, "Actually, the flamingos are a fundraising drive for a local women's shelter." She tore her gaze from his and scanned the fifty or more pink birds scattered across the yard and sighed. "Summer Franklin runs it."

"Darius's wife?"

"Yes. The idea is that whoever receives the pink flamingo flock pays the charity to remove them and pass the birds onto the next 'victim'. Then that person pays and so on and so on…"

Rick laughed, pulled up one of the flamingos and looked it dead in its beady eye. "Sounds like a fun way to make money for a good cause."

"I suppose," she said, and worriedly looked at the hot-pink birds. "But they're so tacky. I'm just grateful my father's not here. He'd have a fit, wondering what the neighbors would be thinking."

Shaking his head, Rick stabbed the flamingo's metal pole back into the lawn and looked at Sadie. "Now that sounds like the prim and proper Sadie Price I used to know. Not the woman I spent that night with."

Prim and proper.

That's how she had lived her entire life. The perfect Price heiress. Always doing and saying the proper thing. But that, she assured herself, was in another life.

"I'm not that girl anymore, believe me." She looked up at him again and said, "Can you come in for a minute? There's something you need to see."

"Okay." He sounded intrigued but confused.

He wouldn't be for long.

She headed for the front door, let herself in and almost sighed with relief as the blissfully cool air-conditioned room welcomed her. A graying blonde woman in her fifties hurried over to her. "Miss Sadie, everything's fine upstairs. They're sleeping like angels."

"Thanks, Hannah," she said with a smile, not bothering to look back at Rick now. It was too late to back out. Her time had come. "I'll just go up and check on them."

The housekeeper gave Rick a long look, shifted her gaze to Sadie and smiled. "I'll be in the kitchen if you need anything."

Rick pulled his hat off and waited until Hannah was gone before he spoke. "Who's asleep? What's this about?"

"You'll see." She still didn't look at him, just walked across the marble floor toward the wide, sweeping staircase. "Come on upstairs."

She slid one hand across the polished walnut banister as she climbed the steps. Her heart was racing and a swarm of butterflies were taking flight in the pit of her stomach.

"What's going on, Sadie? In town, you said we had to talk. Then you say I've got to see something." He stepped around her when they reached the second-floor landing and blocked her way until she looked up at him. "Talk to me."

"I will," she promised, finally staring up into his eyes, reading his frustration easily. "As soon as I show you something."

"All right," he told her, "but I never did care for surprises."

The thick, patterned floor runner muffled their footsteps as they walked down the long hallway. Every step was more difficult than the last for her. But finally, she came to the last door on the left. She took a breath, turned the knob and opened it to a sunlit room.

Inside were two beds, two dressers, two toy boxes. And sitting on the floor, clearly not sleeping like angels, were her twin daughters.

Rick's twin daughters.

The girls looked up. Their brown eyes went wide and bright and they smiled as they spotted their mother. Sadie dropped to her knees to swoop them into her arms. With her girls held tightly to her, she turned her gaze on a stupefied Rick and whispered, "Surprise."

Three

Rick felt like he'd been kicked in the head.

Twin girls.

With *his* eyes.

They were jabbering nonstop as they climbed over their mother.

Their mother.

Sadie Price was the mother of *his* daughters.

Shock slowly gave way to an anger that burned inside him with the heat of a thousand suns. He was blistered by it and forced to contain it all because damned if he'd lose his temper in front of his children.

The girls were wearing matching pink overalls with pink-and-white checked shirts. Tiny pink-and-yellow socks were on their impossibly small feet and they laughed and danced in place as Sadie held on to them.

Sadie's gaze locked with his and he read her guilt in her eyes. Her regret. Well, it was a damned sight late for regret. She'd kept his daughters from him their whole lives.

There would be payment made.

For now though, he dropped to one knee and looked at the girls. Their brown hair curled around their heads, their cheeks were pink and their brown eyes sparkled with life. Love. His heart clenched hard in his chest. One of the girls looked at him warily, and then slowly gave him a smile that tore up his insides.

"Girls," Sadie said, laughing as the twins continued to chatter a mile a minute.

"Birds, Mommy."

"Lots."

"I know," Sadie said, giving first one of her daughters then the other a big kiss. "I saw them."

"Pretty."

"Yes, they are pretty," Sadie agreed.

"Who him?"

Who him. Rick swallowed back the tight ball of anger lodged in his throat. His daughters didn't know him. He was a damn stranger to his own flesh and blood. That knowledge hurt more than he would have thought possible.

"This is your daddy," Sadie said, watching him as she spoke the words that made all of this a reality.

He sat down, drew one knee up and rested his forearm on it. He wasn't going to crowd the little girls. But he wanted more than anything to hold them. Instead, he smiled. "You are the prettiest girls I have ever seen."

The one closest to him gave him a sly smile and looked up at him from beneath lowered lashes that lay like black velvet on her cheeks. Oh, this one was going to be a heartbreaker when she grew up.

"Daddy?" she said and pushed away from Sadie to walk to him.

Rick's heart stopped as she approached him. He was afraid to move. He worried that anything he did now might shatter the moment. And he didn't want to risk it. When she was close enough, the little girl reached out and patted his cheek. Her small hand was feather-soft against his skin and she smelled like shampoo and apple juice.

"Daddy?" She leaned in to give him a hug and Rick held her as carefully as he would have a live grenade. This tiny girl, so perfect, so beautiful, had accepted him without reservation and he'd never been more grateful.

"Daddy!" The second twin rushed him, cuddling up to him just as her sister had and Rick closed his eyes and wrapped his arms around them. He held them close, feeling the warmth of their bodies, the fluttering of their heartbeats. And in one all-encompassing instant had his life, his world, altered forever.

Opening his eyes, he looked at Sadie and saw that she was crying. A single tear rolled down her cheek as she watched him with their children and he asked himself what she was crying for. Was she pleased that he was finally meeting his daughters? Or was she regretting telling him at all?

"Story!" One of the girls blurted the word and pushed away from him, running to a bookcase beneath the window. Meanwhile, her twin settled in on Rick's lap and played with his hat.

"How old are they?" he asked tightly.

"You know exactly how old they are," Sadie whispered.

"What are their names?" That question cost him. He didn't know the names of his children. His heart was being ripped into pieces in his chest and there didn't seem to be a damn thing he could do about it.

Sadie scooted closer to them, reaching out to fix a sliding pink barrette in one of the twins' soft, wispy hair.

"This one is Wendy," she said, dropping a kiss on the girl's nose.

"Wenne!" the toddler repeated with a gleeful shriek. She put her father's hat on and the Stetson completely swallowed her head. Her giggle was as soft as a summer wind.

"Wendy has freckles on her nose."

"Nose!"

Smiling, Sadie captured the returning twin and swooped her up into her lap. She kissed the top of the child's head and met Rick's eyes when she said, "This one is Gail."

Another surprise in a morning full of them.

His heart, which he would have sworn had already been ripped in two, shredded even further as he looked down at the smiling child on Sadie's lap. He actually felt a sharp sting of tears in his eyes and swiped one hand across his face to rid himself of them. Only then did he trust himself to look at Sadie again. "You named her for my mother."

"Yes," she said as the little girl opened the storybook and started "reading" to herself.

"Doggie and a bug and running and..."

Her commentary went on, but Rick hardly heard the mumble of disjointed words and phrases. He was caught in the moment. Struggling hard for the rigid self-control he had always been able to count on.

But he would challenge any man to walk into a situation like this one and not be shaken right down to the bone.

"Gail has a dimple in her left cheek that Wendy doesn't have." She smoothed one hand over her daughter's hair. "And Gail's hair is straighter than Wendy's. When you get to know them, you'll see other differences, too. Their personalities are wildly different."

"Sadie…"

"Wendy is the adventurer. She was getting into things the minute she could crawl," Sadie said, her words coming faster and faster, as if she didn't want to give Rick a chance to say anything. "Gail is the cuddler. Nothing she likes better than curling up on your lap with a book. But she's no pushover, either. She holds her own with her sister and, honestly, the two of them are so stubborn that sometimes…"

"*Sadie,*" he said, his voice deeper, more commanding.

She blew out a breath and slowly lifted her eyes to his. "I know what you're going to say."

"Oh, I don't think you can even guess what I want to say," he told her, anger rippling just beneath the surface of his voice.

"Let me explain, all right?"

"Can't wait to hear it," he assured her, though Rick knew there was absolutely nothing she could say that would make what she had done okay.

He'd been cheated out of his daughter's lives.

Wendy pushed his hat off her head and left him for her mother. Both girls were in Sadie's lap as she read them a story. Their laughter filled his heart even as he struggled with the fury he felt toward their mother.

As he watched her with them, he saw a completely different Sadie than the one he knew. He'd always seen her as an untouchable princess. Born and raised to be the perfect southern lady. Until their one night together, he would have been willing to bet that Sadie Price had never done a damn thing that was even remotely undignified.

Yet here she was now, on the floor, cuddling with two babies like she didn't have a care in the world.

"Daddy! Story!" Wendy reached out a tiny hand to him and Rick's aching heart did a flip-flop in his chest. He would have his answers, he promised himself. But for now, he wanted to make up for lost time. He wanted to be with his children.

And the woman who had kept them from him.

He moved in closer, taking Wendy onto his lap and the four of them became a unit while Sadie's voice wove threads of family around them.

An hour later, the girls were asleep and Sadie and Rick stepped into the hall. She was so tense she was half afraid her spine might snap.

"You just leave them alone up here?" Rick asked as Sadie quietly closed the door behind her.

"There's a baby monitor in the room with receivers downstairs and in my room. I can hear everything that goes on in there."

He nodded and gripped the brim of his hat so tightly his knuckles went white. Sadie could feel anger radiating from him and the worst part was she couldn't blame him for any of it. What man wouldn't be furious to suddenly be faced with the fact that he was a father and hadn't been told about it?

"I think it's time you and I had that talk," Rick said, taking hold of her elbow to steer her down the hall and away from their daughters' bedroom.

"Let's go downstairs, then," Sadie said, pulling free of

his grip. Yes, he had a right to be angry, but she wasn't going to be bullied. Not by anyone. Never again.

She walked ahead of him, head held high, and took the stairs at a brisk clip. Once downstairs, she turned and walked into the family living room. "Have a seat. I'm going to ask Hannah for some iced tea. Do you want anything?"

"Just answers."

"You'll get them." He wouldn't like them, she thought as she walked through the house to the kitchen. But she couldn't help that. What was done was done and they'd just have to go forward from here.

In the cavernous kitchen, Hannah was sitting at a table with a cup of tea and a plate of cookies. "Miss Sadie. Did you want something?"

"Just some iced tea please, Hannah. And some of those cookies if you've got extra."

Hannah grinned. "With those two little angels in the house? I always have spare cookies. You just go on out to the front room. I'll bring it along."

Sadie turned for the door, then stopped as Hannah asked, "Is your friend still here? Would he like some as well?"

"Yes, thanks Hannah. Tea for both of us." As she walked back to the living room, Sadie told herself giving Rick something cold to drink, whether he wanted it or not, might just help cool him off.

Back in the living room, she found him standing at the bank of windows overlooking the front lawn. The pink flamingos looked so silly, she almost smiled. Until Rick turned to give her a glare that could have brought snow to Dallas.

"Start talking," he said thickly, tossing his hat to the nearest chair.

"It's a long story."

"Cut to the part where you give birth to my children and don't bother to tell me."

"Rick, it's just not that simple."

"Sure it is. Lies aren't complicated. It's living with them that makes things tough." He shoved both hands into his jeans pockets. "Though you've managed to do it just fine for nearly three years."

Sunlight streamed into the room and lay across glossy wood floors. Scatter rugs dropped splotches of color in the room and the oversize sofas and chairs gave a cozy feel in spite of the chill she was feeling from Rick. This had always been her favorite room in her family's home. Though now, she had the feeling she would never again walk into it without seeing Rick's accusatory stare.

Sighing, she bent to the baby monitor sitting on a side table and turned up the volume. Then she walked to him and stopped in a patch of sunlight, hoping the warmth would ease some of the cold she was feeling. Rick stood his ground, as immovable as a mountain. He was tall and broad and, right now, he looked like fury personified. His brown eyes flashed with banked anger and his shoulders were so stiff, she could have bounced a quarter off the tendons in his neck.

"You should have told me," he said flatly.

"I wanted to."

"Easy enough to say now."

"Nothing about this is easy, Rick," she countered and wrapped her arms around her middle. She took a deep breath and then continued. "You weren't here, remember? You left the day after we—"

"—made twins?" he finished for her.

"Yeah." Sadie had thought about this moment so many times, she'd even practiced what she would say.

How she would explain. And now that the moment was here, her mind was a total blank.

"By the time I found out I was pregnant, you were in a war zone."

"You could have written," he argued. "My mother had my address. She knew how to get in touch with me."

"I know." Sadie rubbed her hands up and down her arms. "I went to see your mom, actually."

"You what?" He looked stunned.

"When I knew I was pregnant, I went to talk to your mother and—"

"Here we are," Hannah announced as she pushed a rolling cart carrying a pitcher of tea, two glasses filled with ice and a blue-and-white plate full of cookies.

She settled the cart in front of one of the matching sofas, then smiled at the two of them. "You just help yourselves, and don't mind the cart when you're finished, Miss Sadie. I'll come back to collect it later."

"Thank you, Hannah." Desperate for something to do, Sadie hurried to the cart and poured tea into both glasses. "Sure you don't want any?"

"No, thanks. And stop being so damn polite." He walked closer and waited for her to take a sip of her tea. "Why did you go see my mother?"

Sadie set the glass down, sorry now she'd had any. The cold she felt was deeper now, thanks to the icy tea sliding through her system. Looking into Rick's eyes didn't warm her any, either.

Sighing a little, she slumped onto the sofa and leaned back into the cushions. "Because I thought she had the right to know that I was pregnant with her grandchildren."

"She *knew?*" Those two words sounded as if they had been strangled from his throat. Rick shook his head and she knew he was even more shocked than he had been before. "My mother knew you were pregnant and even *she* didn't tell me?"

"We talked about it," Sadie said, turning toward him as he dropped onto the sofa beside her. "We both decided that it wouldn't be right to give you something else to worry about while you were on the battlefield."

He laughed and the short, sharp sound was brittle. "You decided. Between the two of you, you decided to keep this from me." Rick shook his head. "I don't believe any of this."

Sadie reached out and laid one hand on his arm. When he glared at her, she pulled back. "Don't you get it? Your mother was terrified for your safety. She'd already lost your father and the thought of losing you to war was killing her."

His jaw worked as though he was actually biting back words that were struggling to get out.

"She didn't want you distracted. Neither did I," Sadie said. "If you had known, you might have been less focused on what you needed to do."

"I had the right to know."

"We were trying to protect you."

He laughed again and this time Sadie actually winced at the sound.

"That's great. You and my mom protect me by hiding my kids from me. Thanks."

His features were hard and tight, his eyes still flashing with the anger she knew must be pumping thick and rich inside him.

"I know you're mad," she said.

"There's an understatement."

"But I still think we did the right thing," she told him.

"Yeah?" He turned on the sofa to glare at her. "Well,

you didn't. You should have told me. *She* should have told me."

"We were going to tell you," Sadie argued, "when you came home on leave. But—"

"—Mom died in that car wreck and instead of coming home for her funeral, I took R&R in Hawaii. I couldn't face coming back here with her gone."

"Yes."

He scrubbed one hand across his face, then rubbed the back of his neck. "I don't even know what the hell to say about all of this, Sadie." He glanced at her. "There's one more thing I need to know."

"What?"

"If we hadn't run into each other this morning were you ever going to tell me about my children?"

Now it was her turn to be angry. "Of course I would have. You'll notice the girls weren't afraid of you, right? It was almost like they knew you already?"

He frowned, but nodded. "Yeah, I noticed that."

"That's because I showed them your picture. Every day. I told them who you were. That you were their daddy. They knew about you from the first, Rick."

He swallowed hard and took a deep breath. "I don't even know if that makes it better or worse."

Pushing up from the sofa, he stalked across the room, then turned to stare at her. "You showed them pictures of me, but I was never there. Did they wonder why? Do kids realize more than we think they do?"

Sadie stood up, too. Absently, she noted the overloud ticking of the grandfather clock in the corner. It hit the quarter hour and a bell chimed and still the silence between Rick and her continued. When she couldn't stand it any longer, she spoke up. "You're here now. You can get to know each other. I'm not trying to keep your girls from you, Rick. I never was. I just—"

"You moved to Houston because of them, didn't you? Because you were pregnant."

"Yes." She lifted her chin to meet his eyes. She wouldn't apologize for how she'd handled the biggest upset of her life. She had done the best she could and had never once regretted getting pregnant. "I couldn't stay here. Not with the town gossips. I didn't want the girls to suffer because of decisions you and I made."

His frown deepened.

"I wanted a fresh start."

"But you're back in Royal. Why now?"

"It was time. I was…lonely. I missed my home. My family. I wanted the girls to know their grandfather and their uncle."

"And their father?"

"Yes."

"Not so worried about the gossips now? What changed?"

"Me," she said simply. "I love my daughters and I don't care what any gossip has to say. Anyone tries to hurt my girls and they'll have me to deal with."

"And me," he assured her.

She could tell he was having a hard time believing anything she said and she really couldn't blame him for his doubts. But the truth was she had had every intention of telling him. "Honestly, Rick. I was going to be right here in Royal, waiting for you—whenever you came home. I was going to tell you about the girls. I want them to know their daddy."

Shaking his head, he walked toward her, gaze never leaving hers. He moved quietly for such a big man and she sensed the tension still holding him in its grip. When he was near enough, he reached out and grabbed her upper arms, pulling her close.

Sadie felt heat radiating off his body and reaching into hers. Just the touch of his hands on her skin was enough to start small brush fires in her blood. Her heartbeat was thudding in her chest and her mouth was so dry she could hardly swallow.

His gaze moved over her features like a slow caress. And his eyes were still churning with too many emotions to count. "I want to believe you, Sadie."

She tipped her head back to meet his eyes. "You can trust me, Rick."

"That's to be seen. But first things first." He released her, braced his legs in a wide-apart stance and folded his arms over his chest. "There's only one thing to be done now."

A ripple of apprehension scuttled through Sadie and still she asked, "What's that?"

"We're getting married."

Four

"You are completely out of your mind." She took a halting step back, forgetting the couch was right behind her. She toppled onto the cushions, but it took her but a second to scramble back up.

Maybe he was. Rick could admit that getting married wasn't something he had even considered until just a moment ago. Not that he was against marriage—for other people. But as a marine, he had never wanted to go off and leave a wife and kids behind for months at a time. Not to mention the hazards of his job. Why risk making a wife a widow? Sure, it worked for a lot of guys, but he'd seen enough marriages either dissolve or end in grief to not want to take the chance.

Now, though, things were different.

"It's the only honorable thing to do," Rick said, gaze following her as she pushed past him to hurry over to the front window.

"Honorable? You think marrying someone you don't love is honorable?" She laughed, shook her head and pointed one finger at him when he started for her. "You just stay away from me, Rick Pruitt."

"Not a chance," he snapped. He'd been put through an emotional wringer in the last hour or so and damned if he was even seeing straight yet.

He was a *father*.

He had twin girls who had his eyes and their mama's mouth and he hadn't even known they existed a few hours ago. How was that even possible? A man should *know* when he's created a life. When he's got family in the world.

Until today, he had thought himself alone. With both of his parents gone now, he'd had no real reason to leave the Marines. The Corps was his family now, he had told himself. Hell, he hadn't even wanted to come back to Royal on leave. Being in the empty ranch house was... lonely. Too many memories. Too much silence. Still, he had done his duty, come home to check on things, make sure the ranch was still operating as it should.

If he hadn't come home...would he ever have learned of his daughters? Sadie claimed she would have told him, but how did he know that for sure?

"I think we both need a little space right now, Rick," she said stiffly. "Maybe you should go." At her side in a couple of long strides, Rick pulled her in close again and this time wrapped his arms around her to hold her in place.

"You just dropped a bomb on me, Sadie," he ground out. "And if you think I'm gonna walk away from that, you're the one who's crazy."

"I'm not asking you to walk away," she argued, squirming in his grasp, trying to break free of him. "I'm just saying we should take a break. Get our thoughts straight before talking again."

"I don't need time to think," he told her. "I know everything I need to know. You're trying to keep my girls from me. Again."

Her jaw dropped. "Didn't I bring you here? Introduce you to the girls? I want you to be a part of their lives."

"On your terms though," he said, reading the truth in her eyes. "Come and go when you say? Show up for appointed visitation? Damn it, Sadie, I'm their father. I want more than weekends."

"It doesn't have to be like that," she said softly.

"No, it doesn't." The very thought of being cut off from his children was like a knife in the gut to him. He'd already missed too much. He hadn't seen Sadie pregnant. Hadn't heard the first cries of his babies being born. Hadn't seen that first smile or heard that first laugh.

A man alone treasured the thought of family. He wasn't about to lose his chance at having one.

"We can be together." Nodding, he took a breath. "We're their parents. It's only right we be married."

"This isn't a Victorian novel," she argued. "We can coparent successfully even if we're not a couple."

"Coparent." He snorted and looked down at her with a derisive half smile on his face. "Tidy words. Keeping each parent in their place. Is that it? Sounds like it came straight out of a self-help book."

"What if it did?" Her gaze shifted from his. "It makes sense."

"Not to me," Rick said flatly, holding her close enough that her body heat slipped into his. She wriggled some more, but all she succeeded in doing was rubbing herself against him until he was as hard as stone and she was panting with her own needs.

As soon as she realized that he had noticed her reaction, she went completely still. Rick smiled. "I know you can feel what you do to me."

She still wouldn't look him in the eye, but her breathing was heavier and she had stopped trying to pull away.

"I know you're feeling the same things I am," he said, sweeping one hand down her spine to the curve of her behind.

She sighed, closed her eyes and whispered, "It doesn't matter what we feel."

He rubbed her bottom until she was nearly purring in his arms. Rick had discovered on their one night together that beneath the surface of the genteel, aristocratic Sadie Price, there beat the heart and soul of a very sensual woman. He had been thinking about nothing but her for three long years and now that he was holding her again, he didn't want to let her go.

Ever.

All he had to do was convince her to marry him. How hard could it be?

"Baby, we're good together. That's more than a lot of people have when they get married."

Instantly, her eyes flew open and she glared at him. Damn, Rick thought, the woman could turn on a dime and he was never ready for it.

"Do *not* call me 'baby,'" she told him, then added, "I'm not marrying you just because we were good in bed together."

"Fine," he argued, "marry me because we have two children."

"And I thought my brother was the most stubborn male on earth."

Rick shook his head and tried to bite back his own frustrations. Most women in her situation would be leaping at the thought of marriage. Sure, she didn't have to worry about money. He couldn't dangle his own wealth in her face as a lure, because she came from the same kind of hefty bank account he did. But he didn't care how much the world had changed, being a single mother was harder than having a partner to share the work and worry. Why couldn't she see that?

"This isn't about stubborn. This is about you and me and what's best for our daughters."

"And you think that the girls would be better off living with two people who don't love each other?"

Scowling, he let her go when she pushed at him again. "This isn't about love. It's about duty. Our duty to our children."

"Duty isn't a reason for marriage, either. Trust me on this, I know what I'm talking about."

"Fine. Leave duty out of it." Rick shoved his hands into his pockets to keep from reaching for her again. "If we're married, we'll love the girls. That will be enough to build a family."

"No," she said with a harsh laugh. "It isn't enough. I'm not going to marry a man who doesn't love me. Not again."

She backed up a step or two, still shaking her head so firmly, Rick wasn't sure which one of them she was trying to convince.

"If you're talking about that moron you were married to for all of fifteen minutes…" he said.

"It was seven months and ten days," she countered hotly, her blue eyes flashing with the kind of heat that could fry a man. "Seven months before I actually *caught* him cheating on me. I found out later from my 'friends' that he'd been cheating on me all along, but nobody wanted to tell me."

"Don't you compare me to that piece of—" He caught himself and broke off. Then he moved in on her again, stalking her like a cat would a bird. "I don't cheat. And I don't lie. If I make a promise to a woman, I keep it."

"Good for you," she snapped. "I'm still not going to marry you."

Exasperated, he threw both hands high and let them drop. "Why the hell not?"

"I just told you," she muttered, keeping her voice low enough that Hannah wouldn't overhear their argument. "I married Taylor Hawthorne because it was *expected* of me. It was for the family. Good for business," she said and her mouth screwed up as if even the words tasted bitter. "I did what I was told. My father wanted me married, so I married. I was raised to do the right thing. To take one for the team," she said snidely. "To do my duty for the Price family. Well, no more. This is *my* life and I'll do with it what I damn well please."

She was shuddering by the time she stopped talking. Her breaths were coming fast and hard and there were unshed tears glittering in her eyes. Rick felt for her. He'd always known the Price family was far too interested in how things looked. When she married that no-account Hawthorne, Rick had assumed she simply had god-awful taste in men. But damned if he would have guessed that Sadie had laid herself down on a sacrificial altar for the sake of her father.

"I can understand how you're feeling, Sadie. Pisses me off just hearing it, so I imagine living it was that much worse. But it doesn't change a thing."

Stunned, she simply stared at him in confusion. "What?"

"We had children together, Sadie. We should be married." He moved closer, every step small and stealthy. Then he played his ace in the hole. He said the one thing he knew might sway her to accept his proposal. "I don't want my girls being called bastards. Do you?"

"Of course not!" She shook her head and chewed at her bottom lip and he knew he'd gotten to her with that.

The thought of anyone calling his babies names was enough to make him see red. But he knew as well as Sadie did that life in a small town wasn't always pretty. People would talk. Children would overhear it and they would repeat what their parents said.

He didn't want his girls paying for his mistakes.

"But I don't want to get married just for their sakes, either," Sadie said, her voice hardly more than a sigh. "That's not exactly a recipe for happiness, Rick."

A more stubborn woman never drew breath, he thought and swooped in on her, unable to keep from touching her for another minute. If he couldn't sway her to his point of view with logic, then damn it, he'd use whatever weapons he had in his war chest.

He wrapped his arms around her waist and pulled her so close she couldn't help but feel again his body's reaction to her. She wasn't immune to the chemistry sizzling between them. He could feel her heartbeat racing.

She closed her eyes, sighed a little and still shook her head. "No."

"Think about it, Sadie," he murmured, dipping his head to run his lips along the column of her throat.

She shivered and, damn it, so did he. The taste of her filled him. Her scent clouded his brain and shot his body into overdrive. His brain was fogging over and his instincts were clamoring at him to toss her down onto that so-comfortable sofa and lose himself in her. As he'd dreamed of doing for too damn long.

This woman had been in his soul—his bones— for as long as he could remember. Even as a kid, he'd noticed her. Now, as a man, he could admit that though he wouldn't love her, wouldn't love anyone, he felt more for her than he ever had for anyone else.

That would have to be enough.

She moaned, a small sound sliding from her throat as she clung to him, arching into his body with a need that matched his own.

"Remember that night?" he whispered, mouth moving over her throat, up to the line of her jaw and back down again. "How good it was? How good we were? We could have that again, Sadie...."

She cupped his head in the palm of her hand and held him to her as she sighed in pleasure. He ran the tip of his tongue across her skin and nibbled at the throbbing vein at the base of her neck.

"I want you so badly I ache with it," he admitted. "And you want me, too. I can feel it."

"I do," she murmured and he felt a flicker of hope rise up inside him.

"Just think about marrying me, Sadie," he said softly, lifting his head to look down at her.

She swayed a little, opened her eyes, met his and stiffened. "That was so not fair," she muttered.

"Fair?" he countered. "You're the one holding all the cards here, Sadie. I'm just playing the hand you dealt me."

"Oh, stop with the poor-country-boy act," she told him, pushing out of his embrace to glare at him. "You knew exactly what you were doing. You were trying to seduce me into marriage and it's not going to work."

"Why the hell not?"

Sadie smoothed her hair, lifted her chin and said, "Good sex isn't enough to build a marriage on."

"It was *great* sex and it's a lot better than bad sex."

"I am not getting married."

"You surely are."

"You can't force me."

She had him there. He couldn't force her to marry him. But that wasn't saying that he wouldn't do his damnedest to convince her.

Gritting his teeth, Rick took a breath. "You know how you said earlier that Brad was a hardhead? Well, honey, you could give lessons."

"You've been back home one day, Rick. You told me yourself you're only here for a month."

True, he did have only thirty days' leave. But if he decided to get out of the Corps, he could be back in Royal in no time. To stay.

"I'll retire," he blurted the words, surprising even himself.

"Rick, you love being a marine. You told me so yourself not two hours ago." She stared up at him. "What about your duty to country?"

"I have a duty to my kids, too," he argued.

"God, what am I going to do with you?"

"Easily enough answered," he told her. "Marry me."

"Well," a voice said from the hallway, "it's about damn time."

Rick turned to face the man standing in the open doorway of the living room. Brad Price looked grim and his gaze was narrowed and fixed on Rick.

"Brad," Sadie said with a tired sigh, "what're you doing here?"

He came into the room, never taking his eyes off of Rick as he spoke to his sister. "I came to talk to you. Felt bad about our argument at the club."

"Now's not a good time," Sadie said quickly.

"Yeah, I can see that." He walked up to Rick, ignoring Sadie completely. "So you've seen the girls?"

"I have," Rick said, stepping forward and sweeping Sadie to one side of him, keeping his body between her and her brother. This was between him and Sadie and he wasn't about to let Brad push his way into the mix.

"You know," the other man said, "I agreed with Sadie when she decided not to tell you about the girls when you were overseas...."

"Big of you to agree with her to keep my kids from me."

"Brad," she said.

"She did it for you," Brad reminded him.

"Everybody's so thoughtful," Rick said, features hard and tight. "Doing me favors I never asked for. Hiding my children for my own good."

Brad took a step forward. "You ungrateful—"

Rick took a step closer. "You expect me to *thank* you?"

"Stop it," Sadie warned.

"What she did is between Sadie and me," Rick told the man staring him down. "Just like this conversation is. You don't get a vote."

"I'm her brother."

"Which is why I'm still being polite."

Brad's gaze narrowed, but Rick wasn't intimidated. He'd been through firefights, walked down dark streets in enemy territory. He'd had friends die in his arms and been convinced that he wouldn't live to see another sunrise. Nothing Brad Price could show him was going to throw Rick.

"I want to know what you're going to do about my sister and her daughters."

"Brad, honest to God, if you don't get out of here…"

"I'm not going anywhere until he tells me he's going to marry you."

"Not that it's any of your business, but I've already asked her. Twice. You walked in on the second time."

Brad nodded. "Good. When's the wedding?"

"Ask your sister."

Brad looked at her. "Well?"

Sadie stood to one side, arms crossed over her chest, the toe of her shoe tapping frantically against the wooden floor. "There's not going to be a wedding."

"Are you kidding me?" Brad looked at his sister as if he couldn't believe what he was hearing, and Rick was glad to see that someone else was as frustrated with her as he was. "He's finally home and wants to do the right thing by you and his kids and you tell him no? What are you thinking?"

She narrowed her eyes on him. "I'm thinking, Bradford Price, that this is a private argument and none of your business."

"None of my business?" he shouted. "You're my sister, how is this not my business?"

"Don't shout at her," Rick said, his own voice loud enough to command attention.

"Who the hell do you think you are?" Brad demanded, crowding in on Rick.

"I'm the man who's going to marry your sister and you'll watch how you talk to her from here on out."

"Is that right?"

"Damn straight," Rick told him, bristling for a fight. He hadn't come here looking for trouble, but he wouldn't walk away from it, either.

"I don't need you to defend me," Sadie said, turning on Rick with the same vehemence she'd shown to her brother only a moment ago.

"What you need is somebody to talk some sense into you," Brad snapped.

"Amen to that," Rick acknowledged, hating to agree with Brad on anything.

Miss prim-and-proper Sadie Price reached up, and tugged at her own hair in sheer frustration. Letting her hands fall to her sides again a moment later, she shot a glare first at her brother then at Rick. "I've had enough. I'm done talking. That's it. Both of you get out."

Rick dug in his heels. "He can go. I'm not finished."

"Yes, you are."

"Why should I go?" Brad demanded. "This is my house, too."

"Not anymore. Go away," Sadie repeated. "Both of you."

"Sadie, you're not being reasonable," Rick said stubbornly. "We're not finished talking."

"Thank God one of you is making sense," Brad muttered.

"I'm with Sadie on this one, Price," Rick said tightly. "Butt out."

"*Both* of you butt out," Sadie snapped.

"I swear the women in this town are ruining men's lives." Clearly disgusted with his sister, Brad shook his head. "Abby Langley's driving me around the bend and here you are doing the same thing to this poor bastard."

Sadie poked him in the chest with her index finger. "Don't you swear at me." When Rick grinned, she turned on him in a flash. "And I don't want to hear one more word from you, either. Both of you…just get out of my house."

A soft cry sounded and Sadie turned instantly toward the baby monitor on a nearby table. Another halfhearted sniffle and cry came through loudly. At least one of the girls was awake.

"I have to go check on the twins," she said, heading for the doorway.

Rick was right behind her. Hearing that tiny cry had sent an arrow of something sharp and sweet shooting through him. "Are they all right?"

She stopped, looked up at him and put one hand in the middle of his chest to keep him from coming any closer. "They're fine." Then she shot her brother an irritated look. "They probably just heard their daddy and their uncle acting like jackasses."

When she left the room, she never looked back, only called out as she went, "You two can see yourselves out."

Rick looked over to Brad. "Well, that went well, thanks to you."

"Don't blame me if you're fool enough to try to talk sense to a woman," Brad shot right back.

Frustrated beyond belief, Rick grabbed his hat and tugged it on. He shot Brad another hard look and said, "This isn't over between me and your sister."

"I wish you luck with that," Brad muttered. "But I warn you. Sadie's changed since the twins came. Used to be you could predict how she'd react to something. Now…" He shook his head helplessly.

He had already noticed the changes in Sadie, Rick thought, and hadn't needed her brother to clue him in. There was a time when Sadie Price never would have lost her temper. It wouldn't have been ladylike. Her icy coolness had always attracted him for some reason. But Rick had to admit that the wild heat of her now was even more appealing.

A few minutes later, Rick was in his truck, looking up at the facade of the Price mansion. Everything in him urged him to stay. To batter away at Sadie's arguments until they evaporated like shallow creeks in high summer.

But, he thought, as he turned the key and fired up the engine, he was already learning something about Sadie. She was a woman a man would have to sneak up on. She had already dug her heels in, refusing to marry him and she wasn't likely to back down from that.

So, he'd have to seduce her. Charm her. Get her into bed and make love to her until she couldn't think straight.

Then he'd get her to marry him.

Five

The fireworks booth was doing a booming business.

Nothing like a small-town Fourth of July, Sadie thought with a tired smile. She'd missed this when she was living in Houston and now that she was home, she wanted to be a part of it all.

Which was why she was standing behind the counter explaining the finer points of whistling rockets and multicolored fountains to excited kids and their tired parents.

She tried to see past the crowd to where Hannah was watching over her napping twins. But there were just too many people in the town square. Seemed like every citizen of Royal had turned out for the festivities. The noise level alone was almost deafening. Between the crowd itself and the country-and-western band playing at the far edge of the square, peace and quiet would be hard to come by today. But then, who needed peaceful on the Fourth of July?

Summer heat sizzled every breath and the delectable scent of barbecue drifted on a lazy wind. Sadie was having a good time. In fact, the day would have been perfect. If not for thoughts of Rick Pruitt. The man was keeping her on edge, though she hated to admit it, even to herself.

True to his word, he was getting to know his daughters, dropping by the house every day during the last week, playing, reading stories, helping with bath time. And the girls were delighted with the attention. Both Gail and Wendy woke up every morning now asking when Daddy was going to come.

"How you doing, Sadie?"

"What?" She turned and smiled at Abby Langley. "Sorry, I was daydreaming, I guess."

"In this heat, maybe you're just hallucinating."

Sadie laughed and shook her head. "If only…"

Abby leaned one hip against the counter. Handing Sadie a bottle of cold water, she uncapped her own and took a long drink. "Boy, that's good. Okay, so who's the daydream about? A certain marine, I'm guessing."

Sadie took a grateful sip of the icy water and let it slide through her system. Even with the fans behind them stirring the hot July air, it was stifling in the fireworks booth.

"Hey, Abby," one of the other workers called out.

"Sadie and I are on a break," she answered.

"I could use one. Too much heat and too many thoughts," Sadie admitted. "And yes, your guess was right. All of those thoughts are about Rick."

Abby was one of the only people outside her immediate family who knew the truth about the twins' father. Sadie hadn't had many close friends in her life, so she treasured Abby and had really missed their friendship when she and the girls were living in Houston. Abby understood growing up in Royal as the daughter of wealthy parents. But she also knew what it was like to strike out on her own. She had made a dot-com fortune when she lived in Seattle, then come home to Royal to marry her high school sweetheart. Everything had seemed perfect for her.

Of course, nothing had turned out the way she'd expected. What ever did?

"Tell me," Abby urged.

Sighing, Sadie said, "He's been coming over every day. Spending time with the girls…"

"And this is a bad thing?"

"No."

One of the other workers in the booth reached past Sadie for a box of red sparklers. Sadie took Abby's arm and pulled her away a few steps. Lowering her voice, she continued, "It's not that I don't want him to get to know his daughters. They should have a father in their lives and they're already crazy about him—"

"I hear a 'but' in there somewhere."

"*But,*" Sadie acknowledged with a nod, "what happens when he ships out again? He's home on leave. He's still a marine, Abby. Which means he's not staying in Royal. When he leaves, the girls won't understand. They'll just know their daddy's gone."

"Okay, that would be hard," Abby said as they both deliberately ignored the customers starting to stack up on the other side of the counter. "But isn't it still better for them to know him?"

"Yes, of course, it's just…"

"Confusing?"

"Extremely," Sadie said with a sigh. "You know, even when I was a kid, Rick Pruitt...confused me."

Abby laughed. "Sadie, when we were kids, all boys confused us. Hasn't changed much."

"No." A sad smile curved Sadie's mouth as she idly straightened a stack of Magic Wonder fountains. "But for you, it was different. Your family was rich, but they didn't keep you *separate* from everyone in town. Brad and I went to private academies, remember?"

She shrugged as if it didn't bother her, but it still did. When she was a girl, Sadie had wanted friends. She'd seen the other girls her age going shopping or sitting in the diner, laughing together or flirting with boys, and she had desperately wanted to be one of them. But except for Abby, she remained an outsider. Just as she had been for most of her life.

"True, you weren't around much," Abby mused. "Even when you were, your father didn't really like you hanging out at the diner with the rest of us."

Sadie laughed at the image. "The children of Robert Price didn't 'hang out.'" She took another sip of water and looked out over the crowd gathered in the square. "We didn't really belong in Royal, you know? Oh, born and raised here, sure, but we could only see the other kids on the weekends, so we never really built the kind of friendships here that everyone else had. Our father was too determined to keep us isolated for whatever reasons." She smiled, reached over to squeeze Abby's hand. "If not for you, I would have been miserable. It was hard on me, but in a way, I think it was even worse for Brad."

"In what way?"

Sadie pushed a stray lock of blond hair out of her eyes

and shrugged again. "I don't know, he was popular with the girls in town."

"Of course," Abby muttered. "He never did have any trouble attracting girls."

Sadie grinned. "He's my brother and he irritates me beyond all reason at times, but come on. He *is* great-looking."

"Maybe," Abby allowed.

Still chuckling, Sadie said, "Anyway, even though *most*—" she paused for a knowing look at Abby "—of the girls liked him, the guys in town weren't real thrilled with the 'rich guy' swooping in on the weekends."

"Yeah," Abby said softly, reluctantly. "I'd forgotten about that."

Sadie blew out a breath. "God, that sounds so whiny, doesn't it? Poor little rich kids…."

"You're not whiny. Ever. So," Abby prodded, "tell me about Rick?"

Sadie smiled ruefully. "You remember, he was Mr. Popularity even then. Captain of the football team." She shook her head and called up the memory of a teenaged Rick Pruitt, and in response, she felt that odd fluttering in her stomach again just as she had then. "He wore jeans and boots and T-shirts and his hair was too long and his eyes were too dark and he looked like every girl's dream of a bad boy who was really a good guy."

"Yeah," Abby said, smiling with her. "I do remember Rick as a teenager. Pretty studly even then."

Smiling, she looked at Abby. "He would walk into the diner and every girl there would turn to look at him."

"Even you," Abby said.

"Me, too," she admitted, then laughed a little. "But he hardly knew me. Still, anytime he said hello, I'd start burbling and stammering. I felt myself blushing and couldn't stop it. Ridiculous, right?"

"Not really. We all acted like that as kids."

"Yes," Sadie said, "but I'm still doing it. The old Rick was pretty irresistible. Now, though, since those last tours of duty, he's...changed. Become more—I don't know, not closed down, because he's open and loving with the girls. But there's something about him that is shut away. Locked down. And that tears at me, Abby. Oh," she said, pausing to huff out a frustrated breath, "I don't know why he affects me like he does, but it's automatic. Rick Pruitt's around and my brain turns to mush and my body lights up like one of these skyrockets we're selling."

"So having him around all week was a little tough?"

"Just a little."

"I hear that," Abby said, looking past Sadie to frown. "Nothing's as easy as it should be."

Sadie turned to follow her friend's gaze and sighed when she spotted Brad walking through the crowd. "So, you're having a few issues with men right now, too, huh?"

"You know I love you, Sadie," Abby said, scowling at the oblivious man as he stopped to greet a friend. "But your brother sometimes makes me want to scream."

"He has that effect on women. Even his sister," Sadie admitted ruefully.

"Well, this woman isn't going to let him win. He's trying to ignore me at the TCC. Thinks because I'm an 'honorary' member, what I have to say shouldn't matter." Abby winked at her. "He's the most hardheaded man I've ever come across and arguing with him is like trying to talk sense to a wall. But, I don't give up easy and Bradford Price won't know what's hit him when I'm through with him."

Sadie grinned in solidarity. It was nice to know she wasn't the only female being driven slowly insane by a man. "Good to hear. Can't wait to see it."

"There's something else you should see right now."

"Hmm? What?"

Abby turned Sadie toward the counter. "Why don't you take care of this customer?"

Rick Pruitt leaned his forearms on the sun-warmed counter, looked through the screen at Sadie. "So, what kind of fireworks do you have?"

He was in uniform and Sadie felt her breath slide from her lungs in pure, female appreciation. He looked tall and strong and proud. The left side of his chest was covered with rows of colorful ribbons and a few medals glinted dully in the sunlight.

A couple of women walked past behind him and Sadie saw them giving him a slow once-over. Even though a spark of jealousy flared up inside her, she couldn't blame the women a bit. Rick was the kind of man that men wanted to be and women simply wanted. And when one corner of his mouth tipped up in a half smile, Sadie knew she was in very deep trouble.

Just as she had admitted only moments ago, she could actually feel her brain shutting down while her body kicked into high gear.

"Sadie?" he prompted, as if he knew exactly what she was thinking. "Fireworks? What kind are we talking about?"

It wasn't easy, but she managed to get a grip on her imagination and her hormones. "The usual kind. They're safe and sane and very pretty."

Then she sent a frown after Abby who walked away

chuckling. A second ago, she'd been thinking how much she had missed Abby when she was living in Houston. Now, her best friend had left her alone with the very man Sadie had been complaining about. The traitor. Looking back at Rick, she forced her brain to wake up and pay attention, then kept her voice brisk and businesslike.

"What can I get you? All of the proceeds go to the women's shelter."

"Ah," he said. "Like the pink flamingos."

"Exactly." And, Sadie knew that Summer's shelter would be getting a nice donation today, judging from how busy the fireworks stand was. "So, what do you need?"

"Now, that's a tricky question, Sadie," he said, voice dropping to a low rumble that only she could hear.

She couldn't stop the wave of heat that washed through her at the teasing, sexy note in his voice. Despite the crowds surrounding them, it was as if they were suddenly all alone. What was it about him that got to her so completely? Sadie felt as though every nerve in her body was standing straight up and trembling.

Sadie had never felt this way about any other man. Ever.

Certainly not the husband she had married for all the wrong reasons. In fact, up until that one night with Rick, Sadie had been half convinced that she was simply not *meant* to experience the tingling, overpowering pleasures that she read about in romance novels.

But in Rick's arms, she'd found more than she had ever thought possible. Now staring into those brown eyes of his, she was so very tempted to find it all again. He was temptation personified and she was pretty sure he knew it. As if he was aware of her thoughts, his eyes warmed and seemed to twinkle and that's when her breath caught in her lungs and a low, burning ache settled deep inside her.

Somehow, against all odds, she found the strength to rein in her hormones.

Her daughters' faces swam in her mind and that helped. The girls had Rick's eyes, sparkling with mischief. Her twins. The daughters she and Rick had made together on that passion-filled night.

Sadie wasn't a lonely single woman anymore. She couldn't just fall into bed with a man anymore, no matter *how* tempting. She was a mom. A mom who couldn't afford to start something with the father of her girls, because the only reason he wanted her now *was* their girls.

He was charming and attractive and truth be told, a walking orgasm waiting to happen. But if they didn't share two daughters, would he be trying so hard to seduce her? Sadie didn't think so.

Steeling herself, she smiled. "Did you want to buy some fireworks, Rick?"

One eyebrow lifted, but he nodded as if he understood that he wouldn't be drawing her into a flirtatious battle. "Sure." His gaze slipped past her to the shelves stocked with brightly colored boxes of fiery splendor. "Why don't you tell me what kind of fireworks the girls like?"

Her heart twisted. How sweet was that, she thought. He wanted to get something for his daughters to enjoy. Helplessly, she admitted that the one sure way to her heart was through her daughters. And no doubt, a cynical voice inside her whispered, he knew that very well. She ignored that little voice. "They're so little, this will be their first year actually seeing fireworks. I think they're going to be overwhelmed."

"I'm glad I'm here to see it with them," he said.

"I am, too."

"Are you?" he asked, sliding one hand across the counter to sweep beneath the screen to touch her fingers.

A quick bristle of sensation swept through her at his touch and she pulled her hand away. She was standing on a razor's edge here and one push either way was going to dissolve what was left of her balance.

"Of course I am," she said. "The girls will love having you here."

"That's a start," he said.

"Sadie," Abby asked, as she walked up with a smile, "everything okay?"

"Fine," she answered. "Abby, you remember Rick Pruitt."

"Sure. Nice to see you again. Love a man in uniform."

He grinned and Sadie's stomach did a quick flip-flop.

"That's just why we wear them, Abby. Marines like to please their women."

"Women?" Abby asked.

His gaze shot to Sadie. *"Woman,"* he corrected.

Then, as if he hadn't started a brush fire in her bloodstream, he pulled out his wallet. "Give me a few of those red, white and blue sparklers and a couple of the Fiery Fountains."

Getting busy, Sadie grabbed up his order, put it all in a bag and took his money.

"Keep the change for the shelter," he said.

"Thanks. The shelter appreciates it."

"Happy to help." His gaze was locked on hers.

She pulled in a deep breath and sighed. "Rick, what do you really want?"

"You already know the answer to that, Sadie."

Sadie searched for something else to say, but came up empty. What was there left to say? Hadn't they been talking circles around each other for a week now? Nothing had changed. He wanted to marry her for their daughters' sakes and she refused to get married for the wrong reasons. Again.

He picked up the bag and asked, "I'll see you later, then?"

"We'll be here for the fireworks show." Knowing how the girls would be excited to see him, she pointed off to the gigantic black oak that stood in the town square. "Hannah and the girls are over there if you want to say hello."

A wide smile creased his face. "Thanks. Think I will." His gaze shifted to Abby. "Nice to see you."

"Thanks, you, too."

When he walked off, Sadie watched him until he was swallowed up by the slowly moving crowd. Then she sighed and Abby nudged her in the ribs.

"What?"

"He's still gorgeous."

"Yeah?"

"He looks at you like you're the last steak at a barbecue."

"I know." That's just how she felt when he was around.

"So what's the problem?"

"He's not here to stay, Abby," Sadie said, resting one hip against the counter.

"You don't know that. Word is he's thinking about retiring."

"Maybe," she said, looking back over the crowd in the direction Rick went. "But even if he did stay in town, it isn't me he wants. It's his girls."

Abby laughed and dropped one arm around her shoulders. "Not what it looks like to me, Sadie. He's really into you. It's in his eyes."

"He just *desires* me. That's different."

"And could be fun."

She shook her head even though she was smiling. "Fun isn't on my schedule," she said sadly. "I'm a mom now. I have to do what's best for my daughters."

"And what exactly is that?"

"Wish I knew," Sadie whispered as Abby moved off to wait on another customer.

The rest of the day passed in a flurry of activity. There were rides for the twins, a small petting zoo and a country-fair-like atmosphere at the booths filled with pies and handmade crafts.

Sadie had as good a time as a woman could who was twisted into knots. Rick was there. All day. He carried the girls when they got tired, indulged them in ice cream and candy and Sadie could only hope their tummies were tough enough to handle all the sugar. Sadie should probably have drawn a few lines in the sand. Put a lid on sugar consumption at least. But Rick was so excited with his daughters and the girls were simply nuts about their daddy. She simply couldn't force herself to be the disciplinarian at the party when everyone was having so much fun.

They settled on the blanket beneath the tree for a late lunch. It was just the four of them since Hannah had found a group of friends among the crowd. While the girls ate bananas and mac and cheese, Sadie unwrapped the sandwiches Hannah had packed for her. She handed one to Rick.

When he took it, his fingers brushed hers and she gasped a little. He heard it and smiled. "Thanks."

"Don't thank me," she protested. "Hannah packed the lunch."

"I wasn't talking about the sandwich."

"Oh?" She looked at him as she reached over to hand Gail a cup of milk.

"I meant," he said, smoothing one hand over Wendy's dark brown curls, "thanks for sharing our girls with me today."

"You don't have to thank me for that, Rick," she said softly. Yes, he was confusing the hell out of her personally, but his obvious love for the twins warmed her heart. "They're your daughters, too. I want you to know them. I want *them* to know *you*."

He glanced from each of his daughters' tiny faces back to Sadie. Dappled shade danced across his face as the leaves of the black oak dipped and swayed in the sultry breeze.

"I appreciate that. I do." He took a bite of the sandwich, chewed and swallowed. "But I want more than the occasional day with them, Sadie."

"I know that." She picked up the sippy cup of milk Wendy toppled over and set it upright again. "But—"

"No buts about it, Sadie. They're my family. My blood."

"And mine," she reminded him.

"Yeah, which brings me back to my point."

She cut him off. Sadie wasn't going to give him the chance to talk marriage again. Sharing the twins wasn't enough of a reason to get married. She wouldn't take that step again unless she was in love. "I know what your point is, Rick, but I haven't changed my mind."

"Why the he—" he broke off, looked at the girls and gave a rueful smile. "Why the *heck* not? We were good together."

"Yes, for one night."

"Could be every night."

"Marriages aren't only lived in bed."

"Doesn't hurt."

She sighed. "Rick, we've been over this already."

"And will be again," he told her, his brown eyes locked with hers.

"What's the point?"

"We have kids."

"And we can both love them without being married to each other."

"We could be a family," he said softly.

And for one brief moment, that word seemed to reverberate inside her. She had always wanted a family of her own. It was the main reason she had agreed to go along with her father's plan when he married her off to Taylor. She had believed back then that even if a marriage hadn't started out for the right reasons that two people who wanted to badly enough could build something good.

But she'd found out soon enough that a marriage without love wasn't a marriage at all.

"It's a bad idea, Rick," she said finally and met his eyes.

"You don't know that."

She actually laughed and Gail looked up at her with a grin. "Oh, yes," she said, "believe me when I say I do."

"You can't use your marriage as a measure of what we could have."

"It's exactly what I should do," she told him firmly. "My marriage was a misery because there was no love there. I married him for all the wrong reasons and I paid a heavy price." She paused, looked down at her daughters, laughing and babbling to each other, and she felt a well of love fill her. Shaking her head, she looked at Rick. "This time, it wouldn't be only *me* paying the price. And I won't risk putting my girls into an unhappy home."

"You think I would risk that?" Rick picked up a piece of banana and handed it to Wendy. "I only want what's best for them."

"And I believe you," Sadie said. "We just disagree on what's best."

He laughed shortly. "You think you've got your mind made up about me," he said after a long moment, "but things change, Sadie."

"I'm not going to change my mind," she warned.

"Don't make statements that are going to be hard to back down from when I finally convince you to see things my way."

"Are you always this confident?"

"When I know I'm right," he assured her.

A squeal of sound shattered their conversation and had Sadie's ears ringing. Wendy cried for her mommy and Gail crawled to her father and scrambled up onto his lap.

The mayor stood on a hastily built stage at one end of the square. Tapping and blowing into a microphone, the feedback was loud enough to tear paint from walls.

"Sorry about that noise," the mayor said, "but I think we've got it whipped now."

The crowd stirred, then settled down as they waited for the inevitable speeches. Sadie's gaze slid to Rick. He had one arm wrapped around Gail's sturdy little body and jiggled her instinctively to keep her happy.

He did that so easily, Sadie thought with a sigh. He had stepped into fatherhood so smoothly, it was as if he had been with the twins since the beginning. And if he had, she wondered, how would things be different now?

Might they have already become the family he claimed to want?

"I know," the mayor called out, his voice echoing weirdly through the speakers, "that none of you came to listen to speeches..."

"That won't stop you, Jimmy," someone in the crowd shouted.

"That'll be enough outta you, Ben," the mayor chided with a smile. "I'll make this short. But since we're all here and since it's our country's Day of Independence, I wanted to take the time to honor a few of our own."

A ripple of applause skittered through the crowd. Hesitant, since no one was sure what the mayor was up to yet.

Then he let them all know.

"Rick Pruitt?" Mayor Jim called. "I know you're here son, so come on up to the stage, will you?"

Frowning a little, Rick set Gail down on the blanket. His features went dark and his eyes were suddenly shadowed. Dutifully, though, he shrugged, then walked through the other picnickers toward the stage. Meanwhile, the mayor went on with his small roll call.

"Donna Billings. Frank Haley and Dennis Flynn, you come on up here, too."

Sadie's gaze locked on Rick as he walked up the steps to take his place on the stage. The other people who had been called up stood alongside him, each of them in uniform. They all looked as uncomfortable with the attention as Rick did.

Then the mayor announced, "How about we give a big Royal round of applause for our very own finest. Let's thank them all for their service to us and our country."

As the gathered townspeople erupted into wild shouts and thunderous applause, Sadie felt a chill of pride ripple along her spine. From across the square, Rick's gaze locked with hers and she knew that he had been right. If she wasn't careful, he might just change her mind.

Six

During the next week, Rick got reacquainted both with the woman he had spent the last three years thinking about, and with his home.

The Pruitt ranch, under foreman John Henry's stewardship, had continued to thrive. The herd of beef cattle was healthy and growing, and the acreage set aside for raising grain was more productive than he had a right to expect. John had done a hell of a job and Rick was grateful. Knowing his home was in good hands had made it possible for him to follow his own dream of service.

Now, though, he was back and he had to decide for himself if his dreams hadn't changed. Evolved.

Rick's life was more full than he'd ever experienced before. He had once thought that being a marine was the toughest job on the planet. But that was before he became a father. For the last several days he had spent as much time with them and Sadie as he could. Every time he saw those twin smiles beaming at him, his heart wrenched in his chest. It was lowering to admit just how his daughters had him wrapped around their tiny fingers.

There was nothing he wouldn't do for them. Nothing he wouldn't face for them. Their smiles were a benediction. Their laughter the sweetest sound he had ever heard.

Rick had never really thought about becoming a father. And now that it had happened to him, he realized just what a responsibility it really was. Loving a child—a family—was an anchor he didn't believe professional soldiers could afford. That lesson had been brought home to him all too clearly on his last tour.

And the guilt that gnawed on him every second of every day was a constant reminder.

Now, though, he was looking at the situation from a whole different angle. There were two people in the world, alive and breathing because of him and Sadie. Those girls…they needed a father. They needed *him*.

His children should be able to depend on him. To know that he would be there for them. And how the hell could he do that if he was ten thousand miles away, slinking through a desert with a pack and a gun?

Then there was Sadie herself. His feelings for her went deeper than he wanted to admit, but damned if he'd ever call it love. Still, she was a part of him now, as much as the girls were, and he didn't know what the hell to do with that information.

Standing out on the ranch house's wide front lawn, he looked at the place where he'd grown up and felt a stab of affection. The heart of the house was more than a hundred years old. Built by the first Pruitt to settle here—back when Sam Houston was still in charge of Texas.

That small cabin had eventually been added on to with wood, stone and brick until the house itself had sprawled across the land, meandering weirdly with walls jutting out at odd angles. His mother had once told him that when she first saw the ranch house, she thought it had looked like an enchanted cottage. To cement that notion, Rick's father had added a stone tower to the end of the house for his wife to use as a sewing room.

Rick's gaze moved over that tower now and he half expected to see his mother standing in one of the windows waving at him. The fact that she never would again hit him like a fist to the chest. He hadn't been here when she died. Hadn't been able to say goodbye. And that would always haunt him.

Had he given up too much in service to his country? Was it time to step back and let others take over the duties he had always held so dear? Hard to know. Hard to choose which part of your heart to listen to.

Which was why being here was both a balm and a curse. Being on the ranch again fed his soul. Knowing that he might be leaving it again tore at him.

"You look like a man with a lot on his mind."

Rick turned to watch John Henry walk up to him. The older man was in his sixties, but stood as straight and tall as a man forty years younger. His hair was liberally streaked with gray and the moustache drooping over his upper lip was white as snow. The corners of sharp blue eyes was deeply grooved from too many years squinting into the sun and his skin was as tanned as old leather.

John Henry was as much a part of the ranch as Rick himself was. Maybe more so, Rick thought now, since the other man was *here*, taking care of business while he himself was running all over the world taking care of everyone else's concerns.

"Plenty to think about," Rick admitted.

"Anything you want to talk over?"

Rick smiled. John had been on the ranch since Rick was a kid. He was as close to a father as Rick had now and though he appreciated the offer, he didn't see any point in talking about things he hadn't gotten straight in his own mind yet.

"Nope."

"You always were the closed mouth sort," John mused and turned his gaze on the house, too. "It's a good place, you know."

"Yeah, I know."

"But a house needs people living in it. A family. Making memories. It's not good for a house like this to stand empty too long."

"Real subtle," Rick said with a half smile.

"No point in being subtle. If I've got something to say, I just come out and say it."

Rick sighed. John had been warming up to this for a week, he knew. "Let's hear it."

The older man scrubbed one hand across the back of his neck. "You know I was just as proud of you as your folks were when you joined the Corps."

"I know that."

"But that said," John told him quietly, "there's a time for leaving home and there's a time for coming back."

He frowned, shifting his gaze to his mother's window again. If he hadn't left the last time, he'd have been here when Sadie found out she was pregnant. He'd have been here for his mother before she died. Maybe she wouldn't have died.

But the world of ifs was a crowded one with too many possibilities and no changes. Looking backward only fed regrets and that didn't help a damn thing.

"I'm just saying," John continued, "your mom was

real excited to know that Sadie Price was going to have your baby."

Rick snapped him a hard look. "Mom told you?"

"'Course she told me. And Elena. Who the hell else did she have to tell?"

"How about *me?*" he demanded, as a spurt of anger shot through him. "I'm standing here wishing I'd been here for Mom. For Sadie. And now I find out that not only my mother knew about the twins, but you and Elena did, too? Don't you think somebody should have told me that I was going to be a father?"

John didn't even blink in the face of Rick's anger. Instead, he frowned. "Yeah, I did think you should be told. But your mother didn't want you distracted while you were over there. She about wore out her knees praying for you every night and she thought that if you knew about the babies that you wouldn't be focused and could end up getting hurt. Or worse."

The mention of his mother's prayers quelled the fiery anger inside him with a bucket of guilt as effective as ice water. But he had to ask. "When she died, why didn't you write and tell me about the girls then? I could have come home."

"For how long? A two-week leave? Then you head back to a combat zone? What would have been accomplished?" John shook his head and scraped one work-worn hand across a hard jaw covered with gray stubble. "No. Your mother was right not to tell you. Wasn't my call to go against her wishes."

"Fine," he muttered, realizing that this was an ancient argument and nothing would be changed by it, anyway. Besides, maybe John was right. Who the hell knew? He could admit that finding out about his mother's death while he was overseas hadn't been an easy thing. Discovering the truth about the girls might have been even harder to take. "Doesn't matter anymore, anyway. Point is, I'm home now. I know about the twins, now."

"Yeah. The question is, what're you going to do about it?"

"Wish I knew," Rick told him.

"Well," John said, slapping him on the shoulder, "while you're thinking, why don't you ride out with me to check the herd. Get your mind on something else. Maybe the answer will come to you when you're not trying so hard to find it."

Rick grinned. "This just an excuse to get me back in a saddle?"

"Damn straight. Want to see if all that walking you do as a marine has made you forget how to ride a horse."

"That'll be the day," Rick assured him. "But Sadie and the girls are coming here for dinner, so I can't be out long."

"Then we better get moving. Unless like I said, you don't feel comfortable on a horse anymore."

"You want to see comfortable?" Rick steered the older man toward the stable. "I'll race you out to the north pasture."

"What do I get when I win?" John asked.

Rick laughed and, damn, it felt good. The summer sun was shining. Sadie and his daughters would be there soon. He was home, on land that called to his soul, and for the first time in a long time, he began to think that home was right where he belonged.

"Castle!"

"It's not a castle, sweetie," Sadie whispered to Wendy as she set the little girl down beside her sister. Then Sadie picked up the stuffed diaper bags and looked up at Rick's ranch house.

"Is castle," Gail insisted.

"Okay," Sadie said on a sigh, surrendering to the inevitable. After all, there *was* a stone tower at one end of the huge house and that was clearly enough for two girls who enjoyed storybooks about princesses at every bedtime.

Wendy clapped her little hands and took off running. Quickly, Sadie shouted, "Wendy, *freeze*."

The little girl stopped so suddenly, she toppled over, landing on her knees and palms. Her lip curled, her eyes scrunched up and a low-pitched wail slowly built to a scream.

"Hey now!" Rick came out of the house and sprinted across the lawn toward his fallen daughter. Before Sadie and Gail had taken more than a few steps forward, he had the little girl swept into his arms and was soothing her out of her tears.

"You okay, sweet thing?" Rick asked, wiping away tears with his thumb.

"Falled down," Wendy said and dropped her head onto his shoulder with a dramatic slump.

"I know, baby girl," he soothed, running one hand up and down her narrow back while his gaze searched for and found Sadie's. "But you okay now?"

"Okay," she said, lifting her head then patting his cheek. "Down," she ordered.

As he set one daughter down, Gail held her arms up to him. "Up."

"Tag teaming me?" he asked with a smile as he lifted the little girl.

"Welcome to my world," Sadie told him ruefully.

How could a man look *that* sexy while holding a child? Sadie's body was humming, her blood simmering and the low, deep-down ache she'd been carrying around for days began to pulse in time with her heartbeat.

"Happy to be here." His voice was low, a soft touch on her already ragged nerve endings.

Honestly, after being around him so much for the last week, Sadie was in sad, sad shape. Oh, she still wouldn't consider marrying a man who only wanted her because she had given birth to his children. But she wasn't above admitting just how badly she wanted him.

And that was a dangerous feeling.

He was a marine. Trained to spot his opponent's weakness. She sighed to herself. Judging by the wicked gleam in his eye, he was doing just that.

"I'm glad you came," he said after a long moment filled only with the twins' excited jabbering.

Those eyes of his were really lethal weapons, she thought. So dark. So deep. Filled with old pains and secrets, so much so that any woman would be tempted to get closer. To discover the man within. To do just what she had done three years ago, Sadie reminded herself sternly.

She remembered it all so clearly, it could have happened the day before. Sadie had been at Claire's restaurant, trying to look as though she didn't mind eating alone. Rick had walked in, strolled over to her table and asked if he could join her.

She had been so lonely, so…lost, that she had said yes. For once in her oh-so-proper life, Sadie dropped her shields, lowered her guard and had allowed the *real* her to come storming out to play. She had held nothing back that night and, in return, she had experienced real passion. Real fire.

They shared dinner, then a walk around the lake, then a drive to a hotel in Midland, then hours of amazing sex. And over the course of that incredible night, Rick had taught Sadie that her ex-husband had been wrong when he accused her of being a frigid ice queen.

Memories rushed through her mind with a staggering force that left Sadie breathless. Image after image rose up within her, bringing back every second of that long-ago night until Sadie practically vibrated with need.

She dragged air into her lungs and forced herself to keep her gaze locked with his. She had succumbed to those eyes and that mouth once. She wasn't going to do it again. She was stronger than her need.

"The girls have been looking forward to coming," she said, stroking one hand across Wendy's soft curls.

Thank God she had the twins with her, she thought. They would be her safety net. She and Rick couldn't very well indulge in hot, steamy, wonderful, frenzied sex with their daughters in attendance, now could they?

Oh, yeah, she thought. *Sad, sad, shape.*

"Not you though, huh?"

"This isn't about me," Sadie told him, even while her mind was taunting, *liar, liar.* Of course she had been looking forward to seeing him. He was all she thought about lately. The man filled her mind while she was awake and starred in her dreams when she managed to sleep.

"Babe, it's *all* about you."

She stiffened. "I told you once, don't—"

"—call you baby." He grinned. "I didn't. Called you babe."

"That's the same thing," she told him, but couldn't quite seem to keep her lips from twitching.

No other man she had ever known had teased her, flirted with her, treated her like…a woman. Most men around here were so deferential, all they saw was the Price name, never Sadie herself.

"How about *darlin'* then?" he asked, deliberately drawing out the word until it became a deep, Southern caress.

"How about we stick with Sadie?"

He shrugged and smiled again. "That'll do. For now."

She took a breath, hoping to steady herself. Instead, she got a whiff of freshly showered male and felt her ragged nerve endings fray just a little bit more.

"How about we go inside?" That delectable smile of his curved his mouth in invitation. "I want to show the girls their room."

He was already headed for the house, Gail on his hip, Wendy's hand tucked into his when his words finally settled in Sadie's mind.

"Their *room?*"

"Cozy as two kittens, aren't they?" he asked, fifteen minutes later, his gaze never leaving the two little girls.

"Why wouldn't they be?" Sadie shook her head as she looked around the pink-and-white splendor.

Twin youth beds, guardrails in place, were covered by lacy white quilts with pink scrolling spelling out each girl's name in flowing script. White dressers stood alongside each girl's bed and a collection of stuffed animals sat perched on little-girl-size rocking chairs. Pink curtains hung at the wide windows that were also gated for safety. There were matching toy boxes, two rocking horses and two identical castle playhouses, complete with tiny dolls and furniture.

The walls were white, with a mural of spring flowers sprouting up from the gleaming wood floor. A rose-colored braided rug in the center of the room provided warmth and comfort. As if even Heaven approved of what Rick had done here, sunlight speared into the room, dazzling it all with a golden glow.

He had only known about the twins' existence for two weeks and yet he'd managed to create a little girl's paradise. She should be pleased, she knew. Instead, a pang of worry reverberated inside her. This was permanence. Rick was making an important statement here. Letting not only his daughters but Sadie know that he was going to be a part of their lives from here on out.

"You like it?" he asked, shattering her thoughts and dragging her gaze back to his.

"What's not to like?" Sadie walked farther into the room and watched her girls delightedly exploring. "How did you get all of this done so quickly?"

"Amazing what enough money in the right hands can accomplish." He leaned against the doorjamb, folded his arms across his chest and narrowed his eyes on her.

A flicker of heat skittered through her system under that watchful stare. "Why?" she asked. "Why do this if you're leaving again? By the time you get back, they'll be too old for this room."

He frowned and his eyes darkened. "I haven't decided yet what I'm going to do, but whatever it is, the girls will be a part of my life. I wanted them to have a place here. To know this ranch as home."

"Their home is with me," Sadie said quietly with a quick glance at the girls as they squabbled over the stuffed animals.

"Could be with both of us," he pointed out.

"Don't start again, Rick," she said with a shake of her head. "We've been down that road too many times already."

"And never really talked about it."

"There's nothing to say."

When the girls scampered into an adjoining room, Sadie grabbed at the excuse to halt her conversation with Rick and called out, "Hold on, you two...."

"Don't worry," Rick said quickly, reaching out to take her hand. At the first touch of his skin to hers, Sadie sucked in a gulp of air. She felt his reaction as strongly as her own and she knew that whatever else lay between them, the sexual heat was still burning fiercely.

He gave her hand a squeeze and released her reluctantly. "Nothing in here can hurt them. I had experts come in and baby-proof the place. Hell, the whole house has had a toddler remodel."

Sadie curled her fingers into a fist to keep from reaching out to him again just to feel that sizzle of heat. Nodding to him, she relaxed her guard on the girls a little.

She'd already noticed the window gates and the plugs in the electrical outlets. And she had to admit that, even with the worry over Rick trying to swoop her girls out from under her, she was touched that he'd gone to so much trouble. But still... "What's in that room?"

He tucked his hands into his jeans pockets and shrugged. "Not a room. It's their closet."

"Their—" Stunned speechless, she followed her girls and found them pawing through rack after rack of dresses, shirts and jeans. The closet had been designed so that everything was on toddler level, so both girls had no trouble reaching all of the new clothing that had been purchased just for them.

On the floor of the closet, clear boxes of different types of shoes were stacked. Chortling gleefully, the twins indulged themselves. Wendy was tugging at a pair of miniature cowboy boots, while Gail was trying to force her sneaker-clad foot into a princess slipper.

"Sweetie, wait a minute," Sadie said, dropping to her knees and taking the slipper from greedy little hands.

"Wanna," Gail argued, her bottom lip poking out in a pout that was a herald of a tantrum to come.

Sadie braced for it, almost looking forward to seeing Rick handle one of his daughters when she was less than the loveable toddler he knew. But she didn't get a chance. Instead, she listened.

"Well, now, you two girls could play in here...or we could go and see your ponies," he coaxed.

"Pony!" Both of them leaped up and charged to Rick as if he was Santa Claus. And no doubt that's just what he looked like to two dazzled little girls.

Their mother however, was a different story. "Ponies?"

"Tiny ones," Rick assured her, scooping both girls up into his arms. "Really. Hardly even related to horses, they're so small."

"The girls don't need ponies," Sadie said, congratulating herself on the calm even tone of her voice.

He grinned. "Wouldn't be much fun to get things only when you *need* them, would it?"

"Pony, Mommy!" Wendy slapped her hands together and Gail laid her head down on her father's shoulder.

Sadie, looking at the three of them united together against her, knew she'd lost this battle. Rick was making all of her girls' dreams come true. From the castlelike tower on his house, to princess shoes, to ponies. Heaven knew what would be next. Just that thought was enough to have her say quietly, "Rick, you can't keep doing this. You'll spoil them rotten."

Surprise etched itself into his features. "How can you spoil a child by loving her?"

She sighed again. The man was hopeless.

"Sadie, I missed their first two years." He looked from one tiny face to the other. "I missed too much. Let me make it up to them *and* to myself."

She looked at the three of them and something inside her liquefied, becoming a warm, bubbling pool of emotion. How was she supposed to stand firm when he melted her with his love for their girls?

Shaking her head, she said, "I draw the line at them *riding* those ponies. At least not until they're three."

"Riding alone? Absolutely not. But we can hold them in the saddles…" he coaxed.

"You're impossible."

"To resist, you mean," he added with a wink.

"Watch me," she countered.

"I do," he said softly. "Every chance I get."

John Henry's wife Elena had made them dinner. A feast of enchiladas, rice and homemade beans. The twins had their supper upstairs, with the older woman who had insisted on taking care of them to give Rick and Sadie time to talk.

Rick made a mental note to give Elena a raise. He'd been wanting to get Sadie all to himself for hours. God knows, he loved those two girls, but their mother was his main focus. With dinner over, dishes done, he had a chance to simply sit with her in the moonlight.

For two weeks now, he'd spent nearly every day with Sadie and their daughters. And while he was enjoying getting to know his girls, what he craved was getting reacquainted with Sadie. She was making him crazy.

Dinner on the stone patio, with candles in hurricane lamps and music drifting to them from inside the house was as romantic a setting as he could imagine. Having the woman driving him to distraction sitting across from him was just the icing on the proverbial cake.

"That was wonderful," Sadie said, sipping at her wine.

"Elena's the best cook in Texas."

Above them, the moon rose in the sky and a soft wind rattled the leaves of the black oaks standing along the perimeter of the yard. The candle on the table dipped and swayed behind its glass walls and the resulting shadows played across Sadie's features.

"I've thought about you," he said quietly. "A lot over the last few years."

She dipped her head then looked up at him from beneath lowered lashes. "I thought about you a lot, too."

He grinned. "Yeah, I can imagine you did, what with those two little reminders running around."

"It wasn't just the girls," she admitted.

"Glad to hear that," he said, and his pulse quickened. Getting Sadie to acknowledge that there was something between them was just the first step. He had to remind her how good they had been together. Had to show her what they could have together now.

She smiled to herself and lifted her face to the night sky. "It doesn't change anything, Rick. Wanting you, I mean."

"From where I'm sitting it does."

"Excuse me." Elena stepped out onto the patio. "I hate interrupting, but I wanted to let you know, both girls are fast asleep."

"Asleep?" Sadie sat up straighter. "I should just take them home."

"Let them stay," Rick said quietly.

"Honestly, Miss Price," Elena told her, "the two of them were just worn out with excitement. I gave them a bath, put them in their pajamas and tucked them right in. They're just fine. The monitor's been turned on and I brought one of the receivers out here for you to keep tabs on them."

She set the white receiver down onto the table and Sadie looked at it. Rick knew she was thinking about just packing up the girls and running for the hills, but damned if he'd let her. This was working out great. He hadn't planned for the girls to fall asleep, but now that they had, he wouldn't waste his alone time with their mother.

"You two enjoy your evening," Elena said. "I'm just heading home myself." She walked across the patio, slipped through the line of trees and disappeared into the shadows, headed for the Henry house just beyond the stable.

"I didn't plan for the girls to stay here with you tonight." She reached for the monitor and turned up the volume.

"You could all stay," he said, getting up to walk to her side of the table.

"Oh, that's not a good idea," she said, even as he pulled her to her feet.

"Best idea I've heard in three years," Rick argued. He smoothed his hands through her long, blond hair and then cupped her face in his palms.

She shivered and a tiny sigh erupted from her throat. "Rick…"

"Stop thinking, Sadie," he whispered and bent to kiss her briefly, sweetly. "Just for tonight, stop thinking."

"We did that once, remember?" She was arguing, but her hands settled at his waist and he felt the heat of her soaking inside him.

"Yeah. I remember. All of it. The feel of you, the taste

of you." He kissed her again, teasing the part in her lips with the tip of his tongue. Every inch of his body was on fire for her. The last couple of weeks, being close to her and yet so damned separate, had been torture. "Do you know, for months after I deployed, I could close my eyes and smell you on me?"

"Oh, my…"

He bent to kiss the curve of her neck and Sadie swayed into him. Breathing deep, Rick groaned in satisfaction. "There it is," he said, his breath moving over her skin, "that scent that is purely you. Smells like summer. Smells like Heaven."

"Rick, you're not playing fair.…"

"I know," he said, smiling against her skin, then nibbling at the elegant line of her throat until she shivered again. "I don't want to be fair, Sadie. I want *you*."

"*Really* not fair," she murmured, hands sweeping up to splay against his back and hold him closer. "But you know this wouldn't solve anything."

"Not asking it to," he whispered.

"It would probably only make things harder."

"Things are pretty hard right now," he confessed, lifting his head to smile down at her.

She laughed and shook her head. "How am I supposed to fight you?"

"You're not. I'm tired of fighting, Sadie. And so are you." He kissed her then, long and deep, tongue tangling with hers, silently demanding that she feel what he felt, want what he wanted.

Finally, though, he broke the kiss, lifted his head and looked into her eyes. He read passion glittering there and knew he'd won this round. Knew that her needs were going to overpower her sense of propriety. Just as they had that night three years ago.

He dropped his hands to her waist, then skimmed his palms up, beneath the hem of her yellow silk shirt. Her skin was softer than that silk and just touching her again inflamed him more than he had expected. His body went rock-hard and aching. His heartbeat pounded in his chest and need clamped a tight fist around his lungs so that breathing was nearly impossible.

Her eyes locked with his and when he covered her breasts with his hands, he saw the flare of desire quickening in those pale blue depths. Even through the lace of her bra, he felt her nipples pebble at his caress. Felt the sweeping rush of heat that was going to engulf them both.

"I am tired of fighting you. Fighting *this*," she said, arching into him, silently asking for more. "So touch me again. Touch me all over. Make me feel the way you did on that night."

He wouldn't have thought it possible to get even harder, but he did. Hearing her ask for him. Seeing her desire. Feeling her heat.

Rick was lost.

Right where he wanted to be.

Seven

With the summer wind blowing all around them like a soft caress, Sadie forgot about standing her ground and gave herself up to the wonder of being in Rick's arms again.

Her entire life, she had done the right thing, said the right thing, been the perfect daughter. Yes, she'd gotten a divorce, but even society expected that to happen once in a while. Until that night with Rick, she had never really rebelled. And in that one night, she had felt more alive than she ever had before.

She wanted it again.

His kiss enveloped her. Their tongues danced in a sensual feast of sensation until Sadie was panting for air and not really caring if she got her next breath or not. Her hands swept up and down his back, loving the feel of his hard, muscled body pressed against her.

He grabbed her and pulled her abdomen close enough

that she felt the thick heaviness of his body. Desire pumped through them both with a rush that was simply shattering. There were so many sensations. So many emotions churning inside her.

Rick unbuttoned her blouse and slid it off her shoulders and down her arms to puddle on the stone patio at their feet. She lifted her arms to him, encircled his neck and gloried in the feel of his hands moving over her bare flesh. In moments, he had unhooked her bra and dropped it, too, to the patio.

Then he set her back from him and looked his fill. The warm summer air felt cool on her heated skin. He bent his head and took first one hardened nipple then the other into his mouth. His lips, tongue and teeth tortured her gently, sending her mind spinning out of control as her instincts took over.

She groaned and held his head to her breast, smoothing her fingers through his short hair, loving the slide of it against her skin. He suckled her and she felt everything inside her liquefy in a rush of molten heat that settled deep at her core.

"Rick…" She swayed into him as her knees went weak in response to the overload of sensation. "I'm going to fall over here in a minute."

"I'm going to lay you down in a minute."

A stirring of unease mixed with excitement lit up her insides. "Out here?"

"We're alone, honey," he said, kissing her again, lightly, teasingly. "There's not a soul around."

"But Elena. John Henry—"

"Never leave their place at night. No more buts, darlin'," he told her, laying one finger across her lips to keep her protests quiet. "Just relax and trust me. Can you do that?"

She looked up into his eyes and realized that she had already made her decision. She wanted another night with Rick. He was the man who had shown her what real passion and excitement was. Did she really want to back away now?

"I can do that," she said before her rational mind could override her desires.

"Just what I wanted to hear," he said and tore off his own shirt.

She reached for him, unable to keep from stroking her fingertips along that bronzed, sculpted chest. He sucked in some air at her touch and Sadie smiled to know that she was having the same kind of effect on him that he was on her.

A purely female, sexual power swirled through her as she ran her palms across his flat nipples and when his eyes narrowed and his jaw clenched, she loved the rush she felt.

"Sadie, you are making me crazy."

"That's the nicest thing you've ever said to me," she said huskily, leaning in to kiss him.

He chuckled and the sound was dark and rich, rolling through her system like warm wine.

"This is crazy," she murmured, knowing it was true, but not really caring. "Heck, *you're* crazy," she added and even she thought it sounded more like a compliment than an accusation.

"It's part of what you like about me," he said and led her to the double-wide chaise. It was warm from the summer sun and overstuffed to make lounging on the patio as comfortable as possible. And Sadie could hardly believe that she was stripping out of her clothes and lying down on it, naked in the moonlight.

The heavy cotton felt scratchy against her skin, but

any discomfort was lost as she watched Rick quickly get rid of his clothes. She sucked in a gulp of air when she took her first look at his body, hard and ready for her. Then she couldn't think at all because he was there, lying on top of her, flesh to flesh, heat to heat.

She sighed when he rolled to his back and pulled her on top of him. She straddled him then, looking down into dark eyes that flashed with wicked heat. He lifted both hands to cup her bare breasts and at the first touch of his hands, she arched into him, pushing herself into his grasp. Sighing, she let all thought slide away as his fingers and thumbs tweaked at her already sensitive nipples.

She needed to touch as well as be touched. Reaching down, she wrapped her hands around his heavy shaft and smiled when he hissed in a breath through gritted teeth. She stroked him, rubbing her fingers up and down his length and across the very tip of him until he was lifting his hips into her touch.

"You're killing me," he groaned.

"Oh, not my intention at all," Sadie promised. Then, feeling sexy and wild and completely out of control, she went up on her knees and slowly, slowly took him into her body. Inch by glorious inch, she accepted him, giving her own body time to stretch to accommodate his. It was an invasion of the most intimate kind and she wanted all of him within her.

She took her time, prolonging the suspenseful glide of bodies locking together to torture both of them. Her eyes closed and she moaned her pleasure.

"Enough," he grumbled a moment later and rolled them over again, until Sadie was on her back and he was wedged between her thighs.

She smiled up at him. "Impatient."

"Damn right. We've waited three years to do this. So let's get to it."

"You are a romantic, aren't you, Rick Pruitt?"

"Darlin', you, naked, in the moonlight—that's as romantic as it gets."

"Smooth talker." She wrapped her arms around his neck and lifted her hips to him.

He pushed deeper inside her and Sadie gasped, tipping her head back to look up at the stars. He was inside her. Filling her. And for the first time in three years, she felt…complete.

He moved then, rocking his hips, setting a rhythm that she raced to match. Her gaze fixed on his, as if his dark brown eyes held every secret she had ever wanted to know. Breath laboring, bodies straining together, they held on to each other and hurtled toward the explosive release waiting for them.

Rick bent his head to take her mouth with his as the first of the tremors wracked her body. She tasted him as a shattering climax claimed her. Sadie held him tightly, shuddering as ripple after ripple of pleasure roared through her.

And before the last of those tremors died away, he groaned and, still kissing her desperately, emptied all that he was into her depths.

Two hours and lots of sex later, they were lying in Rick's bed, just down the hall from their sleeping daughters. The monitor was on the dresser, their clothes were in a heap on the floor and their heartbeats were just beginning to slow down to normal.

Curled up beside him, Sadie rested her head on Rick's chest and took a long, shaky breath. She hadn't felt this good in years. But she knew there would be a price to pay for it. Sleeping with him was going to reopen the talk of marriage and she had the feeling he wasn't going to like hearing her say no again.

"It's good," he said softly, going up on one elbow to look down at her. "Having you here in my bed. Having our daughters sleeping just down the hall."

Sadie sighed. "Rick, what we did tonight doesn't change anything for me."

He smoothed her hair back from her face and she closed her eyes briefly to enjoy the gentle caress. "It changes everything, darlin'."

"No." Opening her eyes, she swallowed back her own needs and fought to remain logical. "It's not me you really want, Rick—"

"Oh, I think the last couple of hours should have convinced you you're wrong about that."

She had to chuckle at that, since her body was still buzzing from his careful attention to detail. "I *mean,* what you want is family. You just found out about the girls and you want them in your life, I understand that. But this isn't about *me.*"

He took a breath and blew it out before saying quietly, "The first time I saw you, you were about seven years old, I think."

"What?"

"My parents took me to dinner at Claire's restaurant and I saw you at another table with Brad and your folks...."

She scooted out from under his touch and braced her back against the headboard. "I don't see what any of this has to do with—"

"I remember," he continued as if she hadn't spoken, "because I was ten years old and didn't much like girls. But then I saw you. Your long blond hair was pulled back by a pink headband and you were wearing a white dress with ruffles. You looked like a pretty doll sitting there with your hands folded in your lap."

A pretty doll. Funny, Sadie told herself, that was how she'd felt most of her life. Not that her parents hadn't loved her, but she had never really been allowed to be a child. She was always in a dress. Always told to sit up straight. Always expected to be perfect.

Which was why she'd made sure her daughters owned more pairs of play pants than they did dresses. At least until Rick came long.

"And I remember the waitress hurrying past your table and she spilled a Coke. It dropped onto your lap and I can still see your reaction in my mind."

"Oh, God," she whispered, "I remember that."

She hadn't thought about it in years. Now that she had though, the day came back in a rush of memories that had her cringing inside.

Rick sat up beside her, tucked a pillow behind her back and then took her hand in his. "You didn't shout or scream in surprise. You just sat there, your white, lacy lap filled with dark brown cola and you cried." His thumb moved back and forth across her hand. "Big, silent tears, while your mom rushed to clean you up and the waitress babbled apologies. Your dad didn't even look at you, he just took Brad and led him outside."

"He never did like scenes," Sadie whispered.

They were having Sunday dinner at Claire's because her father considered it good business to frequent local establishments. He always said, they were the Price family and it was up to them to set an example for others. He said that it was important that people think well of them so they were always to be on their best behavior.

When they got home that night, her father had made

a point of telling her that she had comported herself well
by not throwing a hissy fit in the diner. He said it was
all the waitress's fault, but that everyone in town would
be talking about what a perfect lady Sadie was.

A lady.

At seven.

It had been a stifling way to grow up, Sadie thought
now.

"You were still a beauty at sixteen," he said, leaning
down now to plant a kiss on her forehead.

Relieved to have a change of subject, Sadie laughed.
"Oh, please. You never knew I was alive when we were
teenagers."

"That right?" He dropped one arm around her
shoulders and pulled her in close to him. "I was playing
basketball with some guys one day at the park when
you walked by with Abby and a couple of other girls.
Don't remember who they were, because my memory's
all about you. Your hair was long and you had it pulled
back into a ponytail. You were wearing white pants and
a red top and you were smiling at something. And I
thought you were the most beautiful thing I'd ever seen."

"You're making that up."

"I called your name and threw the basketball to you.
You were surprised, but you caught it. Then you looked
at me like you didn't have a clue what to do next and you
just set the damn thing down on the grass and walked
away."

Her heart softened at his words as she realized that he
had noticed her all those years ago. And she wondered
what might have happened between them if she'd had
enough courage back then to actually talk to him.

"Oh, God, I remember that, too." She laughed a little
uneasily. "I didn't know what to do. I wanted to throw

it back to you, but I was afraid I'd do it wrong and look foolish in front of everyone. So I didn't do it at all. It's the Price way," she told him softly. "Always worry about what people will think."

"Doesn't matter," he said, "wasn't my point."

"What is the point then, Rick?" Yes, knowing that he noticed her was lovely, but talking about the past didn't change the future.

"You were always the unattainable, beautiful Sadie Price," he told her.

"I was," she said softly, shaking her head at the swarm of memories his words had created. "My parents put me on a shelf and kept me there until I was old enough to marry the 'right' man. Of course, he turned out to be all wrong."

"Maybe," he answered, "what you need to do is marry the 'wrong' man who might turn out to be just right."

She looked at him. "You just don't give up, do you?"

"I'm a marine, darlin'. We never surrender."

"God, why are you so stubborn?"

"When I see something I want, I go get it."

"Why me?"

"Hell, have you *seen* you? You're beautiful. Smart. Sexy as hell. And, oh, yeah. The mother of my children."

"There it is again," she said, pushing out of his arms. Sliding to the edge of the bed, she got up and walked to the window overlooking the front yard. Then she turned and speared him with a hard look. "That's the real reason for your pursuit. For your proposals."

"What's wrong with that?"

"I don't want to be the next duty you pick up and shoulder because you think it's the right thing to do. I want to be wanted for *me*."

Now he pushed off the bed and stalked to her side. "I just proved to you that I do want you."

"Rick, we're arguing in circles," Sadie said, laying both hands on his bare chest. "We don't agree. We're not going to agree. So can we just at least drop it?"

He sighed, then pulled her to him, wrapping his arms around her and holding her close. "We can do that. I don't want to waste what we've got fighting over what we don't. So yeah, we can drop it. For now."

She closed her eyes as she laid her head on his chest. That wasn't a concession, she knew. Rick wasn't the kind of man who would give up and walk away from what he perceived as his duty.

But for tonight at least, there was a ceasefire.

A few days later, Sadie was sitting in the TCC dining room having lunch with Abby. The girls were with Hannah, and Sadie hadn't seen Rick since their amazing night together.

She was torn between relief and fury. She should be happy he was backing off as she had asked him to. On the other hand, for a guy who said he never gave up, he was giving up awfully easily.

"You look serious," Abby commented, lifting her glass of iced tea for a sip. "Or is that furious?"

"A little of both, I guess," Sadie admitted. She gave a quick look around.

The dining room was crowded, as it always was at lunchtime. There were members and their wives, seated at the elegant tables. Whispers of conversation rose and fell like the tide and the smooth wait staff moved in and out of the crowd in a seamless dance that was practically choreographed.

Lowering her voice, Sadie said, "It's Rick, of course."

"Naturally. How're things going with him, anyway? Haven't talked to you since the Fourth."

A flush swept up Sadie's cheeks and she was glad that the lighting in the TCC was so dim. Otherwise, everyone in the room would have seen her pale skin burning red. Bad enough that Abby was close enough to notice.

"Well, that's intriguing," Abby said, flipping her long, dark red hair back over her shoulder. Then she narrowed sharp blue eyes and ordered, "Tell me everything."

Sadie did. Leaving out the details of that sinfully sexy night, she got right down to the bare bones of it.

"Chemistry, oh, yes," she said as she was winding down, "we've got that, there's no doubt. But, Abby, he keeps insisting he wants to marry me despite me telling him no at every turn."

"And why is it again you're turning him down?"

Sadie looked at her friend in stunned surprise. "Because he's only asking because of the girls."

Abby smirked and took a sip of tea. She shook her head. "Doesn't sound like it to me. Sounds like he's asking because he can't keep his hands off of you."

A stir of something hot and wicked whipped through Sadie at the words. But she wouldn't be fooled by her own passions. "No. This is about duty. Plain and simple."

Their waiter appeared to deliver two enormous Cobb salads and when he was gone again, Sadie changed the subject. "I'm so tired of thinking and talking about me. What's going on with you and Brad?"

Abby snorted and picked up her fork to stab a slice of hard-boiled egg. "Firstly there *is* no me and Brad. There is simply me battering away at your thick-as-a-post brother."

"And good luck with that," Sadie told her. "But what's happening with the club?"

Abby looked around now, checking to make sure no one was listening. "Brad is running for president of the club and judging from what I've heard, he's pretty much got the position sewn up."

"Uh-oh," Sadie said, thinking that this couldn't possibly end well.

"Exactly. If Brad wins the presidency, then he'll find a way to not only get rid of me, but to keep all women out of the club forever."

"Sounds like him," Sadie admitted.

"Absolutely it does," Abby told her, dropping her fork with a clatter against the ceramic bowl. "*And* the man will find a way to keep this club locked into the past. Honestly, he is infuriating. He's so hidebound to tradition, he should be living in the nineteenth century."

"Also sounds like him," Sadie concurred.

"Well, he's not going to best me," Abby vowed. "You know, all of this started with the talk of rebuilding the club—which I still think is a great idea."

"I can sort of see Brad's point," Sadie said as she looked around the familiar room. Her father was a member of the club and his family was welcome in the public dining room. She had been going there all her life for special occasions. In a way, the thought of it changing sent a pang through her.

"Are you serious?" Abby asked, dumbfounded. "I mean, yes, tradition is nice, but so is central heating!"

Sadie held up one hand, palm out. "I'm with you. Honest. On your side."

"Glad to hear it. For a second there, I was worried that you were slipping over to the enemy team." Ruefully, Abby smiled and took a breath. "Right. Sorry. I get a little steamed when I start talking about Brad."

"Did you ever notice that it's always *men* making

women insane?" Sadie took a sip of her tea and pushed chopped ham around on top of the bed of lettuce in front of her. She didn't really have an appetite, which she also blamed on Rick.

Why wasn't he getting in touch with her?

Was sex all he had wanted?

Were all of his proposals meaningless?

And *why* did she care? This was what she wanted, right?

She groaned and Abby reached over to pat her shoulder in support. "Of course it's men who make us crazy. Women understand each other. It's the Y chromosome that makes everything so irritating."

"So, have you decided what you're going to do about your irritation?"

"Not yet," Abby admitted, but her eyes took on a calculating gleam. "I do have a few ideas, though. It's time we finally break through and tear down the last of the old boy's club barriers around here."

Sadie laughed and felt a little easier. Sure, her situation with Rick was up in the air and more confusing than ever. But at least she wasn't alone in her confusion.

Before she could so much as start in on her salad again, Sadie sensed a subtle shift in the club's atmosphere. The conversations around them were still going on, but there was more of a hush to them now. As if everyone was suddenly interested in the same thing.

"Oh, my," Abby whispered and tapped Sadie's hand.

When she looked up, she turned her gaze to where Abby was pointing and Sadie actually *felt* her stomach drop. Rick was standing in the entryway, dressed in his uniform, an expression of steely determination carved into his face.

In spite of everything, Sadie's stomach did a quick

lurch and spin as adrenaline-spiked excitement dropped into the pit of her belly. She hadn't seen him in days. And now that he was here, right in front of her, her body was lighting up like a Christmas tree.

Darn it.

His gaze locked with hers, Rick strode across the crowded dining room like a man on a mission. As he came closer and closer, Sadie's heart began to pound in anticipation, even as she fought to keep her emotions off her face.

The crowd around them seemed to sense that something special was up. Conversations dwindled away, and as Rick crossed the room, even the wait staff froze in place. It was like the whole room had taken a breath and held it.

He stopped beside their table and spared a quick look at Abby. "Nice to see you," he said.

"You, too," Abby murmured, her gaze shifting to Sadie.

"Sadie," Rick announced, his voice easily carrying across the crowd. "I've got something to say to you."

"Oh God," she mumbled, trying not to notice the dozens of curious stares directed at her.

"And I don't care if the whole world hears me," Rick continued. "Hell, I want them to hear me."

"Don't do this," Sadie whispered, her eyes on him.

"I have to," Rick said.

He'd finally figured out that the one sure way to get Sadie to agree to marry him was to ask her in front of people. The way she was raised, the woman she was, wouldn't allow her to embarrass either him or herself by refusing him.

So he'd spent the last few days finding the perfect ring and waiting for his best opportunity. When he'd discovered she was going to be here at the club having lunch with Abby, Rick made his move.

She was stunned. He could see it on her face, despite how hard she was trying to hide it. Just like that time when she was a girl in the diner, she wouldn't let anyone know what she was feeling or thinking. She would be a lady and do the only thing she could do.

She would finally say yes.

Keeping his gaze locked with hers, he made an elaborate show of dropping to one knee. Then he opened up the small, navy-blue jeweler's box and showed her the enormous diamond he'd picked out for her, making sure the rest of the crowd got a good look, too.

Their audience took a breath and the sound was audible. Sadie just blinked at him. When he had everyone's attention, he spoke, in a loud, clear voice, "Sadie Price, will you marry me? Will you let me be a father to our children?"

Then he waited for her quiet acceptance.

Eight

"You son of a—" Sadie bit off the last word, but no one in the room had any doubt of what she meant.

Rick slowly stood up and watched as glints of raw, gut-deep anger erupted in her usually placid blue eyes. Okay, maybe he might have made a tactical error here.

Abby was chuckling, covering her mouth with one hand to hide her smile. The rest of the room was blistering with questions and comments. He only caught a handful.

"What'll she say?"

"That's Sadie Price. She'll do the right thing."

"If I was her, I'd slap him for embarrassing me like that."

"Well," another woman mused aloud, "if she doesn't want him, I'll take him."

He didn't care what any of them had to say. The only opinion he was interested in was Sadie's. And it didn't look to him that he was going to get the answer he wanted.

Rick scowled as Sadie pushed herself out of the maroon leather booth seat, grabbed her purse and flung a look back at Abby. "Thanks for lunch but I have to go now."

"I can see that. I'll call you later."

She jerked a fast nod, then fired another look at Rick. "*You,* I want to talk to. *Outside.*"

Then she marched across the crowded dining room like a young queen. People's heads turned to watch her pass and a few of the men shot Rick sympathetic glances.

He wasn't interested in sympathy. Snapping the ring box closed, he stuffed it into his pocket and followed his woman out of the club.

The door hardly had a chance to swing shut behind them when she turned on him like a snake.

"What were you *thinking?*"

The summer sun hammered them both the minute they stepped outside. It was like trying to draw a breath through a wet electric blanket. But the vicious heat had nothing on the fury stamped on Sadie's face.

Gritting his teeth, Rick scrubbed one hand across his face. "I was thinking that I want to marry you. Just like I've been thinking for more than two weeks now."

She threw her hands high then let them fall to her sides again in complete exasperation. "And the fact that I've turned you down countless times didn't enter your head?"

"No," he snapped, irritated as all hell that his plan had fallen so flat. He would have bet cold, hard cash on Sadie Price coming down on the side of decorum. It had never occurred to him that she might not leap into his arms for the sake of the watching crowds.

He could see now, it should have.

"I can't believe you did that in front of half the town."

"Seemed like a good idea at the time," he muttered and flashed a glare at a man who stopped to stare at them. Quickly, the bystander hurried on down the sidewalk.

"And I can guess why," she said, stepping close enough that she could poke her index finger into his chest. "Now that the word's out around town and everyone knows that you're the girls' father, you figured they'd all be on your side. And you thought that I'd say yes to avoid making a scene."

His mouth worked as he fought to keep back the words that would damn him.

"You're a worm for trying to use that against me."

"Darlin', I'm gonna use every weapon I've got when I'm facing down a hardheaded opponent."

"I am *not* hardheaded just because I don't want the same thing you do."

"You are if you refuse to see sense just to prove a point."

She sucked in a gulp of air and stared at him as if he'd just sprouted two heads. "Do you really think I'm that small and petty?" she demanded.

A couple of people strolled past, caught a whiff of their argument and picked up speed.

"I didn't say that," Rick told her.

"You might as well have."

"Don't put words in my mouth."

"Why the hell not? That's exactly what you were trying to do to me." She glared at him with a fire that should have scorched him.

"All I did was ask you a question!"

"In public! Was that your idea of a romantic proposal?"

"I *tried* romance, Sadie!" He loomed over her, but to give her due, she didn't back down an inch. "I had you naked in the moonlight, remember?"

"Well, I never heard such a thing!" An older woman stopped dead as she passed them and slanted Rick a horrified look.

"Mrs. Mulaney," Sadie muttered, never taking her gaze from Rick's.

The older woman gave Rick the evil eye. "You should be ashamed of yourself, Rick Pruitt," she snapped. "Sadie, dear, do you need me to call a policeman?"

"No, ma'am, thank you."

"We're fine, thanks," Rick told the older woman with the iron-gray hair and the sucked-on-a-lemon expression. Mrs. Mulaney was the town librarian and lived her life as though it were her duty to tell people "hush" everywhere in town.

"I wasn't speaking to you, Rick Pruitt! But I should think a United States Marine would know better how to conduct himself." She hurried on as if dogs were chasing her.

"That's just perfect," Sadie muttered. "Now Mrs. Mulaney knows that I was naked in the moonlight with you. Just great. That should take about ten minutes to get all over town."

He smirked at her, knowing he'd just scored a point. "Thought you don't care what anyone thinks about you anymore."

"I don't," she snapped. "Not enough to say yes to a marriage proposal that I know you don't even really want to make."

"You *are* crazy," he countered. "I've been straight up with you, Sadie, right from the beginning. I told you I want to marry you. Be a daddy to our daughters. *You're* the one holding back here."

She took a deep breath, held it for a second and then let it slide from her lungs as she shook her head.

"You know," she finally said, "I should thank you. Only a few years ago, I might have accepted that proposal just to keep from making a scene in the restaurant. But because of *you,* I've found myself."

"What're you talking about?" Rick had the distinct feeling he wasn't going to like this, but he had to hear her out. How else could he plan his next move?

"I moved to Houston when I was pregnant because I didn't want to hear the talk. Didn't want the girls to hear it."

"I know that already."

"But what you don't know is, I'm not that woman anymore." Sadie looked up at him. "I've grown up at last and I like who I am now. These last couple of weeks with you have helped me there, too. I'm not perfect little Sadie Price anymore. I don't *care* what this town has to say about me or you for that matter. Let Mrs. Mulaney spill her guts. I'll hold my head up anyway. And later on, if someone's mean to my girls, I'll handle it, but I'll see to it that Wendy and Gail don't care about gossip, either."

She leaned in until their gazes locked in a silent battle of wills. "I'm going to show them so much love, so much complete acceptance for whoever they are, that *they* won't care what anyone else thinks."

There was that pride in her again. It was good to see her so sure of herself. The only downside was, she seemed to have convinced herself she didn't need *him*. And that he couldn't have.

"Sounds good to me, Sadie," he told her, reaching for her only to have her step back, evading his touch. "All of it sounds just right."

"But you don't believe it. You still think I can be maneuvered into agreeing to marry you."

A stab of shame dug into his chest and Rick didn't like the feel of it. Yes, he had tried to trick her into saying yes. So what did that say about him? That he was a desperate man, that's what.

Damned if he'd apologize for it, either. She's the one who was being unreasonable.

"Maybe I was maneuvering you…"

"Maybe?"

He sighed and felt the weight of the diamond ring in his pocket, dragging at him. This day had really not gone the way he'd planned. But there was a part of him that was standing back enjoying this moment in spite of everything.

Damn, she was magnificent. Her eyes flashing, her skin pink with temper, she was so much more than the porcelain doll her parents had made her. So much more than he had thought her to be. And he wanted her now even more than ever.

"If you're waiting to hear me say sorry," he told her with a grunt of frustration, "you've got a long wait."

"Amazing," she muttered.

"Sadie, I'm not going to keep asking you to marry me only to have you slap me down for it time and again."

"Good." She didn't look particularly happy, though.

He moved in on her, ignored the people streaming past them on the sidewalk and pushed Sadie up against the wall of the club. Hands on her shoulders, he could actually *feel* her tremble under his touch and that reaction gave him hope that all wasn't lost. Not yet, anyway.

Because as he'd warned her, he wasn't a man to give up on what he wanted. He had told her he wouldn't keep asking her to marry him and he meant it. But that didn't mean he was through *demanding* she marry him.

"I didn't get a chance to finish what I was telling you in there," he said, voice low.

"I don't want to hear it," she said and tried to pull free of his grip.

He only tightened his hold and kept her pinned to the wall, where she was so close, he felt the heat of her body radiating toward him and damned if she didn't feel hotter than the Texas sun.

"You're going to, though. This you have to hear."

"Fine." She folded her arms over her chest, cocked her head and glared up at him. "What is it?"

"You should know, I'm not reenlisting."

"What?"

He laughed shortly at the surprise in her eyes. Hell, he'd felt the same way when he'd made his decision a day or so ago. But a part of him had known from the moment he saw his daughters that he was through with the Corps. His wandering days were over and he wasn't sorry to see them go.

There was more for him right here in Royal than anything he could find elsewhere. He loved his daughters and he...cared about Sadie. He didn't love her. Wouldn't allow himself to go that far. But what they shared was important, so his decision to come back home, though not easy, had at least felt right once it was made.

"My hitch is up in two months," he was saying. "In two weeks, I've got to report back to duty, but I'll stay stateside until I'm out. Then I'm coming home. To Royal. To *you*."

"Rick," she said, clearly stunned, "I don't know what to say to you...."

"Don't have to say a thing," he whispered, leaning down until his mouth was just a breath away from hers. "I'm doing this for me as much as for you. It's time I took up the reins on the family ranch. The oil business. John Henry's getting up there in age, though God knows he wouldn't admit that. And I miss home. Have for a long time."

She reached up to cover one of his hands with hers. "This doesn't change anything, Rick."

"Everything changes, Sadie. That's all life is. A series of changes. It's up to us to recognize them when they show up."

"Not all change is for the better," she protested.

"This one is." He kissed her, leaning in until their bodies pressed together and he could feel her heartbeat thundering hard in her chest.

He parted her lips with his tongue, took her breath as his own and gave her everything he had. He poured all that he was feeling into that kiss and when it was over, he had the satisfaction of seeing her stagger unsteadily.

She opened her eyes slowly, blinking up at him as if she was waking from a dream. When their gazes met, he smiled, rubbed his thumb across her lower lip. "I'm not going anywhere, Sadie," he said softly. "I'm going to be here. For you. For our girls. And sooner or later darlin', you're going to be *mine*."

She was still dazed from that kiss, and Rick could admit silently that he felt pretty much the same way. Touching her, tasting her, always left him shaken and craving more. But that kiss would have to do both of them for a while.

"Now," Rick said, taking her arm, "I'll see you back to your table and you can finish your lunch with Abby."

Sadie shook her head. "You don't have to do that."

"Yeah, I do." He opened the door, steered her through the dining room and was completely aware of the gazes locked on him. He couldn't give a good damn. He was a man on the ragged edge of control. Sadie had pushed him about as far as he was willing to be pushed. Now it was time to take a stand.

Let her know that he wasn't going anywhere.

Ignoring everyone else in the place, Rick waited for Sadie to slide into the booth beside Abby. Then he inclined his head. "Ladies…" he said, and left.

As he walked out, he heard the whispers following him and he knew damn well what the folks were wondering.

Did she say yes? Or no?

Well, he thought grimly, let 'em wonder.

By the following afternoon, the whole damn town was speculating about Rick and Sadie. There hadn't been such a flurry of gossip since word got out that Abby Langley was a descendant of Royal's very own Texan outlaw, Jessamine Golden.

Strange how much more interesting gossip seemed when *you* weren't the subject of it.

Scowling into the sun, Rick took a pull on his cold beer and looked out over the ranch lake. He'd thought coming out here today with Joe would get his mind off Sadie, but damned if she didn't haunt him even here.

He could still taste her on his lips. Could still feel the soft, curvy pliancy of her body pressed along his. Hear the soft catch of her breath and smell that tantalizing scent that clung to her skin.

Gritting his teeth, Rick finished the beer and tossed the empty into a nearby bucket. It landed with a clatter that seemed overly loud in the stillness.

"Everybody's talking about you, you know," Joe said, swinging his pole back only to let the line and lure fly out to the center of the lake. It hit with a plunk and ripples rolled across the surface, racing toward shore.

"Yeah," Rick muttered. "I know. Good to be home, huh?"

"Well, hell, can you blame anybody? The show you put on at the TCC?" Joe shook his head. "I only wish I'd been there to see it. You could have given me a heads-up. Let me know that you were going to turn the town on its ear so I could be there to watch."

"Right. Just what I needed. One more spectator."

"People are wondering what Sadie's answer was." Joe looked at him, then snorted a laugh. "Judging from your attitude, I'm guessing she's still saying no."

"Woman won't see reason."

"What's new about that?" Joe cranked on the spinning reel, drawing his line back in so he could recast.

Rick's line lay on the water, drifting with the wind. Some fishing trip this was. He couldn't keep his mind off of Sadie long enough to bother to recast. The woman was invading every damn part of his life.

"You're not doing any of the men in town any favors, you know."

"What?" Rick determinedly picked up his pole and reeled in the line. The whirring sound was almost comforting. He was going to fish and he was going to enjoy it, damn it.

"Abby Langley had a talk with my Tina. Told her how

you're pressuring Sadie to marry you." Joe sighed and cast out again. "Now Tina's giving me grief because you're my friend."

"I'd say I'm sorry about that, but I've got my own problems." Shaking his head at the weird workings of the female mind, Rick set fresh bait on the hook.

"Yeah, well," Joe said, "from what I hear, Tina's not the only wife on the warpath, either."

"That's great." Rick shook his head and sent his newly baited hook flying. Good cast.

"Yeah, I slept on the couch last night thanks to you."

"Hey, don't blame me if Tina finally got wise and tossed your ass onto a couch."

"I'm not blaming you." Joe sighed. "My own damn fault for telling Tina I thought you were right to insist on getting married. Man, you should have heard her after I said that." He stopped and shuddered in memory. "My wife's got a temper that could make a rampaging Apache back up and rethink his options. Hell, even after all that, I still say marrying the mother of your kids is the right thing to do, everybody knows that. Now all of a sudden, that's a bad thing?"

Disgusted, Rick only muttered, "Women."

"That about says it." Joe kicked at the cooler beside him. "Hell, the only reason we've got these sandwiches to eat are because I stopped by the diner on the way over. Tina refused to make me her fried chicken. Said she wouldn't have any part in making you happy when you're making Sadie so miserable." Shaking his head, he mumbled, "Not right, cutting a man off from fried chicken with no warning."

Well, that settled it, Rick thought. Every woman in this town was as nuts as Sadie. Time was, a man who *refused* to marry the mother of his children was treated like an outcast. Now, he was getting the same treatment for *trying* to marry her.

How the hell was a man supposed to make sense of something that had zero logic behind it?

A few minutes of companionable silence passed when the only sounds were a few lazy birds halfheartedly warbling in the heat and the gentle slap of water against the shore. Sunlight glittered on the lake and glanced off it as if it were a mirror. Oaks and summer-brown hills surrounded the place and Rick took a moment to feel the familiar sense of home slide through him.

This was his life. The Corps had been good to him, no doubt. And he had been proud to serve. But his last tour in the Middle East had been a rough one. He'd lost a close friend and come damn close to losing his own life.

Hard to imagine, while standing here in the sun-washed Texas beauty, that half a world away, men and women were dying for their country. He was so accustomed now to the whine and punch of gunfire. To the roar of explosions. To the adrenaline-laced moments of kill or be killed, that coming home was going to take some getting used to.

He wanted it though.

The decision to leave the Corps was the right one for him. Destiny had taken a hand and shown him the road he should be taking and he wasn't going to turn his back on it. What he had to do now was find a way to convince Sadie that they should be walking that road together.

"So," Joe said quietly, "you're really coming home to stay?"

"Yeah." Rick nodded. "It's time. Hell, past time, probably."

Joe set the butt end of his pole down against a rock

and reached into the cooler for another couple of beers. He handed one to Rick and said quietly, "I've been meaning to talk to you about something."

"Yeah?"

"That last letter you sent me…"

Rick frowned and took a long drink. Then he stared at his beer as if looking for something to say. He didn't find anything.

"You said your friend died on a patrol."

"Yeah," Rick said and in a split instant, he was back there. Searing heat, gunfire erupting all around him, men shouting, screaming. He heard it all in his sleep. Saw it all in his dreams. He rubbed his eyes as if he could wipe away the memory, but he knew it would be with him forever.

"He saved your life, didn't he?"

"He did." Rick took a breath, stared out at the lake again because he couldn't look at Joe's friendly, concerned face and talk about what had happened to Jeff Simpson. Hell, he didn't want to talk about it at all. But he knew Joe wouldn't rest until he had the story. And, because Rick was moving back home permanently, best to get it out and done now. He steeled himself against the pain and dove in.

"It was an ambush," he said simply, knowing that there was no way in hell Joe could ever understand what it had been like. No one could who hadn't been there. "I was on point, first man into the village. Unbelievably hot. Sweat rolling down your back under your gear, raining into your eyes until your vision blurred and burned.

"Goats and chickens were scrabbling in the dirt and a couple of kids raced by with a battered soccer ball. Everything looked normal, but I just had a…feeling that something was wrong. A second later, I spotted a shooter in a doorway and turned to take him out." He paused for a sip of beer. "Jeff was right behind me. He spotted a sniper on the roof taking dead aim on my back. Jeff reacted fast. Took me down in a flying tackle. In a heartbeat, I was facedown on the street eating dirt while gunfire erupted all around us—and Jeff took the bullet meant for me."

Joe gave a heavy sigh, then slapped his hand against Rick's back. "I can't know how hard that was for you, buddy. Nobody can. But I'm grateful to Jeff."

Rick turned his head to smile at his old friend. "Yeah," he said. "So am I. Doesn't make it any easier to live with though."

"Can't imagine it would." A second later, Joe *whooped* and grabbed his pole. "Finally got a bite. Looks like fish for supper."

Rick watched Joe reel in a huge bass and thought that there was more he hadn't told his old friend. But what was said in the last few moments of Jeff Simpson's life was nobody else's business. In his mind, Rick heard his friend's strained whisper. Saw the pleading in his eyes and mentally added bricks to the wall he had built around his own heart that day.

Looking around him again, Rick felt the peace of his home ranch slide into him once more, easing the tattered edges of his soul. He took a breath of hot summer air and smiled to himself as he thought that, yeah, he was especially grateful to Jeff Simpson. And maybe that's the main reason Rick was going to leave the Corps. He didn't want to waste the life that Jeff had made possible.

He had a chance here, for more than he ever could have hoped for.

And he was going to take it.

Nine

Later that night, Sadie arrived back at the Price family home exhausted. She'd spent most of the day with Abby, decorating the club for the upcoming TCC Founder's Day dinner and dance. The annual event was the highlight of the year in Royal. Every member of the club would be there with their families, and Abby was bound and determined that this year would be something special.

And once Abby had her mind made up, Sadie thought with a smile, nothing could stop her. Not even Brad—who had, of course, shown up to protest everything they were doing.

"There's nothing wrong with the decorations we use every year," he had said, flatly challenging Abby to fight him on it.

He wasn't disappointed. Abby had climbed down from the ladder she was using to string twists of blue-and-gold crepe paper across the ceiling. Fisting her hands on her hips, she had faced him down.

"And then we can have the same food, the same wine and maybe even the same songs. Heck," Abby told him, "we don't even have to hold new dances, we can just videotape it and play it for the members every year. That way nothing will *ever* change and you'll finally be happy."

"Tradition means something in Texas," Brad had argued.

"Progress means something here, too," Abby countered. "Else we'd all still be riding horses and sending telegrams instead of emails!"

"Progress for progress's sake means nothing."

"Holding on to tradition because you're too *cowardly* to change means even less."

Sadie smiled just thinking about how her brother's face had frozen into a mask of frustration and barely reined-in temper. It was at that point that Brad had stormed from the club, looking as if he was about to explode. To be fair, Abby hadn't been doing any better by the time he left. It was a good hour and a half before Sadie's friend was able to talk without grumbling.

"The man just doesn't know who he's dealing with," Sadie said aloud.

She parked just opposite the front door, shut the engine off and dragged herself out of the car. She just stood there for a long minute, leaning against her SUV, looking up at the night sky, too tired to even walk the short distance to the house. Abby was a hard taskmaster, but Sadie knew this ball was going to be the best one ever.

But, time was passing and she still had to get inside and give the girls their bath and tuck them into bed.

Smiling, she forced herself toward the house only to stop when the front door was flung open. Her father stood in the open doorway, backlit by the hall light.

"Dad." Pleasure warred with a sinking sensation in her chest. She loved her father, but had figured out a long time ago that she was simply never going to be the daughter he wanted her to be. "When did you get home?"

"This afternoon." In his seventies, Robert Price was still a handsome man. His hair was mostly silver now, but he stood tall and straight and still carried the air of authority that had ruled Sadie's entire life.

Summoning a smile, she walked to him, went on her toes and kissed his cheek. "It's good to see you. Did you enjoy the Caribbean? Catch lots of fish?"

"I did," he said grudgingly. "Until I arrived home expecting to get a little time with my granddaughters only to find they're not here."

A ball of lead dropped into the pit of her stomach. Panic clutched at her heart. "Not here? What do you mean they're not here? They have to be here. Hannah babysat them for me today while I was at the club with Abby and—"

None of that mattered. Nothing mattered but finding her daughters. Where was Hannah? What could have happened?

She pushed past her father, headed for the staircase, to the girls' room, but her father's stern, no-nonsense voice stopped her dead.

"Don't bother, they're not in their room. Hannah tells me their *father* picked them up this afternoon and took them out to his ranch."

Slowly, Sadie turned around to face her father. His cool blue eyes were glinting with disapproval. The lead ball in her stomach iced over, then caught fire in a splintering shower of fury that swept through her in such a rush she could hardly draw a breath.

"He did *what?*"

"You heard me, Sadie. Rick Pruitt picked up the girls and took them home with him." Frowning, he asked, "Is this going to be a regular thing now? Are the girls going to be tossed back and forth between you two with no notice at all?"

"No," she told him, feeling the fire of her anger slide through her veins. "They're not."

"Hannah tells me that Pruitt has proposed to you."

"He did." Sadie was already walking out of the house, the heels of her sandals clacking noisily against the floor. Her father kept pace with her, out the door, down the porch steps and across the driveway.

Robert slapped one big hand on the car door to hold it closed when Sadie tried to wrestle it open. "And you turned him down?"

"I did."

"Why the hell would you do that?" he bellowed. "The Pruitt boy wouldn't have been my first choice, but you made that decision when you conceived your girls. Now he's here, ready to do his duty and you tell him *no*?"

"I am so bloody *sick* of the word *duty!*" Sadie shouted it and almost enjoyed seeing the shock written on her father's expression.

"I'll thank you not to raise your voice to me," Robert said coolly.

"It's the only way you'll ever hear me, Dad," she snapped. "I am no one's *duty*. I won't be forced into marriage. Not again."

This time, her father at least had the grace to look abashed. After all, it had been *he* who had forced her to marry Taylor. The man who had shown Sadie up close and personal just how humiliating a life could get.

"You owe it to your children—"

"That's right, Dad," she interrupted him and felt a rush of power inside her. She'd never stood up to him before and at that moment, she couldn't for the life of her fathom why not. "The girls are *my* children. Not yours. I'll make the decisions concerning them and I don't need any help. Not from you. Not from Rick Pruitt."

"You're obviously overwrought," Robert said.

"No, Dad," she countered, "I'm not overwrought. I'm *pissed*." She deliberately used a word she knew her father would find distasteful and felt another wash of freedom sweep through her.

"Sadie," her father said, his voice softer now, his eyes filled with concern.

No doubt, she told herself, he was convinced that she'd had a nervous breakdown. One padded room, coming up.

"I'm not crazy," she said. "I don't need to lie down. And I don't need you telling me what to do. Not anymore."

He opened and closed his mouth several times, but not a sound came out. For the first time in Sadie's memory, she was seeing her ever-so-perfect father speechless.

Sadie looked up at him and realized that the man who had run her life…the man whose approval she had sought for so long…no longer worried her. She was an adult now. A mother. And she didn't owe her father or any other damn person in Royal an explanation for anything she did.

"As for what happens with my girls, that's between me and Rick," she added. "Frankly, Dad, it's none of your business."

"Sadie!"

"Oh," she said, since she was on a roll and why stop now, "I'll be finding a place of my own. The girls and I can't stay here, Dad. I appreciate the interim help but it's time I stood on my own two feet again."

Deliberately, she peeled his fingers off the car door, opened it and slipped inside. She fired up the engine, rolled down her window and said, "I'm going to collect my daughters. I'll talk to you later."

And fatigue forgotten, she stepped on the gas until her tires squealed a protest as she peeled out of the driveway. A quick glance in her rearview mirror showed her that her father was still staring after her, clearly thunderstruck.

She smiled grimly.

He wouldn't be the *last* man she had it out with tonight.

Rick was ready for her.

He had been waiting for this confrontation since bringing the girls home to the ranch a few hours ago. Rick had to admit that without Sadie's housekeeper Hannah's cooperation, he never would have gotten away with it. Thankfully, though, the older woman was on his side in this mess. Also thankfully, Hannah had been with the Price family so long, was so much a mother to Sadie, that she wasn't worried about the possibility of losing her job for helping him.

It had been good, having his kids here for the afternoon. They had explored the stable, petted horses and fed carrots to the two ponies. They visited John Henry's golden retriever, who just happened to have given birth to a litter of pups the week before. The twins had been delighted with those puppies and were already busy claiming all eight of them.

Rick smiled, in spite of the battle that was looming in his immediate future. He was being sucked into a world filled with puppies, ponies and little girls' laughter.

And he loved it.

No way was he going to lose it.

When Sadie brought her car to a screeching halt out front, Rick opened the door and stood on the threshold, arms crossed over his chest, feet braced in a fighting stance. He knew she wouldn't listen to reason, so he had decided to try different ammunition in their private little war.

Looked like he had gotten her attention.

Sadie slammed the car door and shouted, "Where are they?"

"Right here," he said. "Where they belong."

She came around the front of the car like an avenging angel. He wouldn't have been surprised to see sparks flying off the top of her head, she was so furious.

Well, she should join the club because he was pretty mad himself. And he was fed up. Not a good combination.

"The girls *belong* with their mother."

"Wrong," Rick said as she closed on him, fury obviously firing every step she took. "They belong with their parents. Both of us."

She actually growled and threw her hands in the air helplessly. "We are not together! Damn it, Rick…"

"Hey, I tried to be reasonable. I tried to do the right thing. You don't want to hear it."

Her eyes widened and both blond eyebrows shot high on her forehead. "And you think *this* is the way to convince me to marry you? Kidnapping my daughters?"

He snorted derisively. "I didn't kidnap anybody. Those girls are just as much mine as yours."

She stomped up the front steps, stepping into the light thrown from the entryway. Illuminated against the backdrop of night, she looked even more beautiful than ever, he thought. Her long blond hair was loose around her shoulders. Her green T-shirt was wrinkled, her blue jeans were faded and soft and the heeled sandals she wore displayed toenails painted a deep crimson.

He wanted her so badly he could hardly breathe.

She pulled in a deep breath that did wonders for that T-shirt, then she lifted her chin and glared at him with all the freezing power of the ice princess he had once thought her to be.

"I want to see my daughters. Now."

"All you had to do was ask," he said.

"Why should I have to *ask* to see my own kids?" she snapped.

"Huh. Exactly what I've been asking myself," he told her.

Her mouth tightened up and he knew she was gritting her teeth in pure frustration. Good to see she was feeling a little of what he'd been dealing with lately.

"Are you going to let me pass?" she finally managed to grind out.

"Absolutely," he said and stepped to one side, allowing her to slip past him and into the house.

"Where are they?"

"In their room," he told her, following her as she headed for the wide staircase. "They're perfectly happy. Elena made them dinner, they've had a bath and now they're playing before bedtime."

"Their beds are at home."

"This is their home."

The wall along the stairwell was lined with dozens of framed photos. Of Rick's family, going back generations. This was the Pruitt home. Where Pruitt children were raised. Where his girls would grow up, he told himself firmly.

She stopped halfway up, pausing on a wide stair tread, and turned her head to fry him with another hot look. "You had no right."

Rick grabbed her arm and held her in place. "I had every right. I'm their father."

"You should have asked me."

"Right!" He laughed shortly without a trace of humor. "Like you enjoyed just asking me to arrange visits with the girls? I'll be damned if I'm going to ask permission every time I want to see my own kids."

She huffed out a breath, threw a quick glance at the top of the stairs, then turned her gaze back on him. "Rick, we're going to have to work this out. Legally. Visitation. Schedules."

"Do I look like the kind of man who's going to visit his kids according to a schedule some lawyer cooks up?" he asked her, keeping his voice low, so his daughters wouldn't hear him arguing with their mother.

Pulling her arm free of his grasp, she said shortly, "You won't have a choice. This is how things are done, Rick."

"Not in my family," he countered. "In my family, parents and children live together. They love each other. Those girls have a right to grow up on the ranch that will be theirs one day, Sadie. I want them to know it. To love it, like I do." He waved one hand at the wall behind her. "Look at those pictures, Sadie. That's family. The twins' family. They belong here."

"They will be here," she said, clearly trying to appease

him. "But they're not going to live here with you full-time, Rick. They'll be with me. They need their mother."

"Yeah, they do," he acknowledged. "But they need me, too."

He looked into those blue eyes and found himself fighting against his own instincts. Yes, he'd gone to her house to collect the children, not just because he'd wanted to be with them. But because he knew it would be a hard lesson for Sadie. He wasn't going to be cheated out of his kids' lives because their mother was too stubborn to do the right thing.

"I won't be bought off with weekends and part of the summer. I won't be a part-time visitor to my own children."

"I didn't say it would be like that."

"Yeah? How do you see it going, then?"

She sighed heavily and he only now noticed the signs of weariness about her. Her eyes weren't as clear as they usually were and there was a decided droop to her shoulders. Looked to him like she'd been getting by on very little sleep lately. Just like him. He didn't know whether to feel bad about that, or to be pleased knowing that she was as affected by this battle between them as he was.

He went with pleased.

Sagging against the wall, she looked at him for a long minute and finally shook her head. "I came over here ready to skin you alive for taking the girls without so much as telling me what you were up to."

"I can understand that."

"Now, I'm just relieved they're all right and truthfully, I'm too damn tired to fight with you *and* my father all in one night."

One of his eyebrows arched. "Your father? You took him on?"

"I did," she mused, a flicker of pride appearing briefly in her eyes. "In fact, I actually told him to mind his own business."

He whistled and felt a stirring of admiration for her. "Bet that came as a surprise."

"I'm sure," she admitted. "But he's not the only one I'm willing to stand up to, Rick."

"I get that, too." He moved in closer, bracing both hands on the wall on either side of her, effectively bracketing her in a cage of his arms. "But, Sadie, I'm not some trained dog you can tell to come and go as you please."

She laughed at the image. "Trust me, I never thought that of you. No one would."

"Good," he said, nodding. "And I'm not a civilized man, either, and you should know that about me. I'm a Texan and proud of it. I'm not the polite society type of man who'll step aside and say thanks very much for whatever scraps you're willing to hand me."

She sucked in a gulp of air and nodded. "I know."

"I won't be shut out of the girls' lives. I won't take second best. And I won't settle for less than everything I want."

Something hot flashed in the depths of her eyes and Rick felt a like fire start deep inside him. Even furious with her. Even so frustrated he could hardly think straight anymore, he still wanted her. Somehow, in the last couple of weeks, Sadie Price had become *essential* to him.

She was more than the girl he used to dream of on those tours of duty. She was more than that one hot night that had resulted in two children. She was more than his memories of a cool, untouchable girl in a prissy white dress.

Hell.

She was everything.

And suddenly, their battle wasn't as important as having her in his arms again.

"Stay with me tonight," he whispered, leaning in until his mouth was just a kiss from hers.

"I don't think—"

"Good," he interrupted her quickly. "Don't think. Just react, Sadie. To what's between us."

"What would that solve?"

"Why does it have to solve anything?" He kissed her, lightly, delicately, his teeth pulling gently at her bottom lip until she was nearly whimpering. When he let up, he raised his head, looked her in the eye and said, "The girls are ready for bed. You don't want to go back and fight with your father again. So stay. *Stay,* Sadie...."

Closing her eyes briefly, she reached out and wrapped her fists in his black T-shirt, crumpling the fabric. "This isn't why I came here."

"So? Let it be why you don't leave."

"Daddy!"

He jerked his head up at the sound of Wendy's plaintive wail demanding his presence. Then he realized he could already tell the difference in the twins' voices and he smiled. They were a part of him, those girls. His flesh and blood. His family.

"Daaaaaddddddy..." Now Gail sang out, stretching that one word into about a dozen syllables and Rick's grin spread until Sadie couldn't help but return it. Would he ever get tired of hearing his children calling for him? He didn't think so.

"What do you say?" he asked, pushing off from the

wall to fold his fingers around her much smaller hand. "How about both of their parents read them bedtime stories? *Together.*"

She looked down at their joined hands, then back up, into his eyes. He wished he knew what she was thinking because there was pleasure mixed with sorrow in her eyes and that kind of combination could give a man gray hair before his time.

But a moment later, she nodded. "Together. Tonight, at least."

"That's a start," he said and led her up the stairs to where their twin daughters were waiting.

Ten

An hour later, the girls were fast asleep and Sadie was stretched out on Rick's bed. She had to get up and take a shower, but for the moment, she was too tired to even attempt it.

She ran her hand over the heavy, dark red quilt beneath her and felt her insides tremble at what she knew would be coming soon. Maybe this was another huge mistake, she admitted silently. But at the moment, there was nowhere else she'd rather be.

Amazing that this man could infuriate her to the point of mayhem and in the next instant, kiss her until all she could think about was ripping off her clothes and falling into his arms.

"This is *not* a rational way to live," she murmured aloud.

Sitting up, she scooted to the edge of the bed and gave a quick look around. Rick was off in the kitchen getting them something to eat, so she had at least a few minutes to herself.

This wasn't the room she had been in only the week before. He had moved his things into the master suite and she knew that was a sure sign that he meant what he'd said about leaving the Marines and coming home to stay.

There was a bay window at the front of the room and a window seat at its base. A stone fireplace was on one side of the room and on either side of the massive hearth stood floor-to-ceiling bookshelves. There were two comfy chairs drawn up in front of the now cold fireplace and the bed was big enough for four people.

It was a sumptuous room, somehow homey and sensual all at once.

Her thoughts dissolved as she heard the distinctive sound of rushing water. Sliding off the bed, she walked across the room and entered a bathroom that most women would have killed for.

Acres of sky-blue tile with white accents gleamed in the soft light of dozens of lit candles. An oversize tub was frothing with bubbles and a mirror that stretched the length of the room reflected those dancing flames—and the man who had lit all of the candles.

She looked at Rick. "Where did you come from?"

He jerked his thumb at the closed door behind him and grinned. "It's a sitting room my mom used when she wanted to get away from my dad for a while without really leaving the house."

"Handy," she said and looked longingly at the steam and bubbles drifting up out of the tub.

"Come on." He held out one hand to her. "A bath'll make you feel better."

"It'll probably put me to sleep," she warned him.

"Oh, I don't think so," he said. "See, that tub's more than big enough for *two*."

Heat slapped at her and jolted the last bits of fatigue from her system in an instant. Her body flushed and that now familiar, damp ache settled between her thighs.

He smiled at her and what she read in his eyes made that ache pound in time with her heartbeat. Yet, she couldn't resist teasing. "You mean big, bad Texan men take bubble baths?"

"Darlin', if we've got company like you, there's a lot we'll put up with."

He walked toward her and every step he took made the anticipation inside Sadie ratchet up another notch. By the time he reached her, she was hardly able to swallow past the knot of need in her throat.

"Now," he said, taking hold of the hem of her T-shirt to drag it up and over her head, "let's get you undressed and into that tub."

As good as his word, in seconds, Sadie was naked and he turned her so that she was facing herself in the mirror. Any embarrassment she might have felt drained away in an instant. She looked into her own eyes and saw the flash of heat there. Then she lifted her gaze to the reflection of the man who stood behind her.

He covered her breasts with his hands, and as she watched their mirrored images, Sadie felt tingles of excitement light up inside her. His hands were big and tanned and the palms were calloused. She caught her breath and held it.

"Now," he whispered, dipping his head to the curve of her neck, "I want you to watch me touch you."

He looked into the mirror and met her reflected gaze. When she nodded, he slid one hand down her body, along the curve of her waist, back over her abdomen to the juncture of her thighs. A pale brush of blond hair was all that stood between him and the object of his quest.

Sadie couldn't draw another breath. Her head was fuzzy, her legs were weak and all she could do was squirm against him. She felt the cold chill of his belt buckle against her spine and the coarse rub of his jeans. But more importantly, she felt the hard ridge of his body pressed into her bottom.

He sighed as she moved against him, but shook his head at her in the mirror. "First you, darlin'. First I want to watch you come for me. I want *you* to see us together. To know what I see when I look at you. To see my hands on your body. To feel my mouth on your skin."

Every word he whispered was another match adding to the inferno burning within her. Reaching back, Sadie hooked one arm around his neck, holding his head close, even as she parted her thighs for him and silently begged him to ease the throbbing ache at her core.

His gaze caught hers in the mirror as he slowly, slowly lowered his hand to the heart of her body. The first brush of his fingers against her sex brought a whimpered sigh scraping from Sadie's throat. She laid her head back against his shoulder, kept her gaze locked on their mirrored images and concentrated on what he was making her feel.

His fingers moved over her flesh, sliding back and forth, dipping into her heat only to slide out again. His thumb smoothed across that one perfect nub of sensation until Sadie was gasping and writhing against him. Still she watched, unable to look away, unable to tear her eyes from the image of his hands on her body.

With his free hand, he tugged and tweaked at one of her nipples, creating a tangled mass of desires that threatened to choke her with their strength. She was a shivering, trembling knot of raw nerves as he continued to stroke her innermost flesh in the most intimate caresses.

Again and again, he delved deep within her. First one finger and then two, taking her higher, pushing her faster until she was twisting against him and fighting for air as desperately as she fought to reach the climax building within.

"There it is," Rick whispered, obviously sensing her release was close. "Grab it, Sadie. Take what I can give you and let me watch your pleasure."

"Rick...Rick..." She shuddered, gasped, pulled in a desperate, frantic gulp of air and rocked her hips against his hand in a frenzied rush toward completion. "Touch me harder," she whispered. "More...more..."

He looked into her reflected eyes and gave her what she needed. He stroked that nub of flesh where so much pleasure was caged until she splintered in his arms and called his name helplessly.

Minutes, hours might have passed for all Sadie knew. Her hips were still moving on his hand and she didn't want him to ever stop touching her. She was spent. Sated. And still wanted him.

He turned her in his arms, wrapping her up close to him and kissing her until he couldn't breathe, think. Rick thought he had known want before, but those few moments with her, watching her pleasure move across her face, hearing her breathless cries had inflamed him past the point of reason.

Tongues tangling together, hands moving, exploring, bodies pressed together, they stood, locked into an inseparable unit in the middle of the plush bathroom. The world fell away until it was only the two of them with the constant rush and stream of hot water filling an enormous tub to keep them company. The air was hot and sultry. The steam from the tub misted around them like shadow dancers.

Rick tore his mouth from hers, then quickly rid himself of his own clothing. Sweeping her up into his arms, he carried her into the tub and sat down in the hot, frothy water, cradling her on his lap. Her breasts pushed into his chest. Her wet, silky body moved against his. Her hands slid up his neck and framed his face as she kissed him with a heat that was more enveloping than anything that had gone on before.

As if they had each resigned themselves to the inevitable. As if the harsh words between them were forgotten and the problems still waiting for them were resolved.

They were lost, both of them, and together they were found.

He reached down, took her legs and parted them over him. She straddled him easily and moved quickly to take him inside her. There was no slow, deliberate torture this time. No. Now, the torture was being apart. Their only salvation was to join. To lock their two separate bodies into one. To claim the magic that they could only find together.

She impaled herself on him, letting her head fall back as he filled her. Rick kept his hands at her slender waist, then slid them to her hips. He moved her on him, helping her set a fast, breathless rhythm designed to push them both over the edge as quickly as possible.

They'd had the prelude.

Now they each wanted completion.

Still the raging torrent of water rushed into the tub. The jets on the sides of the massive tub pulsed, driving that water into his back, across her skin. More sensations added to those that were born with a touch.

She rode him desperately, rising and falling, releasing him and claiming him again and again. And through it all, her gaze remained fixed with his. As if nothing else existed beyond this room. Beyond this small sea of water that held them in a hot, foaming embrace.

Rick's breath was hard and fast. His needs erupting inside him, quickening with every move she made. He leaned forward, taking first one of her nipples then the other into his mouth, working them with his teeth and tongue. Nibbling. Suckling. Taking her needs into him and giving them back to her mixed with his own.

Her breath sang around him like a damn symphony. She sighed and his heart fisted. She moaned and he got even harder. She twisted her body on his and he felt the tug of release pulling at him.

"Go, darlin'," he urged, rearing back to look up at her fierce, beautiful face. "Take me as only you can."

"I want to watch you now," she said, each word coming in a short, hard gasp. "Come first. I'll follow."

Her gaze locked on him and Rick did as she asked. He released the taut reins of control, surrendered to her heat and allowed his body to erupt into hers.

He called her name on a harsh, guttural groan and before his body had emptied itself, he felt the first tremors shake through her and knew she had kept her word and followed after him.

Sadie slumped against him, her breathing ragged. Rick wrapped his arms around her, murmured her name and even as he held her close, he silently vowed never to let her go.

An hour later, they were lying together in his bed and Sadie was more confused than ever. She ran her fingertips up and down his arm, draped across her middle. She'd come to the ranch tonight, half ready to have him arrested for kidnapping or, at the very least, to hit him with something heavy.

Instead, she'd landed in his bed, in his arms and she couldn't bring herself to regret it. So what did that mean? Her feelings were so convoluted, her mind so tired of going over the same arguments and finding no answers.

"You're thinking," he whispered, tugging her closer.

Her back to his front, she felt his heat sliding into her body. His breath brushed against her hair and the steady thud of his heartbeat pounded in time with hers.

"C'mon, Sadie," he prompted, "I can practically hear the wheels in your mind turning. Tell me what you're thinking."

She turned her head so she could look back at him. Her heart turned over in her chest as her eyes locked with his. How had he become so important to her in so short a time?

Or was it that short? she wondered. Had they been heading here all their lives? Was the crush she'd had on him as a girl only the seeds of what was flowering between them now?

Oh, God. Her stomach pitched as she realized the hard truth she'd been managing to ignore for days. Maybe years.

She was in love with Rick Pruitt.

Her heartbeat sped up and her mouth went dry.

There was no other explanation for her behavior. Why else would she have turned down his marriage proposals time after time? If she didn't love him, she might have married him if only for the sake of the girls.

But loving him, how could she do that? How could she sentence herself to a half life where *she* loved and wasn't loved in return? He'd made no secret of the fact that he wasn't interested in love. What he wanted was his children and a great sex life with her. It wasn't enough.

Her eyes closed as her heart wrenched in her chest. Misery rose up and choked her.

When did this happen? That first night when they made the twins? Or was it before, when a teenaged Rick had smiled at her? Or was it, she asked herself, when he'd stormed back into her life demanding to be a part of it? Or maybe, she thought, it had happened when she had first seen him with their girls? Watched the wonder in his eyes, the pure love radiating from him for those two tiny charmers?

Oh, it didn't matter when it had happened. All that mattered now was the fact that she was in love with a man who felt nothing for her but desire.

Misery spilled into despair. Loving alone was a sentence of loneliness and she didn't see a way out of it.

"Okay," he said, dipping his head to kiss her temple. "Now I have to know what's making you frown when you should be feeling as good as I do right now."

"I do feel good," she said quietly, knowing that statement for being only a half truth. "But—"

He dropped his head onto the pillow. "Knew there had to be a 'but' in there somewhere."

"How can there not be?" She turned around, braced her forearms on his bare chest. Looking into his eyes, she saw everything she could ever want and knew that unless he loved her, too, she would never have any of it. "Nothing's been solved, Rick. We still have a major problem."

"*You* have the problem, darlin'," he said, tapping her nose with his finger. "Me, I'm a happy man. I know what I want. I know what I've *got*." He ran one hand over her back in a slow stroke that had her arching into his touch like a cat.

Sighing, Sadie told herself to get a grip and try to talk. Her body, though, kept turning on her. "I was furious with you today."

"Yeah." He wiggled his eyebrows at her. "May all our fights end just like this one did."

He gave her a quick squeeze and Sadie felt a well of sorrow fill her. Realizing that she was in love should have made her happy. But all she could see was more pain headed her way. And still, she had to know for sure.

"Rick, why do you want to marry me?"

"What?"

"Simple question," she said, hanging onto a slender thread of hope. Maybe he did love her. Maybe he had just assumed that she would know that when he proposed. Maybe there was still a chance that she could have the man—the life—she wanted.

Because she couldn't be a wife only because she was a mother. She couldn't marry a man who simply *desired* her, either. There had to be more, she thought.

There had to be love.

Rick studied her face for a long moment, then used the tips of his fingers to smooth her hair back behind her ear. Emotions churned in his eyes, but they appeared and disappeared so quickly, she couldn't identify them. All she could do was wait and pray that he would say the one thing she needed to hear.

"You know why," he said, and that bubble of hope inside her popped. "We're good together, Sadie. We make a good match. We've got kids and we should be a family."

"We should," she agreed sadly, knowing that it would never happen. Not this way. Not the way he wanted it to.

With no other options open to her, Sadie couldn't stay. She pushed out of his arms, slid off the bed and walked to the chair where she'd dropped her clothes.

He sat up, quilt pooled at his waist. In the soft lamplight, his skin looked like burnished bronze and his brown eyes were shadowed and dark. "What're you doing? What's wrong?"

"I'm going home," she said softly.

"Damn it, Sadie." He jumped out of bed and walked to her, grabbing her arms when he reached her. "Don't do this to us anymore. This game between us is getting old."

"I agree," she said, "and I don't want to play anymore. But, Rick, it isn't *me* doing this."

She tugged her T-shirt over her head and stuffed her arms through the sleeves.

"Well, it's not me. I'm not the one running away."

She cocked her head and looked up at him. "Aren't you?"

"What's that supposed to mean?"

Sadie sighed and lifted both hands in surrender. "Never mind. It's nothing."

"Then why are you leaving?"

"Because you can't give me what I need."

"Bull." He glared down at her and his dark eyes fixed on her mercilessly. "Tell me what you're talking about and I'll get it for you."

"Love."

It was as if the world took a breath and held it. The silence between them was so profound, Sadie heard the drip of the water faucet in the bathroom. The soft sighs their children made, drifting through the baby monitor. The silent crack of her own heart breaking.

"Well," she said, when she couldn't bear the quiet any longer. "That put an end to the conversation, didn't it?"

"Sadie…"

She read regret in his eyes and that tore at her. She didn't want his pity. She wanted his love and, clearly, she wasn't going to get it. Shaking her head, she stepped into her underwear then snatched up her jeans. "I have to go."

"Sadie, I *care* for you," he said tightly. He reached for her, then let his hand drop before he actually touched her. "More than I have for anyone in my life. Isn't that enough?"

She wished it could be. More than anything, she'd love to hold him and have him lead her back to bed. To wake up every morning with his arms wrapped around her. To build the family she had always dreamed of. Yes, she wished caring could be enough. But it wasn't.

"No," she said, flinging her hair back out of her face to look at him. "It's not. I deserve more, Rick. *We* deserve more. We deserve love."

He pushed one hand across the top of his head and bit back a curse. "How do you even know what love *is?*"

She smiled sadly. "You know it when you feel it."

"Well, that's clear as mud."

Now it was her turn to reach for him. She cupped his cheek in her palm. "I love you, Rick. Maybe I always have."

He caught her hand and held it to his face. "Then—"

"No, one person in love isn't a marriage," she said, "it's a recipe for disaster. Remember, I was married to a man who didn't love me. I can't do that again."

"I'm not him."

"No, you're really not," she agreed. "You're a better

man than he ever was. But the next time I get married, it will be because I've found someone who loves me."

"You don't know what you're asking."

"Yeah," she insisted, "I do."

He released her hand and shook his head. "No. You throw the word *love* around, but you don't know. You don't know the pain it brings...what havoc it can cause. Well, I do. I saw what love can do to a man while I was deployed."

Sadie was watching him and saw his features tighten and his eyes fill with shadows. The old pain and secrets she had once glimpsed in those depths were shining there, glittering like diamonds. Every instinct she had urged her to comfort him, but she didn't. Instead, she waited to hear him out. To find out what exactly was at the bottom of his refusal to give and receive love.

He rubbed his jaw as if trying to hold his words in. He shifted his gaze to the wide window and the night beyond as if he couldn't bear to look at her anymore. Several long moments passed and Sadie actually *saw* him regain control.

His shoulders squared, his chin lifted and his eyes narrowed. She wondered if he was ever going to explain, or if he was simply going to let what was between them end without ceremony or reason.

Finally, though, she had her answer when he turned his head toward her. "Love tears people up, Sadie. It makes them miserable. It ruins lives," he said.

It didn't make any sense, but she could see that he believed what he was saying, so her heart ached. "How can you think that?"

"One of my best friends, Jeff, he died during my last tour." He turned his face back to the window and his reflection stared back at him. "He died saving my life and you know what he said with his last breath? 'Tell Lisa I'm sorry. Tell her I love her.'"

Tears filled her eyes and spilled unheeded down her cheeks. Pity swamped her—for Rick, Jeff and mostly, the much-loved Lisa. Yet even knowing what Lisa had lost, Sadie envied her. Though she had lost the man she loved, she had also been truly loved by him. And that was a gift too few people would ever realize.

She looked into the gleaming black surface of the night-shrouded windowpane and met his stony stare. "I'm sorry, Rick. I really am. But I don't understand. What's so horrible about your friend's last words? His love for his wife was beautiful."

"Beautiful." A short, harsh laugh scraped from his throat. "He died in torment because he knew he was leaving Lisa alone. He knew loving her wouldn't be enough and his death was going to kill her."

"Rick…"

He turned, grabbed his own jeans and drew them on with jerky movements. Then he flashed her a hard look. "If he hadn't loved someone, he could have died in peace. He wouldn't have been panic-stricken trying to tell me what he needed Lisa to know. He—" His voice broke off and he shook his head again, then folded his arms across his chest in a classic pose of defensiveness.

Her heart was breaking—for Rick, and for the Jeff she would never meet. But she had to try to get past this. To find a way to make him see that love wasn't a curse, it was a rare gift.

"And you think he regretted loving his wife?"

"I'm betting he regretted it on that day. In that dusty street, in those last few minutes. Yeah." He stalked across the room to the cold fireplace. Fisting his hands on the old oak mantle, he stared into the empty hearth.

"Yeah. I think he did regret it. But it was too late. For him. *And* for Lisa."

"So to save yourself ever feeling that helpless kind of pain, you'll just never love anyone?"

He didn't lift his gaze, but he nodded. "That's right."

"What about the girls?" She walked to his side and waited for him to look at her before adding, "You love them."

His mouth curved in a bitter smile. "That's different and you know it."

"I know you love them, so you're risking the same kind of misery you said your friend experienced. Wanting to be there for them and not being able to. Wanting to tell them everything you're feeling and failing at that, too." She laid one hand on his shoulder and felt him flinch at her touch. "So I ask you, would it be better to never love them at all?"

He turned his gaze from hers and focused again on the empty hearth and the battered old iron grate. "You don't understand."

"No," she said softly, "I don't. I'll never understand turning your back on love because you're afraid of what might happen."

His head snapped up at her choice of the word *afraid* and she knew she'd struck a nerve. "It isn't fear, Sadie. It's a rational decision—and mine to make."

There was a coolness in his eyes now. A distance she'd never seen there before and it saddened her more than she could say. But at the same time, there was a very slender ribbon of hope remaining. It wasn't that he *didn't* love her. He was *refusing* to love her. And that she could fight against. All she had to do was make him change that stubborn mind of his.

Now that she knew what was at the root of his refusal

to love, she knew she'd be able to get through to him eventually. But for right now, there was nothing more she could do.

Suddenly she was more tired than she'd ever been. "I'm going home now, Rick. I'll be back in the morning to pick up the girls."

"Fine," he murmured.

A little stung that he was more than willing to let her leave, Sadie walked out of the room, but couldn't help pausing on the threshold to look back at him. Still hunched over the fireplace, he looked more alone than she'd ever seen him.

Sadie's heart broke a little further. She hated to leave him like this, but maybe it was a good thing. Maybe he'd take out his memories and examine them more closely. If he did, Sadie thought he would discover that, yes, his friend Jeff had lost a lot on that last day—but in loving his wife, he had shown Rick what was really important.

Rick had once told her that he never gave up. Well, she wouldn't give up on him, either. If there was a way to crash past the defenses he had built up around his heart, she told herself as she left the room to walk down the dimly lit hall, she would find it.

Rick heard her leave, and his every instinct urged him to go after her. To never let her walk away. He *needed* her, damn it. He was empty without her.

And in the silent turmoil of his own mind, he heard Jeff's voice again. *Tell Lisa I love her.*

Eleven

Two days later, the Founder's Day dinner and dance at the Texas Cattleman's Club was a success.

That fact would no doubt drive Brad crazy, Sadie thought, but she couldn't help feeling proud. She and Abby and the other women had really worked hard to shake things up a little this year.

There were new decorations—blue-and-gold crepe paper and matching balloons hanging from the ceiling. There were pictures of past parties—blown up poster size—decorating the walls and instead of a boring, sit-down meal, there were two buffet tables practically groaning with delectable choices.

Waiters from the club stood behind the tables making sure the trays were kept full and the steamers were hot. People were laughing, talking, moving around the room and visiting—instead of being trapped at their linen-covered tables as in previous years.

Everyone seemed to be having a wonderful time. Everyone who wasn't her. Idly, she smoothed one hand down the front of her crimson, floor-length gown. She'd looked all over until she had found the perfect dress for tonight—because she had wanted to knock Rick off his feet.

The minute she saw this dress, she'd known it was the one. It molded to her body like a second skin. The neckline was cut deeply enough to display just the right amount of her cleavage and in the back, the fabric swept down to display her entire spine, right down to the top of her behind.

She felt sexy. Beautiful.

And lonely, she thought. *Don't forget lonely.*

Abby was across the room, easy to spot with her long, dark red hair done on top of her head to complement the emerald-green Grecian style gown she wore. Not far from Abby, Brad was holding court with a few of his best friends and judging from her brother's expression, he was probably campaigning again for club president.

She spotted her father in a corner talking to one of the older club members, and Sadie knew that Robert Price was no doubt trying to drum up votes for his son.

After all, *Brad* wasn't the disappointment, *she* was.

Walking to the bar, Sadie caught snatches of conversation as she went.

"I hear that Bradford Price is going to vote to keep the club just the way it is."

"A little change never hurt anybody."

"I don't care for change myself, but I do admit that Abby Langley did a fine job with the party."

"Oh, my, look at Sadie Price…"

Her steps faltered a little, just long enough for her to hear the end of that sentence.

"…She's been keeping company with Rick Pruitt. You know…the *father* of those two little girls? Poor mites."

"If he's their father, why doesn't he marry their mother for pity's sake?"

Good question, Sadie thought and lifted her chin a bit higher as she wended her way through the meandering crowd. The curse of a small town, she told herself, was that absolutely everyone knew your business. The blessing of a small town? Everybody knew your business. The same people who gossiped and spread rumors were also the first ones to show up when there was a call for help.

She knew what she would be letting herself in for in moving back home. And she was prepared for it. All she needed was a little vodka to help her over tonight's bumps in the road.

People carrying loaded plates headed for the tables and waiters drifted through the crowd with bottles of champagne to refill empty glasses. But Sadie wasn't in the mood for a celebratory drink. All she wanted was a little liquor, then she'd get something to eat, say hello to a few people and call it an early night.

If Rick wasn't here, there was no point in her staying.

While she waited at the bar, she watched as a dozen or so couples on the dance floor swayed and spun to the music pouring through the speakers. It was an old song. One of her father's favorites. Frank Sinatra singing about a summer wind.

Unconsciously, she began to sway in time with the music only to jolt to a stop when a voice from behind her spoke up.

"Can I have this dance?"

Her heart did a fast gallop and her mouth went dry as

dust. Sadie turned around slowly and looked up into the warm brown eyes she had most hoped to see that night.

"Rick." He wore his dress blues uniform for the formal occasion and Sadie thought he had never looked more handsome. More…imposing.

Torn between excitement and dread, Sadie didn't know what to think of the way he was looking at her—as if he could devour her with the power of his stare alone.

She hadn't seen him in two days. Not since she'd left him alone in his room in the middle of the night. Her stomach had been in perpetual knots since then and her mind was constantly churning, dragging up one impossible scenario after another.

He loved her, he didn't love her; they married, she died a lonely spinster and he a bitter old man.

Even her normally even-tempered daughters seemed to sense that their mommy was tangled up in her own cascading emotions. As if in sympathy, Wendy and Gail had both been whiny and irritable.

And asking for their daddy.

She knew how they felt because Sadie wanted him too. Now, here he was. And a more gorgeous man she had never seen. The infuriating hardhead.

"Dance with me, Sadie," he said softly, taking her hand in both of his.

She nodded and allowed him to tug her onto the dance floor. Sadie knew that most of the people in the place were watching them, hoping for more fuel for the gossip train. But she didn't care. All she cared about now was the feel of his arm sliding around her. The touch of his warm hand on the small of her back. The feel of her fingers caught in his firm but gentle grip.

He moved into the dance, steering them onto the

middle of the floor and as the music swelled around them, Sadie felt the pain of the last couple of days fall away.

"I've missed you," he said, voice just loud enough for her to hear.

"I've missed you, too." She looked up into his eyes and realized that the cool indifference that had so cut at her the other night was gone.

What did that mean?

"You stayed away on purpose, didn't you?" he asked, spinning her into a tight turn.

"No, I—"

He smiled. "It's okay, Sadie. Probably a good thing you did. Gave me time to think. And there was a lot to think about."

Her heart was stuttering in her chest and the pit of her stomach swarmed with what felt like giant bats. "Come to any conclusions?"

"A few." The song ended and another slow, dreamy romantic tune began.

Rick didn't miss a beat. He kept dancing, holding her even closer as the couples around them danced and laughed.

"Care to tell me what they were?" she asked, silently congratulating herself on being so poised—when what she wanted to do was grab him and kiss him and demand that he love her as much as she loved him.

"I'm getting to it," he said with a half smile that sent shivers of appreciation over her skin.

Glancing across the clubhouse briefly, he turned his gaze back to her. "You remember I once told you that life was all about change?"

"Yes…"

"Well, something occurred to me after you left the other night."

"What?"

"That some change just isn't worth it."

Her heart fell, but then he started talking again.

"Like you leaving me for instance," he said, gaze fixed firmly on hers. "Like me losing the chance to be with you. That's the kind of change that could kill a man."

A ping of guilt came and went in the space of a heartbeat. "I couldn't stay, Rick—"

"I know." He interrupted her, brought her close for a brief, hard hug, then bent his head to hers. "I mean, I understand. Sadie, I want you to know you mean more to me than anything else in this world."

Again, her heartbeat quickened. Honestly, she thought wildly, the ups and downs of this conversation were making her a nervous wreck.

"I'm glad, Rick. But—"

"Not finished," he said, another half smile curving his mouth into a temptation.

"Okay…"

Quiet conversations rippled across the crowded room. The music went on, sliding into one romantic tune after another. The subtle clatter of plates and glasses was nothing more than a vague distraction.

"See," he continued, staring down into her eyes, "I had a meeting with someone yesterday."

"Who?"

He shook his head. "Doesn't matter. What does, is that I realized something important."

Oh, God… If she got her hopes up now only to see them shattered, Sadie thought it might just destroy her. So she tried not to read anything into the gleam in his eyes. But she couldn't keep from wishing for what she most wanted.

"You were right," he told her and this time when the music ended, he steered her off the dance floor and into a shadowed corner of the room.

"Three words every woman loves to hear," she said, bracing her back against the cool, plastered wall.

"I've got three more for you."

She inhaled sharply and felt a warning sting of tears in her eyes. Looking up into his eyes, she saw warmth, she saw passion, and she saw...

"I love you."

Sadie clapped one hand over her mouth to keep from—what? Shrieking? Gasping?

He pulled her hand free, kissed the palm, then drew her into his arms, pressing her entire length to him. "Ah, God, Sadie. I was an idiot."

She nodded, smiling through the tears that brimmed in her eyes and trembled on her lashes.

"I'm over it," he said, smiling as he reached into his jacket pocket. Pulling out that velvet jeweler's box, he opened the lid and showed her the diamond. "So, Sadie Price, will you marry me now?"

"Try to stop me," she said and held out her hand for him to slide that platinum and diamond ring onto her fourth finger.

The oversize stone flashed with light buried in its depths, but when Rick leaned in to kiss her, she saw real stars and felt her life click perfectly into place.

That lasted about an hour.

Which was when the big argument started.

Sadie was showing Abby her ring when Brad stormed up to them.

"Are you serious?" he demanded, ignoring his sister to focus on the redhead glaring at him. "I heard you were actually thinking about running for president of the club. It's a joke, right?"

Whoever was in charge of the stereo shut it off and the abrupt absence of music was startling enough to have everyone in the room turning to watch what would happen next.

With Rick at her side, Sadie spoke softly. "Brad, maybe now isn't the time…"

"You stay out of this," her brother snapped.

"Hey now!" Rick warned, stepping in between Sadie and her brother. "You want to watch how you talk to my fiancée."

"Fiancée?"

More excited whispers raced through the crowd and Sadie rolled her eyes. Trust her brother to speak up and spoil her having the chance to make her own announcement.

"You're getting married?"

"Since when?" her father demanded as he came up to join the fracas.

"Since about an hour ago," Sadie told him proudly and waved her ring in her father's face.

"It's about time," Robert said, fixing Rick with a disapproving stare.

"This isn't about Sadie," Brad said, his voice rising to carry over the crowd's murmuring. "This is about Abby Langley and just what she thinks she's up to."

"I don't owe you an explanation for anything, Bradford Price," Abby told him.

"I want a damn answer," Brad ground out as a few of the older club members drifted up to stand behind his father.

Abby went toe-to-toe with him, tipped her head back and speared him with a glare. "I was going to wait until next week to say this, but you want an answer now? Fine. It's not a joke. I *am* running." Then she raised her voice to match his so that everyone present would hear her. "I'm officially declaring myself a candidate for president of the TCC. Anyone besides Brad have a problem with that?"

Instantly, the crowd was electrified and divided into two separate camps. Snatches of comments rose up into the air.

"Good for her!"

"A *woman* running the club?"

"That Abby was always a troublemaker."

At that comment, Abby and Sadie both turned to fire off angry glances at the speaker. The older man who had spoken a bit too loudly slunk back into the crowd.

"He's just saying what everyone's thinking," Brad told her.

"Is that right? Well, maybe it's time for a troublemaker. At least then," Abby countered, "every meeting won't be so boring the members fall asleep half way through."

"*This* is what's wrong with women being admitted to the club as members," Brad declared and several of the men nodded. "Change for change's sake is stupid. You want to ditch tradition in favor of progress and I don't know if you've noticed or not, but nobody agrees with you."

"I do," Sadie announced.

He brushed her comment away with the wave of a hand. "No one asked you what you thought, Sadie."

"Maybe you should have, Bradford Price. Instead, you're behaving like a spoiled child," Sadie snapped, pushing past Rick to face her brother. "If this is how you behave, then you shouldn't be the president!"

"Sadie!" Robert Price's horrified gasp carried over the crowd.

Sadie knew she'd stepped in it now, siding with an outsider against a member of her own family—in public no less. But Brad was wrong. Why shouldn't she call him on it?

"Sadie's right," Rick said. "You're being a jackass, man. This isn't the way to handle things. You don't want her to be president? Then win the election."

She looked up at her marine and grinned. It felt wonderful to have his support. To know that he would always be by her side. When he looked down at her, she whispered, "My hero."

"My pleasure," he assured her.

"Oh, for God's sake." Brad looked disgusted with all of them. His gaze snapped from Rick to Sadie and, finally, to Abby. "I plan to win. Lady, get used to the idea of losing."

"We'll see, won't we?" Abby said with a sneer.

"You want war, Abby? You got it," Brad said.

Bradford Price was still furious days after the Founder's Day dance. Abby Langley had become the proverbial thorn in his side and he hadn't yet found the way to dig her out. Still, to be fair, it wasn't just Abby getting under his skin. He was on edge all the damn time now. Getting anonymous, vaguely threatening letters in the mail was enough to make any man uneasy.

Which was why he was here at the TCC today. He'd decided to be proactive in figuring out who it was that was harassing him. From the corner of his eye, he caught movement and glance up in time to see Rick Pruitt leaving the club dining room. Briefly, Brad wondered if the man was the right one for his sister. But a second later, he reminded himself that *that* particular problem wasn't what concerned him today.

He looked at the two men at the table with him. Mitch Taylor he'd known most of his life. The interim president of the TCC, Mitch was a star in Texas football, home now recuperating from an injury. Mitch's cool brown eyes met Brad's and he nodded. Mitch already knew about the letters and had suggested he use the club lounge for this meeting with the man Brad hoped would solve the issue.

Zeke Travers was new in town, but he was Darius Franklin's new partner in his security firm. So that was a hell of a recommendation as far as Brad was concerned. If Darius trusted the man, Brad knew he could, too.

Zeke's head was shaved, and his brown eyes were sharp as he watched Brad, waiting. His white shirt accented his dark skin and his black slacks had a crease sharp enough to draw blood. He was all business and Brad could appreciate that.

"Look," he said, lowering his voice as he braced his forearms on the table. "Mitch knows why I asked you to meet me here, Zeke. I've got a situation."

"Tell me."

"I've been getting letters." He dipped one hand into his jacket pocket and drew out a single sheet of paper. Sliding it across the table, he waited as Zeke picked it up and read it.

It didn't take long. The letters were short. Always the same.

Your secret will be revealed.

Zeke's eyes narrowed as he folded the letter again. "Can I hang on to this?"

"Sure."

"How many have you been getting?"

"One a day for weeks now," Brad admitted, shoving one hand through his hair. "I'll admit it's starting to get to me."

Zeke nodded. "I'd be surprised if it wasn't. You want me to look into this for you?"

"That's why we're here," Mitch said, speaking up for the first time. "Darius is a friend of ours and he trusts you."

Zeke smiled briefly and gave a quick nod to Mitch. "He does. So can you."

Brad nodded.

"I'll see what I can do with this," Zeke told him. "I'll get the guys in the lab to go over it. See what they can find out."

Brad released a breath he hadn't realized he'd been holding. It was good to have someone on his side in this. "Appreciate it," he said.

Zeke held out his hand and Brad shook it. "Don't get your hopes up, though. This letter's been handled so much, it's doubtful we'll get much information on it."

When Brad solemnly nodded, Zeke added, "But it's a start."

Standing up, he said simply, "I'll be in touch."

He left and Brad thought that with Zeke Travers in his corner, he could breathe a little easier.

Royal was taking sides.

Taking the twins shopping on Main Street, Sadie was stopped a half a dozen times by women who were absolutely furious with their husbands. All of the women wanted to talk about Abby running for president of the TCC and were thinking of ways they could help get her elected.

The men were up in arms, too. Her own father was hardly speaking to her and she hadn't seen Brad since the night of the dance, three days ago.

But she didn't mind that too much. With her engagement ring on her finger and a smile on her face, she was much more interested in spending every moment she could with Rick before he had to go back to base.

Just thinking about living two months without him was depressing. But once that was done, he'd be home to stay and she'd finally have the kind of marriage and family she'd always wanted.

Sarabeth Allen came bustling out of her flower shop when she spotted Sadie through the window. "Sadie, honey," she crooned, leaning in for a hard hug. "How you doing?"

"I'm fine, Sarabeth," she said, a little confused.

"Good for you, honey," Sarabeth said as she gave a passing woman a hard look. "You pay no attention to wagging tongues, you hear me? Some of these old biddies have nothing better to do than spread rumors."

A small twist of worry tugged at the pit of her stomach. "Thanks, Sarabeth. I'll remember."

"See you do," she said, then pulled a hankie from the sleeve of her shirt and wiped her eyes as she looked down at the smiling twins. She muttered, "Poor little mites," just before turning and heading back into her shop.

"What in the world?" Sadie shook her head and continued to the diner. She pushed open the front door and stepped into the blissful cool. She was already late for lunch with Abby. The hazards of having to get *three* people ready before going anywhere.

The women at the booth closest to her dropped their gazes and lowered their voices. That twist of worry tugged a little sharper. But Sadie was determined to not let anything spoil her happiness.

She felt everyone watching her as she walked down the narrow aisle between the red leather booths and the spinning stools at the counter.

"Poor thing," someone whispered a little too loudly.

"He's a no-account," another voice added. "Just like her last man."

Sadie's stomach started spinning.

"Those poor children…"

In the stroller, Wendy and Gail were babbling to each other and slapping their toys against the stroller tray.

"Tsk. Tsk. Tsk. Such pretty girls, too…"

A little irritated as well as worried, Sadie slid onto the bench seat opposite her friend with relief. She threw a wary glance back over her shoulder, then leaned forward and asked, "What's going on, Abby? What's everyone talking about?"

Abby scowled at the people in the diner and shook her head. "Sweetie, it's just the Royal gossips picking up a juicy tidbit to chew on."

"About me?" she asked, handing a soda cracker each to the twins to keep them happy.

"In a roundabout way," Abby said on a sigh. "Sadie, it's all over town, so you have to know. Someone claims to have seen Rick in Midland a couple days before the dance. Having what looked like a cozy lunch with a beautiful brunette."

Sadie felt a hard punch to the center of her chest. She

couldn't speak. Couldn't think. "No. I don't believe it," she said, shaking her head.

Abby sighed heavily. "I wouldn't, either. Rick just doesn't strike me as the cheating kind."

But then, Sadie told herself grimly, her ex-husband hadn't seemed like a cheater either and turned out, he was the cheat to end all cheats. Worry bounced around in the pit of her stomach like a crazed ping-pong ball.

Had she pushed Rick into this marriage? Was he only claiming to love her to get her to agree to marry him? She bit into her bottom lip and chewed at it as nerves rattled through her system.

"Sadie…"

She shook her head. "I've got to go, Abby. I need to think."

"Honey, don't do anything drastic."

Like give Rick back his ring before she made another horrific mistake?

She glanced at the diamond sparkling on her hand and felt the bottom drop out of her world. She didn't want to believe the gossips. Didn't want to think that what was between her and Rick was nothing but smoke and mirrors.

But could she afford to take the risk?

Twelve

It wasn't a risk.

It was a nightmare.

Sadie hadn't wanted to believe the gossips. Hadn't wanted to pay any attention at all to the rumors flying around town. But the pity-filled looks and the whispers she'd faced at lunch with Abby had convinced her to face the problem head-on.

She wasn't the same woman she had been when Taylor Hawthorne had made her a laughingstock. She was strong enough now to face Rick with what she'd heard. To ask him for an explanation.

Which was why she was here now, feeling her heart shatter in her chest.

Sadie's car was parked on the road outside Rick's ranch. She kept the engine running. She wouldn't be staying.

Behind her, in their car seats, the girls shouted, "Daddy! Want Daddy!"

Every word peeled another little slice of her heart away. She swallowed back the urge to cry, blinked to clear her blurred vision and focused on the view of her fiancé standing in the front yard of his ranch house, arguing with a beautiful brunette. Though the ranch was set far back from the road, there was a wide view of the house and, sadly, Sadie had a front-row seat.

"You wanted proof," Sadie told herself sadly.

Even in her stunned shock, even through the pain, Sadie could admit that whoever the woman was, she and Rick looked good together. They looked very *familiar* with each other, too.

When Rick reached out to grab the woman's shoulders, Sadie hissed in a small, wounded breath. Seeing his hands on another woman was just another tiny stab of an emotional blade. The brunette shook her head at him. She looked furious. Well, Sadie thought, she should join the club.

Rick started talking again and whatever he said must have gotten through to the woman because she nodded and smiled just before throwing her arms around Rick's neck and plastering herself against him for a long hug.

The worst part…Rick hugged her back.

"Oh, God." Sadie swiped away a tear rolling down her cheek.

"Daddy!" Gail shouted. "Want Daddy!"

"Wenne, too!" Wendy cried.

Sadie hardly heard the plaintive cries. She was too busy trying to smother her own as she watched the man she loved hugging another woman in his front yard.

The Royal rumor mill had been right, she thought dismally.

He wasn't even hiding his woman away, the bastard. He was right out in the open. Obviously, he didn't care if Sadie found out about her.

"Just like Taylor," she whispered.

She looked down at the diamond sparkling on her finger. Sunlight caught the facets and dazzled her eyes. For three lovely days, she had been happy. Secure in the knowledge that Rick *did* love her. *Did* want a future with her for all of the right reasons. Turned out, though, that he was simply a better actor than she might have given him credit for.

A pretty ring and promises obviously didn't mean a damn thing if she couldn't trust him.

And clearly, she couldn't.

Anger mixed with hurt churned in her stomach and roiled into a toxic stew. If she hadn't had her daughters with her, Sadie would have confronted him. She'd have walked right up to him and his bimbo and told them both exactly what she thought of them. But she wouldn't do that to her babies. No point in scarring them at this tender age. They would find out in time on their own that their father was no good. She wouldn't have to tell them.

"Sorry, babies," she said aloud, throwing the car into gear again with one last look at the man she loved. Thankfully, he hadn't taken his eyes off the brunette long enough to notice her car idling on the road in front of his place. "We're not going to Daddy's house. We're going to take a trip, okay?"

"Want Daddy," Gail whined, kicking her feet against the car seat.

"No go way!" Wendy wailed.

Shaking her head, Sadie winced as a shaft of light danced off her ring and speared into her eyes. Deliberately, she tore the diamond from her hand and tossed it onto the passenger seat beside her. Without the love and promise it represented, that ring was nothing more than a shiny rock.

Pain wrapped itself around her, but she didn't cry. Her eyes burned, but remained dry. There was an emptiness inside her that felt as wide as the sea. She'd found herself. Found her own confidence and now, even that had been shaken. She'd believed in Rick. Trusted him. Allowed herself to love him completely, and losing all of that now was more painful than anything else she had ever known.

Clutching tight to whatever strength she had left, she drove off without a backward glance—so she didn't see Rick look up at the sound of the engine.

She didn't hear him calling after her, either—and wouldn't have cared if she had.

Two hours later, Rick was at the Price mansion, waiting for *someone* to open the damn door. He glanced around, saw cars in the driveway—though not Sadie's. He was hoping she had parked in the garage, but something inside him had fisted into a knot so tight he was choking on it.

So far, this day had gone from bad to worse. And the bad feeling he had lodged in his chest told him it wasn't going to get any better real soon.

"Damn it, Sadie," he shouted, "open the door!"

Still nothing and the silence was starting to freeze him out in spite of the West-Texas sun blasting down on him from a merciless sky.

He'd tried to call Sadie a dozen times since he'd seen her driving away from the ranch. Rick had known immediately what she must be thinking and he'd wanted nothing more than to kick his own ass for hurting her.

He knew damn well what she must be thinking. Hell, what she'd seen, from her point of view, had probably looked bad. She'd seen him with another woman—hugging another woman—and taking into consideration the fact that her last husband was a cheating no-good snake, Rick knew she was probably now convinced that he was no better.

Well, there was a perfectly reasonable explanation for all of this—which he could prove to her if she'd open the damned door and hear him out.

Rick walked down the four steps to the lawn, looked up at the house and glared at the room he knew was hers. "Sadie, come on!"

His shout went unanswered too.

Gritting his teeth in frustration, he raced back up the steps and slammed his knuckles against the heavy wood door. He'd been doing that off and on now for fifteen minutes with no results. So this time, he pounded on the damn thing in a staccato beat that continued until the door was finally jerked open.

Sadie's brother blocked the doorway. His features were tight and hard and he looked about as welcoming as a rattler eyeing its dinner. "Stop beating the door down."

"Where's Sadie?"

"Why should I tell you?"

"You don't want to get in my way on this," Rick warned.

"Funny," Brad mused. "Seems like a good idea to me."

Fury fisted in his guts. Rick pushed his way past

Sadie's brother and stormed into the Price mansion. His boot heels clacked on the flooring as he walked to the bottom of the staircase and shouted, "Sadie!"

"She's not here."

Rick spun around to face his woman's father. The older man looked cold and dispassionate. Just what he would have expected from a man who would have his only daughter sacrifice her own happiness for the family coffers.

For a long, tension-filled minute, the two men stared at each other. Brad was still standing to Rick's left and the animosity coming off him was thick enough to slice. But Rick's focus was on the older man. "Tell me where she is, Mr. Price."

Even relaxing at home, Robert Price wore an elegantly tailored, three-piece suit. He was an imposing man, but Rick wouldn't have cared if the old boy had been holding a loaded shotgun on him. Nothing was going to stop him from finding and talking to Sadie.

The older man turned his back and walked into the formal living room and Rick was just a step or two behind him. Sunlight washed the room in a bright, golden light. But all Rick noticed was the missing baby monitor that Sadie had kept on a side table by her favorite reading chair.

Ice skimmed over his heart.

"My daughter left here not an hour ago," Robert said, settling into a wing-backed chair that, with the old man sitting in it, resembled a throne. "She specifically said that she didn't want to see you."

Rick pulled in a deep breath and fought to keep from raging at the man. "She's going to anyway."

"Why're you here?" Brad interrupted from behind him and Rick threw him an angry glare.

"That's between me and Sadie," he ground out.

"Not anymore," Brad told him flatly. "The whole town's talking about you and your new girlfriend."

"Ah, God…" Misery pumped through him at a staggering pace.

"That's right," Brad told him. Shaking his head he got closer, his gaze sweeping over Rick dismissively. "Did you really think nobody would know? Hell, you grew up here. You know as well as anyone what the gossips in Royal are like."

"Gossip doesn't mean truth," Rick muttered, his gaze locked now with Brad's. Sadie's brother looked as furious as Rick was. The temperature in this brightly sunny room was close to freezing with the two Price men glowering at him.

And damned if Rick could blame either one of them.

"Close enough," Brad maintained. "Plus, Sadie went to see you, to have you explain, and she got an eyeful of you hugging the other woman."

He knew she'd seen that. Which was why he was here. To explain. To make her see that what she was thinking was all wrong.

"She didn't see what she thought she did," he muttered.

"Right!" Brad laughed and looked past Rick to his father. "Hear that, Dad? Sadie's blind now."

"I heard," Robert said softly.

Rick didn't even glance at the older man. Brad was the one he'd deal with. Rubbing one hand across the back of his neck, he said tightly, "Just tell me where she is, and I can take care of this mess. Five minutes with her, that's all I ask."

"Ask all you want. She doesn't owe you anything anymore." Brad dug one hand into his pocket, pulled something free, then flipped it to Rick.

It hit his palm and the instant his fingers closed over it, something in Rick snapped.

Sadie's engagement ring.

Breath straining in his lungs, heartbeat pounding erratically in his chest, he spoke through tightly gritted teeth. "Tell me where she is, Brad."

"You think I'm gonna stand by and watch while my sister's heart gets kicked around the county again? I don't think so. She's lived through the pity of this town once. Why should I help you put her through that again?"

"I *love* her," Rick managed to say.

"Bull." Brad reared back and threw a punch to Rick's jaw that sent him sprawling onto the floor.

Ears ringing, jaw throbbing, Rick scrambled back up, and threw a punch of his own to Brad's gut. Brad staggered and bent over, wheezing for air.

"I figure as her brother, you were owed one shot at me. But you take another one and I'll put you down. Understand?"

"Try it," Brad said, bracing for a fight.

"That's enough." Robert Price stood up and walked to stand in between the two men. He gave his son a quelling look, then turned his gaze on Rick. "Is it true? Do you love my daughter?"

Rick flashed a furious look at Brad before shifting his gaze to meet the older man's. Rubbing one hand over his sore jaw, he muttered, "Yes. I love her. But it's not easy. The Price family's a hardheaded bunch."

Brad snorted. "It's not this family. It's the women in this town."

Robert, though, simply took a minute or two to study Rick in silence. With their eyes locked, it was as if the older man was trying to see into Rick's heart. And at last, he was satisfied.

"I'll tell you where she went—"

"Dad!"

"But if I'm wrong about you," Robert said tellingly, "I'll turn my son loose on you again."

"You're not wrong," Rick said plainly. "I love her. I love my girls. I'll explain everything to you later, but I owe that explanation to Sadie first."

"Agreed," Robert said. "She and the girls are at the Hilton Plaza in Midland."

Rick started for the door instantly. But at the threshold, he turned back. "Just because your boy got one lucky punch in doesn't mean he could take me."

Robert laughed while Brad fumed.

Rick was already gone.

The girls had cried themselves to sleep.

Sadie's soul ached.

And the hotel was out of chocolate ice cream.

"How does that happen in a civilized world?" Sadie asked, making do with room service vanilla topped with chocolate syrup.

Should have gone back to Houston, she thought sadly. As she had the *last* time she'd run from her troubles. But Houston was so much farther away from Royal and home than Midland was. At least here, she could fool herself into believing that she was still close to... everybody.

Frowning to herself, she had another bite of ice cream and let the bland vanilla slide down her throat. Sadie didn't really like admitting that she had run away. Again. But how could she have stayed in town while Rick was romancing a pretty brunette?

"I bet *she* has chocolate ice cream," Sadie muttered bitterly.

Just as she apparently had *Rick*. But even as she thought that, she wondered about it. Would a man who talked about honor and duty the same way another man talked about his car or job—just another part of his life—cheat?

Had Rick really been lying to her all along? Or had she allowed her own pain and shock to color what she saw?

"Hard to misinterpret a hug like that one," she muttered, remembering how Rick and the brunette had looked, as melded together as...the chocolate syrup on her boring vanilla ice cream.

Sighing, she took a bite, licked the spoon, then lifted one hand to wipe away a stray tear. She hadn't cried until she got to the hotel. But once there, she'd really made up for lost time.

It wasn't easy, hiding her tears from her daughters. But thankfully, the girls were asleep. Which had given Sadie plenty of time to cry herself silly while waiting for ice cream that really wasn't cutting it as far as self-pity-party food.

Now, not only was she unsatisfied in the chocolate department...her chest hurt, her eyes ached and her nose was stuffy. One look in the mirror had told her she was not one of those women who could cry pretty. No, when she cried, her entire body was involved in the process and made her look as though she'd been dragged upside down through hell, feet first.

She used the edge of her spoon to scrape the chocolate syrup off the ice cream. Once it was gone, she sighed unhappily and wondered just how long it would take room service to bring the chocolate cake she had ordered.

The Governor's suite in the Midland Plaza was comfortable, but too darn big for one lonely woman and her twin baby girls. Outside the window, a storm was rolling in, black clouds gathering on the horizon, wind whipping the trees that lined the small lake in front of the hotel. Lightning shimmered in the darkness and the first splats of rain hit the window just as the doorbell of the suite rang.

She hoped the waiter had brought *both* pieces of chocolate cake, Sadie thought. She was going to need them.

Sniffling, she walked to the door, looked through the peephole and gasped when she saw Rick, staring right back at her from the hall. She moved back from the door, shaking her head. She didn't want to see him. Not now. Maybe not ever.

Oh, God. She looked *hideous*.

"Open the door, Sadie."

"No."

"If you don't, I'll make such a big scene out here, people will be talking about it for years."

"That threat would have worked on me once," she said through the door and realized she meant it. She didn't care what anyone thought anymore. She hadn't run away this time because she didn't want to hear gossip.

She'd taken off because she had been too hurt to face Rick.

Okay, yes, she didn't like the pity-filled glances from the gossips in Royal. But the only thing that could *really* hurt her was Rick's betrayal.

"Do you really think I care what anyone in this hotel thinks of me? Or you?" she countered, peering at him through that peephole again. "I don't. And trust me when I say I've seen enough of you today."

She actually heard him sigh. A second later, she was looking through the peephole again, staring into his brown eyes.

"Sadie, what you saw at the ranch—"

Pain slapped at her and her tears dried up. She *really* wanted that chocolate cake. "I already know what I saw. I don't want a recap."

"It wasn't what you think."

"Oh," she said, still watching him, "so she was a stranger and she tripped and you had to catch her in a full-body hug? That must have been terrible for you. *Poor* man."

His jaw worked as if he were biting back a torrent of words. Finally he blew out a frustrated breath, looked directly into the security hole and said, "Fine. You want me to do this in the hallway, I'll do it here."

"I don't want anything from you," she countered hotly. "Except for you to go away."

"Not happening. Not until you hear me out."

"Fine, talk."

He started to, then closed his mouth in irritation before snapping it shut.

"Are you really too big a coward to face me without a door in between us?"

"I'm not a coward. I just don't want you near me."

"So not a coward, just a liar."

Okay, she was lying. She *did* want him. But she wasn't going to share him with a host of women. So she'd just have to learn to do without what she wanted. "Do I have to call security?"

"Sadie," he said on a long sigh, "the woman you saw me with was *Lisa*."

She laughed harshly, then lowered her voice as she heard the girls start to stir in the adjoining bedroom. "You think I care what her name is?"

"She's the widow of my friend, Jeff. The man who saved my life."

Rick waited for what felt like an eternity. But it was only moments before he heard the security chain slide free, the locks turn. Then the door was open and Sadie was standing there, looking at him.

Her blue eyes were rimmed in red and glassy with the sheen of tears. She had a blot of chocolate syrup at one corner of her mouth and her blond hair was pulled into a crooked ponytail.

She looked unbelievably young and vulnerable and his heart melted in his chest. He loved her more with every breath and if he lived to be a hundred, he still would go to his death complaining that he hadn't had enough time with her.

"My God, you're beautiful," he said softly.

She flushed. "Yes, because splotchy girls are all the rage this season," she sputtered.

"Splotchy girls are my weakness."

She hitched an unsteady breath, backed up so he could enter the suite. "Come in."

He took a quick look around as he walked into the room. It was big, with cream-colored walls, stone-gray carpet and a view of the city. There was a blue velvet couch, a couple of tapestry easy chairs and an open door led to what was probably the girls' bedroom.

He heard her close the door quietly before he turned to look at her. Tossing his hat onto the nearby couch, Rick just looked his fill of her. He'd been so worried that he'd lost her. So shaken, thinking about living a life without her, that he hardly knew what to do now that she was standing in front of him again.

"Jeff's widow?" she asked, and her voice was so soft, he almost didn't catch the words.

"Yeah." He didn't go to her. Not yet. He wanted the air clear between them first. They'd been through so much in the last few weeks. Coming together, finding their way and now, he had to make her see that what they had found was real. That she could trust it. And him.

"Lisa and Jeff actually lived in Houston." He laughed a little. "Funny, two Texas boys meeting in the middle of a war zone on the other side of the planet, but—" he broke off. "That doesn't matter now. The point is, I've met with her a couple of times since I've been back."

"Why didn't you tell me?"

"I should have," he admitted. But Jeff was still an open wound in Rick's heart and soul. Talking about him, even with Sadie, wasn't easy. "It's…hard for me to talk about it."

She scrubbed her hands up and down her arms as if she were cold to the bone. "Okay, I can understand that. But tell me. Why was she at the ranch today?"

"Actually, she drove down to Royal to read me the riot act," he admitted and gave her a rueful smile. "In that, the two of you would probably get along great."

Sadie gave him a sad smile in return, but she didn't say anything. She was still waiting for that explanation.

"Lisa was studying medicine," he said on a long, expelled breath. "But she dropped out of school when she and Jeff got married. They couldn't afford it. She came to the ranch today to yell at me because she just found out that I arranged for her to go back to school. I had my lawyers set up a fund for her books and tuition and anything else she needs."

She took a quick breath, then bit down on her bottom lip as fresh tears pooled in her eyes. Immediately, Rick started talking again.

"It's not because I'm having an affair with her or anything," he insisted. "I'm not in love with her, Sadie. I love you and I would never cheat on you with *anybody*. And, damn it, you should know that about me already."

"Rick…"

Her tone gave away none of what she was feeling, so Rick spoke fast, hoping to make her understand.

"I'm sending her to school because it's what Jeff would have done if he'd come home. He used to talk to me about it. How important it was for him that she find her dreams." He ran one hand over his face and shook his head. "Jeff was so damn proud of her, he wanted to make sure she became a great doctor. Well, he didn't come home. Because of me."

"Rick, no," she said. "It was Jeff's choice to sacrifice himself. You shouldn't second-guess him."

"Can't help it," he admitted. "I'll have that guilt riding me for the rest of my life, Sadie. I'll always know that whatever life I have, whatever *love* I have, Jeff bought it for me. He lost everything so I could come home. I owed it to him to make sure Jeff's dreams for Lisa came true."

"Rick, that is the—"

"I wouldn't cheat on you, Sadie," he told her again quickly, interrupting her because he suddenly needed to say everything he was feeling. "I *love* you. I think I've loved you from the time we were kids. Maybe from that day the waitress spilled a soda in your lap."

Tears were streaking her already puffy face in a steady stream now. But she was smiling and that gave Rick the encouragement he needed. He was in front of her in three long strides.

Pulling her up close to him, he wrapped his arms around her, tucked her head beneath his chin. "I've loved you all my life, Sadie Price. And I will go on loving you until we're old and crabby with great-grandbabies crawling all over us."

She laughed and cried a little harder. But her arms snaked around his waist and held him tightly.

"You should have told me, Rick." Tipping her head back, she stared up at him, heart in her eyes. "Why didn't you?"

He shrugged a little uneasily. "Embarrassed, I guess. Or maybe, I don't know. Maybe I thought you wouldn't understand how much I needed to do this."

"How could I not understand? I say a prayer for Jeff every night, thanking him for bringing you home to me."

"Sadie…"

She reached up, cupping his face between her palms. "Why would you be embarrassed to do the right thing for your friend and his wife?"

Rick smirked a little. "Should have told you. With your help it might not have taken so long to convince Lisa to take the damn money."

"So much pride," she whispered with a slow shake of her head. "So much honor. You're an amazing man, Rick Pruitt."

"If you think so, I'm happy." He bent to kiss her hard, fast. The vise around his heart had eased up a little, making breathing easier, but until she agreed to come back to Royal and marry him, he was a man on the edge. "Come home with me, Sadie. Build a family with me. Let's give the twins six or seven brothers and sisters."

"What?" She laughed, astonished. "Are you crazy?"

"Okay, I'll compromise. Four more kids."

"Three."

"It's negotiable."

"Rick—"

"Marry me, Sadie. Whatever it is you want to do, I'll back your play. Go to school. Get that design degree," he urged. "Hell, be Abby's campaign manager against your brother! I'll help."

She laughed again and the sound was like music to him. It was a balm to his soul and a soothing caress to his heart. He'd never be able to hear it enough.

"I'm done with the Corps, Sadie," he added. "I've done my duty and now it's time for me to be with the family I love. With the woman who makes everything in my life absolutely right."

"Are you sure?" she asked. "I don't want you to one day regret leaving the Corps for me."

"I'm not just doing it for you, darlin'. I need this. I need to be with you."

A single tear slid down her cheek. Shaking her head,

she said, "I love you so much it almost scares me, Rick. When I saw you and Lisa together, I felt my heart break—"

"I'm so sorry—"

"No, it's okay." Smiling up at him, she said, "It's my own fault for taking off instead of just *talking* to you. I should have trusted you. Should have trusted *us*. I promise you, from now on, I will."

"From now on? That sounds promising."

"Daddy!" Two voices, one word.

Rick and Sadie turned as one to watch their daughters toddle into the room. Their hair was tousled from sleep and their little faces were bright with delighted smiles.

"So many beautiful women in my life," Rick said, bending down to sweep both girls up in his arms. Then the three of them faced Sadie.

Heart in her eyes, she smiled, went up on her toes to kiss him again and said, "All I want is to be with you and our kids, Rick. I want us to build the kind of family and home that will shine with the love we make together."

He handed Wendy to her, then dug in his pocket for the ring Brad had tossed to him. Holding it up so the light in the room danced off the diamond, he looked at her. "Then I'm guessing you'll want this back?"

Her lips tugged into a smile. "You saw Brad. Does that explain the bruise on your jaw?"

"It does," he said, "but your brother's got a fist-size ache in his belly, so I figure we're even."

"You hit him?"

"He wouldn't tell me where you were. And, he did hit me first."

"Oh, well, then…"

"Can we not talk about Brad right now?" he asked,

grinning as he waved the ring in front of her face again. "Sadie, just tell me straight up. Am I about to be a married man?"

"You bet you are, Marine," she said, holding up her hand so he could slide the ring onto her finger where it belonged.

"Thank God," he whispered, dipping his head to kiss her again.

The twins clapped their tiny hands and that round of applause was the sweetest sound Rick had ever heard.

He was still kissing her when Wendy shouted, "Go castle!"

Gail patted Rick's cheek and solemnly said, "Castle, Daddy. Home."

Rick's gaze met Sadie's. She smiled up at him and said, "You heard your daughters, Rick. It's time to go *home*."

"Darlin'," he whispered huskily, "nothing in my life has ever sounded better."

* * * * *

THE REBEL TYCOON
RETURNS

BY
KATHERINE GARBERA

Katherine Garbera is the *USA Today* bestselling author of more than forty books. She's always believed in happy endings and lives in Southern California with her husband, children and their pampered pet, Godiva. Visit Katherine on the web at www.katherinegarbera.com, or catch up with her on Facebook and Twitter.

This book is dedicated to my sister Linda for always having my back. I love you, Linda.

One

"Go ahead and look, Macy, you are even more beautiful than before," Dr. Justin Webb said.

Macy Reynolds held the mirror loosely in her left hand and slowly lifted it so she could see her face, but she closed her eyes at the last second before she could catch a glimpse. Three years ago she'd been beautiful. She'd even been crowned the Rose Queen of Royal, Texas, as an eighteen-year-old girl. But all that had changed in one fateful car accident. She'd lost her looks, her man and her confidence.

This had supposedly been the last surgery she'd need, but her looks, which she'd once taken for granted, were now the bane of her existence. She was never going to be that beautiful girl again.

Dr. Webb put his hand on her shoulder. "Trust me, Macy."

She wasn't sure she trusted any man but her daddy. He'd stood by her through everything.

Macy and Harrison were all each other had, but she knew she couldn't spend the rest of her life sitting in Dr. Webb's office with her eyes closed.

She thought of the courageous kids in the Burn Unit at this hospital where she volunteered. They weren't afraid to look in the mirror and she shouldn't be either.

She opened one eye and then, surprised by her reflection, she opened the other. Her skin was pale and flawless, the way it used to be. No scars marred the surface. Her pixie nose had been restored to its former shape; she reached up and touched it. Her eyes hadn't been injured in the car accident and her clear green gaze remained the same.

Her lips were the only thing that were really different. A piece of glass had cut her upper lip and now she had a tiny indentation where there used to be none.

"Thank you, Dr. Webb," she said. Still not perfect, but at least she was done with surgeries.

"See. I was right, you are more beautiful than before," he said.

She just smiled and nodded. She put the mirror facedown on the bed next to her. "Don't take this the wrong way, Doc, but I'll be glad not to have to see you again."

Dr. Webb laughed. "Me too, Macy. I'll send the nurse in with some paperwork and then you will be free to go."

He started to leave, but she called him back. "Thank you, Dr. Webb. All your hard work has really made a difference to me."

"You are very welcome," he said and then left.

Her cell phone vibrated as she received a text message and she glanced down at it. The message was from her dad.

How did everything go at the doctor's?

Macy thought about her looks, but she knew she was so much more than just a pretty face now. And Dr. Webb had been a miracle worker to get her face this close to how she'd looked before the accident. She was never going to be exactly the same, but Dr. Webb had done a really good job.

Just fine, Daddy.

I bet you look better than fine. I'll see you when you get home tonight.

Yes. See you then.

Love you, baby girl.

Love you, Daddy.

She and her father were closer now than ever. After her fiancé, Benjamin, left her while she was in the hospital, she'd had no choice but to lean—and lean hard—on her father. The accident had taken everything from her.

But now she was back to her old self. Or at least she really hoped she was. She was ready to stand on her own and she knew she had to get out of her daddy's safe little world and back to her own.

She finished up with the nurse and left the office. And for the first time since then she didn't immediately put on the large sunglasses that covered half her face.

She opened the lobby door and walked right into a man. He caught her shoulders as she tottered on her heels and almost fell over.

"Thank you," she said, looking up into the bluest eyes she'd ever seen. Christopher Richardson…her high school sweetheart and the man she'd broken up with when her daddy had demanded it.

It had been almost fourteen years since they'd last seen each other and she…well, she felt as if no time had passed. Chris looked just as handsome as he had in high school and just as tempting.

"Macy. Some things never change and you get more beautiful each time I see you," he said. There was more than a hint of irony in his voice.

She flushed, remembering how she'd dumped him all those years ago. "You haven't seen me since high school."

"True enough. When a woman tells me to hit the road I tend to do that and not look back," he said. "What are you doing here?"

Should she apologize for what she'd done years earlier? She knew that she owed him way more than a casual "I'm sorry" though. "Um…I had an accident a few years ago," she said. Dang it, why hadn't she lied and said she was here for her charitable work with the Burn Unit.

"I heard about that. Are you okay now?"

She nodded. "Better every day."

"And you, Mr. Big City, what brings you back to Royal?"

"My mom is in the hospital. But I'm back in Royal to bid on rebuilding the Texas Cattleman's Club headquarters."

"Oh. I think I heard something about how you're in real estate like my father," she said.

"I'm bigger than your father, Macy. In fact, Richardson Development is the biggest developer in Texas."

"Wow," she said. She didn't know how to respond. Did he think that she'd be impressed—that she still measured people by their bank accounts?

So she changed the subject. "I hope your mom is okay," Macy said.

She remembered Margaret Richardson as a very kind woman who thought Chris hung the moon.

"She'll be fine. She has a recurring heart problem but the doctors are taking good care of her," Chris said.

An awkward silence lagged between them. He was standing there in front of her looking very sexy and she felt bruised and battered.

"Where are you living now?" Chris asked at last.

"With my dad on our ranch." It had been a hard time when she'd had the accident, and moving back to the ranch had been her only option.

"I never suspected you'd stay with your daddy, but I guess that makes sense," Chris said.

"I moved back to town a little while ago," she said. She didn't have to justify her choices to anyone, but Chris made her feel as if she should explain.

"Go figure. I guess I always thought you'd find a nice rich boy and settle down," Chris said. He rubbed a hand through his shaggy blond hair and gave her that charming grin of his that made her want to melt.

"I did. But he ran away when I proved not to be

the Texas beauty queen he'd hoped for," she said, and thought she didn't sound bitter at all.

"Loser," Chris said.

She laughed. "He was a very respectable man from a good family."

"If he couldn't make you happy then he's a loser. I always loved your spirit."

"Why, thank you, Chris. I think you are just what the doctor ordered."

"While I'm here, I could use the insight of someone who's been living here. Maybe you can tell me a little about what's going on at the club. Would you join me for dinner tonight?"

She thought about it for a minute, but she knew she wanted to go. "I will. If you're lucky I will introduce you to the next president of TCC, Ms. Abigail Langley."

"I'd heard all the wives and daughters were campaigning for Abby. That's the kind of information I need before I put in my bid to do the development," Chris said.

"We are. It's about time women had an equal stake in the Texas Cattleman's Club. My father and his cronies aren't sure what they are going to do. It completely threw them when Abby's husband died and for the first time since Tex Langley founded the club a hundred years ago they didn't have a male-Langley heir as a member. That's the only reason Abby's an honorary member."

"That's not my fight. I'm just the developer they're thinking of hiring. What do you say to six-thirty? If you're staying with your dad, I have the address."

"Sounds perfect. I'll see you then."

Macy walked away very aware that Chris was watching her. The confidence she lost when Benjamin left her was finally coming back. She wanted to pretend that it was because the last of her surgeries was over, but she knew that it was because of Chris.

Chris Richardson had been on the high school varsity football team, which had made him something akin to a god in the tiny town of Royal, Texas. And it hadn't taken Macy too long to set her sights on him. She was used to getting what she'd wanted back then, so he was hers just as junior year ended. They dated over the summer and through homecoming, but then her father had put his foot down.

Harrison Reynolds didn't want his daughter dating a boy whose dad worked for the oil companies instead of owning one. A man who wasn't a member of the Texas Cattleman's Club, ensuring his son would never be one either.

Looking back now, Macy wished she'd been a different sort of girl and had maybe stood up for Chris. But she hadn't been and she wondered sometimes if the accident was what it had taken to really shake things up for her.

One thing she knew for sure was that she'd never really gotten over him and she was glad he was back in Royal.

Chris watched Macy walk away. The sway of her hips and those gorgeous legs going a long way toward reminding him why he'd gone after her in high school. It hadn't mattered to Macy's dad that he was a star wide receiver back then, because he came from the wrong side of town.

But today he was here to visit his mom and to do

a little work on the Texas Cattleman's Club project. It was one of the most exclusive luxury country clubs in Texas. Only families with the right pedigree and the right amount of money could get in. And Chris's working-class dad hadn't provided either for Chris; though today he had more than enough money to buy himself a place in Royal's exclusive club.

He took the elevator to the sixth floor and asked at the reception desk for his mom's room. He walked down the hall to her room and opened the door to see her sitting up in her bed watching TV.

"Hi, Mom."

"Chris! I didn't think you were ever going to get here," she said.

She fumbled around for the remote, but he was at her side before she found it. He leaned down to give her a big bear hug and a kiss. Then handed her the remote. She muted the television, which had been at high volume. Her hearing wasn't as good as it used to be.

"This is extreme, Mom, even for you. Falling down so I'd come and visit you. You knew I'd be here on Texas Cattleman's Club business this weekend."

She shook her head and smiled at him. "I guess the good Lord thought I needed to see you before then. What took you so long to get up here?"

"I ran into Macy Reynolds."

His mom sat up a little straighter. It had never sat right with her that Macy had dumped him just before the senior prom.

"What did you say to her?" Maggie asked.

"Just chitchat. I'm having dinner with her tonight," Chris said. He tried hard to sound casual, but this was his mother and she knew him better than anyone else in the world.

"Is that wise?"

He shrugged. "I have no idea. But it will definitely be fun. She's changed."

"I heard about the accident," Maggie said.

"What happened?" Chris asked as he pulled a chair up close to his mom's bed. She had the same thick blondish hair he did, but she wore hers straight. It hung around her pretty face in a fashionable style. Her eyes were blue like his, but she had a pert little nose and a full bow mouth.

"It was all over the news. Her little BMW convertible was hit from behind in traffic and her car slammed into an eighteen-wheeler. The car was engulfed in flames. She's lucky to be alive. But horribly scarred. At least that's what I heard down at the Royal Diner."

"That place is a hotbed for gossip, but it doesn't mean that any of that is true," Chris said. The diner had the best greasy food in West Texas, but some of the stories to come out of there weren't always the whole truth.

"It was real enough. She had to move back in with Harrison and has spent the past few years having a series of surgeries. It was heartbreaking, Chris, to see that pretty girl in bandages. She couldn't walk for the first six months."

Chris felt weak in the stomach at the thought of Macy in so much pain. He shook his head. "She seems much better now."

"I think she is," Maggie said. "But what about you? Tell me about your work with the Texas Cattleman's Club."

"There isn't much to tell right now, Mom. I'm going

to meet with Brad Price and then start working on my bid to develop and build a new headquarters for the Cattleman's Club. I have a basic idea of what they want, but that's it."

"Are you going out there today?" Maggie asked.

"Yes, I am. I've been granted full privileges to the club while I'm working on the project."

"Where are you staying?" she asked.

"With you. I think you might need someone at home with you when you get out of the hospital. Plus, the doctors still can't figure out why you have these episodes," he said with a grin.

"Good. You don't have to stay with me, but I'm glad for the company. I miss you, Chris."

He stood up and smiled down at his mom. Her face so familiar and dear to him, he brushed a kiss over her forehead and then tucked the covers more closely around her body. "I've missed you too, Mom."

He chatted with her for a few more minutes but then had to leave. He was due to meet Brad. Brad was determined to be the next president of the Texas Cattleman's Club and, given his background as the son of one of Royal's banking families, most people thought he was a shoo-in to win. Chris wanted to take a look at the existing buildings and the property so he knew exactly what he was working with on this project. Everyone who'd grown up in Royal was aware of the club, but Chris wanted to get up to speed on the details of the property.

"I'll stop by tonight before my dinner date," he said to his mom.

"Perfect. Good luck with your business," Maggie said.

Chris left with the impression that his mother had

no idea how successful he was at what he did. But that didn't bother him. He was really only interested in making sure that Macy and Harrison knew how successful he was. And before he went back to Dallas, the Reynoldses definitely would.

As soon as he stepped out of the hospital he was reminded it was August in West Texas and hot as Hades. He loosened his tie and pulled out a pair of sunglasses and hit the remote start button on his Range Rover HSE. He was having his Porsche transported to Royal so he could use that while he was in town.

He wanted the locals to know that Chris Richardson was back and he had plenty of money this time. He may not be a full-fledged member of the Texas Cattleman's Club, but he took a lot of pride in knowing that he had enough money in his bank accounts to be one if he pushed.

He wondered what kind of car Macy drove. He should have asked a few more questions about her accident. It was hard for him to imagine the girl he'd known, who'd lived a decidedly charmed life, having to go through that kind of painful recovery. But then life seldom turned out the way that most people thought it would. Chris had proved that by making a success of himself in the same field as Harrison Reynolds. And tonight he'd be sitting in the dining room of the Texas Cattleman's Club with Macy. Life was sweet.

Macy couldn't stop looking at herself in the mirror and she knew that was a recipe for disaster, so she forced herself away from it and back to her computer. She had a lot of work to get done before her dinner with Chris.

Chris Richardson. Dang, she'd never expected to see him again. She wished she could say that the years hadn't been good to him, but they had. If he'd developed a beer belly and lost some of his hair maybe she wouldn't be quivering in anticipation waiting for six-thirty to roll around.

The doorbell rang and Macy sat up a little straighter, leaving her home office. She heard Jessie, her dad's housekeeper, talking to someone. Macy rose from her chair, and went out into the hallway. She smiled at Abigail Langley.

Abby and Macy went way back to high school, but they had really become closer after Macy's accident when Abby had become her rock. Then last year, unexpectedly, Abby's husband had died of a brain aneurysm and Macy had had a chance to return the favor.

Abby had long wavy red hair and bright blue eyes. She was pretty and tall and walked into the room as if she owned it. Macy envied her friend that confidence. She'd thought the surgeries that restored her looks and her ability to walk would be enough, but this afternoon she'd realized they weren't.

"Hi, there, Abby," Macy said.

"Hello, gorgeous! You look wonderful. No need to ask how the doctor's appointment went."

Macy flushed. "I still don't look like me."

Abby wrapped her arm around Macy's shoulder. "Yes, you do. This is the new you."

"You are right. So…guess who I ran into at the hospital?" Macy asked as she led Abby into the den. The room was richly appointed with deep walnut paneling and oversize leather couches and chairs. This was where her father hosted football parties for his college buddies and where, when Macy had turned sixteen, she'd hosted her first boy-girl party.

On the wall was a portrait of her that her father had commissioned when she was eighteen, and Macy took a seat that deliberately kept her back to the picture. She hated looking at old pictures of herself. She didn't like being reminded of who she used to be.

"Christopher Richardson," Abby said with a twinkle in her eye.

"How did you know?"

"I have my sources. What did he say?"

"Nothing much. We're going to dinner tonight so I can catch him up on all the gossip about the club. He's in town to consult on developing the new clubhouse."

"Well, that's news to me. I'm going to have to have a little discussion with Mr. Bradford Price."

"I wasn't sure if you knew about it or not," Macy confessed. Abby was rumored to be the descendant of infamous Texas outlaw Jessamine Golden and was making history herself as the first female member of the Texas Cattleman's Club.

Abby and Macy had bonded over their shared tragedies. When Macy had been so badly injured and struggling to recover, Abby had been there for her, something Macy would never forget.

Abby didn't say anything else, and Macy was a little worried about her friend. She suspected that Abby was using the connection and campaign to become the next president of the club to distract herself from the fact that Richard was really gone.

"Whose house are we placing the flamingos at next?"

"Mrs. Doubletree has been selected, but we are going to hit TCC first."

"Great. What time and when?"

"Tonight, but if you can't make it due to your dinner date, I will understand. In fact, I think we might be moving them while you are dining. You can help out the next time."

Macy hated to miss out on helping Abby with the flamingos. Since she'd been so badly scarred and had frequently had bandages on to help her healing body stay infection free for the past three years, helping place pink flamingos in the yards of wealthy community members under cover of night had been the only thing she'd really felt comfortable doing to help out.

They placed the flamingos in the yards of different community members, and then the recipient of the flamingoes paid at least ten dollars a bird to have them relocated to another yard. The money was being raised for Helping Hands, a women's shelter run by Summer Franklin in nearby Somerset.

Macy had always been big into causes, having been on the board of the Reynolds Charitable Trust since she turned twenty-one. But normally she just wrote checks and organized galas. Actually getting out and doing things was new to her.

"I will try to make it. It's the only thing I've really been able to do to help," Macy said.

"You've done more than that," Abby said. "You've been helping me out a lot with my campaign."

"I think it's about time that the Texas Cattlemen had some women in their ranks. The shake-up last year helped change it from Daddy's stuffy old men's club into something that our generation can really be a part of."

"I agree. And when I become president of the club, that's not the only change we will be making."

"Good to hear it," Macy said. She and Abby chatted a few minutes longer before Abby had to leave.

After her friend's departure, Macy went upstairs and had a long bath. She didn't want to be nervous about tonight, but it was the first date she'd been on since her fiancé had left her. And that made it important.

She thought about her scarred body and how she still felt like the mess she'd been after that first surgery. She didn't want to stare at herself in the mirror, but her psychiatrist said that she had to accept what she looked like now if she was ever going to move on.

She let the towel drop and stood in front of the mirror, letting her gaze drift down her own body. She saw the scarring on her right side, then the muscle she'd lost on her inner thigh.

She felt tears stir in her eyes and she bit her lower lip. Her body wasn't going to get any better. This was how she'd always look. She glanced back at her face and for a moment almost resented the fact that her face was back to "normal" because the rest of her wasn't. Not even inside was she the same woman she used to be.

She didn't dwell on the fact that the date was with Christopher Richardson. He'd been her first love and she wasn't sure she'd ever really gotten over him. She'd been young and impetuous when they'd met and he'd been forbidden fruit. She'd wanted him because her father hadn't wanted her to have him. It wasn't lost on her that she'd used him and now she was going to have to apologize. The girl she'd been pre-accident would have handled it with her normal panache, but Macy wasn't that woman anymore and she suddenly dreaded the coming evening.

Two

Macy had driven herself to the Texas Cattleman's Club because she was meeting Abby later to move the flamingos. But also because she didn't want to be too dependent on Chris getting her home. The dining room was traditional Texas with lots of big heavy dark wood pieces and portraits of the founding members on the walls.

She went to the bar area and ordered a glass of Chardonnay while she waited for Chris. She hated being alone in a public place. It didn't matter that she'd grown up coming to this club. She felt so exposed because of her accident.

She felt as if everyone was watching her and whispering behind her back. She knew it was her imagination. But Royal was a town that was given to gossip and she hated to be fodder for it. When she'd been younger— before her accident—she'd tried to do daring things to make people notice her, but now she just longed to be invisible.

"Macy?"

She glanced toward the end of the bar where her father stood with one of his business partners. Her dad was one of the old guard at the club. But he was fighting to remain loyal after the scandal involving Sebastian Hunter a few years ago. His friend's embezzlement had shaken him. Sebastian had tried to sabotage the very club he'd been a member of.

"Hello, Dad," she said, turning to give him a kiss when he approached.

He lifted her chin and she knew he was looking for the scar that used to run the length of the left side of her face. Her dad had been the first one to see her after the accident. Her fiancé, Benjamin, didn't think he could handle seeing her that way. So her father had come in and held her hand and told her that she was still his princess.

"Beautiful," he said. He kissed her forehead.

She blinked back tears. "Thanks, Daddy."

He handed her a handkerchief. Then pulled her close for a hug. She hid her face in his shoulder the way she used to when she was little and didn't want to face something.

"What are you doing up here, Mace? Did I forget a dinner date for tonight?" Harrison asked.

"Actually, no. I'm meeting someone," she said. She had no idea how he'd take the news that she was having dinner with Chris. So she decided to keep his name to herself. Chris had certainly changed since high school, but tonight she wanted the fairy tale. She'd felt like the Beast locked away for so long. Now she wanted to feel attractive and to enjoy being out on a date with a good-looking guy. She and Chris Richardson had always made a stunning couple.

"That's good. I wanted to take you out to celebrate the removal of the last bandages, but you know how it is with work. I don't keep banker's hours." She and her dad had been alone since her mother had died when Macy was a toddler. They celebrated things in their own way and on their own time. She knew he'd make it up to her.

"You never have," she said. Macy was very aware of how hard her father worked. He owned one of the largest construction companies in Texas. And flew from Royal to other parts of the state most weeks. He also had his weekly poker game in Midland and a twice-yearly fishing trip with his college buddies.

The waiter called his name and he hesitated. "Do you want me to wait with you?"

She smiled at him. "No, I'm fine. Go on. I'll see you at breakfast tomorrow."

He hugged her quickly and then walked away. She turned back to the bar just as her wine arrived. She took a sip before glancing around the bar. Chris waved at her as he walked toward her.

"Sorry if I kept you waiting," Chris said. "I'll have a Lone Star beer," he told the bartender.

"Right away, sir," the man said.

"You didn't. I was a little early. Since the accident I…I drive a little more slowly," she said. There really wasn't any part of her life that hadn't been affected by it.

"You will have to tell me more about what happened.

Mom knew some of the details," he said. "Let's grab a booth while we wait to be seated for dinner."

She nodded and he led the way to one of the small intimate booths in the corner. Macy slid in and then waited while Chris did the same. He sat directly across from her and put his elbows on the table.

"So what happened? Mom said you'd been burned," he said.

She shrugged. "No one's really ever asked me about it before, because it was on the news."

"Not in Dallas," he said. "But then most of the stuff that happens here doesn't make the headlines there."

"I don't know what to say except my car was hit by a long-haul trucker and that it was a mangled mess… all the rescuers said I was lucky to be alive."

She held her hands loosely together, taking off the ring on her right hand and playing with it before putting it back on. She didn't like to talk about the accident. To be honest, she remembered so little of it.

"I'm glad that you are such a lucky woman, Macy," he said.

The bartender arrived with his beer. She studied him as he took a swallow from it. He hadn't changed at all since high school—well, that wasn't really true. He'd matured into his features; if anything, he was better looking today than he had been back then.

He arched one eyebrow at her and she flushed. "The years have been good to you," she said, trying to find the words to ask him to forgive the immature girl she'd been.

"I can't complain," he said. "I've been working hard building my company, but I play hard too."

"You mentioned that you are here for business."

"That's right. I'm doing consulting work for the expansion of the buildings here on the grounds."

Macy tipped her head to the side and studied him. "Who asked you to do that?"

"Brad Price. We went to college together."

"You went to UT Austin?"

"Yes, ma'am."

"I thought you were going to get the hell out of Texas," she said.

"Plans changed. I graduated at the top of our class... so it was cheaper for me to go to a Texas state university."

"I forgot about that. Beauty and brains," she said.

"Ah, no, you were always the beauty," he said.

She tucked a strand of hair behind her ear. That other girl she'd been was as foreign to her now as the thought of living anywhere other than Royal. "I was a little intolerable back then."

"Not at all. You were pretty and confident. Every boy in school wanted you."

"Not anymore," she said. "And there was only one boy I wanted."

"You had me, if that's what you meant. Why aren't you confident now?"

She realized that she was feeling a little bit funky tonight. Almost blue. She wasn't about to say out loud that she was no longer pretty. Not to Chris. Especially when she realized that he might want a little revenge against her for the way she'd treated him back then.

"Just not as shallow as I used to be. After my accident, I started working with the kids in the hospital's Burn Unit and I came to realize that true beauty has nothing to do with physical appearance."

"What has it got to do with?" he asked, taking another long swallow of his beer.

"I can't define it, but I do know that it comes from deep inside. I think it's how a person deals with others," she said.

He shook his head. "You sure have changed."

His name was called for dinner before she could respond. She slid out of the booth and Chris put his hand on the small of her back as they walked toward the dining room. His hand was big and warm through the fabric of her sundress and she was very glad that she'd run into him today. Being with Chris tonight made her realize just how much she'd been missing.

Chris spent the evening realizing why he'd fallen for Macy in the first place. She was funny and lively and had the kind of dry wit that made him laugh. She was also very intelligent and just a little bit shy. The shyness was new. She used to be a different girl.

He guessed that was what the difference really was. Macy was a woman now and life had handed her more than a few surprises. He was almost afraid to trust the woman she was tonight. He'd been burned by her once before.

"Why are you staring at me like that?" she asked, taking a sip of her wine.

"You aren't what I expected you to be," he said, opting for the truth, as he usually did. When he'd first gotten into the development business he had run into vendors who'd say anything to make their company sound good. And Chris had set Richardson Development apart from them by always being up front and never promising what he couldn't deliver. He did the same thing in his personal life.

"In what way?" she asked, leaning forward as if his answer was something she wanted to hear.

"Well, to be honest, when you dumped me I had sort of hoped the years would be unkind to you and that you'd get fat and sort of dumpy."

"Are you disappointed I'm not?" she asked with a laugh. She had an effervescent laugh that made him smile. Just the sound of it was joy. Though to his ears it sounded a bit rusty. As if she hadn't had much to laugh about in recent years, which he knew she hadn't.

He shook his head. How could he wish for her to be anything but the beautiful, sexy woman he saw in front of him? Even in the August heat, she looked cool and untouchable.

"Not at all. But that's not really why I was staring at you. When we were teenagers you seemed like a girl who was going to lead a charmed life, and I was noticing that you don't seem bitter that you haven't."

She shrugged one delicate shoulder and a strand of her honey-blond hair fell forward; she reached up and tucked it back behind her ear. "I can't change what happened, so there is no use lamenting it, right?"

"Not everyone would see it that way." He realized she didn't see anything special in the way she was, but he did. Nothing she said would convince him that she wasn't heroic. He liked the way she seemed to have adjusted to the changes in her life and he was very glad he was the first man to take her out after her surgeries were complete.

"It's just the way I am now. Plus, if not for the accident I wouldn't have started working in the Burn Unit at the hospital."

"You mentioned that before. Are you in the medical profession now?" he asked.

"No. But I'm the administrator of the Reynolds Trust."

"What is that?" Chris asked.

"It's a charitable organization that my father established after my mother died. They give money to different organizations, some relating to medical research and providing care for the uninsured. I took over after college. After I started volunteering in the children's Burn Unit, I added it to one of our charities at the trust. I am also a financial analyst and work at my dad's company."

"You sound very busy. Do you enjoy your work?" he asked.

"I do. What about you? What is it like being a big real estate developer?"

"I do a fair amount of work around the state."

"More than a fair amount. Every time I open the business page there's a new project with your company's name on it."

"Do you think about me whenever you see them?" he asked.

"Maybe."

"Never thought I'd make good, did you?" he asked. He'd spent more than a few late nights over the years thinking about Macy and wondering what she'd make of his success.

"I was young, Chris. I really didn't think much about you and me, or the future."

"We were both young."

"I wasn't sure enough to stand on my own...despite how confident I may have seemed at school," she confessed.

He took a deep swallow of his beer, not wanting to comment on it. No matter his age, he'd fallen hard for Macy. "And now?"

"I don't know, Chris. I'm just starting to figure out who I am. The accident made me reevaluate my life."

"I can see that," he said. "And now you're one of the rabble-rousers trying to get the club to admit women to its roster."

"Yes, I am. I think it's time we shake things up in this part of Texas."

Chris laughed at the way she said it. His business was headquartered in Dallas, which wasn't at all like this part of Texas. Here, attitudes were slower to change and men were still men.

"It will be interesting to see what happens," Chris said. He had a hard time imagining women as full-fledged members of the Texas Cattleman's Club. The traditions of the club were part of what made it so exclusive.

"I think we will win. Women have always had a certain advantage when it comes to negotiating with men," Macy said with a tip of her head and a wink.

Macy had always known how to get her way. Which was probably how he'd ended up dating her to begin with. But now he was older and wiser. He should know better, but he was still turned on by this woman. It wouldn't take much manipulating on her part to make him want to please her.

"True enough. And the women in Royal know how to use it to their advantage." He had experienced her powers of persuasion when they'd been in high school. He'd never been able to deny her a thing. Even when she broke up with him he hadn't been sure it wasn't his fault.

"You say that like it's a bad thing," she said.

"It's not," he said. Since the beginning of time women had figured out how to get men to do what they wanted and that was the beauty of the opposite sexes. "I always liked seeing you smile, so if I have to do something to make that happen again then I guess I'd do it," he said. Even walking away from her, he'd done that to make her happy because her father had been making their lives hell back then.

"What about now? Still like my smile?" she asked. "My teeth have been professionally whitened and straightened and Daddy has always said I could charm the whiskers off a cat with this smile."

He leaned in closer and put his hand under her chin, tipping her head to the left then the right, studying her very pretty mouth. "Can you frown for me?"

She chuckled but then pouted for him. He rubbed his thumb over her lower lip. "Now smile."

She did and it was like taking a punch to the gut. He'd forgotten how powerful his reaction was to a true smile from Macy. And this was a true smile.

"Yes. I think it's safe to say you still have some power over me with that smile." Even after all this time. No other woman that he had met had affected him the way she had. He didn't want to admit it, but he'd thought of her often over the years, and being here with her tonight was very fulfilling.

"I'll have to remember that. How long are you in town, Chris?"

"At least the rest of August. I have a project that I have to oversee in Dallas that I will need to return to for September. Why, anxious to see me leave?" he asked.

"Not at all." She leaned forward and rubbed her index finger over his knuckles. Then she looked up at him, her green gaze meeting his, and he felt everyone else in the dining room disappear. There was just the two of them.

"I would miss you if you left today," she said. "I'm sorry we didn't keep in touch when you left Royal. I think I missed out on seeing the best of you as you matured into the man you are today."

"Me too," he said. "I would have liked to see you before your accident so I would be able to tell you how much more beautiful you are now."

He lifted her hand to his mouth and brushed his lips across the back of it. That little display of affection was really all that this conservative community would allow, but he wanted so much more from Macy, and this time he wasn't going to leave without taking what he wanted.

"I've got a bone to pick with you, Richardson." A booming voice jarred him back to the present. He looked up just in time to see Harrison Reynolds barreling down on their table like a Texas longhorn on a rampage.

He was a tall man with a big stocky build and he wore his success well with his nine-hundred-dollar boots and a Stetson on his head. If anyone looked as if he belonged in the club, it was Harrison.

Reluctantly, Chris let go of Macy's hand. It seemed more than one thing hadn't changed since he'd left Royal all those years ago. He wondered if he'd ever have enough money or be influential enough for Harrison to accept him. Because it was very clear to him that no matter what he'd done so far, Harrison Reynolds still didn't believe Chris was good enough for Macy.

Macy glared at her father. Couldn't she have one night that wasn't marred by…what? Her father didn't know that this was a date. He probably thought she and Chris were here discussing club business.

"What about, Harrison?" Chris said, turning that affable grin on her father.

She hadn't realized that his smile was just part of an act and now she did. Was he playing her to maybe get back a little of his own after the way she'd dumped him? That hardly seemed likely since high school was eons ago, and Chris didn't strike her as the kind of man to hold a grudge.

"Your prejudice against Reynolds Construction. Is there a reason why we aren't good enough to win a place on any of your projects?" Harrison asked. He grabbed a chair from a neighboring table and sat down with them.

"Hello, Macy."

"Hello, Dad," she said.

"I'm sure you must have been high when you bid with us. I don't give anyone preferential treatment," Chris said.

"Bull. You and I have had past dealings, thanks to Macy here."

"Harrison, I would never let anything stand in the way of making money. You should know that better than anyone. I'm sure your bids were too high. Stop by my office tomorrow and I'll run through the records and see what we can find."

Harrison nodded. "I'll be there. I hear you are in the

running to rebuild the headquarters and other parts of the club. I'd like a piece of that."

"Dad," Macy said, sounding extremely exasperated. It was clear she didn't want to be sitting here with him while her dad tried to talk about business.

"*Macy.* Leave this to me and Christopher," he said.

She rolled her eyes and once again tucked a strand of hair behind her ear. "I'll be happy to, but you are intruding on my date. My first date in nearly three years, so I'd appreciate it if you'd move on."

Her dad turned to her and she realized what she'd said. "Wait a minute. Did you say date?"

"Yes, I did," Macy said a little defiantly.

"With Richardson?"

"He is the biggest developer in Texas, Daddy," she said.

And just like that, Chris knew that, as the son of a working class man, if he hadn't made something of himself, he wouldn't be sitting here with Miss Macy Reynolds.

He shook his head. "I'm not sure how I feel about this."

"Dad, don't even think about saying anything else. This isn't up for debate," Macy said.

"Fine. We'll discuss this tomorrow, Richardson."

Her dad stood up and walked away as quickly as he'd joined them, and Macy could only watch him leave, incredulous that he'd managed to talk about business and threaten Chris in one breath. She never quite got used to her father and his larger-than-life business persona.

"Um…sorry?"

Chris laughed. "I don't think anyone can apologize

for that man. It was nothing. If my company is showing a bias against him then I need to know about it."

"Okay. But what about us? I don't want..."

"Things to be like they were before?" he asked. He didn't have to be on *CSI* to figure out what she wanted. He wanted the same thing. A chance to date her and get to know her without her father and all of Royal looking on.

"Yes. I mean, I know they aren't, but I wanted to make sure you knew. I'm sorry for the way I broke up with you," she said, biting her lower lip as she waited for him to respond.

He nodded. "I am too."

He smiled at her. He really liked this woman and her honesty. She was refreshing compared to the women he'd been dating lately who were always trying to be what he wanted them to be instead of just being themselves. Macy wasn't like that.

"Not a problem. So, where were we? I believe you mentioned that you'd miss me if I weren't here," he said.

"Did I? I can't remember. Why would I miss you?" she asked.

"Because we didn't have a chance to really get to know each other when we were kids," Chris explained. She'd always been the one girl he'd never been able to forget. He hadn't spent the years pining over her or anything like that, but Macy would just pop up in his thoughts from time to time. Like in fall when the bluebells would blanket the fields near his office, he'd always remember the first time he kissed her and how sweet and innocent that kiss had been.

"You might be right. You were really into football back then," she said. "I remember because that is how I first noticed you. Catching all those passes and making touchdowns. You gave me something to cheer about."

"I remember you cheering me on to many touchdowns."

"I sure did. My squad was the best... That sure was a long time ago. I thought the sun rose and fell on Royal and that the rest of the world was missing out on something," she said.

"Did you ever leave?" he asked, and realized aside from the accident he didn't really know much more about the "new" Macy.

"No. I like it here. I guess I'm just a small-town Texas girl at heart. I probably seem a little unsophisticated for the likes of you now that you're a city slicker."

"No one would ever call you unsophisticated," Chris said. He thought that Macy hadn't left Royal because she hadn't needed to. She had always been part of the upper crust and she'd had more opportunities than he'd had.

"Well, I do read all the fashion magazines," she said with a slight flush.

"And shop at the big stores?" he asked.

"Not recently. I...I really haven't left the house much," she said, putting a hand up when he would have interrupted. "I'm not saying that to make you feel sorry for me. I just read *Vogue* and *Cosmo* and *InStyle* and dreamed of a time when I'd look in the mirror again."

He reached over and took her hand. Holding it in his bigger one. He stroked his thumb over her knuckles as a wave of strong emotion washed over him. Macy wasn't putting up any barriers between them. He was getting the real woman and that made him want to protect her. To make sure that the vulnerable woman who was slowly rediscovering herself had the chance to grow. And he knew he would have to tread carefully with Harrison because he didn't want Macy's father to be an obstacle between Macy and him as he had been in the past.

"Surely you don't have those doubts after today," Chris said.

"I…I wish it were that easy, Chris, but to be honest, a part of me is still afraid of seeing the scars when I look in the mirror. Not sure I believe the reflection I saw was real."

He reached up and stroked her cheek, though he knew better than to let this go too far in public. There was something fragile…almost broken…about Macy and he couldn't let it go. No matter that she'd broken his heart in the past, he saw that she was a different woman now. "Let me tell you what I see."

She nodded and held her breath, her pretty white teeth biting her lower lip as he stared at her face. And he wondered how bad her scars had been before the plastic surgery. He'd never met anyone who'd been in a life-threatening accident before.

He traced the high line of her cheekbone over her smooth alabaster skin. Her eyebrows were dark blond. "I see skin like the palest marble, so pretty and smooth."

He moved his finger over her lips. They were full and plump, utterly kissable, and he longed to taste her again. "I see a mouth so pink and delectable it's all I can do to resist kissing you."

He rubbed his finger over the line of her jaw. "This strong jaw tells me that you still haven't lost the stubbornness that's always been a part of you."

She gave him a little half smile. He ran his finger

over the arch of her eyebrows—first one then the other. "These pretty green eyes watch me with a combination of weariness and curiosity. I don't want to disappoint you."

She captured his hand and held it to her cheek. "Thank you, Chris."

He knew whatever else happened between the two of them that he wasn't leaving Royal until Macy was the beautiful flirt she used to be. Confident of herself and her ability to attract every man in the area—especially him.

Three

Macy left Chris after dinner to powder her nose. He was a little intense and she wasn't as ready for him as she might have been, say, four years earlier. Chris had changed in his time away from Royal and her. And she hoped she'd changed as well, but she had the feeling that her changes hadn't taken her as far forward as Chris's had taken him.

"Macy?"

She glanced up in the mirror and saw Abby standing in the doorway. Her friend looked fabulous as always and Macy knew she should stop comparing herself to every woman in the room at some point, but she had no idea when and if that would happen.

"Hello, there. What are you doing here?" she asked Abby.

"Promoting myself to become the next president. I can't let any time slip by. How's dinner?" Abby asked.

She shook her long red wavy hair. Her blue eyes had always made Macy envious. She'd always wanted pretty eyes like that instead of the green ones she had. But after her surgeries she was very happy with her eyes now.

Macy blushed and then shook her head. "Nice. Dad stopped by and read Chris the riot act for not using his company, but Chris calmly stood his ground. I've never seen anyone handle Daddy like that."

Abby laughed and slung her arm around Macy's shoulders. "It's about time. You okay?"

"Yes," Macy said, then realized that she was telling the truth. She hadn't felt like this in a long time. She wanted to laugh for no good reason and just shout at the top of her lungs that life was good. "I really am."

"Good," Abby said.

Macy left the ladies' room and went back to their table. She saw that Chris was talking to a tall handsome African-American man that Macy didn't know. She wasn't sure if she should approach the table because they seemed engrossed in whatever they were discussing, but Chris glanced up and waved her over.

"Zeke, this is Macy Reynolds, Harrison's daughter, Macy this is Zeke Travers. He and I went to college together."

Zeke Travers was solid and muscular with a shaved head and dark brown skin. He had kind eyes and smiled when he glanced over at her.

"It's a pleasure to meet you," Macy said, holding out her hand.

"You as well," Zeke said. "I'll let you get back to dinner. Drinks tomorrow?"

"You're on," Chris said.

Zeke left and Macy watched him go. Brad Price walked straight up to Zeke, and Macy could tell he wasn't happy. The sounds of raised voices could be heard throughout the room and everyone watched them.

"What is going on with them?" Macy asked. She couldn't help herself—she was naturally curious about the spectacle the men were making. Brad pulled a piece of paper from his pocket and waved it at Zeke.

"I have no idea," Chris said. "I'll try to find out more from Zeke tomorrow when we have drinks."

"I sound like a small-town gossip, don't I?" she asked. She wished she wasn't nosy, but she always had been. She liked knowing what was going on in other people's lives.

"It's the nature of Royal to talk," Chris said. Brad looked beet-red with fury. Whatever was upsetting him it had to be serious. She'd never seen Brad in such a state before.

"I hope he's okay," Macy said. She and Brad weren't close friends or anything, but she knew him from Texas Cattleman's Club events when they were children.

"Who is?" Abby said, coming up to their table.

"Brad," Chris said, gesturing to the two men who were arguing.

"He's probably just learned that I am making serious inroads to becoming the next president of the club," Abby said with a confident grin.

"Are you?" Chris asked, arching one eyebrow at her and giving her a hard stare.

"Indeed I am. And you are…?" Abby asked.

"Forgive my manners," Macy said. "Abigail Langley, this is Christopher Richardson. Abby is going to be the next president of the club. Chris has been asked to come up with a development plan for the new headquarters building. He owns his own development company out of Dallas."

Abby and Chris had run in different circles in high school. Well, to be honest, Abby and Macy had run in different circles. Macy's life had been cheerleading and parties at TCC and Chris had fallen in with her crowd by being a football star. Abby and she hadn't had much in common then.

The two shook hands and Abby took a seat in the chair recently vacated by Zeke. Of the three people they'd had at the table she was happiest to have her good friend there now. She wanted Abby's opinion on Chris. It wasn't that she didn't trust her instincts when it came to men—wait a minute, it was exactly that she didn't trust them.

She'd been engaged to a man who'd left her the minute she wasn't the Texas beauty she'd always been. She didn't want to chance getting hurt again.

And though this was only a dinner date, it was with Chris Richardson. The boy she'd defied her father to date. He'd always been attractive to her. Not just physically, though there was that.

"Macy?" Abby asked, startling Macy out of her thoughts.

"Yes?"

"I asked if you thought that Chris and I would work well together when I'm president," Abby said.

She had to give it to Abby for being persistent and determined. There wasn't a person in Royal who didn't know what Abby's intent was. She was focused one hundred percent on becoming the first female president of the Texas Cattleman's Club. "Yes, I do."

Abby smiled at her friend and then reached over to squeeze her hand before getting up. "I'll leave you to your dinner. It was nice meeting you, Chris."

"You too," Chris said.

Abby left and Macy sat back in her chair. "I'd forgotten what it's like to come to dinner at the club. It's such a hub for everyone."

"You really haven't been out for a while?" Chris asked. He took a sip of his drink and leaned forward when he talked to her. It was a very intimate thing to do and made her feel as if they were the only two people here tonight.

"For years." At first she'd been horrified and so traumatized by everything that had happened that she'd been afraid to leave the house. Then she'd wanted to go out, but the few forays she'd made had shown her that people stared. She hadn't been strong enough for that.

"Well, how do you think it went then?" Chris asked. "Your first dinner out in years."

"I think it went well," Macy admitted. "It's also my first date in years."

She'd been hiding away at her father's ranch trying to pretend that she'd just moved from her hometown. It had been hard being so badly injured in a place where she'd known so many people. She had needed to just blend in and that wasn't possible in Royal, so she'd started staying home.

"I'm glad," Chris admitted. "I'm not happy about the circumstances that led to it, but I'm very honored to be the first man you've been out with."

She didn't want to let this mean too much. Chris wasn't in town looking for a small-town girl as his wife, and she knew she was vulnerable right now. But she had enjoyed herself and their date and, if she was honest, she'd have to say she hoped he'd ask her out again.

"I'm glad it was you too," she said. "You have made my night, and celebrating my first day free of bandages couldn't have been nicer. Thank you, Chris."

"It was truly my pleasure, Macy."

The feeling of being in a fishbowl when he went out in Royal was very different from what he usually felt in Dallas. In the big city, no one noticed who he was with, but tonight he was very aware that most of the town knew he and Macy had had dinner together. The gossip had defined who he was and had served to make him want to be better than his dad. He'd been only too happy to shake the dust of this town from his feet.

"I'd kind of forgotten what Royal was like."

"I bet. Don't miss it much, do you?" she asked as he paid the bill and they sat for an extra minute to talk and drink the Baileys that Chris had ordered for them.

"I miss my mom," he admitted. "She's Royal born and bred. I've tried to get her to move up to Dallas but she won't do it, keeps trying to make me move back here instead."

"What about your dad?" Macy asked.

"Nah, he was a Yankee," Chris said with a laugh. "East Coaster who fell in love with the oil industry thanks to the movie *Giant*. Mom used to tease him that he came to Royal looking for Liz Taylor."

"Your mom is pretty enough. Did he think he'd found her?" Macy asked.

"Yes, I think he did. They had a happy marriage until he passed."

"I was sorry to hear about your loss," Macy said. "Did you get the flowers I sent?"

"I don't know. Mom handled all that," he said. That entire time was still a blur for him. He hadn't been old enough to have made his peace with his dad. He had been getting closer to forgiving the old man for all the things he hadn't done for him. Things that a boy had wanted but a man knew weren't really important. "Why didn't you come to the funeral?"

His dad had died when Chris had been a junior in college. It had changed his perspective and sharpened his desires to make his life different. He'd stopped being such a frat boy and focused more on his studies.

"I didn't think I'd be welcome," Macy said. "But I remembered meeting him and how sweet he'd been to me. He was a nice man. Your parents were always so funny at dinner, teasing you and treating you like…the apple of their eye."

"Only when we had company. They had plenty of fault to find when we were alone."

Unlike her dad, who'd forbidden Macy to see Chris, his parents had adored her and really treated her well when she'd come to dinner at his house. But Chris and his dad had butted heads a lot, something his mom had said was due to the fact that they were both stubborn as mules. Chris suspected it was more likely that they both wanted different things for him.

"Ready to go?" he asked, changing the subject.

"I guess so. I've really enjoyed tonight, Chris," she said. In fact, she couldn't remember a date she'd enjoyed more in her adult life. Benjamin had been a coworker of hers and they'd kind of fallen into dating because all their friends were coupled up. They had found each other by default, she thought. Maybe that was why they hadn't lasted.

"Me too," he said, his voice a rich deep baritone that brushed over her senses like a cool breeze on a hot summer's day.

He put his hand on the small of her back as he directed her through the dining room toward the outer doors of the club. He liked the feel of her under his hands. They'd been too young when they'd dated before to get into anything other than heavy petting. And he remembered her teenage body in a bikini from the summer, but that was all. He wondered what she looked like now.

She stopped and started laughing as she saw the sea of pink flamingos.

"What's so funny?" Chris asked.

"The flamingos. I can't believe they showed up here," Macy said. No one was supposed to know who exactly had placed the birds, so she had to pretend she didn't know. The lawn of the club was dotted with gaudy pink flamingos and Chris had a chuckle as well.

"I guess it was the club's time," Chris said. "Mother said one of her neighbors had them a few weeks ago."

"It definitely is the club's time to have them here. I think they're cute," she said.

The conversation trailed off and he could do nothing but stare at her in the moonlight. He took her hand and led her down one of the many paths and out of sight of prying eyes. Her thick honey-blond hair hung loosely around her shoulders.

"Why do you keep looking at me?" she asked.

"I've never seen anyone quite as beautiful," he said.

It was the truth, and all that he knew about her had just been enhanced tonight.

"That's not true, but I'm going to say thank-you anyway."

"It is true," he said. Years ago her question would have been blatant flirting, but today he sensed her genuine unease about her own looks. "How can I convince you of what I see when I look at you?"

She shrugged and nibbled on her lower lip, which drew his eyes to her mouth. He loved her mouth, even with the tiny scar on her upper lip. The full lower lip that made him just want to lean down and taste her. He wanted her.

No big shock there. She was stunningly beautiful, even though she seemed to have forgotten that. He was here for business in the place that he used to call home but where he'd felt he never fit in. And now he didn't want to think about business or fitting in. Macy dominated every thought.

"I don't know. I think I've been afraid to take chances," she said.

"Is dinner with me a chance?" he asked.

She gave him a wistful half smile. "I think it is."

He took her hand in his and led her away from the club toward the flock of pink flamingos. Stopping right in front of them, he pulled her into his arms and tipped her chin up.

"I've been wanting to do this since we ran into each other at the hospital."

"Hold me?" she asked, licking her lips.

"No, I'll kiss you instead," he said. He lowered his head and gave her a chaste kiss. The kind that would have been acceptable when they'd been dating in high school. But her mouth opened on a sigh and her warm breath stole into his. And he groaned because he wanted more.

What he felt for Macy went way beyond the chaste and pure. He angled his mouth over hers and made teasing forays with his tongue. Tasting the essence of this fragile, pretty woman with each sweep of his tongue.

She moaned softly and her hands clung to his shoulders as he slid his hands down her back to her waist and drew her closer to him. He hadn't felt anything this strong…well, in a while. Lust was something he'd dealt with before, but with Macy it was stronger than it ever had been.

He wanted more than to sweep her off her feet and into his bed. That should have been warning, but the only bells going off in his head were screaming for him to remove her clothing and touch her flesh. He wanted her.

He pulled back, but her eyes were closed and her mouth dewy and soft. He couldn't resist coming back for another kiss. Her taste was addictive and the feel of her in his arms even more unforgettable than he'd believed it could be.

"Chris…"

"Yes?"

"I liked that. I can't think of a better gift to celebrate my last surgery than this night and you," she told him once more.

He hugged her close and she rested her head on his shoulder. He stroked his hand down her back. This moment was almost perfect. He was on the lawn of the club that had eluded him as a young man. A place he'd stood looking in on many times, but where he was now welcome.

He held the woman that he hadn't been good enough for all those years ago and she wasn't asking him to sneak around with her, but instead stood here in full view of anyone choosing to glance at them.

And she'd called him a gift. She had no idea how often he'd dreamed of this moment as a teenager or how different it actually was than what he'd fantasized about it. Macy made the difference. Perhaps he still wanted revenge on her dad, but the feeling wasn't as sharp as it once had been.

When Macy had first woken up in the hospital three years ago she hadn't wanted to live. She couldn't accurately describe the pain to anyone who'd never been severely burned, but she'd wanted to die from it. She'd spent each day in an agony of tears and melancholy. Then Dr. Webb had suggested she leave her room and go down to the children's Burn Unit.

One visit was all it had taken for her to stop feeling so overwhelmed. She was amazed at how the kids, some of whom were burned far more badly that she was, just sort of soldiered on. She'd started visiting them at least once a week ever since.

Macy walked into the hospital burn ward the way she always did—feeling as if she was coming home. She had a real job—financial analyst for Reynolds Construction—but this was where she really belonged.

She went immediately to the play area where children scarred by burns and recovering from their own surgeries spent time playing without having anyone stare at them. Sara, a twelve-year-old who'd been trapped in a house fire and had burns on her entire left side, was the first one to notice Macy. The little girl's hair would never grow back, and despite the many surgeries she'd endured, she'd been slow to recover. But Macy had been in worse shape than Sara when she'd come to the hospital.

"You're beautiful," Sara said, a big smile growing across her face. "I know you said you used to be pretty, but you are way better than pretty, Miss Macy."

"Thank you. I wasn't sure what to expect when the bandages came off. I was so scared I almost couldn't look at myself in the mirror."

"Dr. Webb told me that if you recovered I could," Sara said.

She knew that Sara had been anxious for her to complete her surgery so she'd know what it would be like for herself. Who could fault the twelve-year-old for wanting an adult to go through it first? Dr. Webb had suggested Macy start spending time here during her treatment. All the surgeries and the long recovery periods had taken a toll on Macy and she'd felt so isolated, like many of the kids here.

"That's good news. I bet you are going to be even more beautiful than I am when he's done, because you already are," Macy said, rubbing her hand over Sara's head.

Sara smiled at her and gave her a hug. She was in the hospital this time for another surgery on her arms, which had damage as well.

"I brought you a few fashion magazines."

"Yes! I have a new friend here—Jen. She came in yesterday. She's very sad, Macy."

"I'm sorry to hear that. What do you think will cheer her up?" Macy asked.

"Maybe a makeover like we did," Sara said.

Macy nodded. Almost a year ago, when she was feeling at her lowest, she'd had a moment of inspiration. Or maybe it had just been pure stubbornness. Instead of feeling so ugly, she'd decided to hell with it and sponsored an afternoon of fun for the girls in the ward. She'd brought in a local spa company and then gave all the girls pedicures. Just pretty bright nails that they could glance down at and see whenever they felt as if the surgeries were never going to stop and the burns were never going to go away.

"It will take me a few days to arrange it. When does she go home?"

"Not for three weeks. I'm here that long too," Sara said.

"Okay, I will do it."

"Thanks, Macy. I'm ready to look at those magazines now," Sara said.

Macy handed the stack she'd brought to the little girl and then sat next to her on the couch, flipping through the pages. They talked about clothes, and that gave her the idea to maybe have a little fashion show on the ward too. She could bring in some real clothes for the girls to try on. Anything would be better than the hospital gowns the kids were forced to wear.

Then she remembered that Chris's mom was a seamstress and decided to ask her to help design some new gowns for the children. The gowns would have to be lightweight and flowing to accommodate bandages and such. Macy began to feel excited about her idea.

She hoped his mother would feel up to working on the project.

She left the burn ward almost an hour later and stepped out into the August heat. The temperature was in the triple digits and even the linen sundress she wore felt too heavy.

"Macy." Chris called her name just as she got to her car. It was such a hot day that she remote-started it and hit a button to make sure the air conditioner was running before she got in. Summer was one of her favorite seasons, but this August was too hot and she barely tolerated it.

"What are you doing here?" she asked as she turned to face him. He wore a pair of dress pants and a shirt and tie. His thick blond hair hung loosely around the back of his neck and his aviator-style sunglasses blocked his eyes from view.

"Picking my mom up. She's being discharged today," he said. She could tell from the way he said it that he was happy to see his mother recovering, and who could blame him. Macy knew from experience that being in the hospital wasn't fun. And having to visit someone who was ill was even harder.

"That's great news," Macy said. She glanced at her watch and realized she could probably squeeze another hour of time out of her day to go with Chris and help with his mom. "Do you want some company?" She hit the button to turn off her car.

Chris tipped his head. "Your dad and I had a contentious discussion this morning—does that matter to you?"

"Was it about me?" she asked. She really hoped not. Her dad should be able to keep his distance from her personal life. And if he couldn't then she'd have to have a little talk with him. Despite the fact that she'd needed him the past few years, she didn't want him interfering in her budding relationship with Chris.

"No. We were talking about business. He wanted to make sure I didn't forget I'd said I would try to look into the bids he submitted to us," Chris said.

"Then I don't care. I run my little spreadsheets and give Dad the numbers he needs… Oh, no, I hope none of my figures cost him a bid."

"I'm sure you didn't. And I think it's a good idea for you to keep your distance. Your dad is a bull when it comes to that construction company," Chris said. "I'd stay out of it myself if I could. I should have realized coming back to Royal wasn't going to be easy."

"Yes, you should have. Plus, working on the club is highly controversial—everyone has their own ideas about what it is and how it should be," Macy said. "Ask Abby. She is trying so hard to make some changes at the Texas Cattleman's Club, but it isn't as easy as she thought it would be."

"At least I'm just here to bid on a job. I don't know if I could put up with some of the older guard if I was Abby," Chris said.

"She has a way of handling things," Macy said. If there was one thing her redheaded friend had it was determination, and she'd keep on something like the club letting in women until the men simply gave in.

"Dogged stubbornness?" Chris asked.

Macy laughed. That did seem to sum up Abby. "She's not going to back down."

"Reminds me of another woman I know."

"Who do you mean?"

"You," he said. He linked their hands together and drew her back toward the hospital. "You have never given up on yourself when others would have."

"You mean because of the surgeries?" she asked.

"Yes, and the fact that you aren't bitter about anything that's happened to you. You have no idea how remarkable that is," he said.

She was touched that he thought so. There had been times when she'd wanted to lock herself in her room and never leave it again. But she'd always had a reason to leave. Especially once Dr. Webb asked her to visit the kids in the Burn Unit. They gave her so much courage. But she didn't mention that. Didn't want to share something so private with Chris. Not yet. They were still trying to figure out who they were now.

Macy followed Chris into his mother's room. She sat on the edge of her bed wearing a pair of jeans and a sleeveless top. "It's about time you got here."

"Sorry, Mom. I ran into some trouble at the office and then Macy. She's going to keep you company while I go see about your discharge papers." Chris gave his mother a kiss on the cheek and then left the room.

"You look well," Margaret said a little coolly.

"Thank you. I feel good," Macy said. "How about you?"

"Much better. My doctor just worries about my heart, but it's fine."

"Are you sure?" Macy asked, knowing that Chris would be devastated if anything happened to his mom.

"Yes, I am," Margaret said.

It was clear that Margaret hadn't really forgiven Macy for dumping Chris the way she had. And Macy was just now realizing the full extent of her actions back then. The old Macy would have given up, but now she was determined to try to rebuild the trust that Margaret used to have in her.

"I could use your help. I seem to remember you liked to sew."

"I still do," she said defensively. "I don't see what that has to do with you."

She wasn't making this easy on Macy. "Well, I have some friends in the children's Burn Unit and I need someone who can sew who can help me out. Are you interested?"

"Maybe. Tell me more about what you have in mind," she said.

"I want to have a makeover day for the kids in the Burn Unit and I thought we could replicate for them some of the fashions they see in magazines. I can't buy the clothes off the shelves because some of the kids have serious skin-sensitivity issues. If you're interested, I'm going to talk to Dr. Webb and the other specialists and see what they need," Macy said.

"I'd love to help out," Margaret said. "I need a project at home."

"Good," Macy said.

Chris came back a few minutes later with an orderly and a wheelchair and they left the hospital. He kept watching her and she felt a little giddy from the attention. When he asked her if she was available for dinner she said yes.

Four

"Do you think you can do it?" Brad Price asked.

Chris was sitting in the clubhouse throwing back a pint with Brad as they discussed the pros and cons and costs of building a new Texas Cattleman's Club headquarters.

The years had been good to Brad, who'd always been athletic. He was well-groomed and very preppy in his look. Even a stranger would be able to tell he'd been born with a silver spoon in his mouth. His family had long been members of the Texas Cattleman's Club.

"Of course I can," Chris said. "My office is working on the project as we speak and I will have the report to you as soon as it's completed. I think that the new headquarters will be a good direction for the club."

"I do too," Brad said. "I want our generation to make a mark on the club. When I go into the dining room I feel like I'm sixteen and sneaking in without my dad's permission. It should feel like it belongs to us."

"Should I be concerned about the upcoming election?" Chris asked. He didn't want to spend a ton of man-hours working on the project only to have it all be for nothing if Brad didn't win the presidency.

"Why would you?" Brad asked.

"Just in case you aren't elected…"

"That's blasphemy." Brad shook his head. "This is Royal, Texas, not some big city like Dallas. Our members aren't about to vote for a woman president. She's only a member because of how much we all loved Richard."

Chris rubbed the back of his neck. "Damn shock."

"No kidding. We all depended on him here. It's different for you, Chris, because you're new blood as far as the club is concerned but for all of us old-timers who grew up with a Langley in the club—we didn't know what to do. The old guard was feeling sentimental…"

"So they extended an invite to Abby with full privileges never suspecting she was going to stir things up and try to become president."

"Exactly," Brad said, taking a long draw on his beer. "Women!"

Chris lifted his glass in a mock toast and then took a swallow of his beer. Actually, Chris had to admit that he had no problem with any of the changes that the women wanted made at the Texas Cattleman's Club. He thought that it was about time that women had rights at the club. As Brad had said earlier, it wasn't their dads' generation anymore—it was theirs.

"So is everything good with you?" Chris asked, thinking of the fight he'd seen between Zeke and Brad last night. He knew that to Brad, the question might appear to have come out of the blue, but Chris wasn't much on subtlety.

Brad gave him a hard stare and looked distinctly uncomfortable. "Yes. Why do you ask?"

"I saw you and Zeke arguing last night when I was in here having dinner. You're normally not quick-tempered…" Chris let the sentence fall off. He didn't want to push, but he and Brad had been friends in college and, if the other man had troubles, Chris would help him out.

"It was nothing. Just a minor disagreement over something not related to the club," Brad said, looking more than a little distracted. "I noticed you were dining with a woman."

"It was Macy Reynolds."

"I hadn't realized she had fully recovered. That was a really bad accident. Her dad was broken up when it first happened. Spent a lot of nights at the club drinking," Brad said. "She looks good now."

"Well, the bandages from her last surgery came off yesterday. We were having dinner to celebrate," Chris said, not sure he liked the fact that Brad had noticed her looks. "She does look good."

"That's great news. I haven't kept in touch with her, but I guess you did," Brad said.

No one really knew that Macy's dad had forced Chris out of her life. That wasn't the kind of thing that he'd wanted to talk about at UT Austin, so he'd just said they'd drifted apart back then. Who wanted to tell people that he wasn't good enough for the girl he loved? Maybe a different man than he was, but Chris had kept his mouth shut back then.

"No, we didn't. I ran into her at the hospital," Chris said.

Brad nodded at him. "Visiting your mom, right? Is she better?"

"The doctors still don't know what's wrong with her heart. One of them pulled me aside and suggested that since these episodes happen regular as clockwork, perhaps I ought to consider visiting more often."

"Maybe you should."

Chris shrugged. Brad was Royal's golden boy. He himself had been a poor kid. Someone whose parents were around town but weren't part of the in-crowd. He hadn't minded it when he'd been younger. Because when you were in elementary school it didn't matter if you were rich or poor. Everyone played together and got along. Then somewhere around seventh grade everything started changing and groups started forming that had a hard money dividing line.

"I just always wanted more than Royal had to offer," Chris said. And he still did. Though Macy interested him a lot and he could only find her here.

"Do you still want more?" Brad asked. "This little town is changing."

"You just said we aren't like Dallas," Chris pointed out. He liked Dallas. It was more metropolitan than the rest of the state, certainly more so than Royal. There were a lot of people from other parts of the country living in Dallas these days and they'd brought their attitudes with them.

"Well, it would be different for you. Having a woman president of the Texas Cattle*man's* Club isn't going to happen."

"So you say," Chris said. But he knew that all attitudes hadn't changed. The older generation—like Harrison Reynolds—would be only too happy to show Chris the door.

The club looked exactly as it was meant to, a luxury club for the wealthy and privileged in Texas. The heavy furniture was large and comfy for a man, but dwarfed the women when they came to sit in the cozy room. The paneling was dark and on one wall were televisions tuned to industry- and financial-news stations. In another corner, ESPN played. The club wasn't welcoming to women and he didn't see how Abby was going to change that.

As Brad had said, this was Royal. An old Texas oil-rich town with lots of old Texas values. He doubted that anyone who hadn't lived here would get what he meant by that, because Texas was different. Men still held doors open for women and took care of their wives and put God and football first.

Chris shook his head thinking about it.

"Thanks for meeting me today, Chris."

"Not a problem. I'll have some preliminary estimates to you this evening for what it would take to renovate and enhance the existing clubhouse. The new buildings will take me a few days."

"Not a problem."

Brad and he finished their beers and Chris left as one of the other club members drifted over to talk to Brad. It didn't matter that he'd been afforded full privileges as an honorary member, he still felt like an outsider.

He saw Abby standing in the doorway looking in as well. He wondered if she felt the same way. He smiled at her when she looked up and waved as he turned and walked out of the clubhouse.

He toyed with the idea that the situation with Macy

was just like the clubhouse and Abby. She wanted to think the world around her had changed and, since he had money now, her dad wouldn't try to interfere in a relationship between them, but he suspected that old attitudes hadn't changed that much.

His cell phone rang when he got to his car and he glanced at the caller ID before answering it. It was a Royal area code, but he didn't recognize the number.

"This is Richardson."

"Chris? It's Macy."

"Hello, there, what can I do for you?" he asked.

"Um…do you want to meet me for an early-morning horseback ride tomorrow?" she asked.

"At your ranch?"

"No at Tom's Stables. Do you know where it is?"

"I do. Okay, what time?"

"Six," she said.

"That's early but I'll be there," he said.

"Bye."

She hung up before he could say goodbye and he pocketed his phone. He hadn't been on a horse in years but he wasn't about to say no to Macy. It was the one thing he'd wanted her to do back when they were in high school. Take the initiative in their relationship.

Macy woke up at 5:00 a.m. and dressed in her jodhpurs, fitted shirt and riding jacket. She'd pick up her helmet at the stables. Riding had been the one thing that she'd been able to continue doing even when she'd been scarred. She drove through the early-morning streets of Royal. It was warm but not hot on this August morning.

She pulled into the parking lot and saw Chris leaning against the hood of his Porsche. It was a flashy car, and she suspected that was why he'd driven it today. He wore the trappings of his success well, and she regretted she'd let her dad talk her out of dating him so many years before. If they'd stayed together, she probably would have been on a different path, hopefully with him.

"Morning," she said, getting out of her car. She used to drive a cute Audi convertible, but now had a big Cadillac that her father bought for her. It was a heavy car and was one of the top-rated in safety upon impact.

"Morning. I haven't been on a horse in years," Chris said as he walked over to her. "You look like you're ready for a dressage competition."

"I'm not," she said. She'd never been a competitive person by nature, and really it was the routine of riding she liked better than the winning of awards and accolades. "Let me get my crop and helmet out of the trunk."

"Take your time. The stable manager is getting our horses ready. My mom packed us a breakfast picnic." Chris looked so sexy this morning. It didn't help matters that last night all she'd dreamed about was that kiss they'd shared in front of the flamingos. She wanted so much more than just sweet passion-filled kisses from him. But she wasn't sure he was on the same page.

To him she was probably just an old friend that he was spending time with until he left Royal. Maybe not a platonic friend, she thought, remembering the intensity of the kiss they'd shared after dinner. But not a woman he was bent on dating either. She reckoned that had a lot to do with their past and the way she'd treated him.

"That was sweet of her," Macy said as she grabbed her equipment and walked over to Chris.

"She's probably hoping you and I will fall in love and give her some grandbabies."

Macy dropped her crop. *Um...that's a lot more than dating,* she thought. And she'd never imagined he'd even consider that. Now she was hearing… "What? We're barely dating."

Chris laughed. "I told her the same thing. She said a woman can hope, especially a woman who'd just come out of the hospital. I told her she was pushing it. But she just winked and laughed at me."

Macy laughed, as she was sure that Chris intended her to, but inside she was quaking with fear. She had just gotten through a very trying time in her life and she wanted some fun with Chris. She didn't want to think any further than the end of this week.

A big part of her wanted to retreat to her father's house and her bedroom. She wanted to lock herself away and keep herself safe from anything like this. To anyone else, a sexy man saying things about love and babies might be ideal, but not to her. She still wasn't whole and sometimes she felt as if she never would be.

"I'm not—"

"It's okay. I was just being silly. I'm not going to try to talk you into marrying me."

Macy looked at Chris. His tight-fitting jeans and plain black T-shirt so nondescript and yet so defining of the man he was. He might drive a Porsche and run, according to her dad, a billion-dollar development company. But she knew that at heart he was still this man.

If this was six months from now and she'd had time to recover from the past three years of not knowing how she was going to look or when she was going to regain her life, she'd probably do everything in her power to get him to propose. But right now...she just wasn't ready.

"It's not you," she said. "I'm barely able to believe that I have my life back."

"And you're not ready for a commitment. I know. We're just dating and renewing an old friendship," he said.

She tried to read his body language and see if he wanted more than friendship, but it was impossible to tell.

A horse whinnied and they both turned to see Tom, the owner of the stables, walking toward them leading a chestnut horse. "Mr. Richardson, your horse is ready."

"Thank you, Tom."

"Anne will be along with your horse in a minute, Macy," he said to her. "You're looking mighty fine without those bandages on."

"Thank you, Mr. Tom," she said.

"You're welcome, ma'am. Anne's prayer group has been keeping you on the top of their list. I think they will be happy to know that you have recovered."

Macy was touched by his wife's concern. "That means more than I can say."

Tom nodded and then walked away. She hugged herself with one arm, acknowledging that even though she'd felt really alone over the past three years, she hadn't been.

Chris walked over to his horse and took the saddle as if he'd been born in it. She watched as he walked the horse around the yard a few times and then came back to her side just as Anne brought Macy's horse, Buttercup, out.

Macy led the horse to the mounting block, donned her helmet and took her own saddle. She probably didn't need a helmet for this short ride, but her doctors had been adamant when she'd first started riding again that she always don protective gear, and she found she liked doing it now. It was part of her routine and she wasn't going to give it up.

"I'll follow you," Chris said.

Macy glanced over her shoulder at him as she led the way out. Chris followed her down a path through a wooded area behind the stables, and when the path was wide enough he moved his horse up beside her.

"How often do you come out here?" he asked, his deep voice making her want to ask him to just keep on talking.

"Three times a week. It was the only thing I could do for a while. Tom and Anne never stared at my scars or me. And when I was still using a walker, they helped me get onto the horse."

"Wasn't that dangerous?" he asked, concern in his voice.

"What?" she asked. The rides she'd taken while recovering had been the impetus she needed some days not to sink into sadness.

"Riding on your own while you needed a walker?" he asked.

She shook her head. Thinking about how weak she'd been in the beginning. Her damn right thigh with the missing muscle had ached, but once she'd set her mind on riding, she had been determined to see it through. "Tom would follow me about fifty yards or so back."

"Why didn't he just ride with you?" Chris asked.

"I needed to do it on my own," she said, pulling

Buttercup's reins so the horse stopped. Chris stopped riding as well. She remembered those first rides when she'd just cried the entire time. The emotions of being outside and doing something familiar had been more than she could handle at first.

Chris reached over and put his hand on hers. "I'm sorry you had to go through that alone."

"I had to. It was either prove to myself that I could do it or disappear from society completely and just live in Daddy's house the rest of my life."

"But you're not dependent anymore. You're fully healed, so when are you moving out?" Chris asked.

"That's right, I am. I'm going to move back to my own home in a couple of weeks. I don't want you to think I'm weak. The doctors wouldn't let me live on my own when they first released me from the hospital…and Daddy, well, he didn't want to let me out of his sight. I almost died."

Chris leaned over and pulled her toward him. Kissing her hard and passionately. Then he sat back in his own saddle and kicked his horse into a trot. She watched him ride away and then urged Buttercup to follow.

She had the feeling that Chris didn't like hearing about what almost happened to her. None of her friends had, but Chris was the first one who had made her feel as if he would have really missed her if she'd died in the hospital after her accident. As though their journey with each other would have been cut short.

And despite what she'd said earlier, she realized that a part of her did want to have a solid relationship with Chris. She almost felt safe dreaming about a future with him and maybe children of her own. And that was thanks to Chris.

* * *

Chris didn't like thinking about what might have been. He'd left Royal and had shaken the past from his boots like dust as he'd walked away. But if Macy had died three years ago… He didn't like the feeling that thought evoked in him. He was used to being in control and he'd just been presented with the very real proof that he wasn't really in control of anything.

"Chris," Macy called.

He slowed his horse, but seeing her sitting on her own just made him long to pull her into his arms again.

He really needed to get his head together and he didn't want to talk to Macy right now. He felt raw. And the last time he'd felt that way had been when his father had died.

"You okay?" she asked.

He shook his head. "I hate that you might have died and I would never have had the chance to know you again."

She swallowed then edged her horse closer to his. The morning sun shone down on her and she looked so healthy to him that it was hard to believe she'd struggled to get back to this state for the past few years.

"Me too. I feel like you and me have unfinished business," she said.

"We definitely do," he agreed. He wanted to hold her again and do everything he could to keep her safe, which was silly, because there was no threat to her here. "Let's go back to the stables and return the horses. Will you join me for breakfast?"

"After your mom went to all that trouble to make it, I think I'd better."

They returned the horses to the stables and then walked over to their cars. "Should I follow you?"

"Nah, we can take the Porsche. I have a nice spot picked out not too far from here."

"I thought you had a Range Rover," she said.

"I had this one brought out from Dallas. I like the speed of it."

"I'm not much on going fast," she said.

"I won't let anything happen to you," he said. "Do you believe me?"

"Yes. Yes, I do. Okay, I will ride with you. I can't stay long, though. I have to go in to the office this morning."

"Since you know the boss, I don't think he'll fire you if you're not on time," Chris said. Her father was the central man in her life right now and Chris wanted to be that guy instead. He wanted her to depend on him for everything. Dammit, he wanted more from Macy than dating and renewing old ties. He wanted *her.*

That was a given. But he hadn't realized how important it was for her to see him on the same level as her dad. He couldn't believe he was still showing off and trying to impress her. But he knew that was what bringing the Porsche here was all about. There wasn't one other person in Royal who he wanted to see him in this car other than Macy.

"You're right, but I don't like to take advantage… Actually, Dad gives me lots of leeway at the job because I'm still not one hundred percent… Wait a minute, I am. I keep forgetting I've been through my last surgery. Do you know what that means?" she asked, a slow smile spreading across her pretty face.

"No, what?" he asked, playing along with her.

"That I never have to go to the doctor's again and

hear about my options," she said with a smile. "That is such a relief."

"I'm so glad to hear that."

"Me too. I can't believe I didn't think about that until now," she said.

Chris reached over and drew her into his arms. He held her close to him, feeling the soft exhalation of her breath on his neck, and thanked God that she was alive and wholly recovered. He hadn't been there for her during her darkest days, but he was going to make this period of her life the best he could.

She hugged him tight and he held on to her as if his life depended on it. He tried to convey in that embrace all the things he didn't know how to put into words. Like how scary it was to think of her hurt or weighing options.

"So, where are we having breakfast?" she asked.

Reluctantly he let her go and walked over to the Porsche. He opened the passenger door. She eyed the car and then slowly walked over to it. He noticed she was limping a little.

"Is your leg okay?" he asked.

"Just some minor muscle damage, riding makes it act up a little," she said. "You were telling me where we are going for breakfast."

"It's a surprise," he said.

"Um…in Royal?" she asked. "Is that even possible?"

"I don't mean you've never been there," he said. "Just that you don't know where we are going."

"I'll give you that," she said.

He closed the door and went around to get behind the wheel. She'd taken off her helmet and held it on her lap. She tossed her head and fluffed up her hair.

"Um...how do I look?" she asked.

"Gorgeous," he said.

He started the ignition and drove away from the stables. "We're going to a spot I'm thinking of buying."

"Really? Why?"

"My mom needs me to be here more often than twice a year. Her doctors suggested that her heart episodes might be a bid to get to see me more often." He didn't like the fact that she kept having them or that the doctors still hadn't been able to figure out why.

"I'm sorry to hear that. Are you a bad son?" she asked. "You two are all each other has."

"I try very hard not to be," he said. "But I'm busy working all the time and most of what I do when I'm not traveling around the state visiting sites is sit in my office in Dallas and go to meetings. I could easily do that from here if I found a reason to stay," he said.

"Your mom's not reason enough?" Macy asked, tipping her head to the side in a flirtatious manner.

"She's enough for me to come back here more often, but to really stay, I'm going to need something else." Chris would come back here all the time if he and Macy were dating. He wanted to see more of her. When he looked at her now, he wanted her so badly he could hardly think.

"Like a woman to spend your time with?" Macy asked.

"Depends on the woman," he said, signaling then following a dirt road down off the main highway. He stopped the Porsche and laughed.

"What's so funny?" she asked.

"I wanted to impress you with my car, but the Range Rover is better suited for this kind of driving. I should have thought ahead and brought that vehicle instead," he said. But lots of people in Royal had Range Rovers and not that many had Porsches, so he'd chosen his flashy car instead.

"Why did you want to impress me?" she asked. "I'm not judging you."

He shrugged. Chris had always been very competitive, so even if he were only competing against himself he was playing to win. And of course, if he happened to impress Macy so much the better; he wanted her to see only good things when she thought of him.

"Being with you sometimes makes me feel like I did back in high school," he said.

"How did you feel?" she asked.

"Like I didn't have enough money for you...like I wasn't good enough. And I guess a part of me wants you to know that I have plenty now."

She reached across the gearshift and put her hand on his thigh. "Chris, you were always good enough for me. Just you. I don't need fancy cars or big houses."

"Hell," he said. He wasn't able to think with her hand on his leg so close to this groin. He leaned across the seat and kissed her. Put his hands on her shoulders and drew her closer to him. Her mouth opened under his and her fingers dug into his thigh. He sat her back down and then undid his seat belt and opened his door.

"Where are you going?" she asked.

"To get some fresh air. You go to my head, Macy. Make me wish for things that I hadn't even thought mattered. I have always just focused on making money and proving to the people of Royal that I wasn't just an oil worker's son."

"You've done that a million times over," Macy said.

"But it doesn't mean anything if I still don't feel good enough for you."

He got out of the car and closed the door. Looking at the land he'd thought of buying. As a boy he'd never thought of having anything in Royal, and now because of Macy he was seriously considering something he'd never entertained before.

Five

Macy followed Chris away from the dirt road and up a small hill to a copse of trees. He had a blanket under one arm and the picnic basket in the other. She took the blanket from him and spread it on the ground.

"I like this place," she said. "It reminds me a lot of Daddy's ranch."

"Mmm, hmm."

Okay, she guessed he still wasn't ready to talk. What had she done to make him think he had to prove himself to her?

She was afraid to say anything to him. She really didn't know what to think about his comments. And she wanted to say the right thing. She was flattered... because he was trying so hard to prove himself. To show her that he had as much money as her family did.

She sort of understood what he meant. That was what riding had given her. It had been her way of proving to herself that she wasn't as badly injured as she had been.

"Do you think we ever stop trying to prove ourselves?" she asked. "I know that I fight daily with my dad because he still treats me like I'm twelve. I get that I was in a serious accident, but I've recovered now. It's about time for him to treat me like an adult."

He shook his head. "I don't know. There always seems to be another goal lurking on the horizon. Something else that I should be reaching for. No matter what I accomplish, it never fills that empty place inside me."

She reached over and took his hand. He seemed so confident and he was so successful, she thought he didn't have the same concerns that she did. But she liked the fact that they were the same in this.

"Me too. At first it was just live, then it was recover, then regain my looks, now…regain my confidence. When is it going to be enough, you know?"

"I do know," he said. He gestured for her to sit down and then placed the picnic basket near her. He sat down and leaned back against the tree. When she sat down, he drew her between his legs so that her back was resting against his chest.

He wrapped his arms around her and put his head on her shoulder and she leaned into the comfort of his embrace.

"I'm thinking of putting the main house right there."

"So you are definitely getting this property?" she asked, scooting around to face him. She didn't want to get too used to Chris. He wasn't staying here in Royal even if he bought this property. His life was always going to be in Dallas.

"Yes. I'm going to build a little house over there for

my mom," he said, pointing to the left. "I know she likes her independence, but I'd like her closer to me when I'm in town."

He was so sweet with his mom. With families so spread out now, not everyone kept close contact with their parents, and it meant something to her that Chris had.

"Why don't you buy a house in Pine Valley?" she asked, opening the picnic basket and taking out the containers. It seemed as if the upscale neighborhood would be more convenient.

"I want to build my dream home," he said, taking the thermos from her and pouring them both some coffee. The food that Maggie had prepared smelled delicious as she took it out.

"What do you want in a dream home?" she asked. What did he do in his downtime?

"Lots of things. Maybe over dinner tonight, I'll show you the plans I had drawn up."

He was so arrogant sometimes. And she wondered if she was making things just a little too easy for him, but the truth was, she wanted to see him for dinner. She liked this man she was coming to know.

"Are we having dinner?" she asked.

"I'd like to. Not out at the club, but maybe just someplace small, where I don't feel like we're in a fish-bowl."

She smiled over at him. "I'd like that. My dad is going to Midland tonight for his weekly poker game. How about I cook you dinner?"

Chris crossed his arms over his chest. "That feels a bit like the sneaking around we used to do."

"I know, but I don't mean it that way," she said. "My house isn't ready for company yet."

"Why don't I meet you there," he suggested. "We can have dinner and work on *making* it ready for you."

She liked that so she nodded. "I have movers coming to get my stuff next Saturday."

"Are you hiring someone to do the work around the house?" he asked. "Did you rent it out while you lived with your dad?"

Macy shook her head. "I refused. At first it was because I didn't want to face the reality that I wasn't going to be able to go home. Then I didn't want to admit that dad had been right when he said it was going to take me time to recover."

Chris nodded at her. "I can see that. You are very stubborn."

She wriggled her eyebrows at him. Best that he know the truth about her. She never let go of something once she sunk her teeth into it. The accident had slowed her down, but she knew she was gradually coming back into her own.

"Yes, I am. It's part of my charm."

"Only part of it?" he asked with a teasing grin. She loved his smile, which was the slightest bit crooked.

"The best part of it," she said, dishing out the food. They both ate quickly, talking about books they'd read and how funny it was that they'd switched from regular books to e-readers.

"They are just so much easier to manage. Do you know I can read a book exactly where I left off at on my cell phone if I want to? My e-reader was a lifesaver during some of the long nights I spent in the hospital. If

I woke up at 2:00 a.m. and needed something to distract me, I could find a new book and download it."

"Did that happen a lot?" he asked as he cleaned up the remains of their meal.

"Yes. Some of my surgeries were painful. I did discover how much I loved some of those old classics Mrs. Kieffer assigned to us junior year."

"No way," he said, grabbing his chest as if she'd given him a heart attack. "Just playing. She picked some good books for us to read back then. Didn't you mean rediscover?"

She blushed. "I didn't read them the first time. I used to have a friend who'd read them and give me a report on what they were about."

He shook his head at her and she felt as though she'd been caught out, which she had. But back then she'd been a princess and everyone had wanted to help her. So she'd taken the easy way more than once.

"What? Not everyone likes to read. And I was busy cheerleading and sneaking out of the house to meet you."

"I'm glad you could sneak out to meet me. So what book did you discover you liked?"

"*Pride and Prejudice,* which led me to the entire Jane Austen collection. I even watched all the movies."

He shook his head. "Those are okay. I preferred *The Three Musketeers* or *The Count of Monte Cristo.*"

"Nah, I didn't even try those, but I can see where they'd appeal to you. Have you read *Pride and Prejudice?*"

"No, but my secretary has the one with zombies on her desk," Chris said.

"That's not the same, though I did read it. I'm going to lend it to you," she said.

"If you insist, but then you have to read *The Count of Monte Cristo*."

"Deal. We can chat about them next week." She was a quick reader given that all she had been doing was lying in her bed. She might not be able to finish the book as quickly now that she was working for her dad in his office.

"A week? I don't read that fast," Chris said. "I barely have time to catch a game on TV, much less read an entire book in one week."

"I used to. I might not have any time now either. Okay, then we can chat when you say you're done," she said. Today had made her feel normal. Riding was part of her old routine, and Chris, whether she wanted to admit it or not, was part of her new routine. He was a bridge between the pain-filled existence she'd had before and the present.

"Thank you for breakfast. Please tell your mom I enjoyed it," Macy said. She liked that about her small hometown. The fact that many generations still lived there and that for the most part everyone knew of everyone else.

"I'll do that. So, if we are having dinner at your place tonight, I'll need the address," he said.

She nodded and then gave it to him. Reluctantly, she said goodbye to him when he took her back to her car. He didn't try to kiss her again and she hoped he hadn't decided she wanted them to just be friends. Because she wanted so much more from Chris Richardson, more than she'd ever realized before.

* * *

Chris spent a long time at the office and then on the phone with a vendor back in Dallas for a new retail center he was developing in Plano. He rubbed the back of his neck and stood up and stretched. He'd tried not to think too much about Macy today, but his thoughts always strayed back to her.

After that kiss in the car this morning, he'd tried to lighten things up, but he couldn't loosen the knot in his gut. It was more than a knot. It was that same feeling he'd had all those years ago. He was falling for her with her quick smile and teasing ways.

"Chris, Harrison Reynolds is back. He is demanding to see you," Tanja, his administrative assistant, said from the doorway.

Tanja had close-cut hair and pretty features. She was thin and efficient and had moved here when her doctor husband had taken a job at Royal Memorial Hospital. She used to work for Chris in Dallas. He had no true need for an office here, but had opened one so he could keep her on staff.

They did all the West Texas business out of this office and he always had a place to work when he visited his mother.

"Of course he is. Will you send him to the conference room and get him a beverage?" he asked. "I'll be down there in a minute."

"Yes, sir," Tanja said. "I sent the bid for the new headquarters over to Brad Price this morning for you."

"Thank you. I need a meeting with the TCC board on the schedule too. Will you call Brad's secretary and find out when it will work for them?"

"Of course."

Chris waited until Tanja left and then stood up and paced around his desk. Why was Harrison here again? Chris was doing everything he could to look into their bidding processes. He didn't really want to talk to Macy's father. He straightened his tie and put a gracious smile on his face. No matter what transpired between him and Harrison, Macy was still going to see him for dinner tonight.

They weren't teenagers anymore and Harrison had little control over either of their actions. Maybe it was time he let Harrison know that fact in no uncertain terms. But that wasn't his way, Chris thought. He wasn't interested in talking to Harrison about Macy. That was none of the older man's business.

He pushed open the conference room door and entered quietly. Harrison was on the phone, but stood up when he heard the door.

"I'll call you back," Harrison said. "Hello, Chris. Thanks for agreeing to see me."

Chris arched an eyebrow at the older man. Who reminded him a lot of J.R. from the old television show *Dallas*. He was bullheaded and had that Texas attitude. He was going to keep on Chris until Chris gave him the answer he wanted to hear.

"I was under the impression that I didn't have an option," Chris said. "I don't have a lot of time for this meeting, Harrison."

"Sorry about that. I didn't have time to make an appointment and wait to hear back from you. Word at the Texas Cattleman's Club is you are the frontrunner for the new development and I wanted to make sure that Reynolds Construction is the prime choice to do the work." Harrison leaned back in his chair and put his booted feet on the conference table.

"Given that you are a club member, I'm sure you will be chosen by the board for the work," Chris said. The old boys' network was still alive and well in this part of the world. Something Chris had run up against a lot when he'd first started out. It was still amazing to him that now some of those good old boys wanted to do business with him.

"Good. When are you submitting the bid for the work?"

"I've already sent it over to Brad for review. The scope is pretty broad and I want to make sure I've got all the details."

"Good," Harrison said.

"I'm not sure why you're here," Chris said.

"I'm here because…well, you've turned out to be one of the best developers in the state and I don't want to let our past relationship spoil any future endeavors."

"Okay."

"That's why I'm offering to help you out at the club. I may have misjudged you, boy. Now, what's the deal with bids I've submitted to do work for your company?"

Chris shook his head. "I don't know. We are running an internal investigation and going through all the bids that you submitted to us. It's not a quick process."

"Okay, keep me posted," Harrison said.

As if he had a choice. Harrison would probably show up at his office every couple of days until he had an answer on it. The man had a huge ego. And now Harrison had decided they should forget about the fact that he'd forced Macy to break up with Chris in high school. The older man took Chris's forgiveness for granted. "I will, is that all?"

"There is one more thing," Harrison said, standing up and putting both hands on the conference room table. "But it has nothing to do with business."

"Go ahead." Chris had been expecting a warning from Harrison since he'd heard he was here.

"I heard you and Macy went riding together this morning," Harrison said. "I don't want you toying with her. It's one thing to play with me when it comes to business, but Macy is a woman and she doesn't deserve to be treated poorly as some sort of revenge from you."

Chris stood up. He was tempted to not say anything else. To let Harrison stew in his fears for Macy. But he couldn't do it. He wasn't being dishonest with Macy or Harrison about why he was here and what he was doing. "I'm not after revenge. Macy is a special lady to me and I'm not going to use her, and it's an insult to imply I might."

Harrison shook his head. "It's no insult. You and I both know you were pissed as hell at having to leave Royal without her. I just want to make sure you aren't still looking for revenge."

"If I was, it'd be on you, not Macy," Chris said, giving the older man a steely glare. "I'm not the poor boy you rode out of town, Harrison. You should keep that in mind before you make any threats to me."

Harrison held up both hands. "I didn't mean anything by that."

Harrison stared him in the eye and Chris felt the sincerity in the older man's gaze. "It wasn't personal, Richardson, I just want the best for her."

Chris could understand that. He didn't have kids

of his own, but he knew when he did, he'd probably do the same thing. That was the job of the father. "I understand. I want the best for her too. And I think she's forgotten how to let go and just enjoy her life."

"It's been a real struggle," Harrison admitted. "I had to stand back and let her do her own thing. Damn stubborn girl."

"Wonder where she gets that from," Chris said.

That surprised a laugh out of Harrison. "It's a mystery. Thank you for meeting with me. I'll wait to hear from you about the bid for the club."

Harrison shook Chris's hand and then exited the conference room. Chris just watched the older man leave. He would never have guessed he'd have anything in common with Harrison Reynolds.

It was funny how much life and maturity changed a man's perspective. He hadn't realized that love had motivated the older man.

He walked back to his office and put Harrison out of his mind, preferring to think about Macy. Tonight was going to be a special night. The date at the club was too public to be anything other than dinner, and this morning, riding was too... Well, the horses had made it impossible for them to be close. But at her home— that was where he'd have a chance to put some bonds between them that Macy would be hard pressed to undo.

Just thinking about her made him hot and hard. Ready for something that had nothing to do with revenge. And he wanted to make sure that Macy knew he was interested in her, period. There was nothing else motivating him except that pretty smile of hers and her feminine body.

The same things that had drawn him to her the

first time. This time, though, he knew that it was her strength and her intelligence that kept him coming back for more.

Macy didn't expect to feel emotional about returning to her old home, but she did. The grass was neatly trimmed and the entire landscape well cared for by the gardener she'd been paying bimonthly. From the outside it looked as if nothing had changed from the last morning when she'd left the house.

The lights were on and when she pushed the garage-door button and pulled into her garage, it was as if no time had passed. Even her flip-flops were still sitting by the door where she'd left them from a beach trip the weekend before.

The past three years melted away and she thought she'd be meeting her fiancé inside. She had a sort of double vision as she got out of her car and unlocked the door to go into the house. It smelled a little stale and not like the room fresheners she used to keep plugged in all the time.

Her home had remained unchanged, but she had changed in many ways. She flipped on the air-conditioning and slipped off her work shoes, putting on the flip-flops she'd left by the garage door. She went back to her car and started bringing in the cleaning supplies and groceries for the night's meal.

She just needed to do a light cleaning because her father had maintained a cleaning service for her while she'd been living with him. They shared the same cleaning lady, which they'd always done.

She walked through the house, which felt too quiet at first, but then when she hit the button to turn on the radio in the intercom and music from her favorite station filled the house, she started to relax. She walked through the rooms, plugging in the scent of Island Breeze and turning on ceiling fans. She left her bedroom for last and stopped in the doorway.

The bed was draped with a dustcover, as was all the furniture in the house. The dresser top had been cleared off and all the contents taken to her room at her dad's house. She turned on the light and walked inside, her eyes alighting first on the picture of her and her parents that sat on the bedside table.

As she aged, Macy saw herself becoming more like the woman in the picture. She scarcely remembered her mother. That pretty stranger holding her on her lap was more of a feeling—like being wrapped in a hug—than any real person.

The doorbell rang and she glanced at her watch. Though she'd intended to be only a few minutes walking through her two-story ranch-style home, she'd been over an hour.

She pushed the intercom button. This might not have been a good idea. She wasn't sure she wanted company while she sorted through the past that was here.

"Who is it?"

"Chris."

"I'll be right down," she said.

"Take your time."

She hurried down the stairs to the front door and opened it. Chris stood there in a business suit sans the jacket and tie. He'd rolled his sleeves up, but left his shirt tucked into his waistband, accentuating his lean waist.

"Hello," he said.

"Hey. Come on in," she said.

He crossed the threshold and handed her a bottle of wine. She led the way through the house to the kitchen. She was nervous about having him here. The little innocuous dates they'd had so far didn't really have any significance. They were the kind of dates that friends went on. But being here—totally alone with him—was different.

"I haven't started cooking yet."

"No problem. Why don't I get started on the dust-covers while you cook dinner."

"You don't mind?"

"That's why I came over. And that's a fairly simple job that doesn't require you," he said. "I'm going to grab a change of clothes from the car. Where can I get changed?"

"The hall bathroom," she said, gesturing toward the door next to the stairs. She had an open downstairs floor plan. Only the den and kitchen had a wall between them. Otherwise the dining and formal living rooms led smoothly into the family room and dine-in kitchen.

"I'll be right back."

She nodded and watched him leave. Then realized she was staring when he glanced back at her.

"Like what you see?"

She refused to be embarrassed. "Yes, I do."

The man had a nice butt and she cut herself some slack for watching him walk away. She turned quickly toward the refrigerator when he glanced over his shoulder again. She smiled to herself as a feeling of joy washed over her. It had been a long time since she'd experienced something like this.

She put a pot of water on to boil and salted it liberally.

Then set about sautéing mushrooms and some herbs, along with a couple of shallots. As she worked in the kitchen, she felt time slip away from her again.

Chris worked in the house and she heard him moving from room to room upstairs. It was comforting and homey. She hadn't realized how alone she'd been in her father's house until this moment. Her dad had his own life and had of course made time for her in it, but there had been no one to cook for or to share her evenings with.

She made a white sauce and grated some cheese and as soon as the pasta was done she mixed all the ingredients together in a casserole dish and put it in the oven to bake. She made her version of "cheaters" chocolate-mousse pie—a recipe that she'd found in her mother's cookbook. Using whipped cream and melted chocolate, she combined them and then put the combined ingredients in a cookie-crumb piecrust and piped a little cream around the outside of the crust before placing it in the refrigerator to chill.

Then she set the timer and went upstairs to find Chris. He was in her game room, standing in front of the spot where the big-screen TV used to be.

"What happened here?"

"My fiancé. He was the one who bought the TV. I guess he took it back when we broke up."

"Dirtbag," Chris said.

"I scarcely use this room," she said, making excuses for Benjamin, as she had so often when they were together. "He liked the television and I wasn't really using it."

"That's not a good reason to take it. He must not have

been much of a man to have left you while you were so sick."

"He...I guess he wasn't," she said. She walked away from Chris and he cleared his throat.

"You have a very nice house," he said.

"Thank you. I like it. I know it's too big for one person, but I always thought I'd have a family someday. And it was a good investment. My dad's company did the construction of this subdivision, so I got a good deal."

"It makes sense to me," he said. He took the last dustcover off the leather sofa and folded it quickly. He placed it on top of the pile he'd made with the other ones and then walked over to her.

"I've waited all day to do this," he said. He pulled her into his arms and slowly lowered his head. She reached up and put her hands on his shoulders.

"I've waited too," she whispered.

"Good," he said as he kissed her. The warm exhalation of his breath brushed over her and she shivered in his arms. He tasted of that feeling that evoked home. And though the smell of dust covered with Island Breeze filled the room, all she inhaled was the spicy scent of Chris's aftershave. His hands rubbed up and down her back and when he lifted his head, she snaked her arms around his waist and laid her head on his chest right above his heart.

Chris was a good man, the kind she'd always wanted for her own and, standing in this big house in the shadows of her old dreams of the future, she wished somehow their paths had been different and that this could have been their house.

Six

Chris watched Macy move around the kitchen as she prepared their dishes for dinner. He'd washed up and now sat at the counter where she'd set up two place mats. He'd opened the wine, a nice California Merlot that he ordered by the case.

"How was your day?" she asked.

"Had a visit from your dad," he said. He wasn't sure how much he wanted to say about Harrison to Macy, but he thought she should know who was still trying to run her life.

She arched both eyebrows. "Really? Was he still asking about the bids we didn't win?"

"Yes. And the bid I'm working on for the Texas Cattleman's Club," Chris said. "He's a very strong-minded man. I think he just expected me to open up my files and show him everything."

"No kidding," Macy said as she placed a plate of

steaming noodles and cheese in front of him. "Sorry it's only a casserole."

The smells were mouthwatering and, as they ate dinner and talked about the construction business in Royal, he was amazed at the normalcy of the evening. There was something so perfect about being here with Macy. She was smart, funny and had keen insights into the people in their hometown. Something she hadn't had years ago.

"You've changed," he said, realizing that she was a different woman than he'd expected her to be. Part of the transformation had to have come from the accident, but the other part he thought came from her experiences.

"Duh," she said, winking at him.

"No, I mean you seem to really understand what makes people tick. You used to only understand what motivated you."

Macy shrugged and took a sip of her wine. "I spent a lot of time home alone. Aside from reading books, I also surfed the Net and read about our town. And... promise not to tell anyone?"

"What am I promising for?" he asked.

She leaned forward. "My dirty little secret...the thing that has made me so intuitive."

"I promise," he said.

"I watch *Maury*. Once you do that, the human psyche is easy to understand."

That made him laugh. He had never watched the daytime talk show, so he couldn't really say whether or not that was a valid benchmark for human behavior. And it couldn't have surprised him more. That television show wasn't at all what he'd expected her to watch.

"What exactly did you learn from Maury?" he asked, wanting to hear her insights.

She gave him an impish smile. "One thing I love is seeing into other people's lives, especially if they are more messed up than mine. But really I learned why cheaters cheat and why family dynamics get messed up."

"Why is that?" he asked.

"They are searching for someone to love them and listen to them. The problem is that they keep going back to the same type of people. It's an endless cycle."

She was sincere and he had to agree with her. He'd certainly been drawn to the same type of woman all his life. Someone with thick honey-blond hair who was just a little bit out of his league. But in his case it had worked as a catalyst for him to keep working harder and harder until he had improved not only his circumstances but also his life. And now the woman he wanted was no longer out of his league.

"I can see that. What kind of man are you drawn to?" he asked. "Have you learned from your broken engagement?"

"I think so. I spent a lot of time dissecting it. I could see that Benjamin needed something that I could never give him," she said, sounding the tiniest bit sad.

"What was that?"

"He needed a woman who would be happy to be his trophy wife and have his kids but turn a blind eye to his mistresses. He traveled a lot for business. And I'd miss him so much, but he never seemed to mind the separations. Once we broke up, I realized I wasn't really special to him…"

"How did you realize that?" he asked. That's not

something that any woman would just recognize about a man she was going to marry.

"He told me. He only asked me to marry him because…" She paused and looked down at her hands. "This is a little hard to say."

He reached over and took her small, well-manicured hand in his. He really hated that jerk she'd been engaged to. At first it was just because she'd been engaged to him, but now it was full-on hatred because he hadn't realized what a treasure Macy was.

"I'm not going to judge you."

She swallowed hard and then took a deep breath. "I wouldn't sleep with him otherwise. I was saving myself for marriage. I know that it might sound silly, given the morals of today, but I was raised differently and I didn't want to give myself to a man who wasn't committed to me."

"So what happened?" he asked.

"Benjamin asked me to marry him and I said yes. Once we were engaged, we started sleeping together and then…the accident happened."

He stroked his thumb over the back of her knuckles and struggled to keep calm. He didn't like thinking of any man sleeping with Macy, but knowing the bastard had run out on her when she'd needed him made Chris furious.

"I understand," he said, but inside he was writhing, wishing he'd been the man she'd trusted with her virginity and who knew her heart. For Macy it was clear the two had gone together.

"Do you?" she asked. "I'm still not sure I do. The only thing I really know is that I'm mad at myself for trusting Benjamin and not seeing through his lies. Abby says it's because in the first brush of love we don't see the real man—we only see the man we want him to be."

Those words were a bit cynical, but then Abby had lost her husband unexpectedly, so Chris cut her a little slack. "Sometimes you see the real man. I'm not pretending to be anyone I'm not."

She shook her head. "It's not that the man is pretending, it's that...I fill in the missing pieces in my mind because my heart is saying he's the one. Does that make sense?"

He nodded. "I can see that. Like when an older rich man finds a pretty young wife and everyone says she's out for his money but he says she loves him and understands him."

"Exactly. And sometimes he's right, but other times he's not and there might be a bitter divorce a few years later. The hard part—and even Maury can't help me figure this out—is that I can't tell when I'm filling in the blanks and when a guy is the real deal."

He leaned over and pulled her out of her chair and onto his lap. He kissed her again and held her strongly against his chest. "I'm the real thing, Macy."

She tunneled her fingers through his hair and kissed him back with more passion than he'd expected. "I hope so."

"Why don't you see what's on TV while I clean up from dinner," she suggested.

"I was hoping to hold you," he said.

She blushed and stood up. "That would be nice."

"Then leave the dishes and come with me," he said, holding out his hand to her. She took it shyly and he realized something he should have earlier. Macy wasn't just shy about her body postsurgery, she was innocent in general. That was what that tale about her fiancé had shown him.

He settled on the couch. When she sat down, he pulled her close to his side. She curled her legs under her and leaned her head against his shoulder.

He knew of only one way to prove to Macy that he was everything she wanted and needed. And doing so would take time. The more time the better, because he had wanted to caress and kiss this woman for what felt like eons.

Chris put on the Texas Rangers baseball game. And Macy was hyperaware of him sitting next to her on the couch. She liked the way he felt pressed against her side.

After a few minutes, Chris put his hand under her chin and tilted her head back so that he could kiss her more deeply. She wanted this.

She'd always wanted more with Chris than she'd ever gotten. In high school she'd been too into herself to really think about making out, but Chris had ensured each kiss they'd shared had been hotter than the one before it.

Kissing Chris now took her one step closer to reclaiming her femininity and the woman she was becoming. His tongue tangled with hers and the kiss was passionate but not overpowering. Much like Chris himself. His lips were soft against hers and when he pulled back and looked down at her, his blue eyes were filled with passion.

"You taste…like something so irresistible, I want more," he said.

"Me too," she admitted.

"Good."

"Why didn't you kiss me when you dropped me off at my car this morning?"

He kissed her again. "I wasn't sure I wanted to let this go any further."

"Why not?"

"You broke my heart, Macy, when you dumped me. And I know it was just puppy love, but I don't want to let you do that to me again," he said.

She turned on the couch to face him and put her hands on his shoulders. "I'm so sorry, Chris. I wish...I wish I could have been someone else back then. Someone who would have seen you for the wonderful man you are today, but I wasn't."

"I don't want you to be someone else," he said. "I liked that brash, flirty girl who thought she was the center of the universe."

Macy had to laugh at the way he described her. She had been too full of herself. And life had made sure that she had learned the hard way there was more than just Macy Reynolds in it.

"Want to make out?" he asked. "We didn't really get to that much in high school and I want to put my hands on you, Macy."

"I'm not sure...I am still scarred from my accident. And I'm not very experienced. I'm sure you've had lots of experience." *Oh, my God,* she thought, *I'm rambling.* But she couldn't help it.

He ran his hands up and down her back before drawing her hips forward so they were pressed close together. He maneuvered them on the couch so that he was lying against the back and she was cradled in his arms. She wanted this and so much more.

"I knew one kiss wouldn't be enough," he said against her lips.

She shifted against him and continued kissing him as she caressed him through his T-shirt. He'd changed into a pair of khaki shorts and a T-shirt to help her clean her house.

"You feel so muscular," she said.

He laughed a bit self-consciously. "I try to work out at least once a day when I'm in Dallas. I spend so much time sitting at my desk otherwise."

She bit her lower lip as she thought that she'd really like to see what he looked like without his shirt on.

"What?"

"Um…will you take your shirt off?" she asked.

"I'd love to," he said. "But I might ask you to take yours off too."

"I'm not pretty," she said.

"No, you're not," he said. "You're gorgeous. But we can do that on your timetable and not mine."

He sat up and pulled his shirt up over his head and tossed it on the floor. His abs were solid—not a six-pack but still nice-looking.

She ran her fingers over his chest. There was a light dusting of hair on it and it tickled her fingertips as she drew them over him. She leaned forward and lowered her head to kiss his neck and shoulders while letting her hands explore his body.

She liked touching him. She realized that he seemed much more the boy she'd known like this than the tycoon who'd come back to town to prove his worth.

She felt his hands at the small of her back, slipping under her shirt and slowly pulling the material up her body. She put her hands on the waistband of the shirt and held it in place. She wondered if he thought she'd been kidding. She was scarred and she didn't want him to see her like that.

"I won't take off your shirt if you don't want me to," he said. "But I do want to touch you."

She nodded and he slipped his hands under her shirt, skimming them over her body. Finding the burn marks on her right side.

She held her breath waiting for his response to them, but he didn't say anything. As he traced the scar tissue goose bumps spread out from the spot and she shivered. "I'm sorry—"

"Don't," he said, putting his finger over her lips. "You are beautiful. Every inch of you, don't forget that."

He slid off the couch to his knees so that he was next to her. He pushed her shirt up and she watched him instead of looking at her own body. He leaned down and traced the scar with his fingers and then she felt the warm wash of his breath on that area.

A moment later she felt a soft kiss against that damaged area. The scars no longer caused her physical pain, but she hadn't realized how much she resented them until she felt Chris touching her there.

"What are you doing?" she asked.

"Healing this wound."

"Why?" she asked.

"Because I want you to know how sexy this is on your body because it's part of what has made you into the woman you are today," he said.

He lowered his head again and she put her hands on the back of it, feeling his silky blond hair under her fingers. She'd known Chris was different from the other men she'd met and dated, but until this moment she hadn't really understood why.

He shifted and took her mouth again in a sweet, passionate kiss. But she wasn't ready for more tonight. She was vulnerable and more fragile than she would have guessed. She put her hands between them, pushing gently on his shoulders. He lifted his head and looked down at her.

She could only stare into his eyes for a few long moments.

Chris got up and walked out of the living room toward the sliding glass door that led to her backyard. He opened it and the hot August heat rushed over his chest. He wanted more from Macy than she could offer him at this moment.

Plus, he didn't want to pressure her. A moment like this wasn't only going to happen once, and the next time he'd be prepared. He walked around the pool over to the built-in barbecue grill. She had everything in this house that would make it a home.

"Chris?"

"Yes?"

"Do you want a drink?" she asked, sounding a bit disjointed. "I make a mean martini."

He laughed. "Sure, I'll take one."

Her lips were still a little full from his kisses. He wanted to touch her all over again. Just run his hands over that sexy body of hers. But that was a path that would lead to more frustration.

"Actually, I think I'm going to take a rain check on that martini. I better head home now."

"Oh, okay."

He walked over to her and pulled her into his arms, holding her tightly against his chest. And she put her head right over his heart again. "I need some space to breathe or I'm going to be pushing you to make love with me. And I don't want to do that."

"You didn't push me," she said.

"I will if I stay. Are you going to be okay here if I leave?"

She nodded, her head against him. "Yes. I'm going to finish making the beds and wash the dishes, and then I think I'll head back to my dad's."

"Are you available for lunch tomorrow?" he asked.

"I think I have room in my schedule for you. What did you have in mind?"

"Maybe a trip up in my plane?" he asked. He had a small Piper aircraft that he used to commute between Dallas and Royal.

"I'd love it," she said. "I'll pack us a lunch."

"Sounds good," he said. He tilted her head and kissed her again. The embrace was full of passion. He knew he had to let her go or it would blossom into much more than kissing and petting.

But he didn't want to let her go. He liked the way she felt in his arms and letting her go was the absolute last thing he was going to do.

But when she put her hands on his hips and drew him closer to her, so that he was pressed against her thighs, he knew he had to leave.

He pulled back and slowly drew her arms down his body and held both her hands in his.

"Thank you for tonight."

"You're welcome. This might be the best date I've ever been on," she said.

"What about that picnic by the lake back when we were kids?" he asked. That date held many special memories for him.

She shook her head. "This one is better because it is happening now and I think…this time I'm not going to make the same mistakes I did before."

"I hope so," he said. He kissed her again and then walked toward the front door.

He got in the Porsche and drove out of her neighborhood at a sedate speed, but he didn't feel sedate. He felt wild and excited and like everything in his life was about to change. He drove out of town until he was on the long open highway where traffic was light and he put the pedal to the metal, driving as if he could escape the past.

Driving as if he had the answer to his future and there were no questions about himself and Macy and whether or not they really belonged together.

He knew he wasn't back here for revenge and he suspected she did too, but he was afraid that she'd bow to pressure once again to not stay with him. He may have changed on the outside, but he knew he was still the same inside—where it really counted. And as sweet and loving as Macy had seemed in his arms tonight, he also knew that she was just coming back to life after a long dormant period.

He was the first man to kiss her and touch her in three years. And if she were to be believed, only the second man in her entire life.

He started laughing out loud as he realized that once again Macy Reynolds had him tied in knots and he had no idea how to untangle them.

Seven

"Good morning, Dad," Macy said as she entered the kitchen the next morning. She gave her father a kiss on the forehead and then made herself a cup of Earl Grey tea.

"Morning. How was your night?"

"Good," she said, trying not to blush when she thought about her night with Chris. "I worked on my house getting it cleaned up and ready for me to move back in."

"You don't have to move," he said. "I'm fine with you staying here."

"Thanks, Dad. But I think I need to do this. It will make me feel like I'm getting back on my feet."

He squeezed her hand in his. "You're doing an amazing job of recovering. I always knew you had your mother's strength, and you really proved it during this ordeal."

"You always said that I did, but I never felt like it. Everything in my life was just a little too easy, with no real challenges." That might have been why she'd dated Chris. He was the first thing she'd had to work for. She'd enjoyed him, of course; he was such a cute boy back then. And he still was, but there was also the challenge of dating someone forbidden.

"I didn't want you to ever have to struggle for anything you wanted. Grandpa Reynolds didn't give me a dime and made me work twice as hard as everyone else at the construction company to prove myself. I resented my old man and I never wanted you to think of me the same way."

Macy got up and hugged her dad. "I never have. Even when you were imposing your rules about who I could and couldn't date."

He shrugged his big shoulders—the ones that she could remember sitting on and watching parades from when she was little. Her dad had been her first hero and he'd done a good job of making her feel special when she was a child. "I have always tried to protect you."

"And yet I still got hurt," she said. "Isn't life funny that way sometimes?"

No matter what her father had done to protect her, she'd still made mistakes and gotten hurt and made bad decisions, like accepting Benjamin's marriage proposal. Of course, when her dad had said he didn't like Benjamin that had only made her more determined to make the relationship last.

Harrison shrugged. "Yes, it is. All we can do is live by our own code and hope we've not hurt too many people on our journey."

"I think you do a great job of that, Dad."

"Thanks, kiddo. I've got an early-morning meeting at the club to talk about the remodeling they are doing."

"Why are you trying so hard to get that job? We don't need it," Macy said.

"I want to make sure that I'm not affected by Sebastian's misdeeds. He was a friend of mine and I was blind to what he was doing."

"No one blames you," Macy said.

"I blame myself for not catching on," Harrison said. "The club has always been my second home and I want it to continue to be."

She understood that. Her father was fiercely loyal. "Are you eating at home tonight?"

"No, I'll probably work late and stop by the club on my way home. You?"

"Not sure. I have a new book I'm reading."

Harrison laughed at her in a kindly way. Then shook his head before he said, "Girl, you live an exciting life."

She smiled at her dad and lightly hugged him. "I know. Try to keep up."

After he left, Macy finished her tea and then got dressed for work. She was looking forward to her lunch date with Chris. She'd had steamy dreams about him last night. In fact, she hoped to make those dreams a reality today.

She wanted Chris to be hers. Not just some guy from her past or a man she was casually dating. Last night went beyond casual for her.

Was she really going to let things move forward? Could she stop them? For the first time in her life she wanted a lover. Not a fiancé or a boyfriend but a lover. Well sort of. She felt a wave of something wash over her. She glanced at herself in the mirror, seeing her newly repaired face, but also finally starting to accept that the woman in there was her.

That wasn't a stranger staring back at her, but a woman who was strong and confident. A woman who had no problem attracting a sexy man like Chris Richardson.

She drove to the grocery store and picked up everything they needed for lunch and then drove to work. She spent the morning in the orderly world of numbers and formulas. A place where everything added up and no emotions were needed and she liked it. It gave her grounding to her exciting new life. The relationship with Chris was something unfamiliar but so much a part of who she was becoming.

Thinking about him distracted her from her work. But she didn't mind. For too long all she'd had was pain, and work was an escape, but now she had something more fulfilling in her life. Something that she wanted to claim for her own—a man she wanted to claim for her own.

She shut down her computer ten minutes before Chris was supposed to arrive and grabbed her picnic basket to meet him out front. Her dad hadn't said anything to her about dating Chris, but she knew after he'd interrupted their dinner at the Texas Cattleman's Club, he had to have guessed they were seeing each other.

Chris spent most of his morning on the phone with his client in Plano. He really should be focused on his bid to the Texas Cattleman's Club and getting out of Royal and back to his real life. But he was in no hurry to leave.

There was a knock on his office door as he hung up the phone.

"Your mom is here," Tanja said.

His mom eased past his assistant. "Thanks, Tanja."

"You're welcome," Tanja said as she let herself out of the office, closing the door behind her.

"Hi, Mom. What can I do for you this morning?" he asked.

"It's what I can do for you... Amanda Hasher's daughter is coming to town this weekend and I was going to invite her to have dinner with us."

"No."

"But—"

"No. No blind dates. Besides, I'm dating someone," Chris said.

"Who?"

"Macy Reynolds."

"I'm not trying to tell you what to do, darling," Margaret Richardson said, "but is that the smartest thing...?"

"Why wouldn't it be?" Chris asked. "Macy's a different woman now than she used to be."

"I hope so. Are you sure you don't want to just have dinner with Amanda's daughter?"

"Yes, I'm sure."

She sighed.

"What's the matter?"

"I'd like some grandkids. With my heart being the way it is..."

"There's nothing wrong with your heart," Chris said, because he wanted her to start believing that. He wanted his mother to know that he was going to be here for her even if she was healthy, but there was no way to say that.

"The doctors don't know what's the matter with me," she said, giving him her most pitiful look, and if she wasn't a master of manipulation he might have fallen for it, but he'd grown up seeing that look.

"You're right, they don't. But I'm thinking of buying my own place here so I can visit more often...that will probably help," he said, leaning over to kiss her on the cheek. He hugged her and she hugged him back.

"I'm sure it will. If you won't go out with anyone but Macy, then you can both come to my house for dinner."

"Why?" Chris asked.

"I want to see if she's sincere. Macy asked me to work on a project for her and I'd like to see the two of you together."

He shook his head and fought not to roll his eyes. "I'll ask her. But I am working nonstop on this project for the Texas Cattleman's Club and I might not be able to have dinner at a decent hour."

"Great. I will have to figure out what to make. Do you need me to do anything for you today? Dry cleaning or any of that?"

"No, Mom. You just got out of the hospital a few days ago. Shouldn't you be taking it easy?" he asked her. But it was refreshing to see her up and moving around.

"Not at all. Having you home always makes me feel refreshed."

She gave him a kiss. "I'll get out of your hair now. I'm so happy you are home, Chris. I can't tell you how much it means to me that I can stop by your office and see you whenever I want."

She left his office like the whirlwind she was and he

heard Tanja laughing at something his mom said in the outer office. He remembered how desperately he had wanted to get out of Royal, but lately his feelings about the town had changed.

Tanja poked her head back in the doorway. "Chris, I just got the files back from the head office in Dallas on the Reynolds Construction bids. What do you want me to do with them?"

"Go through the ones they submitted and find out who the winning construction company was and then look to see if we awarded to the lowest bid and if there were any special circumstances…like it was a female- or minority-owned business. Also check if there was a specific need of the original bid we did," Chris said.

"Okay. It's going to take me a little while. They've been submitting bids for the past five years," Tanja said.

"Make it a priority. I need to get some answers back to Harrison Reynolds as soon as I can. I'm taking the afternoon off. I'll have my cell phone with me, so you can get me that way if you need me."

"Sounds good. I'll just be working on this project," she said, gesturing to the stack of bids from Harrison's company.

"Thanks, Tanja," he said as she left his office.

He called the airport to make sure that Buck, who managed his private plane, had it stocked with champagne and a few other essentials. He wanted to show Macy all the things that he could give her.

Shaking his head, he stood up and paced around his office. He wasn't about to try to prove himself to her, was he? Why did he keep coming back to this?

His phone rang and he glanced at the caller ID to see it was his college roommate Sam Winston. Sam had come to UT Austin from the Northeast on a football scholarship like Chris. The two of them had become good friends and had stayed close even after they'd graduated. Though it had been a couple of weeks since they had spoken.

"Hey, Sam."

"Chris, man, what's up? I'm in Fort Worth for a conference and I called your office, but they said you weren't here," Sam said.

"I'm back in Royal. My mom was in the hospital."

"Is she okay?" Sam asked.

"Yes. That heart thing the doctors can't figure out," Chris said, catching his friend up on her situation.

"How long are you there? My conference goes until Friday and I can hang out this weekend. Georgia is having a girlfriends-only spa weekend."

"And she told you to stay out of the house?" Chris asked. He'd been the best man at Sam's wedding and he loved Georgia like a sister. She was the only one who knew how to get around Sam.

"Something like that. Are you going to leave me hanging?" Sam asked.

"I'm not going to be in Dallas this weekend. But why don't you come down to Royal?" Chris suggested.

"I could do that. Can I drive?"

"I'll send my private plane to get you. You remember Buck, right?"

"Yes, I do. Great. So I'll be down there on Saturday morning."

"Good. I'm looking forward to seeing you."

He hung up. He wanted the kind of relationship that Sam and Georgia had. They were married but didn't have to be in each other's pockets all the time. And they were happy even after five years of marriage.

That happiness had eluded Chris no matter how many different women he'd pursued. To be fair, he'd only met one woman who had made him want to put his work on hold, and that was Macy.

Maybe that was why being with her felt so different to him. He didn't know. Didn't question it anymore. He wasn't really an introspective guy. He knew what he wanted—Macy Reynolds, and he knew he was going to do whatever he had to to ensure he got her.

He'd been playing his cards close to his vest, afraid to startle Macy and make her retreat, but he was beginning to think that she wasn't running away from him; in fact, the opposite was true.

Macy had a great time at lunch, but they were interrupted by a call from her father about an hour into it. She'd had to ask Chris to take her back to Royal, which he'd done reluctantly.

"I'm sorry."

"It's fine. I know you have to be there when your dad calls."

"Not all the time, but today he needs me," she said. Though privately she wondered why he needed her now, when this morning he'd said the bid they were working on wasn't going in until Friday.

"We can have a more leisurely meal later. Are you free tonight?" he asked.

"Yes. Do you want to go out?" she asked.

"I do. Somewhere we can dance so I can hold you all night."

"Sounds good to me. I can't wear heels the way I used to," she said.

"That's fine with me."

She shook her head. "I was just thinking I wanted to look nice, sorry for blurting that out."

"You always look pretty. What do shoes have to do with that?" he asked as he drove her back to her office.

"They make my legs look longer."

"Macy, if your legs were any longer I'd die. Really, they are terrific whatever shoes you wear."

He might think so, but now that they were dating again old desires were coming back. Desires for things she hadn't thought of since she'd been in the accident. And one of them was that she wanted to put on a slinky dress and some heels.

She thought of little Sara who would be happy to wear anything closely resembling fashion and felt ashamed of herself. She'd grown beyond looks and clothing. "Thank you, Chris."

"For what?"

"Those nice things you said. I was thinking like pre-accident Macy. How shallow was I?"

"Not shallow at all. You were just used to looking at the world in a different way. That's all changed now. Don't get me wrong, I'd love to see you in whatever you think makes you look nice. I like how you were much more confident in your riding clothes than you are in your work clothes," he said. "You walked around the stables like you had the confidence of a hundred women."

His words made sense. But then Chris always seemed to. She had noticed that her clothing made her feel differently. Her riding gear made her feel confident.

She leaned over and kissed him. Nothing passionate, just a little brush of her lips against his suntanned cheek. He was more than a man from her past. More than a man she was dating and who made her feel like a woman again. More than a man she felt casual about. She was falling for him again and she didn't know if she could trust that feeling.

She'd been through so much and he was the first man she'd gone out with after her surgery. She needed to talk to someone; she needed a second opinion. Yet there wasn't really anyone she wanted to trust with these new feelings.

But then, who could tell her what was in her heart? Love wasn't like the numbers she ran in Excel for Reynolds Construction. Love didn't have any guarantees or come with promises. Love gave her this incredible feeling inside, and riding tandem with that were all the doubts and fears she'd never thought to have.

Chris stared at her and she realized she'd let the conversation lag. What had they been talking about? Riding?

"I love riding," she said.

"I could tell."

"Um...do you have plans for Saturday? I'm going over to your mom's house to work on some outfits for my Burn Unit charity. And I'm not sure she likes me."

"I do have plans. My college roommate is in town... Why aren't you sure about my mom?"

"I broke your heart years ago and she knows it. She's helping out with the charity, but she's so cool to me."

"Be yourself and she'll warm up to you," Chris said.

Maybe taking a break from seeing each other every day was a good idea. It would give her a chance to regain her perspective. She needed to make sure that what she thought she felt…love…damn, she hadn't planned on letting any man make her feel anything again. When he'd left, Benjamin had torn her heart into pieces and foolishly she'd thought that meant she'd never have to worry about falling in love again.

That was what scared her. If she let herself care too much for Chris and this was just something temporary for him—he didn't even live in Royal—how was she going to survive?

She wasn't interested in having her heart broken again. She wanted to be cautious and protect herself from the emotions he drew from her so effortlessly, but she knew it was too late. Chris had cast a spell on her whether he'd intended to or not and she wanted him not just in her bed but also in her life.

And that felt foolish to her because her dad didn't really know they were dating. And she'd just come out of a long dark period in her life. But she couldn't stop the feelings she had, and she didn't want to.

Eight

Two days later Macy was still avoiding talking to anyone about Chris. That included Abby, who had called her several times. But Macy just wasn't ready to chat. As she hit Ignore on the cell phone yet again, she heard a rap at her door. She glanced up to see Abby standing there with her phone in hand.

"I can't believe you aren't at least going to answer my call," Abby said.

Macy felt her face get hot. "I am…"

"Avoiding me," Abby said.

"Come in and close my door and I will tell you," Macy said.

Abby did as Macy asked, but instead of sitting in one of the guest chairs, she perched on the edge of Macy's desk.

"Okay, spill, what's so important you don't have time for your good friend anymore."

"I've been dating Chris Richardson."

"The developer?" Abby asked.

"Yes."

"Damn it. I wish I'd known that. I'm bringing another developer to town so that everyone knows I'm serious about my bid to be president."

"Oh," Macy said. "I guess competition is good."

"Of course it is, but I aim to win this and that means Chris might not be in town as long as you'd like him to be," Abby said.

Macy wasn't worried about club business interfering in her life. "Chris and I have some history. I really needed to talk about this, but I didn't know what to say."

"Good thing I decided to stop by and check up on you," Abby said. "Let's get out of this office and go for a walk. You can tell me all about it."

Macy saved her work and then left the office with her friend. There was a large park with several shade trees planted and a pond at the center of it near the Richardson Construction Company main offices. The two women went over there to walk and talk.

"What's up?"

"Chris and I dated briefly in high school, but my dad didn't think he was good enough for me and pressured me to break up with him, which I did."

"I think I remember hearing something about that back in school. But you've never mentioned anything about it," Abby said.

"It was high school and lately I've had something else to talk about."

"Agreed. Let me say once again how happy I am that you have no more surgeries to go through."

"Thanks," Macy said.

"Does your dad object to you dating Chris now?" Abby asked. "I don't see what his grounds would be. I looked Richardson up on the internet and he's very successful."

"I have no idea how my dad feels," Macy said. The hot August morning was starting to make her feel a little sweaty. "I haven't said anything to him about it."

"Why not? Are you afraid to?" Abby asked.

"I don't know. Maybe. It wasn't like there was an official let's-start-dating-again discussion. We just started doing things together and it keeps getting more serious... I think I'm falling for him," Macy said. "I feel like it's too soon after my surgery. What if the emotions are some sort of mirage?"

Abby wrapped her arm around Macy's shoulders, hugging her close for just a minute. "You're grown, so anything your dad says would be moot, but if you think you're sneaking around then I'd clear the air and tell him that you have been dating Chris and intend to continue.

"As for the other...love, only time will tell."

"I'm used to finding answers and plotting and planning things, Abby."

Abby hugged her again. "I know, but real life isn't like that."

Macy was more than aware that her friend was right. She needed to remember that she could plan to her heart's content and still unexpected things were going to occur. She could either go in this new direction with Chris or stop it now and keep herself from being hurt again.

"I'm afraid of getting hurt," Macy said. "I told myself

I was well rid of Benjamin, but sometimes the hurt creeps up on me and I find myself aching again."

"Trust isn't something that comes easy to any of us," Abby said.

"Girl, I thought you had all the answers," Macy said. "Don't tell me you have doubts like the rest of us mortals."

Abby shook her head. "I don't want to tarnish my image."

"You haven't," Macy said. "Thanks for making me talk to you."

"No problem," Abby said.

"Do you fancy helping me out at the children's Burn Unit on Sunday?"

"Sure, what are we doing?" Abby asked.

"A little fashionista day for my friends there. Chris's mom is making some clothes for them to wear from burn-scar-friendly material and I have some ladies from a local spa coming to paint the kids' nails, but I could use some help getting them all dressed up."

"Sounds like fun. What time?" Abby asked.

Macy gave her friend the details as they walked back to the office. And as Abby was getting ready to leave, Macy realized she'd never properly said thank-you to this woman who'd helped her through the darkest period of her life.

"Thanks, Abby."

"You're welcome, but for what?"

"Making sure I was never alone, even when that was all I wanted to be. I don't think you realize what a lifesaver you were."

"You helped me out too, Mace, gave me someone other than myself to think about," Abby said.

"Good," Macy said, hugging her friend and then going back into the office. She saw her dad sitting at his desk on the phone as usual and she hesitated for a moment, contemplating going in to talk to him about Chris. In the end she decided not to. Not yet.

On Saturday morning, as he headed out to meet Sam at the airport, Chris realized that he hadn't seen Macy in almost three days. Was she avoiding him?

Or like him had she simply gotten too busy to keep up with dating? Chris had been busier than he'd expected and had to focus all his energy on the Plano retail facility he'd been working on. They'd run into some snags with the zoning commission and no matter how much talking he did on the phone, no one was willing to speed the process along.

He picked Sam up.

"I'm starving."

"Good. I'll take you to the Royal Diner so you can get something to eat and I can introduce you to my hometown."

"At a diner?"

"Trust me, you'll know more about everyone in a manner of minutes then if you'd lived here your entire life," Chris said.

Sam laughed. They chatted about the conference Sam had been at in Fort Worth, and when they were seated at the diner, Sam caught Chris up on what he and Georgia had been doing around their house all summer. They were having a new pool built.

"Why didn't you ask me to help?"

"Your business is based in Texas. I doubt you could have found a construction crew to come to Connecticut."

"You are probably right."

They both ordered a heavy greasy breakfast of eggs and all the trimmings from a waitress that reminded Chris of Flo, the character from the old television show *Alice*. She had reddish hair that was clearly dyed and wore it in an old-fashioned-looking beehive. She wore bright blue eye shadow and was never without a piece of gum in her mouth.

She was friendly and sweet but a real character.

"Why did you ever leave this place?"

Chris had never talked much about Royal in college. "A girl broke my heart."

"You? I've never known you to let anyone get close enough to do that," Sam said.

"I tend not to make the same mistakes twice," he said. Then privately wondered what he was doing with Macy now. He had no guarantees that she wasn't going to put him through the wringer emotionally again.

"What happened?" Sam asked.

"Her dad didn't approve of me, so she broke up with me. I graduated and left for college. I never looked back."

"If only it were that simple."

"If only. Nothing ever is."

"That's so true. What really happened?" Sam asked.

"That's the truth except for me moving on so easily. I didn't let anyone close because of her and her dad. When I was young, I had this plan to come back here and show them both how successful I'd become. She'd of course beg me to take her back and I'd say no way."

Sam shook his head. "That's a nice fantasy."

"You have no idea. But reality is different. The girl... well, I'm dating her now."

"You are? What about the father?"

"He doesn't know. Isn't that crazy? I'm thirty-two and I'm still not entirely comfortable with her dad."

"Complicated," Sam said. "Things were much easier with Georgia and I. I told her we were in love and going to be happy the rest of our lives and she agreed."

"Liar. You screwed up with her and had to go and beg to get her back. Don't forget who was at your side while you did all that."

Sam chuckled again. "I have started to remember the story differently… I wanted to see you today to tell you that Georgia is pregnant. I'm going to be a father."

Chris was floored and so damn happy for his friend. "Congratulations. I can't believe it."

"We can't either. We'd just about given up on ever having any kids when this happened. Georgia's calling the baby our little miracle, and I told her she has to stop saying how I begged her to marry me…what if I have a son? He's going to want to think his dad was always a great guy."

"You are a great guy, Sam. And you are going to make a really good father. When is the baby due?" Chris asked. Sharing in his friend's happiness made him realize he wanted that too.

"February," Sam said. "We want you to be the godfather."

"I'd be honored. I'll clear my calendar so I can fly up as soon as your baby is born. I can't believe you are going to be a dad."

"Me neither. But it's what Georgia and I have been wanting for a long time. Finding each other, well, Georgia says we were lucky, and I know we were. We've always been sort of yin and yang to each other, but having a child is adding something new to our relationship. I can't explain it."

"You don't have to," Chris said.

They spent the rest of the day in Royal at the Texas Cattleman's Club hanging out and playing poker in one of the rooms. Chris sent a text to Zeke and Brad and they both joined him and Sam for an afternoon of reminiscing about college days and their football glory.

Chris felt more at ease in the club this time. Being with his college-football buddies reminded him that outside of Royal he'd found his place and he'd figured out where he fit in. Coming back here had awakened old fears and attitudes in him.

Maybe his worry that Macy was going to do the same thing to him this time as she'd done in the past was unfounded. She and her father were close, but they were all adults now. Something that was easy to forget since he'd returned home.

He broke even by the end of the night and realized he'd drunk a little too much. But so had the other guys. He and Sam called a cab to take them back to his mom's house.

They tried to be quiet when they entered his mother's house, and were successful. The entire evening was fun, but as Chris lay in his bed drifting off to sleep all he could think about was Macy and how much he wanted her in his arms.

After church on Sunday, Macy and Mrs. Richardson walked into the open play area in the Burn Unit carrying boxes filled with shoes and costume jewelry and found Sara waiting. The little girl had a radiant smile on her face. Next to her was a girl that Macy hadn't met before. She had bandages on the right side of her neck and arm.

"Hi, Miss Macy," Sara said.

"Good morning, Sara. How are you feeling today?"

"Great. I'm going home tomorrow. This is my friend Jen. I'm going to come back and visit her like you do with me," Sara said.

Macy hugged Sara and smiled over at Jen. "I have a surprise for you today."

"What is it?" Sara asked.

"A little fashion makeover," Macy said. Margaret stood beside her with her arms loaded down with clothing in every color of the rainbow.

"Yay!" Sara said. "What can I do to help?"

"Tell Dr. Webb that we are here. And then just get all the girls together and we can get started on our day of fun."

"Come on, Jen," Sara said, taking her new friend by the hand and leading her to the nurses' station.

"Let me help you with that, Mrs. Richardson," Macy said.

"Thanks. By the way, I asked Chris and his friend Sam to help out as well."

"And here I am. Where do you want this stuff, Mom?" Chris asked from the doorway. He held a long metal stand with a bar on it for hanging all the clothes.

Macy was surprised to see him. She hadn't expected him to want to spend his Sunday in the children's ward of the hospital.

"I don't know.... Macy is in charge," Margaret said. "I'm going to get the rest of the things."

Macy took the pile of clothes from Margaret and turned to look at Chris. "Put it over there."

He did as she directed and she brought the clothing over to hang it up. The main difference in the clothes that Margaret had made for the girls and normal clothing was that the garments were made with no inside seams or zippers, which could rub against sensitive skin.

Chris tipped her chin up when she was done hanging the clothes and leaned down to whisper in her ear. "I've missed you."

She'd missed him too. And seeing him again this morning made all the feelings that she'd been so unsure about come rushing back. "Me too. Did you have fun with your friend yesterday?"

"Yes. I did. You can meet him later. He's going to drop by once he wakes up."

"That will be nice," Macy said.

"Come and help me with this load, Chris," Margaret said as she walked back into the room.

Chris went to help his mom and Macy didn't have time to think about Chris or falling in love for a long time. She had little girls to help get dressed up, and tiny, sometimes bandaged feet, to put in oversize shoes.

The day sped by and Macy was surprised that Chris stayed the entire time. She'd catch him staring at her and he'd just wink before he looked away from her.

She basked in the attention from him. She liked the fact that he couldn't keep his eyes off her. And seeing the joy on the little girls' faces just made her even happier.

She felt as if everything in her life had happened for a reason, even that horrible accident. She'd never have taken the time to do something like this before. But this donation of her time was more valuable and rewarding than she'd ever expected it to be.

Abby showed up midway through the morning. "We need to talk."

"Can it wait just a few more minutes? I have one more girl to dress and then the girls are going to do a runway show for us," Macy said.

"Yes, but I heard something important and…we need to talk," Abby said.

"Okay. We will as soon as this is over?"

"Yes," Abby said. There was something about Abby's demeanor that worried Macy. But she didn't let that dampen her mood. The parents of the kids in the Burn Unit were all seated near the red carpet that had been placed on the floor.

Chris had disappeared and she realized she hadn't seen him since everyone had shown up.

"I think we are ready to start the show," Macy said.

"Not yet," Margaret said. "We have a surprise for you."

"What is it?" Macy asked.

"Boys. The girls are going to need escorts on the runway," Margaret said.

All the little boys in the unit were dressed in oversize tuxedo jackets. Underneath, many of them wore their hospital jammies, but they looked wonderful to her.

"How did you do this?" she asked.

"Chris took care of it," Margaret said.

She smiled over and mouthed the word *thanks* at Chris as came back into the room. He just nodded and went to stand behind the parents seated in the chairs. Macy stepped behind the curtain that had been hung so that the parents couldn't see the kids until they stepped out on the runway.

"Is everyone ready?" she asked.

A chorus of yeses filled the air.

Macy stepped out from behind the curtain and looked at all the parents eagerly awaiting their kids. "Thank you for coming to the Royal Memorial Hospital August Fashion Show."

She glanced behind the curtain at Margaret, who pressed Play to start the music. Macy acted as the emcee introducing each girl and her escort as they came out. The afternoon was a huge success and after the event many parents came up to her to say thanks.

Macy was moved by how happy the girls were. Abby waited for her in the hallway though and she knew she needed to go and talk to her friend. As soon as she could, she made her way over to Abby.

"What's up?"

"I heard a piece of gossip this morning at the Royal Diner…"

"About me?" she asked.

"Sort of. I don't know if there is any truth to it, so I'm not sure I should even mention it."

"Just say it. I will consider the source. What did you hear?"

"I heard that Chris is back here for revenge. That he's planning on making you fall in love with him and then dumping you the way you dumped him."

Nine

Abby's source—the Royal Diner—was not surprising. It was the place to hear gossip. Macy felt as if she'd taken a blow to the stomach. She had no idea what she was going to do.

Abby looked mad, and Macy wished she could latch on to the anger instead of feeling this horrible pain inside.

"Thanks for telling me." Her voice sounded weird to her own ears. She was starting to fall for Chris, and the man she knew wouldn't come back here for revenge. Still, she knew she was never going to be able to go back in the room and act as if nothing was wrong.

"I'm sorry to be the one to tell you this, but I didn't want you to hear this from someone else," Abby said.

"What else did he say?"

"I don't know what else was said. One of the wait-resses overheard him and his friend talking and she had to refill someone's coffee, but I thought you should know."

Yes, she should know.

"What are you going to do?"

"Talk to him about it," she said. The accident had taught her that life could end in a moment. She knew how lucky she was to be alive and, honestly, if Chris was the type of man who'd think about doing something like that—then he wasn't the man she was falling for.

That man...well, he was the guy who'd brought tux jackets for the boys today and who cleared his schedule to take her flying even though he probably should have been schmoozing someone from the club to make sure he got the job developing the new headquarters.

"Do you want me to come with you when you talk to him?" Abby asked, holding her hand.

"No, it's okay. I have to do this on my own," Macy said. She had been regaining her confidence with all the dates she'd been on with Chris and just getting out of the house and reclaiming her life. She'd take care of Chris. Confront him and find out if there was any truth to the rumors.

"I'll make sure he doesn't get the job at the club when I become president," Abby said.

"No," Macy said. "Revenge isn't good for anyone. I don't want to disrupt his business. If he feels he needs to get back at me for something that happened almost fourteen years ago, then he's not the kind of man I want in my life."

"That's so true," Abby said.

Macy gave her a forced half smile. She didn't want to think that she had lousy taste in men. She'd kind of always thought that Chris was a good man. And had blamed their problems on her dad. Which made a certain kind of sense, given that she'd been easily influenced by Harrison back then.

"You know I broke up with him so my dad would give me a convertible?"

"Oh, honey," Abby said.

"That's the kind of girl I was. A part of me wouldn't blame him for wanting some kind of revenge, but I'm not like that anymore. I thought he of all people would realize it."

Abby rubbed Macy's arm comfortingly. "The information came from the diner, so who knows what part of it is true."

"There's nothing for it except to ask him and find out what he was thinking," Macy said. She could run over it in her mind a million times, but she wasn't going to be any closer to finding the answers she wanted.

Only Chris could give them to her. She still had to finish up the reception with the parents and then clean up the room they'd used. The last thing she wanted to do was confront him.

She shivered a little thinking about the time they'd spent together, the kisses they'd shared. She'd thought he was being noble, but now everything took on a more sinister meaning.

She turned red, felt her face heating up. Was Chris capable of doing all the things he'd done since they met just to lead her into a trap?

She really hoped not, but hoping wasn't going to do anything. She knew that from her time in the hospital. She had to take action and, even if it was painful, that was what she was going to do. "I'll just ask him straight up if he's here for that. It doesn't seem like something he'd do. I mean, he helped out today without me even asking."

But if his plan had been to lure her into falling for him, she guessed he would do whatever he had to in order to make her feel as if he was doing something that was just for her. She was confused and knew she probably seemed...she had no idea what Abby was thinking.

Probably pitying her because she was once again in a situation where she was—what? Macy had no idea. She was embarrassed that Abby had heard this about her. But grateful that her friend had the courage to tell her.

Abby shrugged. "I have no idea what he's capable of."

"What who is capable of?" Chris asked, coming out into the hallway.

"You," Macy said.

"Call me later," Abby said as she walked by Chris.

Standing there in front of Chris, she searched for the words to ask him if he'd done what Abby had said. But she really couldn't find them. In her head she knew what she had to say, but opening her mouth and asking him if he'd come back here for revenge wasn't easy.

"Macy?"

He sounded sincere and caring and a part of her wanted to believe everything she thought was true about him, but another part of her knew better. She'd been deceived before, agreeing to marry a man because he told her pretty lies. And then when she'd needed him, Benjamin had run away. Now it seemed that Chris, whom she'd thought was different, was cut from the same cloth. That was the part that hurt the most.

* * *

"What's going on?" he asked. Chris knew something was wrong the minute he'd stepped into the hallway and seen the women standing together.

"I'm not sure how to say this."

"Say what? I'm sorry I didn't ask you about the stuff for the boys before I did it, but I thought it would be nice to include them."

She shook her head. "Of course that's fine. I'm sorry I didn't think of it myself. You were so right to do it. Next time I put together a fashion show I'm going to get your mom to make jackets for the boys."

"I know she'll love it. She had such a good time working on the dresses," he said. "But that's not what has you upset. Tell me what's going on."

Chris reached out to touch her shoulder and Macy stepped back, away from him.

"I... Abby heard some gossip at the Royal Diner."

"Not exactly surprising. Did it involve us?"

"Yes," she said. But still didn't go into detail. She wrapped her arms around her waist and hunched into herself.

Whatever was said, it had distressed Macy, and Chris was mad enough that when he found out what was going on, he was going to go to the diner and have a word with whomever was talking about Macy. She didn't need to hear things about herself in the rumor mill. She'd worked hard to recover from an accident that would have sidelined many other people.

"What was said about you?" he asked.

"It was about you and me," she said.

"I have to know what was said," he told her. "I can't tell you if it's true or not unless you open up about it."

She took a deep breath. "Word around the Royal Diner is that you are back here to make me fall in love with you and then break my heart," she said.

Chris shook his head. Dammit, he never said that. Then he remembered his conversation with Sam yesterday morning. Obviously, whoever was listening had only heard part of the conversation. Surely Macy didn't really think he'd do something like that.

"Do you believe that?" he asked.

"Did you say it?" she asked.

"I did."

"Is it true? Why would you do something like that?" she asked. "I trusted you."

"Would you believe me if I said I was talking about the past."

"Is that true? Or have I fooled myself into thinking you are a different kind of man than you really are?"

"No. Hell, no," Chris said, pulling her into his arms. "I think what your source overheard was me telling Sam how I'd felt about you and this town when I left. It didn't take me long to figure out that what happens in high school needs to stay there. I moved on with my life and never thought of revenge again."

He hoped she'd understand where he'd been when he'd left Royal. But that boy had morphed into a man who understood that sometimes getting what he thought he'd wanted wasn't the solution to everything in life. Not getting Macy had challenged him and made him go out and achieve more than he would have otherwise.

But he had no proof to offer her other than his word and, if she didn't believe him, then he'd be in the same place he'd been almost fourteen years ago. It was funny how some patterns in his life always remained the same.

"Well, Macy?"

"Well, what?" she asked.

"Do you believe me? Do you trust your own instincts? That I'm not the kind of man who would plan for almost fourteen years to get back at a girl?"

"When you say it that way…"

"It sounds silly, doesn't it? I was a young man with a bad temper and a big ego. Hell, my own father told me you were too good for me and that I was aiming for someone I should have left alone."

"Did he?"

"Yes, I think he was afraid I'd get hurt and I did. But that doesn't mean I spent the rest of my life plotting revenge on you."

"I wouldn't have blamed you if you had," she said softly. "I broke up with you so I could get a convertible."

He shook his head. "You gave in to the pressure your father put on you. It took me about six months to realize that if I'd put up more of a fight maybe you would have stayed with me. I let you go as easily as you kicked me out of your life."

He reached for her and this time she didn't flinch out of his way. He rubbed her shoulders and then looked down into those pretty eyes of hers.

"Do you believe me?" he asked again.

"I believe you," she said.

"Good," he said, hugging her close. "I wouldn't do anything to hurt you, Macy."

He held her close and kissed her. He tried to convey in that embrace how much she meant to him. He wasn't ready to tell her how important she was to him. But seeing her today with those kids… Seeing the real heart of this woman…had him wondering if Macy was the woman he wanted to have as the mother of his children.

The woman he wanted by his side as he went forward through life. Damn. He hadn't been looking to settle down, but something about Macy made him think of family and home. Those thoughts were uncomfortable, like a too-tight tuxedo jacket, and he wanted to shrug them off.

But Macy had snuck into his affections without him even noticing and, frankly, he didn't want her to leave. He had the feeling that if he let himself fall for her, she'd be everything to him. Like Sam had said of his wife, Georgia—Macy was yin to his yang. Or yang to his yin, whichever way it went.

"I'm so glad you believe me," he said. "I don't know what I'd do if I lost you again."

She looked up at him. "Me neither. I didn't expect you, Chris. I've been on my own for a long time and I had gotten used to living a life that was one of waiting. But you make me want to get out of my shell—to take risks."

"Am I a risk?" he asked her.

"Yes, you are. When Abby told me what she'd heard…I almost didn't blame you for wanting revenge. I was so shallow back then and you said…"

Chris crossed his arms over his chest. "You broke my heart."

"I'm so sorry for that," she said. "I'm not the same woman now."

"I am coming to know that," he said.

Someone called for her. "I have to go back in there."

He watched her as she moved slowly down the hallway, hips swaying with each step she took. He wanted to pretend that he didn't want her to be his completely. To pretend that what was between them was just lust, but he knew deep inside that it was much, much more.

Macy loved the freedom of being on the back of Buttercup. Chris and she had stopped by the stables and brought the horses out to the Reynolds Ranch. Now they were riding out to the swimming hole where, as Macy recalled, they'd spent a lot of time the summer they'd been dating.

It was hot on this August afternoon, but the promise of the cool waters at the swimming hole made up for it.

"I'm sorry again for that rumor getting started," Chris said.

"It's okay. I think maybe we needed to clear the air anyway. Make sure the past is well and truly buried before we can really move on."

Macy had spent a lot of time thinking about that since Abby had told her the gossip. Living in Royal meant people were always going to know her business. She knew that everyone had gossiped about her accident, her fiancé leaving and her recovery. It was the nature of small towns to be in everyone's business and as much as she didn't like being the center of the conversation in town, she did like the fact that she always knew what her neighbors were up to.

"Abby isn't too happy with you," Macy said.

"You're the only woman whose opinion matters to me," he said.

She smiled over at him. "That is very sweet, but if you want to do business with the Texas Cattleman's

Club you have to at least consider her opinion because she is a force to be reckoned with there."

"Brad doesn't think she's going to win the election."

"I don't know if she will or not, but she is bringing another developer into the picture so you aren't the only game in town," Macy said.

"Thanks for the heads-up," Chris said. "I'm going to do what Brad asked me to do and if I can get the work then I will."

"Truly?"

"Yes. I came here for my mom and since Brad asked me to bid on the work, I thought I would, but my fortune isn't tied to the Texas Cattleman's Club."

She thought about that as they rode up to the swimming hole. Was he just making light or did the work really not mean that much to him? In Royal, the club was so exclusive and everyone wanted in. But maybe being away from Royal had given Chris a different perspective.

"Do you come out here often?" Chris asked.

She shook her head. "I mainly ride at the stables. The ranch hands shouldn't have to keep an eye out for me. They have their own work that they do."

"Why would they— Oh, when you first started riding again?" Chris asked.

Macy remembered those early days. She still had scarring and bandages on her body. The last thing she'd wanted was to see anyone. She'd hidden away from the people who worked on her father's ranch.

"Yes. I found I'm a creature of habit. Plus. it was easier to stay away from anyone who might gossip about me. I felt a bit like the Beast in *Beauty and the Beast*."

"I'm sure you were nothing like the Beast," Chris said.

"I was. No one could look right at me when I had the bandages off my face at first. I mean, the skin was trying to heal, but it wasn't pretty. Sometimes I wake up thinking that my face is still so damaged. It's scary."

"I hope that I can somehow find a way of making you forget that you ever had those scars."

"I don't want to forget," she said. "I need them to remind me of what a precious gift my life is."

"It is indeed," Chris said. They arrived at the swimming hole and dismounted.

The horses were all trained to stay when their reins were on the ground and Macy and Chris set up the picnic lunch quickly.

"I don't know about you, but I need a swim before we eat," Chris said.

"It's indelicate of me to say so, but I'm sweating," Macy said.

Chris laughed. "It looks like a healthy glow to me."

She gave him a quick kiss. She felt doubly blessed to be with him this afternoon. First, because of how sexy and attentive he was, but second because of the fear that she'd felt when she'd thought he was back in Royal for revenge.

"Thanks," she said. "Last one in has to cook dinner."

Chris stared at her for a second then said, "You're on."

Macy kicked off her boots and reached for the button at her waistband, undoing it quickly. She pushed her jeans down her legs and whipped her top and hat off at the same time, stripping down to her one-piece bathing suit in no time. She saw Chris hopping on one foot trying to get his pants and boots off at the same time as she scooted around him and ran toward the swimming hole.

His laughter followed her as she ran down the dock and jumped into the water and a second after her toes touched the water she felt Chris beside her and looked over at him as she entered the water.

"Tie," he said as he surfaced.

"I was ahead of you," she said.

"If you say so," he said.

They both treaded water and her smooth leg brushed his hairy one and she saw his pupils dilate. Suddenly it didn't really matter who'd won their little race. Chris kissed her hard and then took her hand and led her to the shallower water where he could stand up.

He pulled her into his arms and the sensation of her bathing suit against his chest was enticing. She wrapped her legs around his narrow waist and held on to his shoulders as she leaned up to kiss him once again.

She felt his hands on her butt as his mouth moved over hers. He thrust his tongue deep into her mouth, but it wasn't enough for her, she wanted more.

She tipped her head to the side to deepen the kiss and lifted her hands to his head to try to control the passion that was rising between them. But there was no controlling it and she felt more alive than she had in a long time as his hands moved over her body.

Ten

Chris felt as if it had been forever since he'd held Macy in his arms, and there was nothing he wanted more than to make her his completely. All his own doubts about her and if she'd leave him the way she had before were taken away.

It was funny that a moment so long ago could so totally define them, but it did. And he was determined to move them past it. They definitely knew each other better today than they had in the past, but that was just one area of their relationship. If pressed, he'd say they'd become good friends. And involving his mother in her project had been a nice gesture on Macy's part.

But he wanted more from her than nice gestures. What he really wanted—no, needed—was to make love to her. To bind her to him with sex and desire. Macy had other friends, but she'd had only one other lover and Chris aimed to erase that man from her memory forever.

He loosened the tie at the top of her halter-top one-piece bathing suit. The wet fabric stuck to her skin and he lowered his head and kissed her neck, rubbing his beard-stubbled cheek against her before taking one of the suit straps and tugging it down until it floated in the water. He kissed her collarbone, tasting the essence of woman and the cool water with it.

He got to the other strap and traced the outline of it with his tongue. Goose bumps spread down her arm and he wondered if her nipples had tightened from that touch of his mouth on her skin.

"Do you like my mouth on you?" he asked, nibbling at her skin while he spoke.

"I do," she said. Her voice was slightly husky and she rocked her pelvis forward so that her mound rubbed over his erection.

"Me too," he said. He put his hands on her waist and lifted her until the tops of her breasts were visible above the water. He leaned down and kissed them and then laved his tongue over the firm white globes.

He snaked his tongue out to caress first one then the other. She moaned and put her hands in his hair, rubbing his scalp as he toyed with her nipples. He straightened and brought her forward with his hands on her back and felt the tips of her breasts brush against his chest.

She arched her back. "I want more. I want to feel your mouth on me."

"My mouth has been on you," he said.

"I know, but it's not enough, Chris. I feel like I'm going to die if I can't touch you all over."

"I don't want that," he said, cupping her butt in his big hands. He rubbed her over his erection.

"Hold on to me," he said.

She tightened her legs around his hips and wrapped her arms around his shoulders. He walked toward the shore, scanning the horizon to make sure they were still alone. No one was out except them. When he got to their picnic blanket, he set her on her feet and stepped back to look at her.

Her thick blond hair was wet and clung to her face and shoulders. Her halter top was still tied under her breasts but the cups and the other strings were draped down on her stomach. He reached behind her and untied the last string of her bathing suit.

She reached for him. Touching his chest and running her fingers around his nipples. His erection hardened even more and the fabric of his swim shorts cut into him. He reached between them and pulled the front of his pants down so his manhood was free.

She gasped when she saw him naked. After a moment's hesitation, she brushed her fingers over his length, then leaned forward bending at the waist. He felt the tip of her tongue on him. He groaned her name and pushed his fingers into her wet hair, holding her to him for a minute and then pulling her up.

"I want to—"

"Not now," he said between gritted teeth. He wanted her to do that as well, but not right now. He was so close to coming and he really wanted to be inside her when he did that.

"Take off your bathing suit," he said.

She arched her eyebrow at him.

"Now," he said in his most commanding voice.

She stepped back and reached down to take it off. When she bent forward, her breasts swayed and he reached out and tweaked both of her nipples. She turned away to toss her suit on the blanket.

He put his hand on her shoulder so he could keep her from turning around and admired her from the back. There was more scarring on her back from the fire. He traced the scars with his finger, then pulled her back against his body and cradled her against him.

He was nestled between her buttocks, and his hands came around to sprawl on her flat stomach. One hand drifted lower to cover her feminine mound; the other drifted higher to tweak one of her nipples.

She shifted in his arms, her hips moving back and forth against him. He parted her nether lips and rubbed his finger lightly over them, and she turned to look at him. Lifting her mouth to his for a kiss.

He took her mouth with his as he let her turn in his arms, and he kept his finger between her legs, making sure she was hot for him. As hot as the late-August summer day. They were incendiary with each other, but he doubted they were going to last long. Even the cool water of the swimming hole hadn't dampened his desire.

He lifted her and slowly bent down until he was kneeling on the blanket and holding her in his arms. He lowered her to the blanket and she lay down on her back, spreading her legs.

He reached over her toward his jeans, which he'd tossed carelessly down, and found the condom he'd put in the back pocket earlier. He ripped open the packet while Macy reached out and cupped him in her hand. He gritted his teeth and let himself enjoy her caresses.

"Do you like that?" she asked.

"Very much."

She brought her other hand to his shaft and stroked him up and down while holding him lightly, and he knew he had to get the condom on quickly and get inside her.

He moved her hands and put the condom on. He came over her. Letting his body rub against hers. His chest over her breasts, his legs against hers and then the tip of his erection against the opening of her body.

He paused there right at the portal of her body and looked down at her. Her skin was flushed, her pretty pink nipples tight with desire and her legs sprawled wide to accommodate his hips.

He slowly entered her inch by inch, taking his time because he wanted this time to last. She caught the back of his neck and drew his head down to hers. "Take me, Chris."

Those words were the goad he needed to forget his control. He thrust hard and deep into her body; turning his head, he caught her mouth with his. Thrust his tongue deep to mirror the thrusting of his hips, and he felt her thighs shift along his and then the heels of her feet at the small of his back. She shifted herself against him. Each thrust into her body drove him closer and closer to his climax. But he didn't want to come without her. He reached between them and found her pleasure center, stroking it as he stroked her inside until she moaned low and deep in her throat and he felt her body tighten around his.

Only then did he give in and let himself come too. When he was spent, he laid his head on her breast, careful to brace his weight on his arms. She cradled him close to her naked body, her fingers toying with the hair at the nape of his neck.

He knew he should say something to her, but he had no words. He only knew that he had found the woman he'd been searching for without even realizing it. It was strange to him that it was Macy, because she was what had driven him from this place. He shifted to his side and cradled her in his arms on this hot afternoon and they both drifted to sleep.

Macy woke to the feel of Chris's mouth against hers. In the distance she heard the horses munching on grass, and a breeze stirred the leaves of the tree above them. She opened her eyes and he was right above her, his blue eyes staring down into hers. She smiled up at him.

She realized he was at her side leaning over her, his weight resting on one elbow. He traced her features with his fingertip. Now that they weren't so hot for each other she felt shy about him seeing her body. She closed her eyes as he fingered lightly over her eyebrows and down her nose. She felt his finger on the scar at the top of her lip and opened her eyes to see his reaction.

She reached for a T-shirt and started to put it on.

"You can't still be shy," he said. "Not now."

"I am. You are so perfect," she said. He was completely naked and she traced a finger over his chest.

"I'm not," he said. He took the T-shirt from her hands and sat up next to her. He traced the lines of her body.

She caught her breath at the way he watched her. It was as if he'd never seen anything as beautiful as her. She reached up, caressing his lips with her fingertips, then rolled to her side so she could see his body.

She felt as if she'd been reborn in his arms. She wasn't afraid of her femininity anymore.

She pushed him onto his back and then knelt beside him.

"What are you doing?"

"I want a chance to explore you," she said.

He propped himself up on his elbows. "Explore away."

She did. She started at his neck and shoulders, touching the strongly muscled part of his body before letting her fingers work their way down. He pulled her closer in his arms, cradling her against his chest. She lay there, just letting the peace of the moment wash over her. It had been too long since she'd experienced anything like this. She'd never felt such complete relaxation with another person.

It was odd to her that it would be with Chris Richardson.

Chris woke just as the sun was setting, waking Macy as well. They got dressed in relative silence. Though Chris had a hard time keeping his hands off her. She had changed his entire perspective today. He'd run the gamut of emotions as he'd realized the type of woman that he'd found in Macy.

He wanted to marry her and he wanted her to know that now, but he wouldn't ask her without a ring. Life was good right now and he had the time to make sure he got the right one. Macy deserved the best and that was exactly what she was going to get from him.

When they were dressed and had their spot cleaned up, he took his cell phone from his pocket and pulled her close to his side, tucking her into his shoulder, and lifted the phone to take a picture of them.

"Looks good. Will you text it to me?" she asked.

"Of course," he said. He took a minute to send it to her and then helped her onto her horse before getting onto his.

He took another picture of Macy on her horse with the breeze stirring her hair. She looked free and happy. Glancing at that picture, no one would ever guess that she'd had a life-threatening accident, and he was glad he'd come back into her life now.

When they reached the Reynolds Ranch, they called Tom, who came and picked up the horses. Macy looked tired, and as much as he wanted to spend the night with her, he knew he couldn't stay at her dad's house or have her to his mom's. He needed his own place in Royal.

"Do you have time for lunch tomorrow?"

"I think I could work you into my busy schedule," she said, smiling up at him.

"I've got a meeting in the morning at the club to discuss the new headquarters. Want to meet me there?" he asked.

"That sounds good," she said. They walked to the ranch house with its big wraparound porch. As a teenager he'd wanted nothing more than to sit on that swing with her and just hold her hand. Well, maybe a little more, but he'd have been happy with some hand-holding, but they'd never had a chance to do that.

"Thank you for everything," she said. "Your help at the fashion show yesterday really made it memorable."

He shook his head and pulled her into his arms. "I should be thanking you."

"Whatever for?"

"Having such a kind heart. Including my mom in your project gave her something to focus on instead of her health. I know you gave those kids in the Burn Unit something other than their pain to think about, and this afternoon you gave me a dream that I thought had been abandoned long ago."

She hugged him and put her head on his chest. "You gave me something special too. The entire day. I was so upset when I thought what Abby had said might be true. I never want to feel that way again."

"I don't want you to either, Macy," he said, tipping her chin up so he could see her eyes. He wanted to be sure she knew that he meant what he said from the bottom of his heart. "I promise never to hurt you."

She nodded. "I know you won't."

He lowered his head and kissed her. Held her in his arms, knowing in his heart that she was his now and he was going to get a ring and, tomorrow at lunch, he'd make it official. Ask her to marry him and then make her his wife as soon as she'd agree.

Macy Reynolds owned his heart and his soul and it was a bit silly to pretend she didn't. He wasn't ready to confess to that just yet. He wondered if he should ask Harrison for her hand.

"Does your dad know we are dating?"

"He may have his suspicions, but we haven't discussed it," she said.

"Does that mean he doesn't object?" Chris asked, pushing for an answer to the one question that really bothered him. Though Harrison had said he regretted interfering when they were younger, that didn't mean the older man would welcome him as a son-in-law.

"I honestly don't know. I'm not going to give you up, Chris. Not for anything."

"Not even a really nice car?" he teased.

She shook her head. "There is no material thing on this earth I want. And you are important to me."

"You're important to me too. I want…" He trailed off as a big Chevy half-ton pickup pulled up in the circle driveway. Harrison Reynolds got out of the truck and waved to the couple.

"Richardson? What are you doing here?" Harrison asked.

"I invited him to come out here and go for a ride," Macy said.

"Great. You are welcome to stay to dinner," Harrison said.

Chris wasn't sure he wanted to stay for the evening meal. Harrison would probably ask about the bids he hadn't won again and Chris didn't want to talk business. "As long as we don't discuss business."

"What else would we talk about?" Harrison asked.

"We could talk about my project at the Burn Unit, Dad. Don't you want to know how it turned out?"

"Of course I do, Mace. Come inside and I'll pour us some drinks."

Harrison held the door and Macy went in first, followed by Chris. He had a strange twilight zone moment as he realized he was having drinks with the very man who'd once told him to stay off his property and away from his daughter. He knew it was a long time ago, but for a second it felt just like yesterday, with Harrison holding the door.

"You okay?" Macy asked under her breath as her dad went to the wet bar.

"Fine." But he really wasn't. He didn't like being in this house with Harrison and Macy. He'd never had a comfortable time here.

"What'll you have, Macy?" Harrison asked.

"Martini, Dad. Do you want me to make it?" she said.

"Not at all. Chris?"

"The same," Chris said. Macy led the way to the big leather sofa and sat down. Chris sat next to her. Macy reached over and took his hand in hers.

Harrison glared at the two of them. Chris felt as if he was eighteen again. Chris dropped Macy's hand and stood up.

"I just remembered I have some work to finish. I better head out. Thanks for a lovely afternoon, Macy."

"You're welcome. I had a very special time."

"What was so special about it?" Harrison said.

"That I spent it with Chris," Macy said.

Harrison gave him another steely-eyed glare and Chris had the feeling that Harrison was more than ready to have him tarred and feathered.

"Walk me out?" he asked Macy.

She nodded and led the way to the door.

"Goodbye," Macy said, giving him a kiss.

"Bye," he said against her lips.

Harrison stood behind Macy, watching him. "Good-bye, sir."

"I'll see you tomorrow at the club for the development meeting, Richardson. We still have a lot to discuss," Harrison said.

Chris left with the feeling that tomorrow he and Harrison were going to be talking about a lot more than just business. And once he was on his own ground,

Chris wouldn't mind it at all. As he got in his car and drove away he shed those reservations of the past. He didn't have to kowtow to Harrison Reynolds. He was more than suitable for Macy, and Chris wasn't going to let anyone stand in the way of his having her.

Eleven

The club was packed full of past and present board members and other interested parties during the planning meeting. Chris already felt as if it was going to be a hell of a day. Abby Langley glared at him as she came into the room with some tall, thin guy with dark curly hair. He suspected that would be the candidate she was pushing for developing the new headquarters.

Brad was already seated and Chris made his way over to his friend and took a seat. "Morning."

"Glad you got here early. I just heard that Abby wants to propose someone else to do the development work," Brad said.

"I heard that last night. Any idea who it is?"

"Unfortunately for us, it's Floyd Waters. He's a member of the club," Brad said.

Chris shook his head. "I guess he's a shoo-in then?"

"Not really. A lot of the old guard isn't happy about

all the waves that Abby's making. I mean, she's only an honorary member," Brad said.

"So what do you want me to do?" Chris asked. "I could approach her and try to incorporate some of her ideas—"

"No. She's made this into a battle. She can have Floyd do her design. You and I will go ahead as we planned. I'm not worried about her or her candidate."

There was a lot of tension in Brad. Something Chris hadn't really seen in the other man before. This election at the club and the possibility of admitting women as members was making everyone here a little on edge. A part of Chris would be glad to return to Dallas where he didn't have to be involved in this intrigue.

"Okay. You should know that Harrison Reynolds will probably throw in with me to sway the vote. He is also a club member, so having the two of you on my side may be helpful."

"That's fine, but Harrison was good friends with Sebastian Hunter, so that may be why he is trying to align himself with me," Brad said.

"What did Hunter do?"

"Embezzled funds."

"Did Harrison profit from any part of the embezzling?" Chris asked. He hoped not, for Macy's sake. Surely if he did then he'd no longer be a member of the club.

"No, he didn't, but he seemed to not notice a few things that made some of the younger members question him."

Chris wasn't here to get involved in the politics, though. He'd present his development plan, talk about his past work and when it was over he'd walk away.

Work may have been the reason he first came here, but Macy and his mom were the main people tying him to Royal now. He touched his jacket pocket and felt the velvet box he'd placed in there earlier. He'd had to pull a few strings to get the local jeweler to open his shop up early this morning, but Chris was happy with the marquis-cut diamond ring he'd picked out.

Slowly a large number of women entered the meeting. All the sisters, wives and daughters of current members trailed in, and Chris shook his head. "This is going to be a long meeting."

"Damn," Brad said. "I should have made this a closed meeting."

"I don't think that would have gone over well," Chris said.

"You're right. Ready?"

"Yes," Chris said. Harrison took a seat next to him as Brad turned to his left to greet another board member.

"We need to talk after the meeting," Harrison said.

"I am supposed to have lunch with Macy."

"You can postpone it. Make it dinner instead," Harrison said.

"I'm not sure I want to do that."

"Yes, you do," Harrison said. "Now that you and Macy are dating again we need to talk."

Chris tightened his fist under the table. So the old man knew about him and Macy. And after all that had happened, Harrison still didn't approve of him. That's what that had to be about. But he had no time to worry about Harrison. He needed to focus on this meeting and on giving the best presentation he could.

A part of Chris felt as if he was on trial in front of all of Royal. Like the son of an oil rig worker wasn't good enough for the Texas Cattleman's Club. Not even for a rabble-rouser like Abby. And he hated that feeling. He'd proved himself on a much larger stage.

"Let's get this meeting started," Brad said, standing up. "Chris Richardson is here today to give us his bid on construction of the new headquarters and some additional buildings that I asked him to develop for the community."

"Before we get started, I'd like to ask for equal time for Floyd Waters," Abby said, also standing up.

"Why would we do that?" Brad asked.

"We are both candidates in this election," Abby said. "As the project won't be funded until after the voting, we should hear from both developers."

There was a lot of grumbling in the room as everyone tried to voice their opinion. Chris quickly realized that he was not going to get out of here in time for lunch. He sent Macy a text message asking if she'd meet him for dinner instead.

Sure. Is everything okay?

No, the club members are having a loud discussion, your friend Abby is stirring up trouble.

Good. TTYL.

Chris pocketed his phone and sat back in his chair waiting until the dust settled. It didn't take long for Abby to get her way, and Brad looked none too happy about it as he took his seat next to Chris again. And her developer was going to present first.

"She just keeps pushing," Brad said under his breath.

"You should be used to it by now. You've always been trying to one-up each other," Chris said.

"True enough, but it would be nice if she'd just once not argue about everything," Brad said.

Chris laughed. "No woman in Royal is ever going to do that."

"You are right, even my sister likes to argue," Brad said.

Chris didn't know Sadie very well, but he imagined she was strong-willed like her brother.

Chris listened to Floyd's ideas and presentation and had to admit they were good. When it came his turn, he did what he always did in these kinds of meetings and pushed everything from his mind except convincing everyone in the room he was the best man for the job. As he spoke, he kept in mind Harrison Reynolds and how he still thought that Chris wasn't good enough for Macy.

It was nearly lunchtime when Macy's phone rang. She hoped it was Chris telling her his meeting had ended. A lot of the other ladies of Royal were at the club observing the meeting as well. Macy had wanted to attend but had a follow-up appointment with Dr. Webb, which had turned out fine.

She had missed Chris last night and really didn't want to wait until tonight to see him. If it was Chris calling, they could still have lunch together.

"Reynolds Construction, this is Macy." She had it bad for Chris.

"Hello, dear, it's Maggie Richardson. Are you available to talk about some jacket designs I have for the boys for our next show?"

"As a matter of fact, I'm free for lunch today. Would that work for you?" Macy asked. Chris's mom had been a godsend at the last show and it was touching that his mother was ready to do another one.

"Yes, it would. I talked to Norma Jones—she's on the board at the hospital—and she would like to make your fashion show available to all the children, not just those in the Burn Unit," Maggie said.

"I like that. We can discuss it with her soon. I will try to set up a meeting," Macy said.

"I'm going to give her a call now and see if she can make it today," Maggie said.

"Okay. We can meet at the Royal Diner in forty-five minutes or so?" Macy suggested.

"That sounds good," Maggie said. "I hope I didn't overstep by instigating this meeting."

"Not at all. I think we had a great event the other day and everyone seemed to really enjoy it. I wanted to do another one," Macy said. "I have a few ideas on themes that we can use the next time."

"I can't wait to hear them," Maggie said. "I'll see you in a little while."

Macy hung up the phone thinking about how busy her life was now. She'd changed so much since her last surgery a few short weeks ago. Before that, she'd work at her home office or go riding, but that was about it. Now she was having lunch out and dating Chris. And she loved it.

She had finally gotten her life back. It wasn't the same one she'd had before and that made her happy. She continued working on the spreadsheet she was putting together and then left a little early to go to lunch. She parked her car off Main Street and walked to the diner.

But when she got there she remembered that someone in here had heard Chris talking about wanting revenge on her and she hesitated for a millisecond before reminding herself that she wasn't going to be daunted by gossip.

She put her shoulders back and walked into the diner with her head held high. She asked for a table near the window so she could see Maggie when she arrived.

Macy thought she saw one of the waitresses staring at her, and boldly Macy returned the stare until the girl walked over to her. "You look so familiar but I can't place the face, do I know you?"

"I'm not sure. I'm Macy Reynolds."

"Lucy Bell, I think we went to high school together."

"We did," Macy said. "You were on the cheer squad with me."

"I was. I just moved back to Royal."

They chatted for a few more minutes and decided to meet for drinks to catch up. Lucy was in touch with the rest of the cheerleaders and they had a weekly gabfest. Lucy invited Macy to join them the next time they met.

Lucy left when Maggie arrived. She was full of ideas. "Let's order and then I want to show you some of the sketches I did. I think I could have made the dresses better if I'd realized what kind of bandages I was dealing with," Maggie said.

"They were perfect."

Both women ordered a salad and diet cola and then started talking about fashion and clothing designs. "I think we should reach out to the parents at the Burn Unit and the patients in the cancer unit too."

"I agree, Macy. I will ask Norma for some names and numbers. Do you want me to call them?" Maggie asked.

"That would be great. I am busy at work."

"What do you do, dear?" Maggie asked.

"I'm a financial analyst for Reynolds Construction," Macy said. But then she felt embarrassed that she worked for her dad. "I used to work for a hotel chain, but after my accident…"

"No explanations are necessary. I am impressed by how much you are doing considering all you've been through."

Macy flushed at the compliment. "Look at you, just out of the hospital as well."

"It's different for me. My condition is a small heart murmur, nothing like recovering from an accident. Is it okay to mention it?"

Macy smiled kindly at the older woman. She was so earnest and blunt she reminded Macy a lot of Chris. "Yes, it is. Chris is very like you."

"Do you think so?"

"Yes, I do. He's a good man, your son," Macy said.

"I've always thought so. I hate that he lives so far away. I really miss having my son close by."

"I bet you do. Hopefully, we can come up with something to get him to come back here more often."

"We?"

"Yes, we. I want him here too," Macy said. "I know that I didn't treat Chris the way I should have in high school. But I've changed, and I really do care for your son now."

"Good. I was hoping that there was something developing between the two of you," Maggie said.

"Me too," Macy said.

The two women enjoyed the rest of their lunch and Macy realized how confident she felt, not just in herself, but also in her new relationship with Chris. It seemed as if she'd had to literally walk through fire to get to this point in her life but it was so worth it.

Chris hadn't been to a meeting this contentious before. Abby had a comment about every single stage of his development plan. He wondered if it was simply, as he and Brad had discussed, that she liked to argue, or if her attitude had anything to do with the fact that she thought he wanted revenge on one of her good friends.

Chris gave her the benefit of the doubt and tried to act as if she just wanted what was best for the club, but to his mind it seemed as though she and the other women wanted equal rights here so badly they were going to turn every decision into a battle.

Once the meeting was over, he and Brad hit the bar for a stiff drink. When Brad left, Chris had a scant minute to himself before Harrison walked up.

"What are you drinking?" the older man asked.

"Scotch neat," Chris said.

"I'll have one too…make mine a double," Harrison said to the bartender. "Let's go over there where we can talk and not be interrupted."

Chris thought about it for a minute and knew he needed to at least let Harrison know that no matter what he said, Chris was going to ask Macy to marry him. Even though he'd had enough arguing for the day, he nodded and walked over to a casual seating group made of large brown leather chairs. He sat down with his back to the door of the room.

Harrison joined him a minute later. "That was one hell of a meeting."

"I'll drink to that. After today I wonder if some of the potential members will change their minds about wanting in so badly," Chris said.

"Doubtful. Those women seem damn serious about it being their time. I liked your development ideas. You seem to know what the club needs."

"Thank you, sir," Chris said. He had thought that Harrison would jump in with his concerns about Macy, but given the long day they'd both spent talking about Texas Cattleman business, Chris guessed he shouldn't have been surprised.

"I still want in on that action."

"I know. We're not to that stage yet, but I will keep you in mind when we are."

"Good," Harrison said, sitting back in his chair. The man should have looked tired or at least a little less like a shark, but the years hadn't taken much of the starch from Harrison Reynolds. "Now, about you and Macy."

"What about us? We're both adults. I've got a good career and can definitely keep her in style.

"I heard a rumor that you only came back for revenge."

"That's not true. I told Macy this as well. What happened between the three of us was a long time ago and I'm not going to lie and say I wasn't pissed off back then, but I don't hold on to things like that. I've always been a man who looks forward to new things."

Harrison nodded. "I want to believe you, son. In fact, I do believe you, but I'm not sure Macy will."

"She does," Chris said. He was so glad that he had

heard about the rumor from Macy before Harrison confronted him. "Was that your only concern?"

"No. Even if you're not here for revenge, I know you live in Dallas. I don't want you playing fast and loose with Macy, so I'll have your word right now that you aren't going to cheat on her."

"Harrison, this entire conversation shows how little you know me. I'm not going to promise you anything," Chris said. His promises were for Macy and Macy alone. What went on between the two of them was private. He took a swallow of his scotch and then rubbed the back of his neck.

"Listen, I agreed to meet with you today and talk because I'm going to marry your daughter with or without your permission. I wanted to ensure there was no bad blood between us and I thought the best way to do that was over a drink."

"Good. I like that. If you marry Macy we can talk about merging our two companies. I like the sound of Reynolds-Richardson Builders."

"I'm not interested in merging our businesses," Chris said. He'd worked hard to have his own company and he liked being his own boss. As much as he wanted Macy in his life, he didn't want to deal with her father on a daily basis.

"I can make it hard for you two if you don't agree to my terms," Harrison said.

Chris couldn't believe what he was hearing, and Harrison was making him angry. "I'm not going to merge with you even if you offered me Macy on a silver platter."

Harrison nodded and then sat forward and motioned for Chris to lean in as well. "I can see now that you are sincere and that Macy means something to you. Do you love her?"

"I think she deserves to hear my feelings before you do. But you can trust me to take good care of her. I mean to ask her to be my wife tonight."

"I'll join you for dinner then," Harrison said.

"No. You won't. I'm going to ask her and not with an audience," Chris said. There were things he wanted to say to Macy, private things that he didn't want Harrison or anyone else to hear.

He'd never been in love with anyone before and he found he was oddly protective of her because of it. He wasn't sure what the future held and if they'd stay in Dallas or move back here, but he knew he was going to always keep an eye on Macy and keep her safe.

"Okay, but I can come over during dessert, and we haven't finished discussing a possible merger," Harrison said.

Chris rolled his eyes. Harrison was going to be an impossible father-in-law. The old man simply bullied and pushed until he got his way. "Did you do this to Macy all those years ago, just keep at her until you wore her down?"

Harrison gave him a cat-got-the-canary grin and nodded. "Hell, yes."

Chris thought it over for a minute and then finished his scotch and put the glass on the table in front of him.

"I guess if you are giving me your daughter's hand in marriage, the least we can do is talk about a merger."

"I knew you'd see it my way," Harrison said, holding out his hand for Chris to shake. "It makes good business sense and you've always been sweet on Macy, so having my approval will pave the way to your proposal and her acceptance."

There was a gasp and Chris glanced up to see Macy standing there wearing a skintight black dress with her hair up and some very sexy red lipstick on her mouth.

"Hey, babe, you look sexy tonight."

"Don't hey, babe, me."

Chris could tell Macy was upset, but for the life of him he couldn't figure out why. He thought she'd be happy he and her father were getting along.

Twelve

Macy was outraged. There was no other word for it. She'd spent the day thinking about what a great guy Chris was and then she walked into the club and heard him making some sort of bargain with her dad.

"I can't believe you two."

"What is it, honey?" her dad said.

"Calm down, Macy. Your dad and I have finally come to an understanding about you."

That made her even crazier. What was it about these men that they would use her as a pawn in their games. "I don't care what your understanding is. I'm not going to be a part of your deals. I thought you of all people would get that, Chris."

"I do, Macy."

But she wasn't listening to anything else he had to say. These men really made her so angry.

"It's not what you are thinking…what are you thinking by the way?" Chris asked.

"That my dad is offering you some kind of bribe."

"Well, that was a little negotiating on my part, Mace. Don't blame Chris."

"Dad, I'm so tired of you trying to plan my life. Didn't you see what happened to me when I thought I was on the road to a certain future? You should realize there are no guarantees."

Her dad stood up and walked over to her. "Now, listen here, girl, I'm not trying to run your life."

"You are, Dad, whether you realize it or not," Macy said. "It's partially my fault because I let you give me a job and moved into your house when I was recovering and then I was afraid to leave, but I'm not anymore."

"Good, that's all good. No need to be mad at me. I just want what's best for you and I know how to—"

"No, Dad. You do not. I quit. I'm not working at Reynolds Construction anymore and I'm going to speed up the timetable for moving out of your house."

"It's not a good idea to quit one job without having another one lined up," her dad said.

"It's not your concern, Dad. I'm taking back my life and I'll make my own decisions from now on."

Harrison shook his head. "Damn stubborn girl. Talk to her, Chris."

"Macy," he said.

But his betrayal hurt worse than her dad's and she held her hand up to him. "I can't talk to you right now, Chris."

"Honey, you are overreacting," he said.

She knew she wasn't. She'd wanted to believe in him, but the truth was, she was only seeing what she wanted to see, not the real man. "I am not overreacting, Chris. I think if you heard your mom and I making a deal for you, you'd be outraged. Why do you men think you can go behind my back and make plans for my life?"

"We don't think that," Chris said.

"Then why are you having a cozy little drink with my dad and saying you're going to ask me to marry you?" she demanded.

"Because I want you to be my wife," Chris said. "I'd think that's obvious. And I know you want to be too because you're not the kind of woman who can be intimate with a man and not want to be married to him," Chris said, leaning forward so that only she heard what he said.

She gasped and took a huge step away from him before she slapped him. How dare he! "I can't believe you just said that to me. I don't want to discuss this anymore. Have dinner with my dad and work on your little plan to make sure you both get the club development deal, but that's all you are getting in Royal, Texas, Christopher Richardson, because I'm not a bargaining chip for either of you to use."

She turned on her heel and stomped out of the club. As soon as she was outside she almost collapsed. She was tired, angry and so hurt she wanted to curl up in a ball and die. But she couldn't—not yet.

She heard the door open behind her. She turned, hoping it would be Chris, but it was a dark-haired man she didn't know.

She walked to her car and got in it. Once she started driving, she had no idea where to go and ended up at a hotel near the highway. She checked in and sat on the bed trying not to cry.

As bad as her car accident had been, she'd never felt this broken on the inside. Her looks could be fixed. Her bones healed and her scars would eventually fade. But this wound on her heart was going to be there for a very long time. She'd never recover from the pain that Chris had given her when he'd bargained with her father for a slice of his business and an opportunity to be a part of the Texas Cattleman's Club in exchange for marrying her.

She rolled onto her side, hugging the pillow close, and let the tears fall. No one was here to see the weakness, so she let her broken heart and her tears fill her for the night. Tomorrow she'd make plans and get ready to move on.

But just lying on the bed crying wasn't good enough for her. She had been through so much pain that wallowing in it didn't suit her at all.

She needed a plan of action. Something to give her focus. She'd have the movers get her stuff from her father's house tomorrow and then she'd call her old boss at Starwood. It was an international company—there had to be positions that would get her out of Royal. Because she thought it was time to leave.

That was the only way her father was going to understand she was serious and that she wasn't going to let anyone use her.

She reached for the notepad on the bedside table and started making a list. Lists appealed to her, so she jotted down a few things, but then her mind turned to Chris. Why couldn't he have just asked her to marry him?

She wouldn't have even minded if later on he tried to finagle some sort of deal with her dad as long as he'd asked her to marry him first.

That wasn't true. She wanted him to love her the way

she loved him and she knew she'd never do anything
to hurt Chris even after he'd made her this mad. She
wanted to make herself fall out of love with him, but
this time she hadn't had a schoolgirl crush on him and
it was going to take a lot of time to heal this wound.

Two days later Macy still wouldn't return any of his
calls and Chris was left with a major decision. He could
either stay in the running to do the development project
and have Macy think that was more important to him
than she was, or drop out and then figure out how to
get her back.

It was surprisingly one of the easiest decisions he'd
ever had to make. He picked up his phone and called
Brad.

"It's Chris," he said when Brad answered. "I'm going
to have to withdraw my name from consideration for
doing the development at the club."

"Why? What happened?" Brad asked.

"I have too many commitments," Chris said. And he
had a big one he was planning to make with Macy. She
was the only thing that mattered. He'd known that when
they'd made love at the swimming hole. He should have
told her how he felt then.

"Is there anything I can say to change your mind?"
Brad asked.

"No, I'm sorry. But Floyd seems like he'll do a good
job for you."

"He does, but Abby found him."

"She will never let you forget it either," Chris said.

"Tell me about it. Thanks for the call," Brad said
before hanging up.

Chris had to make some decisions about his future

and he needed a plan to get Macy back. He had to clear the air with Harrison. He called the older man and got his voice mail. "This is Chris Richardson. I'd like to talk to you. Call me at my office."

Then he called the florist and ordered a dozen roses to be sent to Macy. He knew she was living in her old house now because…well, he'd driven by there last night. And he'd seen her through the window. He'd felt like a creepy stalker, so he hadn't gone to her door.

He didn't want to screw up with her again. The next time they met face-to-face he was going to get her to agree to be his wife and then they'd never be apart again. He could do that, just barely.

He tried to work, but wanted to talk to Harrison. Nothing was going to be okay in his life until he had Macy back by his side. It had been six hours since he'd left his message for Harrison, so he called again and finally got through. Macy's dad agreed to meet him at his office.

Tanja knocked on his door just as he hung up. "Um…a floral-delivery guy just dropped off a dozen roses… He said that the lady who you sent them to refused them."

"Dammit."

"Sorry, Chris. Is there anything I can do?" Tanja asked.

"You can take the roses home," he said. "I'm expecting Harrison Reynolds. Show him in as soon as he gets here."

Chris figured if he had Macy on his home turf he'd have a better chance of winning her over. So he started making plans in his head. He'd have his private plane—no, that wouldn't work—she wouldn't get on his plane if he sent it for her. He'd have to find a plane and then get her to Dallas. He'd have her brought to him and then—what? He'd pour his heart out.

"I'm here. What did you want?" Harrison said as he let himself into the office. The door closed firmly behind him.

"We need to talk and I'm not taking any chances of anyone overhearing what I have to say."

"Fair enough, I owe you at least that. Have you heard from Macy?"

"No," Chris said. "I guess she was good to her word about quitting."

"Hell, yes. She moved out too. Did it while I was at work," Harrison said.

"She's at her old house," Chris said.

"I know," Harrison said. "I sent one of my guys by yesterday to check on her and she sent him back with a mouthful for me."

Chris had to chuckle. Macy was a spitfire and she was his and he wanted her back. "I love your daughter, Harrison, and I'm going to do whatever I have to in order to get her back. I already withdrew from the Texas Cattleman's Club development."

"I figured you would. You don't really need the business," Harrison said.

"Well, no business deal is worth more to me than Macy is and I aim to prove that to her."

"Good. I'm sorry I pushed so hard for the merger the other day. I just...Macy's all I've got and I want the company to be an inheritance for her and her kids. And I know if I let it go to someone who isn't related, it wouldn't be as prosperous as it would be in your hands."

"Thank you for that. We can discuss it after Macy and I have been married at least five years."

Harrison chuckled at that. "I don't think so."

"Harrison," Chris said, leaning forward so the older man would understand how serious he was. "You had better understand that Macy is my one chance at happiness. You ruined it for me once. I'm not going to let you do that again."

"I get that, boy."

"Don't call me boy. I'm not some oil rigger's son anymore. I'm definitely your peer and I am going to be your son-in-law. If we have to have an uneasy truce, that's fine with me, but I'm hoping you will want more than that."

Harrison sat back in his chair studying Chris. "What are you going to do?"

"I'm going to head back to Dallas and then convince her to come back to me. I can't fight for her in Royal. We have too many gossips and all that old history here. I want to start fresh."

"Good. I want to be there. Not when you ask her to marry you, but the next day. Macy's all I've got left in this world and I don't like not seeing and talking to her."

Chris understood that. His mother was the same way. "Okay, will you bring my mom to Dallas with you? We can all have breakfast when she agrees to marry me."

"*If* she agrees," Harrison said.

"I'm banking on the fact that I've only hurt her. Hurt I can make up for. If I've made her stop loving me…"

"I don't think you have," Harrison said. "Did you see the way she yelled at me? I was the one she took most of her anger out on. I think she didn't want to say anything to you she'd regret."

"I hope so," Chris said. But he knew he deserved her anger. Given the situation with Harrison from their youth, Chris should never have been talking to him without Macy by his side. She'd been unsure of him from the beginning.

"I need someone who she will listen to," Chris said, talking more to himself.

"You need Abigail Langley. Macy trusts her. They've been good friends through some dark times. I think she's the one who will be your best bet," Harrison said.

"She hates me," Chris said.

"She doesn't hate me. Let me call her and see what we can do," Harrison said.

"Why are you helping me?" Chris asked.

"I misjudged you, and I have never seen Macy happier than she's been these past few weeks. I know you'll find a way to win her back and I want to be part of it."

"Why?"

"Because you're going to be the father of my grandchildren and I'm going to want to see them."

Chris had a chuckle at that. He was determined to win Macy back, but he was far from sure that he could do it as easily as Harrison seemed to think he could. Chris sat back in his chair ready to put in as many hours as he had to in order to get Macy back.

Macy turned another florist away—this was the fourth one in as many days—and went back to work in her home office. She was still mad. Once she'd decided that crying wasn't part of the solution, she'd been energized working on her to-do list. The list gave her something to focus on instead of missing Chris. And she did miss him.

She couldn't sleep at night because she woke up

dreaming of him. That was the hardest time. During the day she made calls for jobs—her lead at Starwood had fallen through—and worked with the hospital on setting up their next fashion show, which would take place in December. Maggie Richardson's friend Norma from the hospital had been a godsend.

Macy hadn't gone to see Maggie, not wanting to run into Chris. But she was going to have to approve Maggie's new clothing designs sometime this week. She checked her watch and figured that Chris would still be at work at this time of day.

She hopped into her car and made the quick drive across town. Maggie answered the door with a big smile on her face.

"Hello, Macy. I'm so glad you could come over today," she said.

"Me too. Let me see those sketches. I want to get out of here before Chris comes home," Macy said.

"Oh, he's gone back to Dallas," Maggie said. "I thought, well, I thought that was why you came over today."

"I didn't know. What about his work at the club?"

"He withdrew his name, said he was too busy," Maggie said.

Macy didn't know what to say or how to act. She had a million questions, but since she'd refused to answer any of his calls, she didn't think it would be fair to grill his mom about why he'd turned down the business and left Royal.

"I'll go get the sketches for you to approve," Maggie said.

Macy was left alone in the living room and she drifted over to the window to glance out at the backyard.

She was confused. She'd been keeping busy until...until what? She didn't know, but a part of her had hoped that maybe he'd come and beg her forgiveness.

But all those flowers she'd returned must have sent the message that she never wanted to talk to him again. That hadn't been her intent. What *was* her intent? Knowing he'd left cooled her anger. Now she wanted to talk to him. But it was too late. He'd moved on and once again left her behind in Royal.

"Here they are," Maggie said, coming back into the room. Macy took the sketches to the dining room table and spread them out. Since the event would take place in December they were doing a Christmas theme and she looked at the little elf costumes for the boys and girls and wanted to smile.

"Why did he just leave like that?" Macy asked.

"I don't know. He did say he'd be back for the Christmas show."

She didn't want to have to wait until December to see him, but she'd have to. Unless she accepted his flowers. But she wanted more of an apology than a bouquet of roses. He'd really hurt her.

"These are fine, Maggie," Macy said. "I'd love to stay and chat a little more, but I've got another meeting at the hospital." She left a few minutes later and got in her car and just sat there. Chris had left Royal without telling her? What had she expected?

How was she going to make her to-do list keep her from calling Chris? Keep her from trying to figure out if he still wanted her or if he'd given up on her altogether?

She pulled her cell phone from her purse. She unlocked it and hit the pictures icon. There was the photo of her and Chris. The one time they'd made love and it had been glorious. They both looked happy there.

How had things gotten to this point? Had she jumped to conclusions? Should she go and talk to her dad?

"Ugh," she said, leaning forward to rest her head on the steering wheel.

She put the car in drive, and her phone rang as she pulled back into her driveway. It was Abby.

"Hey. What's up?"

"I need your help with the flamingos again."

The last time the flamingos had been moved, it was to the club, and she and Chris had their first kiss right in front of the flock. She felt a sting of tears.

"I can't."

"I haven't even told you when we are doing them," Abby said.

"Chris went back to Dallas."

"Oh, man, you're kidding me. I thought he was still sending you flowers every day," Abby said.

"He is, but I guess today might have been the last time. I don't know what to do."

"Well, getting out of your house might help," Abby said.

"We kissed in front of the flamingos, I just can't help you do them," Macy said.

"Fair enough. Let me think about it and I will call you back."

Macy hung up the phone and went into her house. It was only as she closed the door behind her that she realized she was retreating from the world the way she had when she'd had her accident. Today was the first day she'd left the house since she'd quit her job with her father and told Chris she wouldn't marry him to sweeten a business deal.

She'd turned back into the same woman she'd been before Chris had arrived in Royal. She suspected that if she hadn't run into Chris that day in the hospital she would have just gone back to her routine of not socializing and hiding away from the world.

She didn't want to be that person. She liked getting out. She'd been looking forward to going to the Royal High School Cheerleaders Gabfest, but then had canceled because of Chris. She had to figure out how to live her life.

And she also had to decide if she wanted Chris in her life. She leaned forward and looked in the hall mirror. She had a new face and a body that was fully recovered. Had she worked that hard only to walk away from love?

"Hell, no," she said to her reflection.

She needed a plan and a new to-do list. A list that would get her the one thing she truly wanted—and that was the man she loved as her husband.

Chris was going to learn that if he made her mad they'd fight it out, but he had to stop running away and she had to stop hiding. That was the first thing she'd say to him after she hugged him and told him she loved him.

Now she just had to figure out how to find him in Dallas. She figured she could get Maggie's help if she told the older woman how much she loved Chris.

Thirteen

"There is a call for you from Abigail Langley. She said it's urgent and she must speak with you today," Bettina said. Bettina was Chris's administrative assistant in Dallas.

"Put her through," Chris said. He turned his chair so that he could see downtown Dallas. The city had been home to him for most of his adult life and yet this week he'd felt lost here. Adrift because he didn't know how to get through to Macy. Now he had this one chance to convince Abby to help him.

"This is Chris," he said into the speaker phone. She had to at least be happy that he was out of the running for the Texas Cattleman's Club's new development. Having her man get the job would give her an edge over Brad.

"It's Abby Langley. Harrison said you wanted to talk to me," she said.

"That was three days ago," Chris said. As soon as he said, it he regretted it, but he was tired of waiting to get Macy back and she hadn't returned any of his calls or accepted one bouquet of flowers he'd sent.

"Do you still need me?" she asked, sounding very impatient.

More than he wanted her to know. If he could have figured out how to get Macy back on his own, he'd already have her in his arms, but he needed help to do this. "Yes, I do. I want Macy back and she won't take my calls."

"I don't blame her. Women shouldn't be bartered," Abby said.

Chris was tired of being blamed for something that wasn't entirely his fault. He hadn't bartered for Macy and he never would. He wanted her so badly that he'd pay any price to have her back.

"You should get your facts straight. That wasn't the situation," Chris said.

"Well, that's what Macy thinks. What do you need me to do?" she asked.

Chris had the feeling that if he didn't say the right thing Abby would hang up on him. And as much as that irritated him, it also made him glad that Macy had a friend like Abby who not only had her back but would go to bat for her.

"Can you bring her to Dallas? She won't come for her dad or me, but I thought maybe you could suggest a girls' trip. I'll pay for everything." He'd give up his entire fortune. All the money he'd worked so hard for and saved like a miser to prove to the people of Royal that he was a success—he'd give it all up for her.

"If I do this for you, you will owe me a favor,"

Abby said. He could almost hear the gears turning as she thought of the way to work this situation to her advantage.

"What kind of favor?" he asked.

"Your expertise on Floyd Waters's development efforts," she said.

"Okay, but you do everything the way I ask for it to be done," Chris said. He could handle giving advice to Waters. The man was a solid developer and with some more experience would probably be giving Chris a run for his money. But Macy was something different. He didn't want Abby going off on her own plan. Everything had to be the way he wanted it.

"What do you have in mind?"

"Do you have a plane?"

"Yes. So I'm bringing her to Dallas?"

"She'd be suspicious if she saw my plane."

"Agreed. Why are we coming to Dallas again?" Abby asked.

"Girls' weekend."

"Great, but once you scoop her up what am I going to do?" Abby asked.

"Go back to Royal and continue your campaign to become the next president of the Texas Cattleman's Club."

She laughed. "Why should I help you with this? Are you going to promise to never hurt her again?"

Chris had done little else but think about that very thing for the past four days. "I love her, Abby."

"Do you really?"

"Yes. Would I be begging you for help if I didn't? I could leave Royal and never look back but I can't—won't—leave Macy behind. She's too important to me."

"Promise me you won't hurt her, Chris," Abby said.

"I'd rather die than hurt her again," Chris admitted.

"That's good enough for me," she said after a pause.

"Okay… Thanks… I need you to bring her to Knox Street on Friday. You can say you are going shopping and I will surprise her there. Which store will you go to first?"

"I…I think Pottery Barn. She's just moved back into her house and she needs some stuff for it."

"I'll be there. Can you text me when you land?"

"I will," Abby said. "If she doesn't want to see you, Chris, I'm going to take her back on the plane."

"Fair enough. If she doesn't want me then I will bow out of her life. I want her to be happy and smiling, not hurt because of anything I've done or that she thinks I've done."

"You're a good man, Chris."

"I try," he said and hung up the phone.

He stood up and left his office. "I'm going out for the rest of the afternoon," he said to Bettina on his way out.

He headed downtown to Knox Street and checked out the location where she'd be. There was a big parking lot in the back of Pottery Barn and for the right price Chris was able to secure half of it for Friday afternoon.

He knew everything hinged on his plan. He wanted the right band to be playing and enough flowers to make her think she'd stumbled into the Garden of Eden. He walked up and down Knox Street finding all the right vendors and getting everything set up.

He had to wait two more days to see her again and he wasn't too sure he could do it. So he holed up in his office and started working on the plans for his dream home. Every room he added he imagined Macy in it. He thought about her home in Royal and put in touches of the things that he knew she liked.

It made him feel closer to her doing this. He continued working on the plans day and night until it was Friday morning. He took extra time with his appearance and when he got the text from Abby saying they were landing in Dallas he wiped his sweaty palms on his pants and got in his Porsche.

He drove to Knox Street and waited, hoping that this time when he saw Macy he'd be able to give her the ring he had in his pocket and that she'd say yes to being his wife.

He didn't know if he'd be able to let her go if she didn't say yes. He almost forgot to breathe when he saw the limo pull into the parking lot and then the door opened.

Macy had been more than happy to accept Abby's invitation to come to Dallas. She wanted to be closer to Chris. The flowers had stopped the day she'd found out he'd left Royal, and she had his business address, so she figured while she was here, she'd call him and see if they could talk. She was more than ready to start over with him.

"I'm so glad we can finally come to Dallas to celebrate your recovery."

"Me too," Macy said. "And your suggestion that I buy things for the house was a good one. I need to redo all the rooms. They feel stagnant, as if they are part of my old life."

"I bet they do," Abby said. "After Richard died the house still felt like him. I can't really explain it."

Macy reached across the seat to squeeze her friend's hand. "I understand what you mean. We both need this weekend away. I'm glad you could take a break from campaigning."

"I had a minor victory when Chris withdrew his name," Abby said with a smile.

"Yay!" She was happy for her friend, even though Abby's victory at the Texas Cattleman's Club had directly led to her not knowing where Chris was exactly. Not that she in any way blamed Abby.

"Where are we staying?" Macy asked. She hadn't asked many questions, since Abby's offer to fly them to Dallas for a shopping trip seemed the solution she'd been searching for.

"It's a surprise," Abby said.

The flight was quick and soon they were on the ground and in the limo. "My dad used to bring me here to go back-to-school shopping."

"I remember. He has always doted on you," Abby said.

"Yes, he has. It's been hard not talking to him, but I want him to realize he can't keep playing around with my life."

Abby nodded. "You made the right decision. So when are you going to forgive him?"

"I think I already have. We're all each other has and knowing that he's only looking out for me…well, to be honest, I don't know what he was thinking to try to use his business to schmooze Chris."

Macy had been over that situation in her head several times and no matter how hard she tried she just couldn't figure out why her dad had done that. He was the kind of man who'd never let go of his company to anyone.

The limo pulled to a stop and the driver came around to open the door. Abby gestured for Macy to get out first and she got out and stopped in her tracks. Chris stood in front of her wearing a tux.

A band started playing "You're Beautiful." The lead singer sounded similar enough to James Blunt that she stopped to double-check it wasn't him.

Chris walked over to her holding out his arms. She hesitated, but Abby got out of the car behind her and nudged her toward Chris. "You know you want to go to him."

"I do," she said.

Chris pulled her into his arms. "I would sacrifice anything for you, Macy. You are the true prize of my life and without you I have nothing."

She held him close.

"I love you so much," he said.

"I love you too, Chris. More than I thought I could."

Chris got down on one knee while the band continued to play and took a black velvet box from his pocket. He held it in one hand and opened it. She caught a sparkling glint off the stone before he took her hand in his.

"Macy Reynolds, I fell for you the first time you flashed me that sexy little smile of yours and I was a fool to let you go when I was eighteen. Please let me make up for the years we lost by spending the rest of our lives together."

"Christopher Richardson, there is nothing I want more than to be your wife and spend the rest of my life by your side."

Chris let out a loud whoop of joy and put the ring on her finger. She didn't even have a chance to look at it before he was kissing her and lifting her in his arms and spinning her around.

"We're never going to be apart again," he said.

"That suits me perfectly," she said.

The next morning Chris woke her with a kiss on the lips. "Good morning, my beautiful fiancée."

"Good morning to you, husband-to-be," she said. She'd had time to admire the ring yesterday afternoon and it was exquisite. Even Abby had agreed. She'd stayed for dinner with them but then had gone back to Royal.

"What are our plans for today?" she asked, rolling over on her side so that the sheets fell off her and bared her breasts to his gaze.

"Breakfast and then how about a little venue research," he said, reaching out to cup her breasts in his hands.

"You want to get married in Dallas? I kind of wanted it to be in Royal," she said.

"If that's what you want then we will do it there. Maybe on your father's ranch?"

"Yes, but I think I have to call him and smooth things over with him first."

"We can do that after breakfast," he said, kissing her soundly.

Macy was never going to get used to waking up next to him. She was so happy that Chris had come back to Royal and they'd had this second chance at love. The real tragedy in her life would have been missing out on this.

They made love in the shower and then got dressed. When they got downstairs, Macy saw that Chris's housekeeper had set up a breakfast buffet on the patio and when she stepped out back by the pool she saw why.

"Dad?"

"Hello, Macy. I hope you don't mind, but I wanted to be here to say congratulations and to ask you to forgive me for trying to toy with your life."

Her dad looked tired and worried. She went over to him and gave him a hug. "Of course I forgive you. I know you were only concerned for me."

"And for your future," he said. "Chris has the ability to keep Reynolds Construction going strong long after I'm gone, but I'm not pushing for that anymore. This is about you and him now."

She kissed his cheek, realizing that her dad wasn't going to stop pushing for what he wanted and she knew now that Chris loved her and didn't need anything else in his life to be happy.

"Thank you, Daddy. I'm so glad you are here this morning."

"Me too," he said, giving her one of his big bear hugs that made her feel wrapped up in his love.

Maggie walked out on the patio next and Macy went over and gave Chris's mom a kiss. She looked happy this morning as she lifted Macy's hand to look at her engagement ring.

"I'm so glad you two resolved your problems. I didn't like it when you were split up."

"Me neither," Chris said.

"Me neither," Macy said at the same time.

He twined their hands together and led the way to the table for breakfast. They spent the morning talking about their plans for the future and Macy knew she'd found more than she'd ever expected to when she found

Chris. She'd found love and the promise of a future that had everything she'd ever dreamed of.

Chris lifted her hand to his mouth and kissed the back of it.

"What are you thinking about?" he asked.

"How great our future is going to be," she said.

"It is going to be great," Chris agreed. "And we have a great story to tell our kids about how Grandpa tried to break us up, but we didn't let him."

"You might not want to tell that story, Chris," Harrison said.

"Why not?"

"What if you end up with a headstrong girl like Macy? She'll be running wild with all kinds of boys and telling you that you are acting like me if you try to stop her," Harrison said with a big laugh.

Chris shook his head. He looked forward to having a girl with Macy's pretty eyes and features who'd make him crazy as long as she had. With Macy by his side he could do anything and would be very happy.

"Are you two planning to settle down in Royal?" Harrison asked.

"We haven't really had a chance to discuss that, but I'd like to divide our time between Dallas and Royal," Chris said.

"I like that idea," Macy added.

"Me too," said Maggie.

"We can still do business together," Harrison added. "Now that we've cleared up our misunderstanding—"

"Misunderstanding? My company didn't do anything wrong. You consistently bid higher than everyone else," Chris said goodnaturedly.

"You get what you pay for in the building business,"

Harrison said. "But now that you and Macy are settling down I might give you a family discount."

Macy couldn't help but laugh at the way her father said that. She suspected that despite the respect he and Chris held for each other they'd continue to butt heads.

She didn't let that bother her. Everything that Chris did seemed to please Macy, and they both looked forward to a life of happiness and love and laughter together.

* * * * *

AN AFTER-HOURS AFFAIR

BY
BARBARA DUNLOP

Barbara Dunlop writes romantic stories while curled up in a log cabin in Canada's far north, where bears outnumber people and it snows six months of the year. Fortunately she has a brawny husband and two teenage children to haul firewood and clear the driveway while she sips cocoa and muses about her upcoming chapters. Barbara loves to hear from readers. You can contact her through her website at www.barbaradunlop.com.

For Marcelle
in honor of our final writers conference.

One

Jenny Watson knew a bad idea when she heard one.

"It's not a date," she tartly informed her best friend, Emily Kiley, kicking off her shoes and curling one jean-clad leg beneath her on Emily's bed.

Emily called from the depths of her closet. "Just because he doesn't call it a date, doesn't mean you can't look your best."

"He's my boss. And it's a business function."

"It's a wedding."

"A Texas Cattleman's Club wedding," Jenny corrected. "And he was invited in his capacity as Interim President."

Emily emerged from the closet carrying something made of dark burgundy chiffon. "I was thinking this one." She draped the dress along her body, revealing a one-shoulder, sleeveless creation with a wide-fitted waist, and a two-layer, A-line skirt that dropped to midthigh.

"Ha, ha," Jenny mocked, leaning back against the oak headboard.

Emily knew full well that Jenny would never touch a style

that was so off-the-runway sophisticated, and she'd definitely never wear a color that bold.

"It'll look great with an updo." Emily swirled around to the corners of the room as if she was waltzing. "You can borrow my black rhinestone sandals. And I've got those fabulous teardrop earrings and the matching necklace. The diamonds are synthetic, but there's no way to tell."

"I'm not wearing that dress," Jenny insisted.

"Why not?"

"Do you need me to write you a list?"

"Come on," Emily cajoled. "Live a little, girl. You'll look gorgeous, and Mitch will absolutely sit up and take notice."

"I'll look foolish." Jenny wasn't showing up in front of her friends and neighbors in Royal, Texas, looking like some kind of Manhattan diva. "There's nothing wrong with my black dress."

It was her perennial favorite—a sleeveless, square-necked jersey knit that flowed to her knees. She combined it with a short, sheer black cover that fastened at her throat. It was the perfect combination of classic and chic.

"And how many times has Mitch Hayward seen you in that?"

"A couple," Jenny admitted, seeing no need to do the math.

Mitch didn't care what she wore. He wanted an uncomplicated woman on his arm, someone to help him work the event. Her boss liked to keep tabs on the members of the Texas Cattleman's Club. He prided himself on recalling details of everyone's lives, and Jenny knew she was a big help in that department.

"You've had a crush on him since you were twelve," Emily pointed out.

"'Crush' being the operative word," Jenny put in. And it had been over a long time ago. "The man left town when I was only sixteen."

Quarterback Mitch Hayward had gone to college in Dallas on a full football scholarship. He'd come back to work in Royal for the first two summers. But after that, his successful sports career had kept him on the road. Up until last year, when a shoulder injury had brought him back home.

"He's been back for twelve months," Emily pointed out.

"That long?" Jenny plucked at the bedspread, pretending she didn't remember the exact date, the exact hour, the exact minute Mitch Hayward had returned to Royal. "I guess time flies."

Emily plunked down on the bed beside her. "You are *such* a bad liar."

Jenny heaved a sigh, feeling the need to inject some reality into the situation. "I am not going to make a fool of myself by dressing up for Mitch."

"Then dress up for Rick Pruitt and Sadie Price." Emily referred to the bride and groom. Rick was a longtime member of the Texas Cattleman's Club and well respected throughout the region.

"Like they're going to care what I'm wearing," said Jenny.

Since Rick had rushed off to Houston in July to bring Sadie and their two-year-old twins back home to Royal, the ecstatic couple had eyes only for each other.

Emily reached out to grasp Jenny's forearm, her voice taking on a tone of urgency. "It's do or die, Jen."

Talk about melodramatic. "Do or die, what?"

"I've watched you pine away over him for a year now. Either make a play for Mitch, or start dating other guys."

"I'm not pining away."

But as Emily stated the bald truth, Jenny felt her chest tighten and her stomach contract with apprehension. All year long, she'd tried desperately to ignore her attraction to Mitch, telling herself it was a childhood crush that she was long since over.

"You're about to turn thirty," said Emily.

"So are you."

"That's right. And I have a plan."

"A plan for turning thirty?"

"A plan for my life," said Emily, her gaze taking on a dreamy quality and drifting to the window behind Jenny. "If I don't meet a man, *the* man…" Then she frowned, and her eyes narrowed. "Well, at least a man who might be the man, by my birthday next month, I'm going to have a baby anyway."

Jenny straightened in shock. She couldn't believe what she was hearing. "A single mom? Are you kidding me? Do you have any idea—"

"I want children."

"I know from experience how bad that can turn out."

"We're not talking about your childhood." Emily glanced at her watch and hopped up from the bed. "In fact, we're still talking about the wedding tonight. I can tell you, if I had a thing for a guy like Mitch, and if that guy was anywhere within a hundred miles of here, I'd damn well be doing something about it."

"You would not."

"I would." Emily nodded decisively. "Come on, Jen. What's the risk? He doesn't notice, no harm done. You simply showed up to some friends' wedding in a nice dress. But if he notices, it's a whole new ball game."

"If he doesn't notice," Jenny began, telling herself it was an academic argument, since she wasn't really considering the dress, "then it's game over."

Compassion rose in Emily's blue eyes. "If he doesn't notice you in this, it was game over anyway. Wouldn't you rather know?"

Jenny started to shake her head, but then she stopped. Did she truly want to spend the next year, or two, or three, longing for a man who wasn't remotely interested in her? Would she rather keep the fantasy alive, or would she rather face the truth, no matter how hurtful?

"If he's not into you, Jen, then you can move on. You have to move on."

Jenny catalogued her options, considering every angle as dispassionately as humanly possible. But, despite her efforts to be strictly analytical, her emotions crowded in. Her heart rate increased, heat prickling her skin, as she silently admitted Emily's advice had merit.

Perhaps it truly was now or never.

"Be a woman about it," said Emily, holding the dress forward, an expression of hopeful encouragement in her eyes.

Jenny steeled her nerves.

She took a bracing breath and rose from the bed, snatching the dress from Emily's grasp. "I can't believe I'm doing this."

"Shower first," cautioned Emily, taking back the dress. "And shave your legs. We have exactly four hours to completely make you over."

"I'm not—"

Emily gave her a gentle shove toward the bathroom. "Oh, yes, you *are.*"

By the time Emily had styled Jenny's hair, applied her makeup, helped her into the dress and clipped on some jewelry, Jenny was a nervous wreck. Emily had refused to let her look in the mirror until the process was complete, and Jenny now stood in the middle of the bedroom balancing on dainty, high-heeled sandals. The fancy dress rustled against her thighs. Her face was tight with carefully applied makeup. And she had walked through a mist of Emily's most expensive perfume.

Finally, Emily stood back to survey her. "You ready?"

"I've been ready for three hours."

Emily's grin went from ear to ear. "You look amazing."

"I'm going to fall off the shoes."

"No, you won't."

"I hate wearing my contacts."

"Buck up. This is going to be worth it."

"The black dress would have been perfectly fine."

"The black dress wouldn't have changed your life."

Jenny frowned at her friend. Nobody's life was getting changed tonight. Mitch wasn't going to spy her from across the Texas Cattleman's Club hall, realize he'd never seen the real Jenny before and rush to pull her into his arms.

Never going to happen.

Which was depressing.

After tonight, she'd never be able to delude herself again.

"Here we go," said Emily, pulling her walk-in closet door closed to line up the full-length mirror.

Jenny looked into the mirror. Her eyes focused, and she blinked in astonishment.

The woman staring back didn't look anything like her.

"Something's wrong," she said to Emily.

"Huh?"

"That's not me."

Emily laughed. "*That* most certainly is you."

Jenny shifted experimentally. The sandals elongated her calves, tanned from swimming in the lake all summer. Her neck looked longer than usual, her arms more graceful, and the updo of her thick strawberry blond hair was complemented by Emily's glamorous earrings. The necklace winked at her, while her artificially lengthened lashes blinked heavily over her green eyes.

The neck of the dress made the most of her cleavage. And her bare shoulder felt decadently sexy. For some reason, her waist seemed narrower than usual. Maybe it was the full skirt, or the way the cut of the bodice accentuated her breasts.

Nervous sweat popped out on her brow. "I can't go out like this."

"What? Afraid you'll stop traffic?"

"Afraid I'll get propositioned."

"Good grief. You look like a movie star, not a hooker."

"I feel like a hooker."

"Yeah? Tell me, what does a hooker feel like?" Emily pulled a small jeweled purse out of her top drawer and snagged Jenny's bag from where she'd dropped it on the bay window's padded bench seat.

"This isn't funny." Panic began to swell in Jenny.

The makeover was all fine and good as a fantasy, but there

was no way she could leave Emily's house looking like this. The gossip would swirl around Royal for months to come.

How could she have let this happen?

How could she have been so foolish?

She swallowed. "We have to take it off."

"There's no time."

"There's—"

"If you don't leave now, the bride will beat you to the church." Emily stuffed the vital contents of Jenny's bag into the jeweled clutch.

"I'm serious, Em."

"So am I." Emily pressed the purse into Jenny's hand and held out her car keys. "You gotta go."

"But—"

"You want to be late?"

"Of course not." Jenny prided herself on her meticulous punctuality. And even if she didn't, she'd never insult such a respected TCC member by rushing in at the last minute for his wedding.

Emily gave her a gentle shove toward the door. "Have a great time, Cinderella."

Mitch Hayward was going to be late. Of all the days, of all the events, of all the stupid, stupid fiascos, it had to be this. At this rate, Rick and Sadie would be standing under the Leadership, Justice and Peace plaque at the Texas Cattleman's Club clubhouse with a preacher pronouncing them man and wife, by the time Mitch made it into the parking lot.

He zipped past the diner in his vintage red Corvette and geared down for the corner at River Road, his back tires breaking loose against the hot asphalt. But he stomped defiantly on the gas pedal, muscled the car to head straight and prayed that Officer Brendall wasn't out on traffic patrol at this particular moment.

The roof of the clubhouse came into view in the distance

amongst the oak trees, at the same time as he spotted a long white limousine on the road in front of him. It had to be Sadie and her bridesmaids. He geared down and put the pedal to the floor, pulling around the limousine, hoping against hope that Sadie would forgive him for the stunt.

He screeched to a halt in the clubhouse lot, parking illegally before springing from the car and running up the stairs.

His assistant, Jenny Watson, was waiting by the door to the foyer.

He was conscious of a flash of bold burgundy, before snagging her arm and towing her toward the club lounge entrance.

"What happened?" she rasped, trotting to keep up with him.

"A flock of flamingos," he growled, scanning the rows of folding chairs for vacancies.

"What?"

He spotted a pair at the opposite side of the flower-and-candle-bedecked room, and he beelined for them.

"Those plastic flamingos for the charity fundraiser," he whispered to her, ignoring the censorious stares sent his way by the Texas Cattleman's Club members assembled for the wedding. "The whole flock was planted on my front lawn."

He plunked Jenny into a chair and seated himself, just as the piano music changed, and all heads turned to watch the first bridesmaid start her way down the aisle.

The attendants were pretty in pale lilac dresses, but Sadie and Rick's two-year-old twin daughters all but stole the show. They were dressed identically in ivory lace dresses, accented with lilac ribbons and bows. They had flowers braided into their hair, and they dutifully dropped multicolored handfuls of rose petals from their baskets as they walked.

Then the pianist began the wedding march, and the guests rose as Sadie appeared in a stunning white gown, flowers woven into her hair, and a tremulous smile on her face as she approached Rick. Mitch was about as far from a romantic as a guy could get, but even he couldn't help feeling a warm glow for the couple who had been through so much, were so obviously in love and were about to create a family with their two young daughters.

As the preacher pronounced the couple man and wife, the guests spontaneously burst into applause. And by the time Rick kissed his bride, most of the women, and even some of the men, were wiping misty eyes while they smiled with pure joy. Camera flashes went off and Rick and Sadie each picked up one of their daughters to make their way back down the aisle.

"That was lovely," said Jenny, tucking her tissue back into her compact purse.

"You can't help but be happy for them," Mitch replied.

Then she pressed an elbow into his ribs. "Did the game go into overtime or something?"

"Sorry," he apologized, his mind going back to the debacle of getting out of his driveway.

Truth was, he had been further delayed when a football buddy, Jeffrey Porter, his teammate on the Texas Tigers, had called on the road from Chicago. Jeffrey's girlfriend of two years had caught him cheating and abruptly ended the relationship.

Mitch was intimately familiar with the temptation of beautiful women when a guy was on the road with the team. There was never a shortage of dates. It was one of the reasons Mitch had always avoided serious romantic relationships. If he couldn't trust himself to be faithful, he wasn't going to make any promises to anyone.

It was probably past time someone called Jeffrey on his behavior. Quite frankly, with the way his attention strayed, Mitch was surprised his buddy hadn't been caught long before this. Still, he'd felt duty bound to sympathize with the wide receiver.

"What happened?" Jenny asked as the front rows of guests began surging down the aisle, following the wedding party out into the foyer.

"It was mostly the flamingos." Mitch repeated the part of the story he'd decided to use as an excuse, while they waited their turn to exit the lounge. "Somebody obviously paid to have the flock planted on my lawn, and it was all I could do to navigate through the mess."

She looked up at him, skepticism clear as her brows lifted above her green eyes. "What? Did they gang up on you?"

He did a double take. There was something different about Jenny today. He tried to put his finger on it.

"I took one of them out," he grumbled. He'd been in a hurry after his phone call with Jeffrey, and one of the flamingos had scratched the front bumper of his 'Vette. He sure hoped he didn't have to repaint.

"Did you hurt it?" Jenny asked with a carefully schooled, straight face. It was obvious she found the mishap amusing.

"It'll live," he responded without missing a beat. "You know, I'd have given them an extra donation without the birds," he griped. A time-honored local form of extortion, the recipient of the flamingos was compelled to pay a donation to get the birds moved to another unwitting victim's yard. "A phone call would have worked just as well." He was a strong supporter of the local women's shelter that ran the flamingo fundraiser, and he'd have happily bumped up his annual contribution.

"The flamingos are more fun," said Jenny, turning as the people toward the middle aisle started to move. "I'll help you pick the new target. Maybe we can plant them on Cole's lawn next." Cole Maddison, Mitch's friend, neighbor and fellow TCC board member had deep pockets.

"Sure," Mitch answered absently, still trying to figure out what was different about her.

The glasses.

She wasn't wearing her glasses.

That was unusual for Jenny.

He wondered if she'd forgotten them, or if she'd decided the wedding was an occasion formal enough to warrant wearing her contacts. He knew she didn't like them.

She started to walk away, and his gaze caught on her short dress. That was also unusual. She normally wore knee-length skirts, or slacks, a crisp blouse and a blazer. Jenny was as buttoned-up and tailored as a woman could get. It suited her precise and meticulous personality. But today, puffy, bold burgundy fabric swirled around her thighs. One of her shoulders was bare, and she was wearing unusually flashy earrings.

What was up?

"Jenny?"

She turned.

Holy cow. From this angle the entire package nearly took his breath away. What had happened to his no-nonsense, efficient assistant?

"Yes?" she prompted.

"Nothing." He started to move with the rest of the crowd, embarrassed by the reaction he was having to her makeover. She was perfectly entitled to dress up for a wedding, and he had absolutely no business ogling her.

They made their way through the double doors, outside to the back of the clubhouse overlooking the expansive grounds. When Mitch stopped at the rail of the back veranda, Jenny kept going, making her way down the wide stairs toward the lawn and the gardens. He was a little surprised she hadn't stuck by his side like she usually did. Perhaps she needed to talk to some of the Cattleman's Club members or to some friends.

As Interim President, Mitch had been aware of the reception preparations for several weeks now. A few days ago, they'd erected a huge canopy tent in case of rain, but the Monday Labor Day evening was clear and warm. A band had set up on the gazebo, and a temporary dance floor had been built on the knoll overlooking the pond. Round, white-linen-covered tables dotted the lawn, and tall propane heaters were discretely placed throughout the dining area to keep guests warm once the sun went down.

The wedding party had assembled in front of the clubhouse

gardens for photos. Even from this distance, Mitch could see the tension between maid of honor Abigail Langley and best man Brad Price. As the last remaining descendant of the TCC founder by marriage, Abigail was also the Club's sole female member.

It was no secret that Brad resented having a woman as a full member of the Cattleman's Club. He'd taken to using the term "cattle-people's club," and suggested they put up lacy curtains and buy a pink gavel for monthly meetings.

Most of the men brushed the jokes off as harmless, but Abigail had recently gotten wind of Brad's behavior and had been highly insulted. She even challenged him in his run for TCC president. Mitch got the feeling that she avoided Brad as much as possible. But today they'd been thrown intimately together as members of the wedding party.

He scanned the sharply dressed crowd, easily spotting Jenny where she stood beside the dining area talking to Cole Maddison. She laughed at something he said, and rested her hand briefly on his arm. For some reason, Mitch felt a surge of jealousy.

Ridiculous.

Just because he'd never known Jenny to date, didn't mean she shouldn't date. Hey, if she liked Cole and if Cole liked her…

Mitch found his feet taking him down the stairway and across the lawn toward them.

"Hey, Mitch," Cole greeted easily as he approached.

Mitch gave his friend a nod.

Jenny didn't glance his way.

"Nice ceremony," Mitch offered, wondering why he felt awkward.

"I'm not sure Brad's going to survive the night," Cole returned, canting his head in the direction of the tuxedo-clad Brad, who was on the receiving end of a glare from Abigail.

"She's a pistol," Mitch agreed.

"Excuse me a moment," Jenny put in, moving away.

Mitch's gaze reflexively followed her as she made her way toward the bride and groom.

"That's a shocker," said Cole.

"What?" Mitch pulled his attention away from Jenny's tanned legs and the sexy little sandals that accented her dainty feet. Her toenails were polished a bright plum, he'd noticed.

Cole's expression was incredulous. "I'm talking about Jenny. She looks like a million bucks."

"It's a nice dress," Mitch allowed, telling himself to get a grip. It was Jenny—sensible, efficient, professional Jenny.

"She's a stunning woman," said Cole. "I wonder why she dresses down all the time."

Mitch frowned. "I wouldn't call it dressing down. She looks completely professional at the office."

Cole drew back. "I didn't mean it as an insult. But you have to admit, it's a shocker."

What was shocking was that Mitch couldn't seem to tear his gaze from her.

"I may ask her to dance," Cole declared.

"With what intention?" Mitch demanded before he could stop himself.

"*Intention?* What are you, her chaperone?"

"Jenny's a nice girl. Just because the woman puts on a pretty dress, doesn't mean she's fair game." But even as he spoke, Mitch realized just how ridiculous his words sounded. Who Jenny danced with was absolutely none of his business. Neither was who she dated, or slept with for that matter. He was her boss, not her keeper.

Cole's eyes narrowed speculatively. "Have you got designs on her?"

"No, I do *not* have designs on her. We're colleagues. I see her every day at the office." Theirs was a professional relationship, nothing more.

"Not like that, you don't," Cole muttered.

"Quit obsessing about Jenny."

"Me?" Cole gave a hollow chuckle. "You're the one who can't keep his eyes off her."

Mitch realized he was watching her yet again, marveling at her grace and glamour. He dragged his attention back to Cole, meeting the man's smirk.

"Back off," Mitch growled.

Cole accepted a glass of champagne from a passing waiter, and Mitch did the same.

"Admit it," said Cole. "You think she's hot."

"I think she's efficient." And that was all that mattered in Mitch's world, no matter how tempting she looked tonight.

Two

Jenny's evening had been an abject failure.

Mitch hadn't been wowed by her new appearance. He'd barely seemed to notice her, and he didn't ask her to dance, not one single time. Through dinner, the toasts and speeches, the cake cutting and finally the dancing, she'd grown more and more depressed.

Now that the bouquet had been thrown and the newly married couple had officially left for their honeymoon, she was going straight home to take down her hair, take out her contacts, scrub off the makeup and send the dress back to Emily via the dry cleaners. She never wanted to look at it again.

Outside in the parking lot, she hunted through the small jeweled purse for her car keys.

To think she'd felt beautiful at the beginning of the evening. She'd let Emily's optimism rub off on her. Then, standing next to Mitch while the bride marched down the aisle, she had actually felt a little like Cinderella.

She retrieved her car keys as she made her way across the

asphalt, feet aching from the high heels and a blister burning on her left baby toe. Her car was parked under one of the many overhead parking lot lights, but as she approached it, she realized something was wrong. Her taillights seemed to be faintly glowing.

She quickly inserted the key and opened the driver's door to find her headlight switch on. She flicked it off, frowning, because it had been broad daylight when she arrived for the ceremony. She slipped into the driver's seat, pulling the door shut and inserting her key into the ignition.

"Come on," she muttered, holding her breath as she turned the key.

It clicked. The engine clunked. A brief grinding noise came from under the hood. And then silence.

Jenny cursed under her breath.

She tried the key one more time but was met with stubborn silence. She smacked her palms down on the steering wheel in frustration.

She did not feel like waiting for a taxi to take her home. And now she'd have to come back tomorrow and get her car. Though it was a workday tomorrow, she'd decided to call in sick for the first time in, well, ever. She was going to pull the covers up over her head and wallow in self-pity. She swore that a pint of gourmet ice cream and a sappy movie were as close as she was coming to activity tomorrow.

She scooped up her purse and reached for the door handle, when she noticed something on her dashboard. It was a folded piece of paper, and she was certain it hadn't been there when she parked the car.

Confused, Jenny reached out and unfolded it, leaning forward and squinting in the illumination from the parking lot's overhead light. *You'll thank me tomorrow,* it said. And it was signed *Emily*.

Jenny couldn't believe it. Her best friend had actually sabotaged her car? Had Emily lost her mind?

Someone rapped on the window, and Jenny nearly jumped out of her skin.

"You okay?" came Mitch's deep voice.

Jenny crumpled the paper into her palm.

He lifted the handle and pulled open her door.

"I'm fine," said Jenny, hoping he'd accept her answer and go away.

"Car trouble?" he asked.

She shook her head, still staring straight ahead. She just wanted to get home, away from Mitch and away from the humiliating memories of this night.

"I heard you cranking it over. Want me to take a look?"

"It's fine," she insisted.

He was silent for a moment. "Are you mad at me?"

"Of course not," she lied.

"Your car's broken down, Jenny."

She closed her eyes for a long moment. "I know. I'm tired. I was going to call a cab."

"Don't be ridiculous. Pop the hood."

She turned to look at him. "You're not exactly dressed for mechanical repairs."

He glanced down at his pristine white shirt and silk tie. "Good point." Then he held out his broad hand. "Come on. I'll take you home."

Jenny glanced around the parking lot, desperately searching for someone else who could serve as her knight in shining armor. The very last thing in the world she wanted right now was to spend more time in Mitch's company while he failed to notice the new, improved and sexy Jenny. But nobody else was around to save her.

"I'll just go back inside," she began.

"Will you *stop?*" He reached down and snagged her hand, drawing her gently but firmly from her vehicle.

She grabbed her purse and came steady on her feet just as he slammed the door shut behind her, obviously annoyed. Well, she was annoyed, too. Even if he hadn't been bowled over by her chic new look, he could have at least complimented *something*. The hair, the dress, the shoes. But he couldn't even throw her a crumb.

He kept hold of her hand. "This way."

She spotted his sleek, gleaming Corvette parked haphazardly next to the front garden. "That's not an authorized parking spot."

"I was late. I'll pay the fine tomorrow." He swung open the door. "Now, get in."

She huffed out a breath, and braced her hand against the back of the bucket seat, stepping one foot inside the car and nearly losing her balance on the high heels.

His arm snaked around her waist, and she felt her dress hike high on her thighs. Her bottom pressed against his leg as he braced her steady.

"I'm fine," she ground out.

"You're grumpy," he responded, a trace of humor in the voice that was close to her ear.

"Will you let go?" Her pulse was doing unnatural things under his touch. Her face flushed hot, and her knees suddenly felt unsteady. She determinedly pulled herself into the car.

He let her go, and she dropped onto the seat. She quickly straightened her skirt, covering as much of her thighs as possible. Then she glanced down to catch an expansive view of her cleavage. She adjusted the shoulder of the dress and tugged at the bodice.

Mitch had paused, watching her, the door still open. But she refused to glance up. He was probably laughing at her clumsiness.

After a long moment, he stepped back and firmly closed the door, moving around to the driver's side. There, he climbed inside without a word, started the engine and pulled the sports car smoothly out of the parking lot.

As their speed increased, the overhead lights flashed above them, alternating with the branches of stately oak trees lining the street. The silence stretched out between them. A mile farther down, they turned off River Road to take the shortcut along Rooster Lane. Given the potholes and sharp gravel on the little-used road, and Mitch's deep love of his Corvette, Jenny could only assume he was in a hurry to get rid of her.

Fine by her. She couldn't wait to get home.

Then, abruptly, he pulled off the road onto a grassy patch beneath the oak trees, rocked the car to a halt and set the emergency brake.

"What are you doing?" she asked in confusion, wondering if something was wrong with his car. Surely, Emily couldn't have sabotaged them both.

But he turned in his seat, draping his arm across the back of hers. "Spill, Jenny. What's wrong?"

His abrupt question took her by surprise. But she quickly regrouped. "I'm tired and I want to go home." That was definitely part of the truth.

"You've been acting weird all night," he pressed.

"I have not." She folded her hands primly on her lap.

"You didn't even dance with me."

The accusation in his voice made her own tone rise along with her blood pressure. She spoke past a clenched jaw. "You didn't even ask."

"I had to ask?" he retorted.

"It's kind of traditional."

"Like you needed extra partners," he scoffed.

She turned to look at him. "What's that supposed to mean?"

"It means—" he gestured with one hand "—the way you're dressed tonight, there was a line around the block."

"Nice that *some people* noticed."

His eyes glittered in the dash lights, and there was a long moment of tense silence. When he spoke, his voice was a throaty rasp. "You think I didn't notice?"

Jenny wasn't sure how to answer that. If he'd noticed, he'd done a darn good job of hiding it.

"You think I didn't notice?" he repeated, louder this time, crowding her.

Was the car getting smaller?

"You didn't say anything," she pointed out, fighting the urge to shrink back against the door.

"What, exactly, was it that you wanted me to say?" He leaned closer still, and a few beats of silence ticked past. "That your eyes look like emeralds without your glasses? That you have unbelievably sexy legs? That you should show off more often, by the way."

The front of his shoulder brushed the tip of hers, and Jenny swallowed against the electric sensation that passed between them.

His voice went lower. "That those shoes were designed to keep a man awake at night? That I've been watching the wisp of your hair, curling over your temple and resisting the urge to smooth it back all night long?"

Jenny couldn't move. She couldn't breathe. Her chest was frozen in place, while her pulse tripped over itself.

His fingertips fluttered against her temple, touching her hair. "Or that your red lips look soft, smooth, delicious?" His hand eased around to the back of her head, fingers splaying into her hair, as he drew her forward, his mouth coming down on hers in slow motion.

What was happening? What was going—

And then he was kissing her.

He was *kissing* her.

Sparks flew out from every corner of her body. Her skin prickled hot in the sultry car. Her belly buzzed and her thighs twitched, and her body leaned subconsciously toward him.

He parted his lips, deepening the kiss. His free arm slid around her waist, pulling her tight to his chest, while his tongue tested the seam of her lips.

She opened for him, and he invaded, spreading new waves of desire throughout her body. She whimpered, grasping his broad shoulders through his jacket for support while her world tipped on its axis.

He finally broke the kiss, touching his forehead gently against hers. "I noticed," he breathed.

With her brain struggling to grasp the enormity of what had just happened, "Oh," was all she managed.

He let her go, leaning back in his seat, closing his eyes for a long moment. "Sorry about that."

"It's, uh…" She straightened her dress again, sitting back in her own seat. "Fine," she ended.

It was more than fine. It had been amazing.

He'd noticed. He'd *noticed*. And he'd kissed her.

Wow, had he ever kissed her. She'd never been kissed like that in her life.

Mitch let off the emergency brake and put the Corvette in gear.

He pulled onto the gravel road and continued toward Jenny's small house beside Frost Lake.

She hadn't the first idea of what to say or do.

Mitch pulled his Corvette into Jenny's short driveway, his brain a jumble of lust and recrimination as he automatically turned off the headlights and killed the engine. He pushed open his door and rounded the hood to open hers.

In the ten minutes since he'd kissed her, neither of them had said a word. But inside his head, he'd given himself about a dozen stern lectures. What the hell did he think he was doing? Jenny was a nice girl, a great girl, a wonderful girl, and she worked for him.

She wasn't one of the sophisticated women he met at parties in New York and L.A., who wanted nothing more than a famous football player as a companion for the evening or the night. She was honest, uncomplicated, and he was a cad for giving in to his baser instincts.

He pulled open her door, forcing himself to concentrate on the treetops, the full moon hanging on the horizon and the darkened outline of her little house—anything, anything but looking at Jenny again.

He knew he should get the heck out of here without delay, but her porch light was out, and the gentleman in him wouldn't send her up the uneven pathway and the dark stairs on her own. He offered his arm, ignoring her light touch, looking straight ahead as they made their way along the stepping stones in her front garden.

They walked up the stairs and across the porch, then she stopped and turned toward him.

"I'm—" she began, and he made the mistake of meeting her gaze.

Her eyes were opaque jade in the faint moonlight, her lips red and swollen from his kiss. Her hair was disheveled, her cleavage highlighted by the sexy dress and those legs went on forever, ending in those fantasy shoes that somehow hijacked his primal brain. He groaned in instant surrender and swooped in for another kiss.

She tipped her head to accommodate him, soft lips parting, tongue answering his own, even as her slim arms wound around his neck. He wrapped his own arms around her narrow waist and pulled her against him once more, those luscious breasts flush to his chest. Her mouth was hot on his, her thighs taut, the feel of them hardening his body beyond imagination. He stroked a hand over her messy hair, releasing the clip that held it back, so that it tumbled free.

He kissed her temple, her ear, her neck, making his way along her bare shoulder.

"Mitch," she gasped, her breath hot puffs against his chest.

He drew back, looking into her soft green eyes. Her cheeks were flushed, her lips parted, and her shiny strawberry blond hair framed her face like a halo.

Walk away, he ordered himself. *Walk the hell away.*

But she pressed a key into his palm.

On automatic pilot, he unlatched the door, pushing it wide. He scooped her into his arms and carried her inside, slamming the door firmly behind them and making his way straight down the back hallway to her bedroom.

There, he lowered her gently to her feet.

"Jenny," he breathed, reminding himself of who this was, trying one more time to convince himself to do the right thing.

But she came up on her toes and kissed him passionately, and he'd spent far too many years being self-indulgent to summon self-discipline now. His hand moved reflexively to her breast, grasping the soft mound beneath the silky dress. She parted his suit jacket, her small hands sliding around his back, their heat searing through the thin cotton of his shirt.

He shrugged out of the jacket, and it fell to the floor. One of his thighs pressed between hers, easing her dress out of the way. She gasped, as the fabric of his slacks obviously hit home. Her hands fumbled with his tie, and he gave into temptation, slipping the single shoulder of the dress down her arm.

Their movements grew faster, more frantic.

She popped the buttons of his shirt, while he found the zipper at the back of her dress. In seconds, they were chest to chest, skin to skin, and he pressed long, deep, fiery kisses on her mouth.

Her dress slipped to the floor. Her scant panties combined with those shoes nearly sent him over the edge. He stripped off the remainder of his clothes and eased her down on the big bed, into the neatly pressed quilt and the plump, perfect pillows.

She was all motion beneath him, heat, softness, kisses and breathy cries. Her fingernails dug into his back, while he kissed her lips, her neck, her breasts, kneading his hands along her thighs, up and around. Impatiently, he tore off her panties. She gasped, then moaned and arched against his fingers.

He kissed her hard and deep, strumming her nipples. Her hands roamed his body. He shifted over her, and her legs wrapped around him, her hips arched against his weight in an invitation he couldn't ignore.

He grabbed for his slacks, quickly retrieving a condom before instinct obliterated reason. He thrust into her exquisite heat, his primal brain telling him to make it last and last and last. Pillows flew to the floor. The bed rocked on its brass foundation, while the stars through her bedroom window melted and slid from the sky.

She cried his name just as his own passion crested. His breathing went hoarse, and long minutes throbbed past before sanity returned. Exhausted, he rolled to his side, taking him with her, pulling her deep into his arms.

Once again, words eluded him. He had absolutely no idea what to say to her. He wasn't sorry. He didn't regret it. But, oh boy, had he ever made a big mistake.

Instead of speaking, he cradled her against his body, held her close until she was safely asleep. Then he held her an hour longer. He knew he'd be facing the stupidity of his actions full-on in the morning, but he was in no hurry to get there.

It wasn't until the moon was high in the sky, and Mitch knew he was in real danger of falling asleep right there next to Jenny, that he eased her from his arms and tucked the covers around her. He risked a gentle kiss at her hairline, before slipping into his clothes and leaving her sleeping.

Jenny wasn't surprised to wake up alone in the morning. Since the wedding had taken place on the holiday Monday, her alarm went off as usual for the workday on Tuesday. She had a few unfamiliar aches and pains in the shower, but she didn't mind. Mitch had noticed her. Boy, had he noticed her.

She was a little embarrassed about tumbling into bed with him so quickly. But it wasn't as though they were strangers. They were both adults, and he'd spent years living in big cities and moving in sophisticated social circles. She knew it was an entirely different dating world out there.

She dressed neatly and professionally for the office, her

glasses back in place, and took a cab to the TCC. She'd call the auto club and get a boost sometime during the morning.

As usual, she arrived before Mitch. She put on the coffee in their three-room, second-floor office area, booted up her computer, checked both her and Mitch's voice mail boxes for weekend messages and pulled her pending files out of the locked cabinet, sorting the issues in priority order on her desktop.

She was halfway through her new emails, when the door opened. She felt an excited hitch in her stomach and looked up to see Mitch walk into the office. A reflexive smile formed on her face. Should she stand? Would he hug her this morning? Kiss her? Or would they leave that kind of behavior outside the office?

He clicked the door shut. And when he turned back, she was surprised to see him scowling. Her smile drooped.

"Good morning," she offered, studying his expression. Was something wrong? Was there a problem she hadn't heard about? The rivalry over the upcoming club presidency election was well known. Had something more happened between Abigail and Brad?

Crisply dressed in his usual business suit, he set his jaw, squared his shoulders and crossed toward her.

She stood. "Mitch?"

"I owe you an apology," he began without preamble, his focus settling somewhere beyond her left ear.

"You don't—"

"My behavior last night was completely unforgivable."

What did he mean? That he hadn't danced with her, complimented her at the reception or that he'd left in the middle of the night without a word? Whichever it was, he was already forgiven.

"I took advantage of you, and I am profoundly sorry."

Now she was completely confused. Was he talking about their lovemaking? Because she had been as willing and eager as him.

"I stepped way out of line," Mitch continued, still not looking her in the eye. "You deserve better than that. You deserve better than me."

Wait a minute. She didn't want better than Mitch. She wanted Mitch.

He finally flicked a glance directly at her. "I hope you'll still be comfortable working here. I'll do everything in my power to make sure our professional relationship is not impacted." His dark eyes softened slightly. "Can you forgive me, Jenny? Can we possibly forget it ever happened?"

A lead weight pressed down on Jenny's chest, and her knees nearly buckled from lack of breath. Forget it ever happened? He wanted to forget he'd made love with her? Go on as if everything was normal, as if she was…was…some kind of one-night stand?

Reality washed over her like ice water.

She was a one-night stand.

Mitch had thought she was pretty, sexy, desirable and available last night, period. The sophisticated dress, heavy makeup and fancy hairdo hadn't given him romantic thoughts. They had given him lustful thoughts.

A clipped laugh of embarrassment slipped out, and she quickly covered her lips with her fingers.

What a fool she'd been.

His gaze narrowed. "Jenny?"

She scrambled to gather her emotions. This was one of those moments. She'd been stupid. She'd made a complete fool of herself. In the aftermath, she could pull it together and pretend she was as sophisticated and aloof as him, or she could break down altogether, and he'd remember forever that she behaved like a gauche teenager the morning after.

She wouldn't let that happen. She was tough. She was controlled. She could do this.

"No problem," she managed to assure him with a dismissive wave of her hand, sitting down and turning back to her computer. "Business as usual. I get it. We slipped up. Hey, it happens."

"Are you sure—"

"I'm fine," she said with forced brightness. "If you don't mind, I'd really like to get through these emails before coffee. The auto club will be here—" She stopped right there. No point in bringing up any reminders of their one-night fling. It was over and done, and she wasn't going to think about it ever again.

The desk phone rang, and she scooped it up, turning her back completely on Mitch. "Texas Cattleman's Club."

"What happened?" It was Emily's voice.

A flush prickled Jenny's scalp. "Can I call you back?"

"Is he there?"

"Yes."

"Roger. Got it. Call me back as soon as you can, okay?"

"I will." Just as soon as she went to the bathroom and threw up.

She hung up the phone and stared at her computer, the characters blurring in front of her eyes.

He was still standing behind her.

She could feel his heat and hear his breathing.

She schooled her features and turned. "Is there anything else?"

He looked lost, and a little confused—an unheard of state for Mitch Hayward. "I really am sorry."

Jenny gathered every bit of dignity she could muster. "So you said."

"Maybe we could—"

"I don't think talking about it is going to help."

He paused for a moment. "Right. I guess not."

"Like you said." She turned and punched a couple of random computer keys. "We'll simply forget it ever happened. Carry on as usual." And she was absolutely, positively going to date other men. This silly fantasy of hers had gone on far too long. She was nearly thirty. Mitch was nowhere in her future, and she was ready to fully accept that reality.

* * *

When Jenny finally left the office at the end of the workday, Emily was there in the parking lot, leaning up against Jenny's car, looking very impatient. Jenny's steps faltered, but she knew she couldn't avoid Emily forever.

"You didn't call me back," Emily accused, straightening away from the door panel.

"You sabotaged my car," Jenny pointed out. The auto club guy had boosted it midmorning, and the battery was back in shape now.

"For a good cause." Emily peered at Jenny's expression. "Seriously. What on earth happened last night?"

"My life's not going to change, that's for sure." Jenny focused on unlocking the car door.

"Did he insult you? Ignore you? What?"

Though she'd like nothing better than to take Mitch's advice and forget last night ever happened, Jenny knew she couldn't keep a secret like that from her best friend. It was too big, too devastating. It would eat her alive if she didn't share it. Though it might eat her alive even if she did.

"Get in," she told Emily, hitting the unlock button for the passenger side.

Emily quickly rounded the car and hopped in, pulling her seat belt into place. "Spill."

Jenny cranked the engine, putting the car into Reverse, swinging around to head for the parking lot exit. She needed to get clear of the TCC building and the feeling of having Mitch close by before she spoke.

She followed the curve of the road and put her mouth on automatic pilot, struggling to stay detached from the words she was uttering. She tried to pretend she was talking about someone else, some poor, hapless woman who'd let her emotions rule her logic and who got exactly what she'd deserved.

"At first," she told Emily, "it seemed like he didn't notice me at all. Nothing was different. Except he didn't ask me to dance.

He always asks me to dance. As if he has to. Like it's his duty. Since I'm technically his 'date.'"

"Jen? You're babbling."

"Right." Jenny's moist hands slipped on the warm steering wheel. "He didn't ask me to dance."

"I got that."

"I got ticked off and left. I mean, the hair, the dress, the makeup, the *shoes*. Do you blame me for being upset? Don't you think any normal, red-blooded guy would have asked me to dance?"

"I don't blame you for getting ticked off. And, for what it's worth, I thought you looked hot."

"Thank you. I agree. I felt like a fool. But I looked hot."

Emily smirked and snorted out a laugh.

"So, I leave the reception. I head for my car."

"Which I'd incapacitated."

Jenny nodded her acknowledgment. "Which you'd incapacitated. Thank you *very* much, by the way."

"Did it work?"

"Like a charm."

"I knew it would."

"He drove me home."

"I knew he would."

"And I slept with him."

"I knew—" Emily twisted in her seat. "Wait a minute. *What?*"

"I slept with Mitch." Jenny was really quite proud of how detached she sounded as she went into the sordid details. "I tore off my clothes. Or maybe I tore off his clothes, I can't quite remember the details. In any event, we were both naked."

Emily's voice rose to a squeal. "You *slept* with Mitch Hayward?"

Jenny glanced at her friend's incredulous expression. "Am I not saying this right?"

"On the first date?"

"Well, technically, it wasn't a date. Or I guess you could say it was our twelfth date, if you count dates that aren't really dates. But, really, at this point, I'm planning to take credit for them all. It makes me seem less slutty, don't you think?"

"You're not slutty."

"I slept with a guy on the first date."

"Twelfth date. And I thought you said your life wasn't going to change?"

Jenny missed a stop sign and sucked in a shocked breath when she realized what she'd done. She was a careful, conscientious driver. Fortunately for her, there was no cross traffic.

"Maybe you better pull over," Emily suggested in a worried tone.

"Yeah," Jenny agreed. She eased her car into the gravel parking lot of the Royal Diner. She kept a death grip on the steering wheel until she came to a complete stop.

"What happened?" Emily asked gently. When Jenny didn't answer, she put a comforting hand on her shoulder. "Jen?"

"This morning…" Jenny swallowed. She wasn't going to cry. She was an adult, and she would not cry over a cad like Mitch. "When he got to the office. He told me he was sorry, and he hoped we could forget all about it, carry on as usual, as if nothing had happened."

"I can't imagine Mitch—seriously?"

"Yes."

"Did he say anything else?"

"That I deserved better than him."

It was Emily's turn to go silent. They both reflexively watched while a car pulled past them and turned into a spot near the diner's front door. The car doors opened, and two teenagers hopped out.

Jenny was pretty sure she knew what Emily was thinking. It was what Jenny was thinking. It was what any reasonably intelligent adult would conclude.

"Yeah," she voiced it out loud, her tone mocking. "He gave me the old, 'it's not you, it's me, babe' brush-off."

"Ouch," Emily whispered.

"I can't believe I was a one-night stand. I'd have bet money against that ever happening. To me of all people. I'm not stupid, Em."

"Of course you're not stupid," Emily staunchly defended. "I never would have guessed that Mitch of all people—"

"He's a football star," Jenny reminded her, feeling defeated. She wished she'd remembered that important fact last night. "He's a celebrity, and the world is his oyster. I bet he does this kind of thing all the time."

"But not with you."

"He has now."

Emily gestured with a spread palm. "But, you're not... You know."

"I am now."

Emily thwacked her head against the seatback. "This is ridiculous."

"I'm over it."

"You are not."

"I am. I have no choice. What you told me last night was spot-on. And I promised myself if this didn't work out, I'd date other men. That's exactly what I'm going to do. Pining away over Mitch Hayward has gotten me exactly nowhere in the past, and it will get me exactly nowhere in the future. I *refuse* to do something so illogical."

Emily sat up straighter, eyes narrowing, forehead creasing. "Are you serious?"

"Absolutely." Jenny had never been more serious in her life.

Emily smacked the dashboard. "Then let's get going."

"Where?"

"Take Bainbridge to Payton for Harper's Boutique. You're going to need a new wardrobe."

Three

After an excruciatingly long day at work, followed by a grueling physiotherapy session for his injured shoulder, Mitch pulled his Corvette in front of the garage of his rented, split-level house. The pain in his shoulder was bad enough, but then there were some of Jenny's words that he couldn't seem to get out of his mind.

"We slipped up," she'd said. "Hey, it happens." As if it was the kind of thing that had happened to her in the past. As if anything like their lovemaking had *ever* happened to him.

Sure, he'd dated his share of women. He was on the road, in the public eye, invited to parties and publicity events where supermodels wanted to hobnob with athletes.

But it wasn't the same thing. There had never been anything like his night—well, his half night—with Jenny.

He exited the cool car, using his left arm to push the door shut, cursing the fact that his shoulder wasn't healing as quickly as he'd hoped. He knew he wasn't eighteen anymore, but he was in top physical shape, and he'd done every single thing the doctors and physiotherapists had told him to do.

He heard the sound of footsteps and looked up to see Cole, who lived across the street, pacing his way down the driveway.

"Hey," Cole greeted with a nod, striding forward. Living so close to one another, the two men spent many casual evenings in each other's company.

"Hey," Mitch returned, hitting the lock button on his key fob.

"Shoulder okay?"

"It will be. But my physio is a sadist."

"Poor baby."

Mitch grunted.

"Got a beer?" asked Cole.

"Sure," Mitch answered as he started for the front door. He'd rather have a double shot of single malt. But he'd read studies that told him drinking alcohol to relieve pain was a dangerous path to start down. He wondered if it was as dangerous for emotional pain as it was for physical pain.

"You took Jenny home last night," Cole stated as he followed behind.

"So?" Mitch's tone came out uncharacteristically sharp. But the last thing he wanted to do was talk about Jenny. "Her car broke down."

"I saw she left it in the TCC parking lot."

Case closed. There was nothing unusual about Mitch offering Jenny a ride home. He didn't owe anybody any explanation.

He inserted his key and swung open the front door. He retrieved his *Royal Crier* newspaper from the metal bracket beside his house, and grabbed a handful of mail from his mailbox. Then he tossed it all, along with the keys, onto the side table in his small foyer.

The house was cool and dark, and he breathed a sigh of relief at being home. Maybe he'd take some pain pills later tonight. He had a feeling it was going to be a challenge to get to sleep.

"I was on the phone with Abigail for an hour today," he told

Cole, changing the subject from Jenny and choosing something familiar and safe as he crossed the living room to open the blinds. The direct sunlight had passed over his house hours ago and would now be shining on the back deck.

"Does she know that Brad's being threatened with blackmail?" Cole asked. Few people knew about the blackmail threats to Brad, but Cole was a trusted confidant of most TCC board members and had been brought into the loop.

Mitch shook his head. "Not yet. At least not that she mentioned. She has some strong opinions on the design for the new clubhouse."

Brad and Abigail were locked in a bitter fight for the upcoming presidential election at the Texas Cattleman's Club. Mitch was pretty sure that Abigail would have spoken up if she knew that Brad was receiving vague, threatening notes that talked about exposing his "secret."

"Whatever it is, it's going to come out sooner or later."

"I'm betting sooner." Mitch opened the refrigerator and snagged two icy cold imported beers. "That's the thing about secrets."

"That's the thing about secrets," said Cole, an oblique look in his eyes as he accepted one of the chilled, green bottles. He twisted off the cap and tossed it into the trash.

Ignoring Cole's dire tone, Mitch opened his own bottle and headed for the back deck. He settled into a padded chair beneath the shade of the awning, propping up his right arm to relieve the stress on his shoulder.

The deck provided a view across the seventh green of the Royal Golf Club. Two men were putting in the distance, while a foursome, two men and two women, made their way to the eighth tee. A breeze rippled the leaves on the perimeter oaks, bringing with it the scent of freshly cut grass.

Cole sat down. "Secrets," he said, then took a swig.

"You got one that matters?" asked Mitch, trying to gauge his friend's expression.

Cole smiled. "I think you do."

Mitch squinted. "You know something I don't?" Most of his life had been splashed across the national tabloids. Everybody in the country knew his yardage, his college grades, his weight. They'd even done a spread on his new haircut last fall.

"You got home at 4:00 a.m."

Mitch stilled, and his voice lowered to a warning growl. He did not need to defend himself to Cole. "Last time I checked, I was over twenty-one."

"You were with Jenny." Cole's tone wasn't exactly judgmental, but there was a steadiness in his eyes that made Mitch feel like he was under interrogation.

Mitch didn't want to lie, but he wasn't about to tarnish Jenny's reputation, either. So, he didn't respond.

"Are you sure that was such a good idea?" asked Cole.

Mitch felt his heartbeat deepen, while adrenaline trickled into his system. "You might want to think about exiting this conversation along about now."

"I'm worried about Jenny."

"Jenny's fine."

"How would you know that?"

Mitch forced in a calming breath and took a long pull on his beer. He knew he should never have kissed her. And after she'd made his blood pressure skyrocket there in the car, he should never have walked her to the door.

But it was done. And he couldn't change it. And it was none of anybody else's damn business.

"What are your intentions?" ask Cole, his gaze steely.

"Is this a joke?"

"I'm dead serious. I've known Jenny since she was a little girl—"

"And I haven't?"

"I didn't sleep with her."

Mitch came instantly to his feet, pain throbbing through his shoulder. He hated mounting an argument when he was in the wrong. Oh, he could do it. But he sure hated it. "Jenny is an adult. We talked this morning and—"

"And she told you she was fine?" Cole asked, brow arched.

Mitch came clean. "She said 'we slipped up' and 'hey, it happens.'"

"Does that sound like Jenny to you?"

And that was where Mitch's logic fell off the rails. It didn't sound remotely like Jenny.

The accusation went out of Cole's eyes, and Mitch felt his guard slip a notch.

Both men were silent for a few minutes, while the wind picked up, and the golf games continued on the course.

"What were you *thinking?*" asked Cole.

Mitch eased back down in his seat. "You saw her last night."

"Yet I didn't sleep with her." Then Cole's gaze grew contemplative, as if he was questioning his own judgment on that front.

Something dark burst to life inside Mitch, and he reflexively jerked forward. "Don't you dare even think about sleeping with Jenny."

Cole looked amused now. He obviously saw some kind of twisted humor in Mitch's predicament. "That sounded a whole lot like jealousy. Why don't you tell me again how you have no intentions toward her?"

Mitch could tell where Cole was going. But there was absolutely no future for him and Jenny. Jenny was a great girl, and Mitch was only human. "You know what I'm like."

He and Cole had been friends since elementary school. Cole had played baseball instead of football, his smaller stature making that game a better fit. But he was fully aware of the perks available to elite athletes. And he was under no illusions about Mitch's lifestyle.

"You're not the guy I'd pick for my sister, that's for sure," Cole agreed.

"You don't have a sister."

"If I had one."

"I'll be leaving town after the election, or as soon as my shoulder heals," Mitch added to the discussion. There was absolutely no future for the two of them. And Jenny deserved a guy who could give her a future.

Nipping things in the bud was the only way to keep from hurting her even more.

"I talked with Jeffrey Porter last night," he put in, knowing it was a way to further emphasis his undesirability as a match for Jenny. Cole was well aware of Jeffrey's many indiscretions.

Cole lifted his beer bottle in a mock toast. "Is he serving as your cautionary tale?"

"His girlfriend caught him cheating. You know," Mitch mused aloud, "I honestly think Jeffrey said 'no' to the first hundred propositions. Then maybe one night he was alone. Maybe we'd lost the game. Maybe he got hurt on the field. Maybe the coach had reamed him out for something, and maybe he'd had a fight over the phone with Celeste. And there she was, a fresh, pretty, willing little sweet thing that would make all his problems go away. At least for a while. And so, he stumbled. And once he'd done it the first time, well..."

Mitch had watched the same scenario play out with dozens of players. His teammates tried to make relationships work, yet, inevitably, they were spectacular failures.

"You don't have to sell me on the general sleaziness of professional athletes," said Cole.

"I'm trying to sell you on the general sleaziness of *me*. I'm going back to that world, Cole. And I'm no different than any other guy on the team."

"Then you had no business sleeping with Jenny."

Mitch grunted out a cold laugh.

He ought to be drawn and quartered for what he'd done to Jenny. Guys like him had no business sniffing around caring, wholesome, defenseless girls like her.

* * *

Jenny was keeping a sinful secret. It had to do with her updated wardrobe. Though she'd worn her usual Friday outfit of gray linen slacks, matching blazer and her favorite aqua silk blouse to the office this morning, underneath it all, she wore skimpy purple lace panties and a matching push-up bra.

She and Emily had spent every evening this week shopping for new clothes. They'd started Tuesday at Harper's Boutique. Then, they'd moved on to every high-fashion store within a fifty-mile radius.

Even if nobody had a clue, Jenny felt a little bit sexy. It was good for her bruised ego. As Emily had said on the drive home last night, Mitch had no idea what he was missing.

The outer office door opened with a rattle, and a uniformed courier entered, a white cardboard envelope in one hand and his electronic tracking device in the other.

"Delivery for Mr. Hayward," the young man announced. He crossed the room and perched the envelope against her upright in-basket, holding out the tracking device.

Jenny took it and scrolled her signature across the grayed window. "Thanks."

"Have a good day." He gave her a salute of acknowledgment while he turned to leave.

As the door swung shut behind him, she ripped the perforated tab and reached into the depths of the cardboard pouch, extracting a smaller manila envelope. She retrieved a letter opener and sliced through the paper. Inside, she discovered four VIP tickets to tonight's football game in Houston. The Texas Tigers versus the Chicago Crushers.

Her mood slipped another notch.

Like any good Texan, she loved football. And the last three times Mitch had been sent complimentary tickets to a nearby game, he'd invited her to join the group. But those days were obviously over.

A folded note slipped out of the envelope, and she opened it up. *The jet will be at the airport at four,* it read. *Bring a date.* It was signed by Mitch's friend and teammate Jeffrey Porter.

"Jenny, can you please look up—" Mitch stopped short.

A jolt of guilt hit her. Which was ridiculous. She opened Mitch's mail all the time. There was nothing on this package to indicate it was personal. And it wasn't. He was a football player. He received packages from his team with some regularity.

"The tickets?" he asked, moving forward.

She nodded. Bundling them along with the note back into the manila envelope, pretending everything was perfectly normal in her world. "They say the jet will be at the airport at four." For a split second, she wondered who his date might be, but then she quickly cut off that line of thinking, mentally admonishing herself.

She rose to deposit the empty cardboard packaging into the recycling bin.

She heard Mitch behind her, the envelope rustling. He was clearly reading the enclosed note.

Determined to banish the annoying jealousy, she turned and moved briskly back to her chair.

But she no sooner sat down than perversity made her speak out. "So, who are you taking?"

He went still, and she had to fight the urge to glance at his expression. She focused on picking up the scattered bits of cardboard from the envelope tab. She rolled them between her fingers and tossed them in the wastebasket.

Then she straightened a stack of papers on her desk, returned her letter opener to the drawer and lined up three pens in front of her phone.

Mitch's voice was a deep rumble. "Do you want to come to the game, Jenny?"

She forced out a little laugh. "Of course not. That would be silly."

"You can join me if you'd like."

She looked up to where he stood above her, tone tart. "I would not like."

Her words dropped into silence.

His gaze held hers, and for a long moment she couldn't breathe. He seemed to be searching deep into her eyes.

Then his lips compressed, and his broad shoulders drew back beneath his suit. "You do understand why I'm no good for you, right?"

"Absolutely."

He was no good for her because there were hundreds of beautiful women out there who were perfectly willing to throw themselves at a star quarterback. And Mitch was a star quarterback who wanted to be in a position to catch them.

She was a fool to ever think she could hold his attention. She wasn't a movie star. She wasn't a supermodel. And she sure wasn't a bored debutante looking for a walk on the wild side.

"It has everything to do with me, and nothing to do with you," he said.

"You do know that's the oldest line in the book."

"In this case, it happens to be true."

"Well, that would be a first."

His eyes narrowed. "You've heard it before?"

"Not me, specifically," she admitted.

He snorted out a cold laugh. "Can we stop?"

"Sure." She turned to her computer, pretending to read an email while she waited for him to walk away.

"That's not what I meant," he finally said.

She didn't turn back. "Then what did you mean?"

"I'm inviting you to a football game."

"And I'm turning you down."

Mitch tapped the envelope against the desktop. "You're making way too much of this."

At that, she did turn. "You're the one who won't go away."

"Because you're being ridiculously stubborn. You love football. Come out and have some fun."

"I have plans with Emily tonight." They were going out manhunting, tonight and every Friday night until they found the right guys.

"Bring her along," Mitch countered.

"She doesn't like football."

"She likes private jets. And there'll be a VIP party after the game."

Jenny found herself hesitating. He was right about Emily liking the VIP world. In fact, she could almost hear Emily's voice now, extolling the virtues of a party chockablock with single male notables from the Houston area. A target-rich environment was how she'd describe it.

And Jenny did want Emily to find the right man. Emily's talk of getting pregnant while she was still single had Jenny worried. Single parenthood was a grueling struggle, and she wouldn't wish it on anyone.

It wasn't like she'd have to stick to Mitch's side, either at the game or at the party. In fact, she could mostly ignore him. It would be a big party, full of other guests.

"You and I won't be alone at all," Mitch assured her, breaking the silence.

The unexpected statement surprised a laugh out of Jenny. "Are you afraid I won't be able to keep my hands off you?"

"No." He didn't smile, and he didn't elaborate. His gaze remained steady on her eyes, and for some reason she thought he meant the opposite. But that was crazy. Sexy, famous Mitch could easily keep his hands off staid, plain Jenny.

Still, a buzz of awareness shimmied through her system, and she silently berated herself for the weakness. How long was it going to take for these ridiculous feelings to go away?

"Fifty-yard line," he added.

"You think that'll tempt me?"

"Yes, I do. Row four."

Okay, she was tempted. But she promised herself that it had nothing to do with spending time with Mitch. They were great

seats. And it would be a great party. And she had four brand-
new outfits to choose from.

Plus, she knew Emily would love the trip. Emily had been
incredibly supportive and unbelievably patient all week long.
The very least Jenny owed her was a target-rich VIP party.

An optimistic smile twitched Mitch's lips. "You'll be able to
smell the sweat and hear the cuss words."

Jenny made up her mind. "Wow. What girl could say no to
that?"

The Tigers won the game twenty-one to six, so the mood
afterward at the Moberly Club party on Galveston Bay was
celebratory. With Emily's wholehearted approval, Jenny had
worn navy leggings and royal blue leather ankle boots, topped
with a flirty denim miniskirt and a shimmering peach tank top.
They'd done the makeup thing again, put in her contacts and
pulled her hair back in a messy knot, topping the whole outfit
off with dangling silver earrings.

Jenny wasn't used to men's interested gazes following her
progress while she crossed a room. But she steeled herself,
squared her shoulders and ordered herself to relax and have
a good time. There was a dance band playing in the corner.
She'd ordered a bright-colored cranberry martini and took a
first sip. When Cole Maddison asked her to dance, she accepted
cheerfully and slid off the bar stool.

The club had been closed for the team's private party, and
everyone seemed to know everyone else. Most of the players
were built for strength and not agility, so the dancing caliber
was mixed. Their laughing efforts made Jenny relax, and she
gave herself over to the music.

Across from her, Cole did the same. He was under six feet,
and much slighter than all the other men around him. But his
movements were smooth and practiced. His smile was broad.
And she felt emotionally safe in his company.

"May I cut in?" came a deep voice at her side.

Jenny glanced up to see Jeffrey Porter's bright smile. She'd met him a few times over the years, and she knew he was a good friend of Mitch's.

She looked to Cole, who shrugged his shoulders and raised his palms, backing away to the beat of the band.

Jeffrey wore a white cotton dress shirt and black jeans. His skin was olive-toned, and his jet-black hair was pulled back in a ponytail at the base of his neck. In her experience, he was invariably friendly and jovial. All the other players seemed to like him.

The band switched to a slower number, and he drew her into his massive arms. "We should take this nice and slow," he spoke in her ear. "I'm not the most graceful guy on the floor."

"No spins or dips?" she teased.

"It's for your own safety, ma'am."

She laughed. "Nice catch out there, by the way." She referred to a late game play in the end zone where Jeffrey had leaped a good five feet to snag the ball and score a touchdown before smacking into the turf.

"Thank you. Mitch would have drilled it straight to me, saved me a bruise or two."

"You think?"

"Don't get me wrong. Cooper's a decent quarterback. But Mitch is psychic."

Jenny drew back. "Psychic?"

"Yes, ma'am."

"Does he ever give you any stock tips?"

It was Jeffrey's turn to laugh, and his brown eyes crinkled up at the corners. "Wouldn't that be something?"

"My 401(k) could sure use the help." Jenny spotted Emily across the dance floor in Cole's arms. In her ultrahigh heels, they were nearly nose to nose. Her expression looked tense, her movements stiff, and Jenny couldn't help but wonder what was wrong.

"My salary's just fine," said Jeffrey. "But I expect my career to be short."

Jenny's attention went back to Jeffrey. "You do? Is something wrong?"

"I'm going by the mathematical odds. It's tough out there."

Jenny cringed reflexively in sympathy, remembering some of the hits Jeffrey had received in the game. She leaned in. "Are you in pain?"

"I'm always in pain. But that's not the same as being injured." He nodded toward the perimeter tables. "Now, Mitch there. He's injured. And his physiotherapy regime is brutal."

Jenny glanced sideways to where Mitch stood in a group of other players. He gazed intently at her, with what looked like anger simmering in his darkened eyes.

She missed a step, but Jeffrey quickly caught her, tugging her close. "Whoa, there, missy."

"Sorry," she breathed, refocusing her attention. What on earth was the matter with Mitch now?

Four

Mitch watched from the sidelines at the Moberly Club, while out on the dance floor Jeffrey flirted with Jenny. Though he knew she was too smart to be taken in by Jeffrey's smooth talk, he was tempted to warn her away from the man. Or maybe he should order Jeffrey to stay away from her. It might be his responsibility to make it clear, in no uncertain terms, that Jeffrey was to stay well away from his assistant.

He straightened away from bar, intending to do just that.

"Well, hello, stranger." A tall, leggy blonde sidled up to him.

"Misha," he greeted, recognizing the former wife of one of Houston's many oil executives. "I didn't know you were in town."

"Back from Paris last week," she purred, resting her elegant, manicured hand on the arm of his suit jacket. She was a former model, born and raised in Germany. She'd had a brief but profitable marriage in Houston. Word on the street was that he'd ended up with the sports cars, while she got the Tigers' season tickets.

"Would you care to dance?" he asked dutifully, even though he'd prefer to spend his time confronting Jeffrey.

"But, of course." She took his hand and moved to the dance floor.

Misha, it turned out, had spent the past few months traveling, perfecting her tan in Tahiti, visiting a game preserve in South Africa and dedicating a new museum wing in Prague. She offered to show him her all-over tan, but Mitch graciously declined.

His next dance partner was just back from St. Kitts. It seemed she'd bought a little bungalow beside the ocean. She'd taken up snorkeling. She throatily informed him there was a hot tub on the balcony of her hotel suite, and then hinted that she'd like to show him how long she could hold her breath.

Mitch honestly didn't remember these parties being quite so crass. By midnight, all he wanted to do was head for the hotel, take an aspirin and crawl under the covers.

Alone.

But then his gaze caught Jenny.

She was in the corner talking to Emily, being handed another martini. A green one this time. She seemed to have developed a taste for exotic drinks. And he didn't know what had gotten into her with the clothes lately.

That short skirt showed off her incredible legs, and their navy silhouette made a man's mind go all kinds of places. She'd worn her contacts again, and her ornate earrings sparkled whenever she moved her head. His gaze rested on the shimmering peach tank top, making out the rounded curves of her breasts against the slinky fabric. It was obvious she'd forgone a bra.

He couldn't remember ever seeing her braless. Then again, he supposed he hadn't been looking. Why was he looking now? What the hell was the matter with him? What, exactly, would it take for him to learn his lesson?

He caught sight of Jeffrey. The man was heading in Jenny's

direction again, a predatory gleam in his eyes. This time, Mitch did make his move. And he didn't let anyone stop him along the way.

"Jeffrey," he greeted heartily, falling into step with the man.

"Hey, Mitch. Glad you could make it."

Mitch would just bet Jeffrey was glad he'd shown up with Jenny. "I see you've met Jenny."

Jeffrey frowned. "I've met her lots of times before."

"You didn't dance with her before."

"Her hotness factor's gone way up in my books."

"You keep her out of your books."

Jeffrey turned his head to look at Mitch. "Huh? What are you talking about?"

"She's my assistant, you moron. Keep your hands off her."

"We were only dancing."

Mitch shot Jeffrey a dark look. "You're talking to me here, Jeff."

Jeffrey gave a sheepish smile. "Point taken."

"She's a nice girl."

"Then she'll slap me across the face, won't she?"

"You give her any reason to slap you across the face, and your face will be meeting up with my fist."

Jeffrey sputtered out a laugh. "So says the cripple."

"I've still got my left."

In answer, Jeffrey looped an arm over Mitch's shoulder. "Careful, buddy. You're starting to sound territorial."

"I told you, she's my assistant."

"And that's all she is?"

"Absolutely." If Mitch said it out loud often enough, maybe it would come true.

"Why don't I believe you?"

Probably because Mitch was lying. "Because your brain's in the gutter."

"Your brain and mine have been partying together down there for quite a few years."

Mitch spoke slowly and deliberately. "Not with Jenny."

"Hey, Jenny," Jeffrey sang out as they approached. He did a few mock dance steps, making her smile. "Got time for one more spin around the floor?"

Jenny turned and stumbled ever so slightly on her high-heeled boots, bracing herself against the bar. Her green eyes were bright, her smile more dazzling than usual. Mitch had seen her with only the two, but how many drinks had she had?

"We have to head out," Mitch interrupted before she could answer. If there was any chance her judgment was clouded, Jeffrey was the last guy she needed to be around.

"It's barely midnight," Jeffrey protested.

"We've planned an early flight in the morning," Mitch lied again. They could take the jet back to Royal anytime they wanted. But he stepped up beside Jenny, threading her arm through his.

"Cole around?" he asked Emily.

The woman sniffed her delicate nose. "How would I know?"

"You were dancing with him."

"Only till I could get rid of him."

Jenny pointed. "Over there. Behind the pillar." She started to move, but Mitch held on, causing her to trip again.

"How many martinis did you drink?" he asked.

She looked up at him, blinking her long lashes as if to bring him into focus. "I ordered two. But I barely sipped either of them. Why?"

"Because you're a lightweight," he murmured.

"Thank you." She nodded sarcastically. "I just lost three pounds."

He couldn't stop a grin at her joke as he ushered her forward to where they could meet up with Cole. "Time for bed, princess."

As they passed Jeffrey, the man shook his head, chuckling darkly at Mitch. "Assistant. Right."

Mitch threw a surreptitious elbow into Jeffrey's rib cage.

* * *

"I'm starving," said Jenny from the third-row seat in the chauffeur-driven Escalade as they sped along the shore of Galveston Bay.

Mitch twisted his head to look at her. "That's probably a good idea. A little food in your stomach along with the liquor."

"Will you stop," Jenny huffed. "I sipped on two teeny little martinis. I'm just hungry because it's late. Look." She pointed out the tinted window, turning her head as they cruised past the red neon sign. "Cara Mia Trattoria. And it's open."

Cole spoke up from the bucket seat next to Mitch's in the middle row. "If she can read Italian, she can't be that bad off."

Jenny smacked the back of Cole's bucket seat. "I'm perfectly sober, people."

Cole grinned, while Emily gave a shrug. "I could eat."

Mitch turned forward to address the driver. "Can you take us back to Cara Mia?"

"Of course, sir," the uniformed man responded. He checked the rearview mirror, then pulled a U-turn in advance of an upcoming red light, taking up the right-hand lane, before signaling to pull up to Cara Mia's front door.

As the SUV came to a smooth halt, Mitch handed the man a twenty-dollar tip.

"Thank you, sir. You have the service's number?"

"I do," Mitch confirmed, yawning the door open.

"We're on duty for the team until three."

Mitch nodded his thanks and stepped out of the vehicle. He turned to offer his hand to Emily, who'd been sitting behind him, but his gaze moved reflexively to Jenny's flirty skirt as she exited from Cole's side.

"They have a deck," she announced as she rounded the back of the SUV. Wisps of hair had worked loose from her knot and curled enchantingly around her bright face. "Do you think we can sit out there?"

Mitch curled her arm around his own, steadying her across

the cobblestone drive. "I'm sure they'll let us sit wherever we want."

She inhaled. "I love the ocean."

Wind bent the palm leaves, and rolling waves sounded rhythmically in the distance.

"Fresh air's probably good for you," he observed while she disentangled her arm from his and stepped toward the restaurant stairs.

The hostess wove her way in front of them through the crowded tables on the restaurant's deck. She showed them to a view table, overlooking lighted gardens, an expansive lawn and stone walkways that led down to a sandy beach. The tide was in, and the surf was up. Propane heaters warmed the air, and a floral centerpiece anchored the billowing white cloth on the round table.

Jenny plunked into a padded wicker chair and snagged a leather-bound menu.

A waiter filled their water glasses and offered cocktails, but they all opted for iced tea.

"Isn't that gorgeous?" Jenny's attention was distracted by the tiny pink lights decorating the flower gardens. In an instant, she was on her feet, crossing to the rail of the sundeck for a better look.

"Chicken marsala pizza?" suggested Cole. "With avocado and eggplant."

Emily peered over her menu at him. "What is that? Like, nerd pizza?"

"Are you calling me a nerd?"

She smirked. "Just commenting on your taste in pizza."

"Well, what do you suggest?"

"Sausage, ham, peppers, mushrooms, onions, pepperoni."

"What are you, pledging a fraternity?"

"It's a classic."

"You want me to order a pitcher of draft to go with it?" asked Cole. "We could have a chugging contest."

Emily stuck out her tongue at him.

Mitch chuckled low at the pair's antics, glancing to check out Jenny at the rail of the deck.

She was gone.

He straightened in his chair, gaze darting from table to table. Had she gone to the ladies' room?

He stood.

"What?" Emily asked.

"Where's Jenny?"

Emily and Cole peered around the busy deck.

Mitch's gaze snagged on her boots, discarded beneath her chair at the table. He instantly shifted his attention to the lighted gardens. There she was, halfway down the stone path, meandering her way toward the ocean.

"Got her." He pointed, tossing his napkin onto the table. "I'll be right back."

He trotted down the stairs and strode his way through the quiet gardens toward the beach. The salt tang grew stronger, and the roar of the waves filled his ears as he caught up to Jenny.

"Going somewhere?" he asked as her feet hit the sand.

"Just breathing the night air," she responded, and turned in a circle.

"Only two drinks?" he confirmed.

She shook her head and rolled her eyes.

"I was afraid you'd decided to take a swim," he admitted.

"It'll take more than a few sips of a martini to get me into the ocean in September." She plunked down on the soft sand.

Once again, he was struck by how different she seemed from the regular Jenny who masterminded his financial spreadsheets, deftly handled demanding club members and wrote concise, informative month-end reports. The transformation was more than a little disconcerting.

He eased down beside her, taking in her little skirt spread out in the sand. The shimmering top left most of her tanned back bare, while her breasts pressed teasingly against the thin fabric, nipples pebbled in the cool air.

"Interesting outfits you've been choosing lately," he heard himself observe, dragging his gaze away from her sexiness.

"I needed a new look," she told him, nodding out to sea. "If I want to snag a man."

Something hitched in Mitch's stomach. "You want to find a man?"

"Of course I want to find a man. All women want to find a man." She turned back to him and pointed her index finger for emphasis. "And if they tell you they don't, well… Well, maybe they don't. But most of them do. And I do."

Her eyes were round and soft in the glow from the gardens. Her cheeks were flushed, and her lips were pursed in a determined little moue that he wanted so badly to kiss. He gritted his teeth against the unruly urge, his stomach tightening.

"You had them lining up at the Moberly Club," he pointed out. "You must have danced with Jeffrey five times."

"Jeffrey's nice," she sighed.

Mitch felt his gut clench tighter. He needed to nip this Jeffrey fixation in the bud. "Jeffrey's not a good guy for you."

"I'm not that crazy about his ponytail."

"Well. Good." Not that the ponytail was the biggest worry by any stretch of the imagination.

"Jeffrey likes you a lot." She smoothed out a patch of sand with her palm, then traced her fingertips in a pattern through it.

At the moment, Mitch couldn't say he was exactly returning the favor. What if Jeffrey decided to cut his ponytail? Mitch would cut off a ponytail. For the right woman.

Wait a minute. What was he saying? There was no right woman. There were only women. Plural. Sophisticated and uncomplicated, and in keeping with his pro-football lifestyle.

Jenny smoothed out the sandy patch again, then drew a big heart with her index finger.

Mitch found himself waiting for her to draw initials.

"Jeffrey says you're psychic," she put in instead.

Mitch glanced up. "He what?"

"He told me you were psychic." She pushed the sand off her hand and held it out to him, palm up. "Go ahead. Read my future." She came to her knees looking decidedly earnest. "Tell me about the tall, dark, handsome dream man I'm going to marry. I'd like two kids, a white picket fence. And throw in a dog, will you?"

He took her hand, realizing it was just an excuse to touch her, but not particularly caring.

She looked so sweet in the dappled light.

"What kind of dog?" he asked, pretending to take her seriously.

"A Dalmatian."

"Isn't that a little big?"

She gazed up at him. "This isn't how it's supposed to work. You tell me what kind of dog."

"Oh. All right." He obediently looked down at her outspread hand.

He gave in to the temptation to run the pad of his thumb over her palm, tracing the faint lines on her soft skin. "I predict a long and happy life."

"That's lame."

"I thought everybody wanted a long and happy life."

"You need to be more specific."

"Okay." He squinted. "Here we go. Next Tuesday." He paused. "You're going to buy a purple dress."

She tipped her head, peering closer. "Will it help me snag a man?"

"Tall, dark and handsome," he put in, ignoring the jolt of emotion at the thought of her on a honeymoon with some random stranger. It was bad enough watching her dance with Jeffrey.

A serene smile grew on her face. "That sounds nice."

Mitch found he didn't like her reaction, not one little bit. "Wait a minute," he elaborated. "He cheats on you and you kick him to the curb."

"What? No. No way."

Mitch shrugged. "Afraid so."

"You're lying."

"I calls 'em as I sees 'em."

She tugged her hand away and gazed out across the bay. "You're a terrible fortune-teller."

He couldn't help but chuckle at her outrage. To make amends, he held out his own hand. "Here, you predict mine."

She didn't even bother to look at it. "You're going to die alone and lonely."

"What did I do to deserve that?" Not that he was denying it. It was most likely true.

"You're a heartbreaker, Mitch."

"Not on purpose." There had been a few women who'd expressed disappointment that he didn't want to get into a serious relationship. He'd always chalked it up to the fame and money factors. He knew he wasn't enough of a prize that a woman might actually miss him for himself.

"Result's the same," she told him. And she looked so dejected, that he found himself desperate to put the smile back on her face.

"How 'bout I make up for being such a cad," he teased. "I could get you a Dalmatian puppy. Or a kitten. Kittens are a lot less work."

She gave him a look of exasperation. "I don't want a pet."

She wanted a man. He got it. He hated it, but he got it. She wanted the kind of man Mitch would never be. He knew what he should say, knew what he had to say and what he had to do.

His tone was decisive. "I'll help you find one."

"A pet?"

"A man."

Jenny's eyes went wide. *"What?"*

"If you're sure that's what you want." His voice grew stronger.

"I'm here for you, Jenny. I know a lot of men. Jeffrey's a bad choice, but—"

She jumped to her feet, swiping the sand off the back of her denim skirt. "Have you lost your mind?"

He watched the strokes of her palms for a moment, but then quickly checked his wandering imagination. "I'm happy to help out," he lied, rising with her.

"You are *not* going to fix me up with your friends."

It certainly wasn't his first choice, but it was a perfectly practical approach to her problem. And to his. Since mooning after her like a lovesick adolescent wasn't getting him anywhere. "I don't see why not."

"Because it's insulting, for one."

"How is that insulting? I have nice friends. Most of them are physically fit. Most have money. Many of them are considered handsome."

"Read my lips." She stared up at him in the dim light.

His gaze went obediently to her mouth.

"No," she enunciated.

"Wow. Such a coherent and cohesive argument."

Her eyes crackled emerald. "Hell, no."

He couldn't help but grin.

"Mr. Hayward?" came a stranger's voice.

Mitch swiftly cut his attention to a cluster of teenage boys tentatively approaching across the sand.

"Is that you?"

Mitch inwardly sighed but mustered up a hearty professional smile for the teenagers. "It sure is."

There were five in all, maybe sixteen or seventeen years old. Barefoot, they wore knee-length, brightly colored shorts topped with an assortment of team T-shirts.

"Wow," one breathed, while a couple of the boys elbowed each other playfully.

"We play varsity for Gulfport Collegiate."

"Took State last year."

"I'm a quarterback, just like you."

Mitch widened his smile. "Congratulations," he offered to them collectively.

"Man, I wish we had something he could sign."

"I wish we had a ball."

The tallest jumped up and made a mock catch. "Mitch Hayward, right on the money."

His friends chuckled at their own cleverness.

"Except for Davey, here," one spoke up, taking the smallest of the group in a headlock.

The short boy struggled to get out.

"Davey doesn't play," said the tall one.

"Too puny," voiced another.

"One of my best friends is your size, Davey," Mitch offered, and the larger boy immediately let him go.

"He played baseball in high school." Mitch folded his arms across his chest. "But he spent most of his time in the computer lab. His software company now owns twenty percent of the Texas Tigers." Mitch's gaze took in the rest of the group. "You'll want to treat Davey with a little respect. One day, he might be signing your paychecks."

Davey grinned, while the rest of the boys sobered, obviously absorbing the information.

"Tell you what," said Mitch. "I think I can do a little better than an autograph. Davey, you drop me an email through the Tigers' website, and I'll hook us up with some tickets to the next Houston game."

Five sets of eyes went wide. "Seriously, man?"

"You bet." He draped an arm across Jenny's shoulders. "But right now I've got some pizza getting cold."

"Oh, man!"

"That's awesome!"

"Thank you, sir!"

The boys' calls of appreciation followed them as he steered Jenny along the path to the restaurant veranda.

"Were you serious about that?" she asked.

"The tickets?"

"No. Well, you better have been serious about the tickets."

"I was."

"I meant about Cole. I assume Cole was the baseball player in your story."

"He was."

She twisted her head to stare up at him. "Cole *owns* part of the Texas Tigers?"

"He owns a company that owns part of the Texas Tigers."

"Why hasn't he ever said anything?"

"To who? I knew. I expect plenty of other people did, too."

"I never knew."

He gave her shoulder a reflexive squeeze. "You're smart, Jenny. But nobody knows everything."

She harrumphed. "Well, now I know this."

"Does that put him on your husband list?"

Jenny immediately jerked away from Mitch's arm, glaring at him, putting a few feet of distance between them while her voice ramped up an octave. "How dare you?"

He wasn't really sure how he'd dared. The question had just popped out.

"Have I ever done anything to make you think I'd marry a man for his money?"

"I only just found out you wanted to get married at all." Though he supposed he'd long since suspected. Jenny was exactly the kind of girl who should settle down with a family. She'd be a great mother, an amazing wife.

He swallowed against a dry throat.

"And I am exceedingly sorry I ever told you that." She put her nose in the air and flounced toward the veranda, ending the conversation.

Five

Jenny kicked off her boots and tossed her small purse onto one of the two queen-size beds in the opulent hotel room in downtown Houston. It was nearly two in the morning. The excitement of the game and party had long since worn off, and now she was simply exhausted.

"I don't understand why you said no," Emily said as she dropped down onto the couch that faced two blue upholstered armchairs in front of a bay window offering a view of the night-time city.

"To Mitch, fixing me up? You don't see an inherent conflict there?"

"You mean because you're in love with him?"

"I am *not* in love with him," she quickly denied. "I was temporarily infatuated with him. And, sure, I slept with him. But I recognized my mistake, and I'm moving on."

"So, where's the conflict? Heck, I'd like him to set me up. Did you get a look at some of his friends?"

Jenny sat down in one of the armchairs, curling her feet

beneath her. "Like Cole? You two looked pretty cozy when we got back to the table."

Emily blew out a disgusted breath and waved her hand through the air. "Cole? Why do you think I'd handicap my children's genetics by hooking up with Cole?"

"Cole's brilliant."

"He's barely five foot ten. And this is Texas. You don't think my sons will want to try out for the football team someday?"

"Cole plays baseball."

Emily arched a brow. "This is Texas," she repeated.

"You don't even like football."

"But my kids will. And I can rah rah on the sidelines along with any good mother."

"Okay. How about this? Cole owns twenty percent of the Texas Tigers."

That information seemed to give Emily pause. "Seriously?"

"That's what Mitch just told me." Jenny's thoughts went back to their conversation. "You know, Mitch was awfully good with those teenagers. We were right in the middle of an argument, but he just switched on the charm."

"That's our Mitch. Diplomatic and charming, no matter what the circumstances."

As she digested Emily's words, an unsettling thought crept into Jenny's mind, hollowing out her stomach. "Do you think…" she began slowly. "Do you think he does it with me?"

"Does what?"

"Turns on the diplomacy. In the office. When we're together. Do you think I've been seeing the polished, professional Mitch, and not the real guy?"

"It's possible," Emily ventured. "It does seem to be second nature to him."

"And it's exactly why they appointed him to the interim presidency. He can smooth things over, make everyone feel happy, even when he's telling them no." Jenny swallowed. "Oh, dear. This is humiliating."

"Why?"

"He's been handling me, just like he handles everyone else. I had a crush on the persona. I don't even know the real guy." Jenny stood up and paced across the room. "Do you think that's why he slept with me?" When she thought back to the conversation, she felt the blood drain from her face. "The last thing I said to him before he got all gooey and romantic was that I was upset he hadn't noticed my new look. Then, all of a sudden, he couldn't say enough flowery things."

She hung her head, shoulders drooping. "He fed me a line. He told me exactly what I wanted to hear. Good grief, I've seen him do it to a hundred different people. And then, when I practically threw myself into his arms…" Jenny couldn't bring herself to finish the thought. She could never, ever face Mitch again.

"It was a mercy—" Emily pressed her lips shut.

"Just kill me," Jenny squeaked. "Toss me off the balcony, and put me out of my misery."

Emily came to her feet. "It's not that bad."

"Not that *bad?*"

Emily braced her hands on Jenny's shoulders. "He can't read your mind. All he knows is that the two of you had a one-night fling. If it was an unemotional fling for him, there's no reason it wasn't an unemotional fling for you. He wants to put it behind you. You do, too. Case closed."

"Case closed?" Jenny found her voice trembling.

"You're a logical woman, Jenny. And putting it behind you makes good sense. Heck, you've seen him a dozen times since that night. You've made it through the awkwardness. The tough part is over."

"Yes." Jenny forced herself to nod in agreement. The tough part was over. She'd do her job, professionally and thoroughly, just like she'd always done. Mitch was diplomatic. She could be just as diplomatic. And she'd keep her emotions well away from anything to do with Mitch.

"You going to let him fix you up?" asked Emily.

"Not a chance."

"You want Cole?"

"I think of Cole as a brother."

An odd expression flitted across Emily's face. "Really?"

"He's a sweetheart."

"He's stubborn as a mule. I think it's short-man syndrome."

"He's barely under six feet. And he's incredibly fit." Jenny knew that Cole was involved in martial arts. He also still played baseball, and he loved the outdoors.

"Whatever," said Emily. "He's off the list. Fortunately for us, there are still ten million other men in Texas."

And Jenny was going to be happy with one of those ten million men. She was going to find someone kind and honest, who was as interested as she was in building a loving family.

It was nearly four o'clock the following Saturday. Jenny was at the Cattleman's Club offices, finishing work on her database before the office opened up again on Monday. She'd taken over the big boardroom, spreading the membership correspondence out in a way that wasn't possible at her desk.

Her laptop was at one end of the oval table, and she had letters, emails, reports and drawings sorted in neat piles over its expanse. She was almost finished with the metadata, and she'd already scanned each of the paper documents to provide easy access for the Board of Directors.

"Jenny?" Mitch's voice echoed from outside in the hallway, footsteps coming closer. "Is that you?"

"In here," she called, trying hard not to react emotionally to his presence. She'd never had any problem with equanimity before, dealing with all kinds of people on all kinds of issues. But with Mitch logic and reason seemed to fly out the window.

"What are you doing here?" he asked through the doorway.

"I needed to finish up and get this table cleared off," she replied without looking up. She pointed from pile to pile in explanation. "Letters against a new clubhouse. Letters against a female president. Pledges to vote for a female president. Letters in support of a new clubhouse. Suggestions for elements of a new clubhouse. And, actual spec, architectural drawings of a new clubhouse. Oh, and these ones are miscellaneous, save the whales, ban antibiotics in dairy cattle, nationalize the high-tech sector and turn the stop sign at Fifth and Continental into a traffic light. I wasn't going to include them in the database."

"Somebody thinks we control the traffic lights?"

"Apparently. Can you get right on that? The letter writer believes it's a serious problem." She glanced up to see not just Mitch, but Mitch, Jeffrey and two other men that she vaguely remembered from the football team clustered in the doorway.

Her face heated. "Uh…"

Mitch strode into the room. "Jenny, these are some of my teammates. Emilio, Nathan and you already know Jeffrey."

"Of course I do. Hi, Jeffrey." She greeted the other two with a smile and a nod.

"Hey, Jenny." Jeffrey made his way around the table toward her.

The man named Emilio spoke up. He was huge, with an impossibly deep chest, jet-black hair and no discernible neck. He took in the piles on the boardroom table. "You ever want an administrative job with a football team, I'll give you a good reference."

"Back off," Mitch growled. "I'd be lost without her."

Jenny ruthlessly reminded herself that Mitch meant in a professional way. On the personal side, she was just another in a long line of dalliances.

"It's easy enough to see why," said Nathan. He was blond, and slighter than the other three, with a wide, white smile. "Great to meet you, Jenny."

"I'm giving the guys a tour of the clubhouse," Mitch explained. "But, do you want some help here?"

She quickly shook her head. "I'm almost done. The boardroom's booked by the Hospital Fundraising Auxiliary at ten tomorrow, and I wanted to make sure my mess was out of the way."

Jeffrey moved closer. "I don't mind lending a hand."

"Ten minutes, tops," Jenny assured him.

"Then I'll still be around and help you carry it all back to the office," said Jeffrey.

Mitch stepped in, an edge to his voice. "Leave everything here. We'll move it after you're done."

"But—" She caught Mitch's expression and stopped short. "Sure. Okay. Give me fifteen?"

"We'll be back," said Mitch.

Nathan spoke up. "And then you can come to dinner with us."

"Barbecue at Mitch's place," Emilio sang, clapping Mitch on the shoulder with a meaty hand.

Jenny automatically cringed, knowing it was Mitch's injured shoulder, and that he'd had a physio session scheduled for this morning. But, other than a slight tightening of his lips, Mitch didn't react.

"And bring Emily," said Jeffrey, doing a mock golf swing. "We're hitting the links first, and I need to show off to someone."

Jenny couldn't help but smile at that. She appreciated Jeffrey's happy-go-lucky approach to life. "You mean a hundred thousand screaming fans doesn't do it for you?"

"We don't have a game this week. Besides, I prefer my adoration up close and personal."

"Fifteen minutes?" Mitch confirmed, with a scowl at Jeffrey.

Jenny noticed that Mitch didn't echo the dinner invitation. Just as well. The last thing she needed was to hang out and get personal at Mitch's house. It had been a long week, with Jenny sticking carefully to professional topics only, fearing he'd bring up matchmaking again.

After the men filed out, she quickly finished the data entry, saved everything to the server and shut down her laptop. She took it back to the office, fully intending to clean up the boardroom and escape before the men made it back from the club-house tour.

Her plan failed.

She met them in the hallway on her second trip, her arms full of paper.

"I thought I told you to leave it," Mitch barked.

She immediately understood her blunder. Mitch had been trying to help her graciously exit. He'd expected her to leave the mess and clear out before they got back.

"Sorry, boss," she mumbled, feeling foolish. She could have escaped, should have escaped. This was one time when she should have ignored her instincts to finish a job before leaving work.

"It's not a problem, Mitch," Nathan put in. "I'll grab the rest, and we can head over to the golf course."

They all looked expectantly at Jenny.

"Um." She bit down on her lip, mind scrambling for an excuse. She'd never been a good liar, and trying to do it under pressure made it that much worse. "I don't think I can—" Her glance darted automatically to Mitch.

"Mitch wants you to come." Emilio clapped him on the shoulder again.

This time Mitch did cringe with obvious pain. "Of course you're welcome to come along, Jenny. Call Emily. Let's make it a party."

"Emily's hot," said Jeffrey, and Nathan and Emilio each gave a whoop of approval.

Mitch turned on them. "If you guys are going to behave like children…"

The men immediately sobered and shook their heads. "Nope. Not us. We'll be perfect gentlemen."

"Listen," Jenny put in. "It's not the most convenient day for me—"

"Call Emily," Jeffrey interrupted. "I want to impress her with my 9-iron."

Nathan and Emilio guffawed, and Mitch compressed his lips.

"I'm going to assume you didn't mean that the way it sounded," Jenny couldn't help putting in.

"Absolutely not." Jeffrey gave Nathan a shove with his shoulder. "I meant it literally."

Jenny looked to Mitch once more. His eyes were softer this time, and there was a hint of a smile on his face. "You want me to call her?" he asked.

"I can do it," Jenny capitulated.

There was every chance Emily would enjoy meeting Mitch's other teammates. They were certainly larger than Cole. Emilio, for example, could probably give her some monster, future linebacker sons.

Emily and Emilio.

It could work.

Since Mitch had his own clubs, he waited outside the pro shop while the attendant got the others outfitted.

To his surprise, Jenny joined him there. She'd avoided him as much as possible all week. And when they did end up together, both of them danced around each other, keeping the conversation strictly business. Mitch knew he should step up and make good on his offer to matchmake. It would be better for both of them if she was taken by some nice guy who'd give her that dream life. But he couldn't seem to bring himself to do it.

She came closer now, lowering her voice, suspicion written all over her face. "Please tell me this isn't a setup."

He kept his own tone low. "You think I've set you up to look bad at golf?"

Her expression shifted to a look that clearly questioned his intellect. "Not golf."

It took him a moment to realize she was talking about the matchmaking. And in that instant, he realized he could never do it. He especially couldn't set her up with his friends or teammates. Because, if Jeffrey or one of the other guys actually did date her, fall in love with her and marry her, there was a good chance Mitch would end up lusting after a friend's wife.

If that happened, he'd have to move to Mongolia. He didn't think they played a lot of ball in Mongolia.

"It's not a setup," he assured her.

"Why don't I believe you?"

"I'm not even the one who invited you along."

"You didn't uninvite me, either."

"And you didn't come up with an excuse not to come. Even though I gave you every opportunity."

"I'm a bad liar. Sue me."

She was right about that. Jenny was smart, efficient and dedicated. But she couldn't tell a lie to save her life.

"I think Jeffrey likes you," Mitch found himself taunting.

He didn't know why he did it. Frustration, maybe. Or maybe he simply wanted to elicit an emotional reaction. Jenny was back in her uptight clothes, white blouse, pressed slacks, her glasses perched on her nose, her features carefully controlled.

He wanted more. And it worked.

Behind the glasses, her green eyes blazed defiance. "Well, I like Jeffrey."

Mitch fought his instincts. "Good."

"Darn right, it's good."

"Then he can golf with us. Hey, Jeffrey. You, me and Jenny. The rest of you can make a foursome."

Cole, who had met up with them when Mitch picked up his clubs, beamed at the groupings. There was no denying he had a thing for Emily. The woman didn't seem inclined to give him the time of day, but Cole was nothing if not tenacious. And as a baseball player in football-crazy Royal, he'd dealt with adversity his entire life.

"You're golfing with *me?*" Jenny demanded.

"How else am I going to throw you at Jeffrey?"

"But you said—"

"I guess I lied."

After a moment's silence, she stuck her prim, little nose in the air and gave a toss of her sleek hair. "Fine. Go for it. Throw us together. Let's see what happens." She sashayed back to the clubhouse.

Watching her leave, Mitch's hand tightened on his golf bag. Despite his threat, he was not going to throw Jenny and Jeffrey together, not today, not ever.

Every instinct he had told him to go after her and claim her for himself. But he had no right to do that. So instead, he hoisted his clubs and stalked toward the cart parking area.

He stuffed his clubs in the back of a cart and sat down to cool off.

When he saw the other six approach, Emilio and Jeffrey each with two golf bags on their broad shoulders, he realized he'd left Jenny to manage her own clubs. What the hell was the matter with him? Jenny was going to think he was a cad.

He sighed.

Just as well.

She might as well know the truth.

He turned on the cart ignition, while Jeffrey climbed in beside him, and Jenny sat stiffly down in the backseat.

"We're going to tee off first," said Jeffrey.

That made sense, since the three of them would complete the game faster than the other four.

They drove to the first tee.

Mitch's first swing sent his ball to the far end of the fairway, while Jeffrey's hit the green. Jenny's shot came up short, off in the rough, only a third of the way down the fairway.

"Sorry," she mumbled, shoving her 3-wood back in the bag.

"You need a few pointers?" asked Jeffrey, swinging himself into the backseat of the cart to sit next to her, leaving Mitch to be the chauffeur.

"Sure," she responded with what sounded to Mitch like enthusiasm.

"She's doing fine," Mitch intervened. "The poor woman's up against two pro football players."

"Doesn't mean she can't improve her stance and her follow-through," Jeffrey argued.

Mitch spent the next six holes watching Jeffrey play the attentive instructor to Jenny the naive golf student. He had her listening with rapt attention, concentrating, improving her swing, laughing at her own mistakes, while Mitch's mood darkened along with the clouds rolling in from the Gulf.

On the seventh fairway, the first raindrops splattered down.

"Let's finish this one and head back," Mitch called down the fairway to Jeffrey, relieved that the torturous afternoon was about to end.

He waited while Jenny lined up a shot on the far side of the fairway.

Suddenly, thunder split the sky above them, lightning tracing its way across the arc of the black clouds.

"Don't swing!" he yelled to Jenny, abandoning his ball to sprint toward her.

She twisted her head to stare at him in confusion.

He pointed to the sky. "There's lightning up there. Your club's a conductor."

As he reached her and snagged the club from her hands, the skies opened up above them.

Mitch quickly glanced around for shelter. "The gazebo," he called, grabbing her hand to make a run for it. The golf cart was farther away, where Jeffrey had left it on the path.

Jeffrey saw their move, and dashed in the same direction.

By the time the three of them made it to the small open-sided cedar gazebo, it was pouring rain, and they were soaked to the skin.

"Crap," Jeffrey sputtered, running his hand over his wet hair and shaking out the droplets.

Jenny was in a short-sleeved white blouse, topping a pair

of pale gray slacks. The blouse clung to her torso, outlining a lacy bra.

Jeffrey's brows went up as he took in an eyeful, but Mitch stepped between them, warning Jeffrey off with a glare.

Mitch quickly stripped off his navy golf shirt and handed it to Jenny.

She looked perplexed. "What are you—"

"You're translucent," he explained.

She glanced down. "Oh."

"Put it on, Jenny."

She snagged the shirt from his hand and tugged it over her head, settling the hem around her thighs, then finger combing her damp hair.

"I didn't expect to go swimming," she huffed.

Jeffrey grinned, peeping over Mitch's shoulder. "No complaints from me."

"Back off," Mitch warned.

"It's a forty-dollar bra." Jenny brushed off the incident. "Models wear them on the runway all the time, in nationally televised shows no less."

"You want to give me my shirt back?" he challenged.

"Not really." Then her gaze froze for a moment on his bare chest.

He dared to hope she liked what she saw. Then he gave himself an instant rebuke. How would that be good? This physical attraction between him and Jenny was the root cause of all their problems.

The lightning flashed, the thunder boomed and the rain came down even harder.

"You want me to go get the cart?" Jeffrey offered.

"We might as well wait it out a few minutes," said Mitch. "This might not last long."

Jenny's cell phone rang.

She pulled up the tail of Mitch's shirt and dug into the pocket of her slacks. "It's probably Emily. I hope they're all okay. Hello?" she said into the phone.

She listened for a moment, eyes narrowing, mouth turning into a frown.

"Everything all right?" Mitch couldn't help but ask, but she waved him to silence and turned her back.

He glanced to Jeffrey, whose brow furrowed in concern. Had somebody been hurt?

"Uh-huh," Jenny was saying, her tone grave. "No. No, I don't." Her free hand went to her forehead, and Mitch reflexively stepped toward her.

"Jenny?" He put a hand on her shoulder.

"As soon as I can," she said without acknowledging him. "Yes. Of course." She blew out a breath.

"Jenny?" Mitch repeated.

She turned to him, her face pale, hands shaking as she lowered the phone. "My house is on fire."

"*What?* What happened? Who was on the phone?"

"My neighbor. It was a lightning strike." Jenny held up helpless palms. "The roof burst into flames."

Mitch grabbed her phone before it could slide off to the floor. "Has the fire department been notified?"

"They're on the way there."

"I'll get the cart," said Jeffrey, bounding down the two stairs to sprint across the course.

Mitch reached out to touch Jenny's arm, longing to pull her into his embrace. "No pets, right?"

"That's what Clara, my neighbor, asked. No. No pets. I'm allergic to cats."

Mitch hadn't known that. He tried to rub the chill from her shoulders. "It might not be so bad. The rain will help put the fire out. And the fire department's close by."

Jenny nodded numbly. Then she seemed to gather herself. "You're right. No sense borrowing trouble." She gave a decisive nod. "We need the facts. Let's get the facts, and go from there." She stepped away from his hand.

Mitch's protective instincts nearly blinded him. Jenny belonged in the comfort of his arms, not standing there all alone and dripping wet, trying to cope with the disaster that had suddenly befallen her life.

He made a move toward her, giving in, anticipating the feel of her small body against his.

But Jeffrey was pulling up in the cart. And Jenny was darting for the gazebo stairs. And the moment was gone.

Six

Red-and-blue lights flashed against the chaos that was once Jenny's home. A dozen firemen sprayed water into her windows, where orange flames leaped out in the darkening evening. Neighbors stood on the sidewalks, huddled under umbrellas, avoiding the runoff that had turned to a gushing river cascading down the street. The rain remained steady, but Jenny barely noticed.

Emily linked an arm with hers, squeezing tight. "Thank goodness you weren't home."

Jenny swallowed. She hadn't thought of that. But it was true. If the guys hadn't invited her to go golfing, she might have been sitting in her living room, directly below the lightning strike.

She shuddered reflexively at the thought.

"It's going to be okay," Emily continued.

Jenny nodded, trying to force her rational mind to engage. There was a lot to be thankful for here.

"I know," she finally said. "Nobody was hurt. And everything else is just stuff. It can all be replaced." She paused, a dark shot of humor piercing her numbness. "It's not like I had boxes of precious mementos from my happy childhood."

"Okay, that was impressive," said Emily.

"What?"

"You. Looking on the bright side so quickly."

Jenny shrugged. "I suppose I could curl up in a fetal position somewhere and cry instead."

"Many people would."

"I think I'm in shock."

"Yes, well, that's to be expected. You've got insurance, right?"

Jenny nodded. She was well insured. Everything being destroyed by the fire could be replaced.

Her brain automatically began to catalog the possessions in her house. She started in the living room, where the fire was worst, then she mentally worked her way through the dining room, kitchen and bedroom.

"We are going to have to replace my new wardrobe," she pointed out to Emily.

"That part'll be fun," Emily responded with determined cheerfulness.

Jenny didn't disagree. Shopping for new clothes with Emily had been a lot of fun. Of course, shopping for every single possession a person needed in life was a little more daunting.

She told herself she was lucky. The circumstances of her childhood made very little of her life irreplaceable.

"At least there are no homemade quilts. No heirloom jewelry," she reminded Emily.

"That's a good thing," said Emily. Then she gestured to the fire. "At a time like this."

Emily knew all about Jenny's complicated upbringing. Her parents had gotten married because her mother was pregnant with Jenny. The marriage was a mistake, and after five rocky years, her father had left them for good. After the breakup, her mother's psychological and emotional issues had grown worse, making life chaotic for young Jenny.

Just then, a section of the carport caved in, landing with a resounding crash on top of her car. She started at the sound, blowing out a breath.

"Gonna need a new car, too." Emily's voice was hoarse.

"This is unbelievable." Jenny struggled to keep her equilibrium. Her possessions were disintegrating in front of her eyes.

She caught a glimpse of Mitch where he stood next to the fire truck. He seemed to sense something, turning to scan the crowd. When he came to Jenny and Emily, the scan stopped. He looked directly into her eyes for a moment before returning to his conversation with the fire chief. Meanwhile Cole and the teammates looked on, obviously ready for action, and just as obviously frustrated by their inability to pitch in.

"Do you think this is a sign?" Emily asked.

Jenny dragged her gaze away from Mitch. "A sign of what?"

"That it's time to start a new life?"

"You mean leave town?" Leave Royal, the TCC, Mitch?

"No. No. I was thinking that when you rebuild, you could go sleek and modern, instead of boxy and practical."

"You didn't like my house?" Jenny was surprised to hear that. It was… Her gaze fixed on the flames once more. Well, at least it had once been very functional and livable. It had everything Jenny needed, and the mortgage was very nearly paid off.

"I'm just saying, maybe something that goes along with the new clothes, the new hairstyle, the new makeup and, soon, the new man."

Jenny pondered the suggestion.

A fresh start. Wasn't that exactly what she'd been telling herself she needed? Was the universe trying to help her out?

"The TCC is awash with both professional and amateur architects," she noted. "The building project is bringing everyone with a drafting table out of the woodwork."

"Anyone have a style you particularly like?"

"A couple, for sure." Jenny nodded. There were some incredibly creative people living in Royal.

"There you go. Think about it. Maybe do something completely different, fun, exciting."

"You suppose there's something wrong with us?" Jenny took a step back as the flames grew hotter on her face.

"Not a thing," said Emily.

"We're standing here planning my new house while the old one burns."

"It means we're practical," Emily stated with conviction. "Practical and realistic. Those are both very admirable traits."

Jenny watched while a fireman doused the oak tree overhanging her living room roof. The roof was blackened, and sagging at an unnatural angle. She couldn't help picturing the armchair that sat in front of the bay window. She'd bought it last year on sale over in Westbury County. There was a tear on the back now, and she'd never been really crazy about the plaid pattern.

Truth be told, she'd also been thinking about replacing her television set. Though, in this day and age, maybe a larger computer monitor made more sense.

"You must be getting cold." Mitch's voice startled her, and she realized he'd moved up next to her in the darkening night. The lights seemed to flash brighter now, the flames more vivid, though she knew the fire was coming under control.

"I'm hot," she responded, wiping her damp hands across her fire-warmed cheeks.

"The fire will be out soon. And you're still soaking wet."

"So is everybody else." She couldn't help stealing a glance at Mitch's bare, glistening chest. She was still wearing his T-shirt, and he looked magnificent, somehow all-powerful standing amidst the chaos.

"I talked to the chief," he continued. "They think the lightning fried your entire electrical system and started a bunch of smaller fires inside the walls. There's really nothing more you can do here tonight." His gaze shifted to Emily. "Is Jenny going to stay with you?"

"Not unless she wants to swell up like a blowfish."

Mitch's brows went up in an unspoken question.

"My cats," said Emily.

Jenny's nose twitched and her sinuses tingled just thinking about Powder and Puff, Emily's long-haired Persians. She was good for a couple of hours at Emily's. But she'd never be able to sleep overnight. "I guess it'll have to be a hotel."

The Family Inn by the highway had kitchenettes, and their rates were reasonable. She struggled not to feel overwhelmed by the logistics of the next few days. There'd be necessities to purchase, insurance forms to fill out, and soon, very soon, she was sure the magnitude of her loss would hit her.

"Why don't we all head for my place for now," Mitch suggested, his broad hand coming down on Jenny's shoulder. The gesture felt far too comforting, so she quickly shrugged it off. She couldn't let herself depend on Mitch.

"We'll get everybody dried off," he continued, clearing his throat and letting his hand drop to his side. "We can have something to eat and figure out your next steps."

"Good idea," Emily quickly agreed.

Jenny followed up on Emily's agreement with a nod. The chill of the night air was setting in as the bright flames turned to billowing smoke, and the mist from the fire hoses mixed with the steady rain coming down on them.

Jenny couldn't stay here and stare much longer. She had to get started on the logistics of the rest of her life.

Since Jenny's entire wardrobe had gone up in smoke, Mitch had asked Cole to stop at the Quick-Mart and pick her up a pair of sweatpants and a warm shirt that would fit. He'd offered her his shower, then put a barbecued cheeseburger directly into her hands, making sure she had a comfortable place to sit and an opportunity to collect her thoughts.

Now, with the barbecue finished and cleaned up, and a friendly poker game underway in his dining room, he watched

Jenny wander out onto his deck alone. She stopped at the rail to gaze across the lights of the golf course. The rain had stopped about an hour ago, and the moon was peeking out from behind the dissipating storm clouds.

Mitch waved off an invitation to join in the game and followed her outside.

Her feet were bare on the damp deck, since Cole hadn't thought to buy socks or shoes, and hers were still in a heap in Mitch's laundry room. Mitch briefly glanced to where the fleece pants covered her rear end and wondered if Cole had thought to buy underwear. But he quickly squelched that picture, admonishing his wandering imagination.

If there was a scrap of a gentleman inside him, she needed it right now. He made himself promise to provide her with support, not lust.

"Hey," he offered softly, padding across the cool, smooth deck, his own feet also bare after he'd changed from wet clothes to a pair of faded jeans and a well-worn Tigers T-shirt.

She turned her head to profile, mustering up a weak smile. The hoots and good-natured ribbing of the poker game faded behind him.

"You okay?" His voice was gentle as he came to a halt next to her at the rail.

She shrugged her slim shoulders, turning her attention back to the view. For some reason, she looked particularly delicate beneath the oversized navy hooded shirt. "I'm fine."

He didn't believe that for a minute. "Yeah, right."

"I'm really fine."

"You've just lost everything you own." Mitch couldn't imagine every treasure and memento of his entire life, his childhood trophies, the faded football jerseys, certificates, photographs, letters, gifts from his parents' travels around the world, going up in flames before his eyes.

She turned to look at him, tone going a bit brittle. "Thank you so much for pointing that out."

"Jenny."

"No, really. I'd almost forgotten."

He set his jaw. He could take this. She deserved to be upset. And if she needed to rail, it might as well be at him.

But she fell silent.

"Go ahead," he invited.

"What?"

"Get it out. Yell at me."

Her tone had returned to normal. "How would that help?"

Now, he was the one feeling frustrated. "Quit being so damn logical and analytical. You do what you have to do."

She glanced down at the baggy clothes. "What I have to do is go shopping. I may be a little late for work tomorrow, boss."

"You know that's not what I meant."

"What did you mean?"

"I meant emotionally. You deserve to be angry, to rail at the universe. Let it out, Jenny."

Nobody, not even logical, practical, two-feet-firmly-planted-on-the-ground Jenny could go through a disaster like this and not feel distraught.

"There's nothing to let out," she told him.

"Yes, there is."

But instead of answering, she got a faraway look in her green eyes. Moments ticked by. But, finally, she spoke. "I know you must find it odd."

Since he hadn't a clue what she was talking about, he waited for her to elaborate.

"Emily said I should rebuild." Jenny leaned back, holding herself steady with a firm grip around the top rail. "That sounded good to me. I rather like the idea of starting from scratch, building a life that reflects who I am today, and not…" Her voice trailed away.

He waited.

"What must I find odd?" he finally asked.

"I hear what you're saying." She seemed to wander off on yet another conversational tangent. "A normal person would be a little upset that everything she owned had just turned to ashes."

"A little upset?"

Jenny did have a gift for understatement.

"Thing is," she continued. "I don't really care."

"Of course you care." Clearly, the woman was in shock. Or maybe she was in denial. Was there something he ought to do about either of those conditions? Or did they simply work themselves out over time?

She shook her head. "I don't care. It's stuff, Mitch. I can get new stuff."

"It's not the stuff itself," he felt compelled to point out. "It's stuff as the representation of your life, your achievements, your milestones."

"I guess I have no achievements."

"That's ridiculous."

Jenny was one of the most accomplished people he knew. The TCC couldn't run without her. Mitch wouldn't even want to try.

She gave a little shiver. "Maybe this isn't the best time—" Then she laughed. "Or maybe you're not the best person."

He reflexively reached for the propane heater switch, flicking it on, causing three tall, strategically placed heaters to glow to life. He sure didn't like thinking that he wasn't the best person to help Jenny.

"We should drop it," she told him.

"You have dozens, maybe hundreds of accomplishments," he told her. "Ask ten other people in Royal, and they'll tell you exactly the same thing."

"You're not dropping it," she pointed out.

"Because you're not making sense."

"My house just burned down. I'm allowed to not make sense."

"Are you in shock?" He scanned her face. She wasn't pale, and she wasn't shaking. In fact, all things considered, she looked remarkably calm.

"Just because I don't have a stash of silly little life mementos that are vulnerable to loss or destruction, doesn't mean I'm in shock."

Mitch tried to figure out what she meant. "Everybody has mementos." Whatever they were, she had to be upset at losing them.

She gave a cold laugh. "Hard for the all-American kid to understand, huh? We didn't all live that storybook childhood, Mitch."

Mitch hadn't lived a perfect childhood. Far from it. "Are you angry with me?"

"No. I'm not angry with anyone." She backed away from the rail and plunked down on one of the couches. "Let's talk about you instead."

Mitch hesitated. But he knew people reacted to stress in different ways, and he should probably humor her. He took the chair across from her. "What do you want to know?"

"Tell me about your mementos. What would it absolutely kill you to lose in a fire?"

Besides Jenny?

Not a good answer.

He gave it some thought. "My Fitzpatrick Trophy."

"Why?"

"Because they're hard to win. And it's the rookie of the year award. It's not like I'm ever going to be a rookie again."

"So, it reminds you of something good?"

"Yeah." Well, sort of. It mostly reminded him of his hard-ass dad, and how Mitch had finally stuck it to the old man by proving that he wasn't a complete screwup. Still, who wouldn't hate to lose the Fitzpatrick in a fire?

"Winning it was immensely satisfying," he said to Jenny.

She gazed at him for a long moment. "What else?"

"I don't know. The usual stuff. Pictures, certificates, ribbons, my college diploma. Why are we talking about me?"

"Because it's more fun than talking about me."

"No, it's not." Mitch would rather talk about Jenny any day of the week. In fact, now that the subject had come up, he found himself with a burning curiosity. "What, exactly, did you lose tonight?"

"Well, it sure wasn't any rookie of the year trophy," she finally offered.

"Other things are just as important as sports trophies. Pictures of your tenth birthday party, for instance. Or that stellar report card I just know you got in first grade and every other grade after that." He'd be willing to bet that even back then, Jenny had been pretty much perfect, always punctual, always neat, all work complete and in on time. In short, a teacher's dream.

He smiled encouragingly, but Jenny's eyes had clouded to jade. Had he just reminded her that she'd lost all her childhood photographs?

What a complete cad.

Impulsively, he moved to the couch beside her.

"No tenth birthday pictures," she said.

Not anymore. Mitch could have kicked himself.

"No report cards." Using both hands, she raked her fingers through her damp hair. "Funny thing about my mother." She leaned back and tipped her head against the couch.

Mitch wanted to reach out to her, but he forced himself to stay still. Something important was obviously going on inside her head.

"She liked to clean," said Jenny.

Okay, that wasn't what he'd expected. "Clean?" he prompted.

"A lot." Jenny stifled a small laugh with the back of her hand. "You've heard of hoarders?"

"Of course."

"Mom was the opposite. It was some kind of an obsessive-compulsive disorder. She's on medication now. But, well, let's just say I'm pretty accustomed to starting over when it comes to worldly possessions."

Mitch found himself moving closer. "What are you saying?"

"I'm saying she got rid of things. Every year or so, in a fit of psychological confusion, she would throw out every single thing in my bedroom."

Mitch was struck silent.

"I tried so hard when I was little," Jenny continued, a faraway look coming into her eyes. "I thought if I kept everything in my room just so." She gestured with both hands. "Neat as a pin, dolls lined up by size, their clothes ironed, pictures alphabetical, socks in the top drawer, underwear next, pajamas, tops and skirts and slacks." Her voice faded away.

"You ironed your doll clothes?" He couldn't keep the incredulity out of his tone.

"It didn't help. She cleaned them all out anyway."

Mitch felt as though he'd been given an astonishing window into Jenny's makeup. "Is that why you're so meticulous and efficient?"

"In small doses, it's a good thing."

"But do you like being meticulous and efficient?" It had never once occurred to him that she might not. Did she get satisfaction out of running a tight ship at the office, or was it a leftover compulsion from her childhood?

Laughter wafted out from the raucous poker game, as Emily accused Cole of being a jinx.

Jenny didn't answer, and Mitch realized he didn't know her nearly as well as he thought he had. Was she unhappy? Did she struggle emotionally?

"You can change, you know," he told her.

"I have changed."

"I don't mean putting on a sexy dress for a wedding and getting all gorgeous—"

She laid her index finger across his lips, but it was too late. The image was already coursing through his brain. And the touch of her finger put a physical element into the fantasy.

He was going to kiss her again.

Unless lightning struck him dead, he was going to lean in, capture her lips and drag her into his arms all over again.

From the poker table, Cole gloated in triumph, reminding Mitch that they were in full view of five other people. But he didn't even care.

He captured her hand, holding it tight against his cheek. When he spoke, his voice was strangled. "What am I going to do about you, Jenny?"

A beat went past.

"Take me to a hotel."

For a split second, he misunderstood and desire roared to life. But then he got it. "You meant without me."

Her cheeks flushed bright, and her lips flattened together, her entire body stiffening with anger. "It's not fair for you to send me mixed signals like that. What is it you want, Mitch?"

"What I want, and what I can have are two completely different things." He knew he was wrong. He was doubly wrong to say it out loud, and it was unforgivable to say it to Jenny. But that didn't change the way he felt.

"You were the one who called a halt to everything," she reminded him.

The heated air suddenly felt stifling. "I explained to you why I had to do that."

"You never did."

He cataloged their conversations through his brain. Of course he'd explained it to her. What exactly had he said to her? "It's because you are you, and I am me."

She came to her feet, expression closed off. "Nice. You're the big celebrity, and I'm a boring small-town girl."

"No, you don't—"

"I understand perfectly, Mitch." Her eyes blazed, and she held up her hands. "Do me a favor. Let's keep it strictly professional from here on in. I don't want to know about your childhood, and I don't want you to know about mine."

"I threw smelly socks in the corner."

She blinked in incomprehension.

"When I was a kid," he elaborated, for some reason, refusing to let the conversation end. He wanted to know about her, and he wanted her to know about him. "And as a teenager. I used to drop my socks, my jerseys, shorts, pretty much anything, wherever they fell, and let 'em sit."

"Why are you—"

"It ticked my mother off something fierce. And my dad yelled at me for doing it. Then again, he yelled at me for every little mistake. Especially on the football field."

"Mitch—"

He ignored her interruption. "From the time I was nine years old. It didn't matter if a receiver was out of place, or if a blocker screwed up. Everything that happened on that football field was my fault. The pass wasn't long enough. It wasn't accurate enough. I should have run. I should have faked. I should have found a hole, handed off or cut back."

Mitch couldn't believe the words were tumbling out of him. He'd never shared this with anyone. "When I wasn't a first-round draft pick, he called me an abject failure. He said I hadn't put my heart into it."

Jenny was looking at him with pity now. He hated pity. But from her, he'd take it. It was better than indifference.

"But your interviews," she put into the silence. "The two of you go on camera together. And you rave about his inspiration and support."

Mitch gave a cold laugh. "I do, don't I?"

"It's all an act?"

"We have an unspoken agreement to revise history."

Jenny sat back down. "Are you trying to make me care about you?"

"Yes. No." What the hell was he trying to do here?

He took her hand, and mustered every scrap of honor in his disreputable soul. "I'm a cad and a womanizer, and I can smooth talk my way into or out of just about anything. Like touchdown passes, most things in life come way too easily to me, and I don't appreciate them nearly as much as I should."

Her eyes had softened, and he felt the danger of her compassion right down to his toes.

"Is that what your dad told you?" she asked.

"He was right."

"What if he wasn't?"

Mitch shook his head. "Don't do it, Jenny. Don't convince yourself that I'm worthy."

"Don't convince yourself that you're not."

"I'm—"

"You are a glib smooth talker, Mitch. You're smart and you're diplomatic, and I know you've been handling me just like you handle everyone else in your life. But there's more to you than that. You just proved it."

"Hate me, Jenny."

"I can't."

"If you could see inside my head right now, you'd have no trouble at all."

"Tell me what's inside your head."

No way, no how was he going to do that.

But her gaze was steady, and the heated air thickened between them.

"You are," he finally said, determined to put an end to this once and for all. It was true that he could talk his way out of anything, and right now he was going to talk his way out of Jenny. "And you're naked. On top of me. Your hair is wild, and your breasts are gleaming in the moonlight."

Her eyes went round, and her lips parted.

"You've kissed every inch of my body, and I've kissed every inch of yours. You're crying out my name, begging for more, harder, deeper. Your nails dig into my shoulder, but it feels good, because it's you. And we come together, and it lasts forever, and it's the best freaking sex I've ever had."

She gave a long, slow blink, her cheeks flushed red, and her shoulders drooping in the still, heated air.

"But guess what, Jenny?" he spat. "It's a one-night stand. The next day I go back on the road, back to the team, back to the parties and the girls, and I leave you far behind."

He let his words drop to cold silence.

Her eyes narrowed, and her lips pressed together. "You're lying."

He gave a harsh chuckle. "That's the bald-faced truth, darlin'. I'd be lying if I told you anything else."

She straightened and drew away from him.

He hated the suspicion in her eyes, but he knew it was for the best. "You're right to suspect that I'm handling you, Jenny. I can talk my way into your pants then out of your life without breaking a sweat. When it comes to sex, don't trust me for an instant."

She rose shakily to her feet, and took a couple of backward steps, staring at him in obvious shock.

It was only then that he realized Emily, Cole and Jeffrey had overheard the tail end of his little speech.

Emily quickly swooped in and put an arm around Jenny, ushering her swiftly toward the front door.

Cole gave Mitch a glare of disgust and followed the two women.

Jeffrey ambled onto the deck and took a seat as the front door slammed firmly behind the trio.

"Harsh," Jeffrey observed.

"Necessary," Mitch responded, feeling lower than turf grass.

"I've sure never seen you do that before."

"She deserves to know the truth."

"That wasn't the truth. That was you protecting someone you care about," said Jeffrey. "You were trying to scare her off."

Seven

Jenny was still stunned from Mitch's words as she blindly followed Emily and Cole into Cole's front foyer. The terra-cotta tiles were smooth and cool under her bare feet. Clearly, there was something wrong with her. Otherwise, she would simply walk away from Mitch and be done with it.

"What is the *matter* with you people?" Emily demanded of Cole as he secured the door behind them.

"Don't lump me in with him." Cole strode through a plaster archway and into the living room of his large, airy house. He swept an arm toward a curving staircase, looking at Jenny. "There are three bedrooms up there. Take whichever one you want. But you're not going anywhere near a hotel tonight or any other night."

Jenny was nearly overcome with gratitude. She just wanted everything to stop for tonight. She was tired, battered and bruised.

"He was a colossal jerk," Emily stated, stomping her way behind Cole as he moved farther into the house.

"You won't get an argument from me," Cole tossed over his shoulder.

"Maybe I should quit my job?" Jenny ventured, bringing up the rear, struggling to keep her feelings in some semblance of order. Mitch had hurt her, there was no doubt about that. But he'd also outlined the bald truth in no uncertain terms. There was absolutely no future for the two of them.

"No," was Emily's quick response.

"You'll outlast him," said Cole. "Wine, anyone? Whiskey? Beer?"

The more Jenny thought about it, the more handing in her resignation made sense. Mitch had made it as plain as possible that he wasn't interested in a relationship. But despite her vows to both herself and Emily, she couldn't seem to get him out of her head. Seeing him every day would only make things worse.

"I don't think I can face him," she told Emily.

"It's *him* that shouldn't be able to face *you,*" Emily put in with staunch loyalty.

Maybe that was fair, but it wasn't reality. "Do you suppose he'd give me a reference?"

Cole chose a crystal bottle filled with amber liquid from the bar situated between the two walls of glass that showed off his backyard. "I'd give you a reference. Hell, I'll give you a job. You just say the word, Jenny. Tell me what kind of career you want, and I'll make it happen."

Jenny couldn't help but smile at Cole's generous offer. She felt immeasurably better being around such loyal friends. "You know any nice guys, Cole? Are there any nice guys left in the world?"

"I'm a nice guy." Cole splashed some whiskey into a heavy crystal tumbler.

"Would you date me?"

"You bet." But his glance flicked to Emily.

Jenny smiled at the telltale action. "Or maybe you have a

nice friend?" she amended her request. "The four of us could double."

"Excuse me?" Emily put in.

Jenny ignored her. "Anybody but Mitch."

Cole grunted at that. "You want me to fix you up?"

"I want you to fix me up."

"Don't count me in on this plan," said Emily.

Cole placed the tumbler in her hand, his fingers lingering against hers for a moment. "Nobody asked for your opinion."

"You're getting it anyway."

His gaze bore into hers. "You pick the time, the date and the location. We'll do anything you want."

Emily glared back. "It's not the location that's the problem."

"Then what's the problem?"

"You're the problem," Emily stated bluntly.

"You barely know me," Cole countered.

"You're short."

"I'm taller than you."

"Ha."

"I'm five-eleven. What are you? Five-six? Five-seven?"

"Five-six," Emily admitted.

"There you go. As long as you keep your heels below five inches, we're good. Now, where do you want to go?"

"Nowhere."

Jenny watched the battle of wills with fascination, wondering who'd come out on top. Emily was self-assured and very determined, but Cole seemed to be holding his own against her.

He cocked his head toward Jenny. "You'd abandon your best friend in her time of need?"

"Jenny has nothing to do with this."

"I'm fixing her up, helping mend her broken heart."

"My heart's not broken," Jenny felt compelled to add. Bruised, maybe. And definitely the worse for wear. But she wasn't about to let some silly schoolgirl crush incapacitate her.

"Her heart's not broken," Emily repeated, staring pointedly into Cole's eyes.

"She asked me to fix her up."

"*Her,* not *me.*"

"She needs moral support. Now, where do you want to go?"

Emily pressed her lips mulishly together and, despite everything that had happened over this hellish day, Jenny fought an urge to laugh.

"I have tickets to the Longhorn Banquet in Austin next weekend," Cole offered with a sly smile.

Jenny silently awarded him a point for that one. The Longhorn Banquet was the hottest ticket of the year. Held in the state capital, it included the who's who, and celebrated prominent Texas citizens' annual accomplishments. The governor would attend, as would business, arts and sports notables from around the state.

"Wait 'til you see my jet," Cole added. "And I've rented a house on Lake Austin. Waterfront, six bedrooms, spa, pool and a full staff. Jenny can stay with us. And, I'll get her a date."

"I'm in," said Jenny. In her books, anticipating a luxurious weekend away was definitely better than wallowing in self-pity for the next week.

Emily turned to her. "You're not buying this," she exclaimed. "He's bribing us with staff, and a spa, and a private jet." Then her words trailed away.

"If I'm going to get bribed," Jenny put in philosophically. "It might as well be by the best."

Emily stared at Jenny for a long moment. Then her hand went to Cole's chest. "She's smiling. You made her smile."

"I did." Cole accepted the credit, leaning ever so imperceptibly toward Emily.

Then while Emily crossed the big room to Jenny, Cole's hungry gaze stayed glued to her every move.

"You really want to do this?" Emily asked her. "You think it'll make you feel better?"

"I sure don't want to sit on my butt and pine away for Mitch."

"He's a jerk."

"He truly is." But even as she voiced her agreement, Jenny couldn't help remembering the expression on his face when he'd told her about his father. She'd never have imagined all-American Mitch Hayward was hiding a crappy childhood. They had that in common.

"Okay." Emily nodded.

"So, it's a go?" Cole asked hopefully.

Emily shot him a warning glare. "This weekend is all about Jenny, not about you."

"Yes, ma'am." Cole grinned. "You ladies just tell me what you'd like. Meal suggestions for the chef, preferences for floral arrangements, wines, special sheets on the beds? They have chauffeur-driven SUVs, but I can get a stretch limo if you'd prefer."

Jenny nudged her friend. "How are you not dating this guy already?"

"He's too short," said Emily.

"I'll buy lifts," Cole put in.

"Short is a state of mind."

"It's a state in *your* mind, woman, not mine."

Emily sniffed her disapproval, and Jenny couldn't help but laugh.

"I'm leaving now," said Emily, and disappointment flickered in Cole's blue eyes.

Emily missed it because her attention was focused on Jenny. "I'm going to grab you some of my clothes and a few personal things. Tomorrow, we'll stock you up. But I'll be back in an hour with the essentials."

Since there was nothing left to salvage from her house, the insurance forms were straightforward, and the cleanup started right away. Jenny drove by it once, on Sunday morning, but she quickly decided it was time to focus on the future, not to dwell on the past.

The house was gone for good. But the lake was still beautiful, and the black scars on the land would heal. Emily was right. There was a lot to be said for rebuilding something brand-new, right here.

Jenny took Monday off work to dash through a long list of errands and settle into Cole's guest room. She'd offered once more to get a room at the Family Inn. But Cole was adamant, and Emily backed him up. He had plenty of room, and it would take months for her new house to be built.

It was a shock for her to find out that Cole had a housekeeping staff. He had a cook, a gardener and a housekeeper. All were incredibly friendly and seemed determined to treat Jenny like royalty. When she'd mentioned that she usually took baking to the office on Tuesdays for the TCC's youth outreach program, Maria, the cook, had insisted on pitching in to make cupcakes.

So, the mound of jumbo gourmet-frosted chocolate creations that Jenny carried outside to the athletic field late Tuesday afternoon attracted more than the usual hungry glances from the thirty or so teenage boys practicing football passes.

Mitch had started the youth outreach during his first month at TCC. He was a strong advocate for youth in sports, and his star power had ensured participation from the local teenage boys. The program had grown, and now several members of the TCC were working with the teenagers on everything from algebra to career planning. But Tuesday after school was still devoted to sports, and Jenny had taken up the habit of providing a baked treat for the kids at the end of the session.

Normally, she left the baking next to their water jug, gave everyone a wave and went back to work. But today, she found herself pausing. As angry as she wished she could be with Mitch, she couldn't help noting how great he was with the kids. And she couldn't help remembering the story about his father.

Were the two related in some way? Was he trying to do for

other kids what his own father never did for him? She recalled the encounter on the beach in Galveston. Mitch had stuck up for the smaller kid. In a few short moments, he'd obviously boosted the boy's self-esteem, and very likely given him a whole new perspective on life and on his future opportunities.

Jenny watched while Mitch gave a few pointers on passing the football to one of the boys. Again, it was one of the smaller boys, someone who might easily get picked on in a group. The boy nodded, gave another throw and was rewarded by Mitch's clap on the shoulder and what were obviously words of praise.

How on earth could Mitch think of himself as a bad guy?

Then his gaze caught Jenny's.

Since she'd skipped work yesterday, and since today he'd had back-to-back meetings out of the office, they'd barely spoken. On the upside, there'd been no time for awkward conversation. On the downside, she knew that conversation was looming in their future.

She'd written and discarded three letters of resignation yesterday. Part of her longed to walk away from the emotional minefield of working for Mitch, but the other part of her loved her job at TCC and told herself she was adult enough to stick this out.

Cole was right. One way or another, Mitch would be gone from Royal very soon, and he'd be completely out of her life. At the latest, he'd leave after the TCC presidential election in December. That wasn't so far away. Jenny could keep her head down and her focus on business until then. Heaven knew the issues surrounding the new clubhouse and the presidency were coming at them faster and more furious by the day. Who'd have time to talk about anything personal before the election?

Now Mitch was moving toward her.

The TCC building and emotional safety were just fifty yards away. She could make it if she left right now. She doubted very much that he'd sprint after her. Then, while he finished up with the boys, she could shut down her computer, gather her purse, head for the parking lot and drive her rental car back to Cole's house and hide in the back sunroom, where Mitch's house wasn't even visible.

He was closer now.

She had one minute to make a decision.

Leaving would be easy.

Staying would be fraught with—

"Hello, Jenny." His long strides quickly covered the last few yards between them.

"Hello, Mitch," she offered evenly.

His glance went to the big tray of chocolate cupcakes sitting on the table. "The boys'll like those."

"Maria made them."

He nodded. "So you did decide to stay at Cole's?"

"He didn't tell you?" That surprised Jenny. Cole and Mitch were very close friends.

"I don't believe he's speaking to me at the moment."

She didn't know how to respond to that. Emily and Cole hadn't overheard Mitch's entire kiss-off speech, thank goodness, but they'd heard enough to be very angry with Mitch. Still, she couldn't help hoping the incident wouldn't drive a wedge between the two men.

"I'm, uh, sorry," she tried.

"*You're* sorry?"

"That Cole's angry with you."

"He'll get over it." Mitch paused. "And you?"

"Me?" Was he asking if she'd get over being angry with him for not wanting a relationship with her? It sounded quite petty when she thought about it that way. It was entirely Mitch's business who he chose to date or not to date. If he wasn't interested, he wasn't interested. That surely wasn't his fault.

Still, she couldn't seem to find a coherent answer to his question, and the silence stretched between them.

He was the one to break it. "Are you going to quit, Jenny?"

She drew a breath. Mostly, she thought no. But in the dark

of night, when Mitch's words ran around and around inside her head, she sometimes felt like she had to make a clean break, if only to save her sanity.

"Let me be the one to quit," he put in before she could answer.

"What? No." She shook her head firmly in denial. "You can't quit." She gestured to the field. "The boys, the members, everyone depends on you. I'm completely expendable."

He took a step closer. "You've got it backward. I'm a figurehead. You're the one who's indispensable."

It wasn't true, but the earnestness in his eyes suddenly brought home the humor of the conversation. "Is it just me," she asked him, "or is our mutual admiration society a little nauseating?"

Mitch broke into a familiar grin, and a wave of relief coursed through Jenny's stomach. He stage whispered, "I'll keep it a secret if you do."

"Definitely."

His expression sobered again. "And I'll stay if you will."

Jenny gathered her courage. "Okay. I'll stay." She risked another joke. "But you have to promise to keep your hands to yourself."

"You're a pistol, Jenny."

"I'm a survivor, Mitch."

A funny expression crossed his face. "You don't have to *survive* the TCC, Jenny. You're fantastic at your job. Don't worry so much about being careful and meticulous. Relax a little. You can make mistakes and mess things up. Nobody will die."

She understood what he was saying. She didn't have to be perfect for him. For some reason, his words made her eyes sting.

She blinked quickly to get rid of the sensation. "Does that sound like me? Messing things up?"

"I don't know," he said with sincerity. "But I'd like to find out."

Out of the corner of her eye, Jenny saw the boys making a move for the cupcakes. "Tell you what," she said to Mitch, knowing they'd be overrun in a matter of moments. "I'll stop organizing the whiteboard pens in the order of the color spectrum."

He lifted a hand to his chin and pretended to ponder. "I don't know, Jenny. Loosening the color spectrum rules? Can anarchy be far behind?"

The first of the teenage boys reached the table. "Hey, Mr. H. Jenny. Those look fantastic!"

"Help yourself, Scott." She gestured to the thick-frosted, color-sprinkled cupcakes.

"Awesome," came another boy's voice.

"You're the best!" shouted Terry.

Jenny took a step backward to avoid the fray. She could feel Mitch's gaze on her, but kept herself from looking back at him again as she headed toward the clubhouse. They'd ended their conversation on a joke. It was a lot more than she'd hoped for today.

"I can't believe things are moving along so fast," Jenny said to Emily as she peered down at several sets of house plans spread out across the glass-topped table in Cole's formal dining room.

Cole was off to one side, sprawled out in an armchair next to the open French doors, typing away on his laptop. His shirt-sleeves were rolled up, and his tie loosened. "If there's going to be a change in the foundation footprint, they might as well know about it while the loaders are on site." He glanced up. "It'll save money in the long run."

"You know something about construction?" asked Emily, an edge to her voice.

"A little."

"Is there anything you don't know about?" She stared back at him with what Jenny had come to recognize as her clash-of-wills expression.

Cole paused in what looked like contemplation. "Women," he finally answered. "Specifically, you."

Jenny couldn't help but laugh.

"You're a nerd," Emily accused.

"Yeah? Well, you're dating me."

"Not after Saturday night."

"We'll see." Cole smiled confidently, going back to his work on the laptop. "You may find 12:01 comes around pretty fast. And then you'll also be dating me on Sunday."

"Conceited," Emily muttered under her breath.

"I think he's cute," Jenny whispered back.

Emily kept her voice low, leaning her head close to Jenny's. "I don't want to sleep with cute."

"Why not?" Jenny whispered back, giving Cole a surreptitious once-over. He was a very attractive man. He was in excellent physical shape. He was smart, successful, had a good sense of humor. And he was definitely one of the few males on the planet who could hold his own against Emily.

"I'm looking to get pregnant, remember?"

Ah, yes. The linebacker factor. "Would you rather sleep with Emilio?"

"Huh?"

"He's tall, brawny, definite football genes in that guy's DNA."

Emily's eyes narrowed. "Maybe. But he's kind of...I don't know. Do you think he's sexy?"

"It's not what I think that matters." Jenny thought Mitch was the one who was sexy, and look how far that had gotten her. "Who do you find sexy?"

Emily shot a fleeting, telltale glance at Cole who was typing away on his laptop. "I'm still looking," she whispered with a thread of determination.

"You two do realize I can hear you," Cole drawled.

Emily's face flushed red as she straightened in her chair. "We're not talking about you," she snapped.

"I know. You're talking about Emilio." Cole looked up again, his gaze boring deep into Emily's this time, anger lurking in the sapphire depths of his eyes.

As the tension thickened in the room, Jenny started to rise from her chair. "Why don't I just leave you two—"

"No!" Emily snapped. "Sit down. We're choosing your new house. This one." She pointed to a set of plans. "I like the contemporary hardwood floors, and all that glass."

Jenny turned her attention to the blueprints for the two-thousand square foot single-story custom house. The floor plan looked very elegant, ultramodern, with lots of planes and angles, and great circulation space between the bedrooms, kitchen and a glassed-in deck which could overlook the lake.

The front doorbell sounded, and Cole rose swiftly from his chair. Since any one of his staff members would answer, Jenny assumed it was his excuse to leave. She also didn't expect him to come back.

"Look at all those built-in closets." Emily spoke with what sounded like false cheer. "You'd have tons of room for the new wardrobe. I can picture it now, entertaining, dinner parties."

"Emily—" Jenny began.

"What?"

"This thing with Cole. Are you feeling—"

"I'm fine."

"But—"

The front door banged shut, and footsteps sounded down the hallway.

"He's coming back," said Emily. "Don't worry about it. I can handle Cole."

"...only if she's not too busy," came the sound of Mitch's voice.

Jenny stilled, her stomach clenching.

"She's in the dining room," Cole responded, and Jenny met Emily's eyes.

Emily reached out and squeezed her hand. "Are you okay?"

Jenny gave a determined nod, ignoring the butterflies circling in the pit of her stomach. "I can handle it. We spoke a few times at the office today. It was fine. I'm doing fine."

"Emily?" came Cole's voice as he appeared in the arched doorway. "Mitch needs to talk to Jenny."

Emily pivoted in her chair. "I'm not going to—"

"Emily," Cole growled. He jerked his thumb toward the hallway. "Now."

She opened her mouth, obviously about to refuse his command, but then something in his expression seemed to stop her.

"Fine," she ground out, bringing her hands down on the glass surface of the table as she rose from her chair. "But I'm not going out of earshot." She gave Jenny a significant glance. "Call me if you need me."

"I will." Jenny fought a smile. She was warmed by Emily's protective instincts. Not that they'd be remotely necessary.

Then, head held high, Emily crossed the room to Cole. Jenny noted that he put his hand on the small of her back as he ushered her out of the room.

Mitch immediately filled the empty doorway, tall, broad-shouldered, magnificently handsome as ever. She sure wished her chest wouldn't do that little hitch whenever he entered the room.

She needed to strive for equanimity. She had to stop being attracted to him. Then again, being angry with him was only marginally better. It was just as emotionally unsettling.

"Jenny." He nodded, his deep voice impacting her even more than his appearance. "Sorry to bother you after working hours."

"No problem," she automatically responded, her attention piqued. Had something gone wrong at TCC?

His gaze stopped on the paperwork in front of her.

"We were just looking at house plans," she explained.

"Pick something yet?"

Jenny shook her head. "Is everything okay at TCC?"

Mitch strode into the room, taking the chair Emily had vacated. That put him right next to Jenny, making her body respond to whatever male pheromones radiated from his pores. Her skin tingled, and her palms began to sweat.

So much for equanimity.

"I was looking for the letter to the senator. The one on the subsidies from last week."

"You couldn't find it in the directory? It should be under federal government, financial issues, political support." Jenny hated the thought that she might have misfiled something.

"Oh." He nodded. "Political support. I'll look there."

"Did you need it tonight? I can log in and get it for you. Cole probably won't mind if I use his laptop."

But Mitch was shaking his head. "I can get it in the morning."

"Okay," she agreed. But his words surprised her. If it could wait until morning, why had he gone to all the trouble to come over here?

Eight

Mitch hadn't lost the letter to the senator. He couldn't care less about the letter to the senator. All he was looking for was an excuse to come and see Jenny. She'd seemed like she was doing okay at work today, but he was still guilt-ridden over the way he'd treated her. His instinct was to apologize again. But he didn't want to belabor the issue. He supposed he wanted the best of both worlds, for Jenny to understand why they couldn't have a relationship, but for her to still like him.

Now he glanced down at the three sets of building plans. "Which way are you leaning?" he asked in an effort to keep the conversation going.

"You sure you don't need me to—"

"Don't worry about it." He waved away her question. "Tell me about your house plans."

"I haven't decided yet." She reflexively glanced down at the three drawings on the table.

Mitch swiveled the pages to face him, finding the contrast

among the three designs fascinating. It was as if completely different people had picked them out.

The first was an ultramodern contemporary, plenty of glass and sharp angles, long rooms, with sleek storage systems and display cases for art. The second was attractive, but practical. Two stories, it had three bedrooms on the top floor, a nice-sized ensuite in the master bedroom and a small balcony off the bedroom that would overlook the lake. The kitchen and dining room were L-shaped, while the living room boasted a big stone fireplace. With the exception of the skylight in the entry hall, there wasn't a lot to distinguish it from thousands of other practical houses in thousands of other residential neighborhoods around the state.

It was the third set of plans that had Mitch pondering. It was all arches and detail, softness and whimsy. It seemed to have a French provincial influence, and the demo pictures showed deep carpets, scrollwork on the wood and etching on the glass. The ceilings were high, with open beams, many of the walls were on forty-five degree angles, keeping the rooms from sitting square, while little wrought-iron balconies and bay windows gave the interior a wealth of nooks and crannies and the exterior complex detail.

He lifted one of the large sheets of blue line paper. "Did Emily pick this one?"

"Emily picked the contemporary. That one's really a token plan. You know, included so we can have three distinct choices."

"Did you pick it?"

"I did," she acknowledged.

Now Mitch was even more curious. This plan was very unlike Jenny. Well, unlike the Jenny he thought he'd known for the past year.

"Why?" he asked her.

"What do you mean?"

"I mean, out of all the thousands of house plans in all the world, why choose this one as a top three pick?"

There was a definite note of defensiveness in Jenny's tone as she responded. "I wanted to look at something completely different."

"I like it," he said.

"I find it impractical." She pointed to the living room, the dining room and one of the bedrooms. "How could you possibly arrange furniture in there?"

"I guess you'd turn it on an angle. Or have something custom designed." He pointed to an alcove in the kitchen. "You could put a half-octagonal breakfast nook in there. Or a window seat and a planter. There are a thousand things—"

"I don't know why I even added it to the list." Her lips compressed into a line, and she folded her hands primly in her lap.

He covered her hands with his own. "I'm not your mother, Jenny."

"What is that supposed to mean?" She pulled herself free.

"It means, you're allowed to like something, just because you like it. You don't need an excuse, and it doesn't always need to be functional, practical and utilitarian."

"I'm not about to build an impractical house."

"I would," said Mitch, meaning it. He'd build whatever house struck his fancy. And he'd build it in the blink of an eye if Jenny wanted it.

He gave his head a shake, chasing away that ridiculous thought. Jenny's taste was irrelevant when it came to his house.

"Those bay windows all add cost," she told him. "They'll be a pain to clean, and I can't afford custom furniture."

"You'll have the insurance settlement to spend."

She gave him a sharp glance. "You know what I mean."

"What if you had an unlimited budget?"

"I don't."

"Play along with me for a second. *If* you had an unlimited budget?"

She mulishly set her jaw.

But he waited her out.

"Fine," she capitulated, pointing to the French country plans. "If I had an unlimited budget, I'd add a big deck out back overlooking the lake, and a turret up front." She moved her finger. "Right there. With a round room on the top floor that had window seating all round. I'd buy dozens of pillows and curtains with ruffles, in a floral pattern that looked like a country garden. It would have deep, cushy seats, and a thick green carpet."

"Green?"

"Like grass. And everything would be soft."

He took in her rosy cheeks, the pout of her mouth, the moss green of her eyes and the way her dark lashes slowly stroked with each blink. "Soft is nice."

"This is ridiculous. I don't know how you talked me into daydreaming." She shook her head, moving back, appearing to physically distance herself from the whimsical house plans.

He continued to study her expression. As usual, his desire for her battled its way to the surface. But it was tempered this time, tempered by something warm, something soft and protective. His voice went husky. "It's not ridiculous to have dreams."

She twisted her head to look at him. "A person should stay away from dreams that have no hope of coming true."

On impulse, he smoothed a stray lock of her hair back, tucking it behind one ear. "Those are the only kind worth having."

She rubbed her cheek where his hand had touched it. "Really? So, what are your dreams, Mitch?"

It was impossible for him to answer. Because right then, he was toying with a dream that involved Jenny and forever.

He took a safe answer. "I want to play professional football."

But she shook her head. "Come on, Mitch. That's not a dream. That was already your reality. We're playing a game. You have to come up with something you could never have in a million years."

He searched his brain for an acceptable answer and ended

up stalling. "I don't know, Jenny. There aren't a lot of things I can't buy."

"Something money can't buy."

"Happiness?"

"Sure." She waited for him to elaborate.

This time, he tried to be honest. "I want the TCC to have a successful election that brings the membership together under a good leader."

She rolled her eyes. "Lame."

"You don't want that?"

"Of course I want it. But that's motherhood and apple pie. Who doesn't want it? Plus, it's not for you personally. Tell me something that's for you."

"I can't think of anything off the top of my head."

"Oh, yes, you can." She was obviously not going to let this go. "I owned up to secretly wanting a silly, whimsical house. Spill."

"You should build that house."

"Quit stalling."

But he had to stall, because he knew exactly what it was that would make him happy. Something he could dream about and never have. But he wasn't going to tell Jenny. He refused to hurt her all over again.

He shook his head. "I can't tell you."

"Yes, you can."

"No, I really can't." Inside his head, he was asking himself what the hell he thought he was doing even flirting with the truth. He needed a lie, and he needed one quick.

"Why not?" she pressed.

"Let it go."

"You wouldn't let me off the hook."

He thought about it for a moment longer. And then he gave her a different truth. "I want a miracle cure for my shoulder. I want to be back to one hundred percent."

"You will be—"

But he shook his head. "I keep telling myself it's getting better." He hadn't voiced his deep-seated fear out loud to anyone. He didn't really know why he was doing it now. "But it's not."

She reached out and touched his arm, her sympathies obviously engaged. "You just have to be patient."

"This isn't about patience. It's about the physical limitations on the human body." Now that he'd stuck his toe in the pool of bald honesty, he plunged all the way under. "I see the expression on the physiotherapist's face, the expression on my doctor's face. They told me six months. Well, it's been a year. And there's been no discernable progress for the last six weeks."

"I understand these things can plateau."

He sent her a look that told her to stop lying.

She swallowed. "That's your secret dream?"

"Yes." It was the only secret dream he could tell her about. The other was a relationship between the two of them where she didn't get hurt in the end. Impossible.

"Is there anything I can do to help?" she asked.

The genuine caring in her eyes blew him away. After all that had happened, all he'd done to her, that she could muster up this kind of compassion for him was nothing short of amazing.

"Anybody ever tell you you're a saint?"

She coughed out a laugh. "Good grief, no. My mother used to tell me I was the devil in disguise."

"Your mother had no right to say that."

"She was ill."

"She was nasty."

Jenny gave a philosophical shrug. "She's out of the state now, and out of my day-to-day life."

On impulse, Mitch brushed the pad of his index finger across Jenny's temple. "Don't let her live on up here."

"I'm not."

"Build the house, Jenny. The one you love."

"Are you going to pay for it?"

It took everything Mitch had not to say yes.

* * *

Wednesday evening, Jenny determinedly rolled up the plans for the French country house and slid them into a cardboard tube. It was all well and good for Mitch to tell her to dream. But reality was reality. She wasn't building it.

"Jenny?" Cole called from the front room. He was home earlier than usual, and she hadn't heard him come in.

"Back here," she answered in response, tucking the plans to the back of a shelf on his built-in china cabinet.

Cole had been incredibly generous about letting her stay with him. She was becoming positively spoiled by the cook and the housekeeper, and she now teased him about never leaving.

He'd told her she was welcome to stay as long as she liked. He said he'd begun to think of her as the sister he'd never had. Since Jenny had always wanted siblings of her own, his words had touched her on a very deep, emotional level.

He strode into the dining room, loosening his tie, having already discarded his suit jacket somewhere along the way. "Can I ask you a huge favor?" He winked and grinned. "Sis?"

"Am I going to hate this?" she teased in return.

"I hope not. You can say no if you really hate it."

"What if I only sort of hate it?"

"Then you should say yes and make me happy."

"Go ahead." She pretended to brace herself against the back of a chair. "Hit me with it."

"Jeffrey Porter called today. From the Tigers."

"I know who you mean."

"He offered a fifty-thousand-dollar contribution to my hospital charity if I gave him my fourth ticket for the Longhorn Banquet."

The fourth ticket? So, he'd be attending with them.

"He'd be my date?" Jenny asked.

"He would. Tickets have been sold out for months."

Jenny didn't have anything against Jeffrey. She didn't see her and Jeffrey going anywhere on the relationship front. But fifty thousand dollars was a lot of money.

"It's a good charity?" she asked Cole.

"They're building a new pediatric wing."

"He won't think he and I are on a real date, right?"

Cole shook his head.

Jenny analyzed the request for a downside. It was a lost opportunity to date someone new. Then again, there'd be a whole lot of new people at the party.

"What do you think?" Cole put in.

"As long as you don't think I'll be misleading him."

"Don't worry. He just broke up with his girlfriend. But he's not looking for a replacement. Trust me when I tell you you're not going to break Jeffrey's heart."

"That did sound kind of conceited, didn't it?"

"It sounded very sweet. You're a caring person, Jenny Watson."

"And so are you."

"You'll tell Emily that?"

"I already have."

"I like having you in my corner, sis."

"And I like having you in mine." She hesitated. "Bro." Then she giggled. "I've never called anyone that in my life."

"Then, I stand adopted. Did you pick out a dress yet?"

She shook her head. "I was thinking about going to look for something tonight." She made a show of inhaling the spicy aroma of the cook's baking lasagna. "After dinner."

Cole reached into the pocket of his slacks. "Here, take my credit card."

"Don't be ridiculous." Jenny might not be able to afford custom furniture, but she could definitely afford her own clothes.

He flipped open his leather wallet. "I want you to get something special."

"I'm not taking your credit card, Cole."

He seemed to be ignoring her. "In fact, why don't you call Emily. Go to Maximillians. Tell her I'm buying for you both."

Jenny felt her jaw drop open. "*The* Maximillians?"

Had he lost his mind? The purses alone at that store cost three thousand dollars.

But he held out the slim platinum credit card. "If you don't let me buy a dress for you, Emily will never let me buy one for her."

"You can't spend that kind of— You can't spend *any* kind of money on our dresses."

"But I can. That's one of the perks of making a whole lot of money. You get to spend it on anything you want."

"I'm saying no, Cole." She took a backward step. There was no way he was talking her into doing this.

He stepped forward. "I *need* you to do this."

"You don't—"

"Correct me if I'm wrong, but I think Emily might, just might, be slightly attracted to me."

Slightly attracted? Jenny was pretty sure it was a lot more than slightly attracted. She also realized Emily was fighting it for all she was worth.

"I want to see what she'll do. If she has the chance to pick out a dress, a no-holds-barred, money-is-no-object dress, just for a date with me, I really need to know what it is she'll choose. Do me this favor, sis."

Jenny rolled her eyes. "I can't believe it." She socked Cole playfully on the shoulder. "I cannot believe you just made the one and only argument that could get me to use your credit card to buy a three thousand dollar dress."

"Don't restrict yourself to three thousand." Cole grinned. "And don't restrict yourself to a dress. You're going to need shoes and accessories. And so will Emily."

Jenny continued to shake her head. This was surreal.

He took her hand and placed the credit card firmly in her

palm. "I mean it. You have to go wild. If you do it, Emily will do it, and then I'll know whether or not I've got a shot."

"She might just spend your money out of spite," Jenny felt compelled to warn him. While she was pretty sure Emily harbored a secret attraction to Cole, she was also sure Emily had a very strong will. She didn't want to fall for Cole, and she was annoyed at him for chasing her.

"I won't get my answer because she spends my money. I'll get my answer from what she spends it on."

The edges of the credit card were hard against Jenny's palm. "Are you sure about this?"

"I am positive about this. Call her. Right now."

Jenny tucked the credit card away and reached for her phone. "What are you hoping she'll buy?"

Cole gave a shrug. "I'll know it when I see it."

Jenny pressed her speed dial. Then she listened to Emily's gasp of disbelief, followed by her growing conviction that Jenny should absolutely indulge herself at Cole's expense and, finally, her mounting excitement as she bought fully into the plan.

Mitch had watched Jenny drive off from Cole's house half an hour ago, so he knew Cole would be alone. He knew he had no one but himself to blame, but he missed the days of being able to wander over to Cole's house on a whim, or having Cole wander over to his house to share the interesting bits of information from their lives. It never had to be earth-shattering, not the kind of thing where you pick up the phone to call your family or whoop it up with the gang, just the everyday, normal things that you wanted to share with another human being.

But he felt like he couldn't invade Jenny's space every evening. So, instead, now Cole was with Jenny, while Mitch was alone. He felt as if he'd screwed up two relationships in his life.

As he started up the driveway, Cole came out the front door, car keys in his hand, striding toward his Mustang.

"Hey, Cole," Mitch called out, in case Cole hadn't spotted him.

It appeared he hadn't, because he turned guiltily. "Oh, hey, Mitch."

"Got a hot date?" Mitch joked, striding closer.

"No. I'm…" He pocketed the keys. "It's nothing." He hesitated a moment longer. "You up for a beer?"

"I don't want to hold you up."

"No. Not at all. No big deal."

"Where were you going?" Mitch couldn't help but ask. It wasn't like Cole to act all twitchy like this.

"Errands. Come on." Cole turned back for the house. "I've got a couple of lagers on ice."

Feeling vaguely like an interloper, Mitch followed along. "I got some news a few days ago." For some reason he felt like he ought to get straight to the point.

"Good news?" asked Cole as they made their way through the house.

"Pretty good."

Cole reached for the refrigerator door.

"I've been short-listed for the Youth Outreach Award at the Longhorn Banquet."

Cole's reach faltered. "On Saturday?"

"Yeah." What other Longhorn Banquet was there in Texas?

There was something wrong with Cole. "And you just found out?"

"Last week, actually. But with everything that's been going on, I didn't want to…you know, intrude over here."

Cole swung open the door, his voice hearty. "That's great. Congratulations, buddy." He snagged two bottles and pressed one into Mitch's hand.

"What's wrong?" Mitch had known Cole way too long to fall for this act.

"Nothing's wrong."

Now Mitch was getting mad. It was one thing to be ostracized by Jenny. He deserved that. But he was still Cole's friend. "What the hell?"

"Fine." Cole twisted off the cap. "I had four tickets. So I invited Emily. And Jeffrey is taking Jenny."

Mitch felt as though someone had punched him in the solar plexus. "You're double-dating?"

Cole nodded, then took a swig of the beer.

"With Jenny and *Jeffrey?*"

"Yes."

"Son of a bitch."

"Me?"

"No. Jeffrey. I'm assuming you're just trying to get into Emily's pants."

Cole frowned. "That's not exactly what I had—"

"*You* didn't know I'd be there. I get that. But Jeffrey." Mitch's anger bubbled boldly to the surface.

He'd told himself a thousand times that Jenny was allowed to date anyone she wanted. He'd forfeited his right to an opinion a couple of weeks back. But he'd warned Jeffrey away. He'd warned Jeffrey in no uncertain terms that he was to stay away from Jenny.

"Jeffrey knew you'd be there?" For some reason, that revelation made Cole smile.

"Don't you dare laugh."

"He's messin' with you, Mitch."

"Of course he's messin' with me. I told him to stay away from her. I warned him not to hurt her."

Cole looked like he had something more to say. But instead, he took the bottle of beer back from Mitch and placed them both on the granite countertop. "I sent them shopping."

"Who?"

"Emily and Jenny. I gave them my credit card and sent them to Maximillians to buy dresses for the banquet."

That didn't sound right. "Jenny won't spend your money."

"That's where I was headed when you showed up just now," Cole responded. "To make sure she did."

"You were going to Maximillians?"

"I was."

"I'm coming, too." Mitch pivoted to head for the front door. "And you're not buying Jenny a dress."

"Yes, I am."

"No, *I* am."

The thread of a chuckle was back in Cole's voice. "Why does that not surprise me?"

Mitch turned to glare at his friend.

"And good luck with that," Cole added.

Mitch didn't need luck. He was a professional football player. He had strength, guts, agility and endless determination. He'd already defied the odds nine ways to Sunday. He could get one woman to buy one single dress. And since it was for a date with Jeffrey, he'd push for something that went from wrists to ankles, no cleavage, preferably in a sedate gray woolen blend.

By the time they arrived at Maximillians, Mitch had decided on exactly the dress Jenny should wear. But when he entered the store and made his way to the changing area, honing in on the sounds of Jenny and Emily's voices, the nun outfit flew right from his head.

Jenny stood in front of the three-way mirror in a black strapless sheath of a full-length dress that flared out at the knees. The top was sequined and dipped low between her breasts, clinging like a second skin.

His mouth went dry, and his knees went weak.

"You'll have all the men at the gala panting after you like Labrador retrievers." Emily laughed.

That was Mitch's fear, too.

Emily was dressed in a short, full-skirted deep-blue satin dress. It was also strapless, and flared from the waist to reveal a black crinoline peeking out at the hem.

Mitch felt Cole come to a halt beside him.

Jenny gazed wide-eyed at herself in the mirror and seemed to stumble for words. "It's too…too…"

Too *everything,* Mitch wanted to shout. If she was dating

him, sure, it was a perfect dress. But not when she was dating Jeffrey.

"Perhaps the silver?" a sales clerk offered, holding up a slinky, short dress with capped sleeves and ties that crisscrossed the open back.

Jenny frowned at it uncertainly.

"I'll try that one," Emily put in, scooping the hanger from the sales clerk.

"Go with the blue," Cole muttered under his breath.

"Can you grab me some shoes?" Emily called as she pulled the heavy curtain shut.

"Sure." Jenny turned and immediately spotted Mitch. Her jaw dropped open, and she glanced to the right and to the left, as if looking for the punch line to a joke.

She made her way toward him, every movement sinuous and graceful. Her voice, however, was an accusatory hiss. "What are you doing here?"

"He came with me," Cole put in, and Jenny seemed to notice Cole for the first time.

"Why?"

"I got curious," said Cole. "I couldn't wait to see what she picked out."

"I meant why did you bring Mitch?"

"We were having a beer."

Jenny compressed her lips.

"I won't get in the way," Mitch found himself promising.

"I'm going to ignore you," Jenny announced.

"Fair enough. Do you want to know what I think of that dress?"

She glared at him. "Absolutely not."

"Okay," he agreed.

But when she stared at him a moment longer, he found his gaze dropping to the cleavage, to the nipped-in waist and to the clingy fabric where it hugged her hips.

"You don't like it," she stated.

"That's not the problem."

"Then what's the problem? You're grimacing."

"That style isn't you."

"It is now." She brushed past him. "I have to get Emily some silver shoes."

"Get her a bag, too," called Cole, and Jenny cracked what looked like a reluctant grin as she shook her head.

Mitch watched as she made her way across the store. She consulted with the shoe salesman, chose two pairs, then started back. On the way, she paused at a rack, taking out something gauzy and pastel, her expression softening as she ran her fingers over the fabric. But when the sales clerk approached her with two more dresses, she let the gauzy one fall back on the rack. The two women chatted on their way back to the changing area.

Curious, Mitch went to see what had caught her eye.

He couldn't have been more surprised. It was a V-necked, spaghetti-strapped dress made of pale, mottled rainbow silk. The soft, romantic colors were very unlike Jenny, as was the swish of the layered skirt that came to points at the hem, and the tiny jewels that adorned the neck and the waist.

For some reason, the dress reminded him of the house plans. Did Jenny have a secret romantic side? Instead of geometric lines and practicality, did she truly long for swirls and irreverence? The idea intrigued him.

"Hand-painted," came the clerk's voice from behind his shoulder. "One of my favorite designers. Brand-new in today. Is it for someone special?"

Mitch was willing to bet every item in the store was made by one of the clerk's favorite designers. But if this particular one had caught Jenny's eye, he wanted to see her in it.

He nodded to the changing rooms. "Can you take it to the woman who's trying things on? The one with the strawberry blond hair?"

"Of course." The clerk smiled, removing the dress from the display.

"Don't tell her it's from me."

The woman touched her finger to her lips to promise her silence, and Mitch gave her a nod of appreciation.

He moved to another section of the store, pretending to ignore Jenny. In his peripheral vision, he caught her puzzled frown and her initial head shake to the clerk. But the persistent clerk prevailed, and Jenny took the dress into her cubical.

Mitch made his way casually back to the changing area.

"Are you going to offer an opinion?" Emily was demanding of Cole as she modeled the silver dress. "Or just stand there and gawk?"

"I'm here to make sure you don't go overboard with my credit card."

"Oh, I'm going overboard all right." She held out one of her silver sandaled feet. "See these? They're Amerelda, three-inch heels, and I'm buying them."

"What about the blue dress?"

"You liked the blue dress?"

"Your choice."

"Well, I like them both."

"Then buy them both."

Emily put her nose in the air as she flounced off. "I think I will."

Mitch turned to Cole and raised his brows, wondering if his friend had a master plan. "This is going to be an awfully expensive date."

"Like I care."

Mitch considered Cole's determined expression, and came to the simple conclusion that he had it very, very bad for Emily Kiley. In a misery-loves-company way, it made him feel better. But only by a very small margin.

"I hope she's worth it," he offered to Cole.

"I figure I'll know by the end of the weekend."

Then Jenny appeared in the hand-painted silk, and the breath left Mitch's body. She looked like a goddess, a fairy nymph who wandered out of a mystical garden. The colors set off her honey-toned skin, meshing perfectly with her minimal makeup and her delicate features. Her limbs were long and graceful, and he immediately pictured her with wild flowers in her hair, tiny white satin sandals and a trailing bouquet.

He found his feet moving, taking him closer to where she swayed one way then the other in front of the mirror. The words *buy it, buy it, buy it* echoed through his head, but he kept himself determinedly silent.

"It's really not me," she said to no one in particular.

Mitch moved closer still. "Pretend for a minute," he said softly. "That you're not you."

"Well, that's ridiculous." But she smiled as she said it, and a warmth invaded his system.

"It goes with your eyes," he offered, easing closer still, turning the conversation more intimate.

"It would have to. There's every color in the universe on this."

"Do you like it?"

"Maybe if I was a fairy princess. But I'd never wear it again."

"So what?"

"I'm not going to buy a dress this expensive to wear once."

"I'll buy it for you," Mitch found himself vowing. Then he instantly regretted the words when her smile disappeared.

"Cole told me his plan," Mitch quickly amended, backpedaling fast. "I only meant that anything that won't fit on his credit card will fit on mine. Don't you want to be a fairy princess for just one night?"

A longing burned deep in Jenny's green eyes, and he knew in that instant she was the fairy princess. She'd been the cautious, perfect child for her mother, the professional, meticulous employee at the TCC, and the chic, sophisticated city girl for Emily, but deep down inside, Jenny wanted to be the princess.

She needed this dress. And she needed the whimsical house and the custom furniture. And Mitch vowed to himself that he would move heaven and earth to make those things happen for her.

Suddenly, Emily appeared from her change room, and her eyes went wide when she saw Jenny. "Wow. That's sure not you."

"It's not, is it?" And some of the light went out of Jenny's eyes.

Cole moved closer to stand next to Mitch.

"But isn't that the point?" Mitch quickly put in, feeling almost desperate. "For Jenny to buy something completely different? When is she going to get a chance like this again? It's hand-painted silk," he parroted the sales clerk. "Just came into the store today. One of her—" he gestured vaguely to the clerk across the store "—favorite designers."

Both Jenny and Emily blinked at him in surprise.

"I overheard," he defended.

Emily took another look at the dress. "Well, maybe," she allowed.

"Once in a lifetime," Mitch repeated. Then he lowered his voice for Jenny's ears alone. "A dream."

Jenny hesitated for a long moment. Then she turned back to the mirror. She pivoted, letting the skirt swirl around her thighs.

"It'll look great on the dance floor," Mitch dared. "You need some white satin sandals, low heels, maybe a ribbon at the ankle."

"What the hell's up with you?" Cole muttered beside him.

"Shut up."

"That might look good," said Emily. "Really, what the heck?"

Jenny smiled, and Mitch's chest went tight. It was a perfectly natural reaction, he assured himself. He'd never claimed that he didn't admire Jenny, only that he wasn't any good for her. He wanted her to be happy. She deserved it.

Nine

The awards had been handed out by the governor, the speeches made, dinner was finished and Mitch's distinguished plaque for the Youth Outreach Award was parked with the others on a table for attendees to admire. As the best days in Mitch's life went, this would probably rank as the worst.

He'd made it through his short speech, thanking all the right people, but all he could see was that Jenny was with Jeffrey instead of him. And echoing inside his brain were his doctor's words from earlier this morning. His worst fear had been realized today. Mitch was never going to play football again.

He hadn't said a word to anyone, and now he was standing on the sidelines as the dancing began, accepting congratulations from friends, acquaintances and strangers while watching Jenny in Jeffrey's arms.

He should have talked her into the gray wool blend instead of the rainbow silk after all. He resented the way the delicate dress flowed around her sexy legs, a splash of color in a sea of monochrome. Her hair was styled in a crown of braids, wisps flowing free over her temples and along her neck. And she'd found a pair of white silk sandals. The heels were higher than he'd pictured, but they were strappy and delicate, rhinestones winking around her slim ankles.

She was perfect, and it was all for another man.

He took a deep drink of his single malt.

She disappeared from his view, and he reflexively shifted, nearly knocking into an older gentleman in a tux, who scowled at Mitch, his bushy brows drawing together. Mitch gave a perfunctory apology, not particularly caring that the man might be someone important.

He wove his way through the crowd, trying to come to terms with the fact that he wasn't a pro football player anymore. What was he now? Just a guy with a nest egg and no career, whose services would soon not even be required at the TCC. They'd have a new president, and Mitch would have little to do and nothing of value to contribute to the community.

He came closer to the edge of the dance floor, telling himself to stop wallowing in self-pity. But watching Jenny laugh in Jeffrey's arms made everything that much worse. Jeffrey should let go of her. He needed to let go of her right now. In Mitch's raw, emotional state, he needed Jenny in *his* arms, not in his teammate's.

Scratch that. He and Jeffrey weren't teammates anymore.

Mitch stuck his glass on an empty tray stand as the music changed from one song to the next. The band was sticking to classics, with the occasional jazz tune tossed in. No pop and no rock, and apparently no country, even though this was Texas.

When the floral arrangements were two feet high, the main course was Kobe beef and Newfoundland lobster, and the average carat weight per woman was in the low double digits, he supposed Keith Urban was out of the question. Still, he had an urge to scoop Jenny up, get rid of his bow tie and jacket, and head for the nearest honky-tonk where they could kick back.

He craned his neck, scanning the floor. Where had she gone?

"Having a good time so far?" came Jeffrey's deep voice.

"A blast," Mitch responded drily, determinedly swallowing his misery, bracing himself for an up close view of Jenny in the dress. But when he turned his head, she wasn't with Jeffrey.

"She's out on the dance floor." Jeffrey had correctly interpreted Mitch's expression.

"You left her there alone?" That was even worse.

"She's got a new partner."

"Who?" Mitch demanded.

Jeffrey chuckled. "I didn't get his name."

Mitch strained to look, but couldn't catch a glimpse of her dress. "You didn't tell her I was going to be here, did you?"

"Was I supposed to tell her that?" Jeffrey accepted a glass of wine from a passing waiter.

Mitch declined another drink. "I saw her expression of shock when my name was called at the podium."

"Yet she wasn't sitting anywhere close to you."

"Don't get cute. I thought you would have given her a heads-up is all." Mitch took a step back to get out of the line of circulation around the dance floor.

"Why didn't you tell her yourself?"

"I barely saw her this week." Except in the office. And in the office, they were being careful to stick to business.

"She told me about the dress," said Jeffrey.

"That was Cole."

"Cole said it was you."

"Cole has a big mouth." Mitch changed his mind about the wine and caught the next waiter who came by.

"So, why are you turning yourself inside out watching me dance with her?"

Mitch grunted a noncommittal answer. So he didn't want Jenny at the mercy of a player like Jeffrey. That was simply good taste.

"You don't want to date her," Jeffrey pointed out, watching Mitch a little too closely.

"Of course I don't want to date her. But I don't want you to date her, either."

"Noble sentiment. If you were her father, and if this was the nineteenth century."

"Ha, ha," Mitch mocked.

"Seriously, Mitch. Am I making my point out there?" He cocked his head to the dance floor. "You need to either start dating her yourself or step aside."

"I already stepped aside."

"The hell you did. You haven't taken your eyes off her all night."

"I can't see her now."

"She's to the left of the band."

Mitch zeroed in. He felt a little buzz of relief at seeing her proper stance with her dance partner. He could live with those six inches of airspace between them. But he wasn't so crazy about the guy's expression, nor about the way he kept glancing at her cleavage.

"Tell me something, Mitch."

"Yeah?"

"That guy she's dancing with? What do you want to do to him?"

"Rip his head off and kick it through the uprights."

"I rest my case."

"You have no case."

"You can't take out every guy who wants to sleep with her. Because take a good look at her, Mitch, lots of guys are going to want to sleep with her."

"It better not frickin' be you."

"It'll never be me."

Mitch didn't trust that promise, not one little bit. "Why not?"

"Because you're my friend, and because I know what's going on here."

For a split second, Mitch thought Jeffrey meant his shoulder injury. But he quickly realized it was impossible for Jeffrey to know what the doctor had said.

"What's going on here?" Mitch asked.

"What's going on here is that you've been sacked one too many times behind the line of scrimmage, and it's resulted in serious brain damage. Otherwise, you'd be out there on that dance floor with Jenny. She's incredible, Mitch. And she said she wants to date you. But, oh, no, you're so busy protecting your dating future with generic blonde bombshells, that you—"

"That's not what this is about," Mitch growled.

Jeffrey snorted. "The hell it's not."

"Give me one reason why I should take advice from you."

"Because I screwed up. I had my chance with Celeste, and I blew it. I have to start all over again." His voice went lower. "You watched me screw up, so now you don't have to."

"It's not that simple," said Mitch, even as his thigh muscles quivered with the need to cross the hall to Jenny. He tried to tell himself it wasn't fair to Jenny to date her. But a growing chorus in his brain kept telling him he wouldn't hurt her. He liked her too much to ever let himself hurt her. He honestly didn't know which side of the argument to believe anymore.

"Song's about to change," Jeffrey warned.

Mitch swore under his breath. Giving in, he took the first few steps toward the dance floor.

Mitch was heading her way. Jenny watched him weave through the crowd on the dance floor. His gaze had locked on hers, and his jaw was set to a determined angle, shoulders square, stride eating up the distance between them. Judging by the flare in his blue eyes, he was either going to ask her to dance or have her arrested.

The strains of the music faded around her, and she relaxed her hold on her partner, stepping away.

"Thank you." She smiled and nodded to the man she'd just met, drawing away and switching her attention back to Mitch.

She drew a little hitch of a breath, letting her arms fall to her sides and reflexively moistening her lips. She felt pretty tonight in a way she never had before. It was the dress, the hairstyle, the subtle makeup and the delicate shoes. And there was no denying, it was also the way men regarded her.

Normally, she caught very few eyes. At the wedding and the football party, when she'd been dressed in such sophisticated clothes, their interest had been frankly sexual. But tonight was different. There was respect in their eyes, a deference in their tone when they asked for a dance.

Jenny smiled to herself, thinking she could get used to this.

Mitch was thirty feet away now. She definitely wasn't seeing deference in his expression. Still, she found herself eagerly anticipating his arrival.

Would he ask her to dance? Would she say yes? What would happen when she was in his arms again? Would all her well-laid plans fly out the window? Because the one thing she definitely could not achieve with Mitch was equanimity.

He came to a halt in front of her.

Neither of them spoke, but his expression softened.

"I like your dress," he finally spoke.

"Thank you."

The music came up again, and she felt self-conscious standing still in the middle of the swaying couples.

"Did you want to dance?" she asked him, taking away her option to say no. Not that she realistically thought she'd say no to him.

"No," he told her, making her feel more self-conscious than ever. "I want to get out of here," he finished.

She wasn't sure how to take that. Was he saying goodbye? She couldn't control a wash of disappointment.

He steadily held her gaze. "Come with me."

Yes, yes, yes. "I came here with Jeffrey," she reluctantly replied. "I can't just leave him."

But Mitch took her hand, something that looked like pain

filtering through his eyes. "Only as far as the grounds. I've got to get away from this crowd for a few minutes."

"Is something wrong?" She couldn't imagine why Mitch would feel a need to leave. He was a celebrity tonight. She'd been surreptitiously watching him while she danced, and he'd had a steady stream of congratulations, everyone from the governor to movie stars.

"Yeah," he told her, towing her along. "Something's wrong."

He shouldered his way through the crowd, her hand still firmly clasped in his as he cleared a path to the bank of French doors that led to a huge concrete veranda.

It was a warm, humid night, and a few couples were engaged in conversation around the lighted deck, drinks in hand, dresses sparkling along with the laughter.

Mitch glanced around, then headed for the stairs that led down to the gardens and manicured lawn of the River Bend Club.

Clouds had obscured the moon, and the only illumination came from the windows of the club behind them, discrete pot lighting in the gardens and the residential buildings far across the river.

At the bottom of the stairs, her heels sank into the soft grass. "Wait," she gasped.

He abruptly stopped, turning.

"My—" She shook her hand free from his, lifting her feet one at a time and peeling off her sandals and dangling them from one hand. "How far are we going?"

He gazed out ahead of them. "I don't know. Until we're away." His voice was stark, his jaw clenched, his eyes slate gray.

"Mitch, what's wrong?" She was getting worried.

"Do you mind if we walk?"

"Of course not." She fell into step, glancing up at his profile every few feet, wondering if he was going to tell her why he was upset.

Finally, she couldn't stand it anymore. "What's going on, Mitch. Has somebody been hurt?"

"Yeah." His voice was flat.

Oh, no. "Who?"

"Me."

"What?" She froze. "How?"

He halted and turned back to face her, voice hoarse. "I spoke to the team doctor today. It's official. I'm never going to play football again."

Jenny's stomach sank. "No," she rasped.

It wasn't possible. He'd worked so hard. He'd done everything they'd told him to do. He had the best physiotherapist, the best surgeons. He was young and fit and incredibly healthy.

"Are you sure?"

"Yes."

"I mean, is there—"

His voice went raw. "You don't think I asked them to double-check? To triple-check? To call Sweden and see if there was a new procedure or a miracle cure?"

Of course he'd done all that. What a stupid, stupid question.

"It's done, Jenny." Now, his voice was devoid of emotion. "It's over. I'm thirty years old, and my career is finished."

"Oh, Mitch." She blinked back the sting of tears, swallowing hard as her throat closed in.

Mitch's gaze went to the brightly lit castlelike building behind her. "I'm sorry. I didn't mean to be selfish and drag you into this. You should get back inside."

"But—"

"Jeffrey's waiting."

"Jeffrey will understand."

"I wouldn't."

She stepped boldly forward. "I'm not leaving you."

"I don't deserve that."

It didn't matter what he deserved or didn't deserve. There

was no way she was leaving him right now. "Do you need to yell? Scream? Get it out of your system?"

"I'm not going to yell at you."

"You can," she offered.

"It's not your fault."

"That doesn't matter. If you need to—"

He reached out to her, gently grasping her upper arm. "Stop. You are *not* going to be my whipping post."

"I am so sorry, Mitch." She placed a hand on his chest, feeling his heat, feeling his heartbeat, wishing there was something she could do to help.

"Jenny, don't."

But she stepped into the touch and pressed more firmly. "You don't deserve this, Mitch."

He gave a weak laugh. "And you don't deserve the likes of me."

"I don't have you," she pointed out.

"Don't you?" His deep gaze bore into hers.

He trapped her hand, squeezing it tight against his hard chest, his voice hollow and haunted. "I try and I try. But I can't seem to stay away."

The shoes slipped from her fingertips, landing softly on the lawn below. Before she could censor them, her feelings whispered out. "Then stop trying."

Her voice was deep and throaty. And she realized she didn't want to censor the words. She meant them with all her heart.

She shifted closer still, her breasts brushing the back of his hand. If there was a small measure of comfort she could give him, even if it was only temporary, she was willing.

His chest heaved.

She walked her fingers up the front of his dress shirt, stopping at the black bow tie.

"We can't," he strained.

"We can," she countered. "In fact, we already have."

He trapped her wandering hand once more. "This will only make it worse."

She swore she could feel his hurt throbbing tight in his chest. She couldn't bear to leave him. "Or, it might make it better."

"And if it ends?" he rasped. "When it ends?"

"When it ends, I'll survive. You said it yourself, Mitch. Everything in my life doesn't have to be planned, controlled and logical. Deep down inside, I'm impulsive and wild."

He groaned her name.

"Let me be impulsive and wild."

His hand convulsed over hers, tugging it tight against his chest, the blue flame of his gaze heating her through to the core.

"I wish I could make a guarantee," he rasped.

She smiled serenely, certain of her decision. "I don't want a guarantee."

All the way back to his hotel suite, Mitch expected Jenny to change her mind, or else to evaporate from his dream, leaving him to wake up alone, sweating and frustrated in a tangle of sheets.

But she didn't.

And he closed the suite door behind them, leaning back against it as the latch clicked into place. He watched her walk across the plush carpet, into the dimly lit sitting area.

"You forgot your shoes," he pointed out.

She turned. "You want to go back?"

He shook his head, stepping forward, tugging the loose end of his bow tie and tossing it on a chair. His tux jacket followed as he moved toward her. He was about to make the biggest mistake of his life, but he couldn't bring himself to care. He was too raw with emotional pain, too tired of fighting his feelings for Jenny. He didn't have it in him to be strong. Reality would to have to wait for tomorrow.

He reached out to touch her face, stroking his rough fingertips along the smooth satin of her cheek. "How is it possible for you to be so beautiful?"

Her smile widened, green eyes glowing jade.

He cupped her ear, the back of her neck, bending and drawing her close. His lips touched hers, and his eyes closed shut in response to her sweet taste, the moist heat of her mouth.

He wrapped an arm around her waist, drawing her close and feeling her lithe curves mold against him. She fit so perfectly. Though he fought for control, and he strained to take this slow, raw desire throbbed its way insistently into his system. His kisses grew harder, longer, deeper. His skin caught fire, and his muscles turned to tempered steel.

She met his tongue, and he bent her backward, his hand roaming from her neck, to her shoulder, along the side of her breast, whispering over the thin silk that covered her body. From the second he saw her in this dress, he'd longed to feel her heat through the gossamer fabric.

His palm rounded her buttocks, pressing her against his taut thighs. He groaned as the soft curve of her belly came up against him.

She clung to his shoulders, while he kissed her temple, her ear, her neck, skipping over the jeweled trim of her dress to press his hot lips against the smooth honey-tone of her shoulder.

Her lips touched his chest, kissing him through the pressed fabric of his shirt. For some reason, the gesture seemed intensely erotic, and he threw back his head to savor the sensation. Her fingers fumbled with his buttons then. She kissed his bare chest, and lust ricocheted from his brain to his toes and all points in between.

He scooped her into his arms, capturing her swollen mouth with his own, kissing her hard while she cradled his head, curling her body against him. He strode for the bedroom, ignoring the light switch, navigating by the dim glow of the city lights that filtered through the gauzy curtains.

He lowered himself to the bed, falling backward onto the

thick quilt, pulling her down on top of him and running his hands up the back of her thighs, finding the lace of her tiny panties, then drawing her softness more solidly against him.

Between hot kisses, she pushed off his shirt. He pulled down the zipper at the back of her dress. But she drew back and shook her head, catching her bottom lip with her white teeth. Her hair had come loose from the braids, and her eyes simmered with deep desire.

He forced his hands to still. He'd be as patient as she needed, even though it might kill him. To his surprise, she rolled the lace panties down the length of her legs, tossing them aside. Then she pulled upright, sitting astride him.

"Is this what you pictured?" she asked in a throaty voice. "Was this your fantasy?"

The dress had fallen off one shoulder, and her messy strawberry blond hair framed her face in the fragile light.

"It's better than the fantasy," he whispered. "You're better than the fantasy." He traced his thumbs along the inside of her thighs. Her dress whispered out of the way, and his thumbs met in the middle, sliding slick while her eyes fluttered closed and her head tipped back.

The strap of the dress slipped farther down her arm, the fabric sliding over one breast, revealing her pert pink nipple.

"Much better," he rasped, drawing her down to take the nipple into his mouth.

He was rewarded with her gasp. She rocked forward, bracing herself with her hands in his hair, kneading his scalp while her thighs twitched under his hands.

The dress fell to her waist, and her writhing movements brought him close to the edge of control. He swiftly unfastened his pants, shoving them out of the way after retrieving a condom from his pocket.

He shifted to move on top, but she pinned down his shoulders, thighs bracing his.

"Remember," she whispered, bending to kiss him, her breasts

brushing the bare skin of his chest. "You told me how this goes when you described your fantasy."

She sat up straight, trapping his gaze with her own, lowering herself onto him, smooth and slow, until his hips bucked to meet her. His hands twisted in the quilt in a desperate attempt to keep hold of control. But there was no turning back. She was too sexy, too sweet, too passionately perfect.

He grasped her hips, holding her firm, matching her movements, and nearly dislodging them from the bed with the force of his thrusts.

She leaned forward to kiss him, and he flipped them both over, adjusting his angle and covering her with kisses, while she curled herself around him.

His brain roared for release, but he held on to paradise just as long as he could. When her cries found his ears, and her body arched high, he let the world melt around them in waves.

She was heat and sweat and scent in his arms. Her breathing was raspy, and her heart pounded hard against his own.

He smoothed back her hair, kissing her temple, then her cheek, then her hot, moist lips. He smoothed her hair again, pulling back to gaze at her exquisite face. Her eyes were closed, cheeks flushed, lips abraded in a way that made him twinge with guilt.

He wanted to say something. There had to be the perfect words for this perfect moment. But he couldn't come up with anything that didn't sound trite.

He settled on, "You're beautiful," and kissed her again.

She blinked open her eyes, her voice sleepy. "You're not so bad yourself."

"Thank you." He couldn't help but smile. "I was really hoping for 'not so bad.'"

She cocked her head, and her smile turned impish. "Do you need me to tell you you're the best I ever had?"

"Only if it's true."

"You're the best I ever had."

He searched her expression, hoping against hope that it wasn't a joke. He'd rather be the only one she'd ever had. But he knew that was ridiculous.

"I lost my virginity in college."

"So did everybody else."

"It really wasn't that great."

"It never is."

She smirked. "My point is, you didn't have much competition."

He paused, her words filling him with some unnamed emotion. "Just the one guy in college?"

She nodded.

"And it wasn't very good?" He felt a smile of pride grow on his face.

"It was terrible. Quit laughing."

"I'm not laughing."

"You're insufferable."

He hugged her close, savoring the feel of her naked body, the curl of her limbs, the softness of her breasts. "You're a treasure."

"Can you put that on my next performance evaluation?"

"Absolutely. You want me to include the rationale?"

She playfully smacked him on the arm. "I want you to approve a raise."

"You need money?" He found himself ready to step in if she did.

"I've developed expensive taste in clothes. And you just ruined a three thousand dollar dress."

He reached to where the dress was bunched at her waist and ran the filmy fabric through his fingers. "It was *so* worth it."

Ten

Jenny awoke cocooned in Mitch's arms. Sunlight was streaming through the big bedroom window, the split beam catching on the rumple of her dress discarded on an armchair beside them. A cool breeze wafted lazily down from the ceiling fan.

Mitch's body was warm where he curled around her back, one arm draped across her stomach. She shifted experimentally, stretching sore muscles.

He nuzzled her neck with a whisker-roughened face, kissing his way to the tip of her shoulder. "You okay?" he asked gently, voice morning-husky.

She shifted onto her back, taking in his sleep-crinkled eyes and beard-shadowed chin. "I'm fine." She gently touched his bare chest, concern growing as she recalled the terrible news he'd received yesterday. "You?"

"Fine," he responded, dipping to kiss her gently on the lips.

"You know what I mean," she pressed.

He slipped an arm beneath the small of her back, drawing her naked body against his own, kissing her again. "I think I'm in denial. Or maybe you're just too distracting for me to dwell on anything else." He pressed himself meaningfully against her.

"Again?" She quirked a brow, shifting one more time to test the extent of her soreness.

"Always," he muttered, his hand closing over her breast.

Her nipple instantly peaked, and desire flooded her system. Okay, so maybe she wasn't that sore.

Surprisingly, he drew back. "But you're not ready."

"I could—"

He put a finger across her lips, trailing it downward. "You've been out of practice since college."

"I was never in practice *in* college."

His grin looked decidedly possessive. "Hungry?"

She nodded, touched by his tender consideration. "Famished. And I'd kill for some coffee."

"Regular? Latte?"

"Whatever you've got."

He reached for the bedside phone. "What I've got is room service. Name your pleasure."

It was on the tip of her tongue to say him.

"Don't look at me like that," he scolded. "I'm trying to be a gentleman."

"Croissants, strawberries and regular coffee."

"You never used to play with fire," he mumbled.

"You never used to look so sexy."

He punched a button on the phone. "Tell me what's different, and I'll do it all the time."

"You're going to stay sleep-rumpled, unshaven and naked?"

"Yes," he said, staring straight at her, even though he spoke into the phone. "We'd like some croissants, some fresh strawberries and a pot of coffee."

She scooted close and whispered in his ear. "That's impractical."

His arm closed around her, and he shifted the mouthpiece to beneath his chin. "It's okay. I think they're in season." Then he spoke into the phone again. "Thank you." And he hung it up, turning back to her, grinning. "Or did you mean the naked part?"

"I meant the naked part."

"You like me naked?" he confirmed.

Jenny made a show of pulling up the sheet to peep underneath, gazing unabashedly at his sleekly muscled, magnificent body. Oh, yes. She liked him naked.

"That's it." He shifted abruptly to the edge of the bed. "I'm outta here."

She felt a jolt of unease, and pushed up on an elbow. "Did I do something wrong?"

"No." He slid his legs into last night's pants. "You're doing everything absolutely right. And if I don't leave now, I'll be all over you again."

She felt a satisfied smile grow on her face, and she let her head fall back on the pillow.

He hesitated for a split second. "You're a dangerous woman, Jenny Watson."

"Nobody's ever called me dangerous before."

"That's because they didn't see you in that dress."

She gave an exaggerated sigh. "And I guess they never will, since you tore it."

"I'll buy you a new one."

"That's silly."

"I loved you in that dress."

"You loved me out of it more," she singsonged.

He pointed through the doorway to the living room. "I'm getting the room service now, and then I'll meet you on the deck for breakfast."

Breakfast. With Mitch. After a long night of…

An unsettling thought raced into her mind, and she sat upright. She hadn't meant to ditch Jeffrey, but that had been the upshot of her behavior. "Do you think Jeffrey's mad at me?" she called out.

Mitch paused in the doorway. "I think Jeffrey's laughing at *me*."

"I don't understand."

He turned. "He all but dared me...in fact, he did dare me to dance with you."

She still didn't understand.

"He's not mad," said Mitch. "Trust me on that."

There was a knock on the suite's outer door.

"Meet me on the balcony?" Mitch repeated.

Jenny nodded, swallowing her worry. Mitch and Jeffrey were very good friends. She had to trust that Mitch knew what he was talking about.

She stayed in bed until the voices disappeared and the suite door whooshed shut. A few seconds later, she heard the balcony door slide open.

She made a quick trip to the bathroom to freshen up, then she glanced around the bedroom for something to wear. Her crumpled, stale dress seemed to be the only option. But then Mitch's tux jacket caught her eye.

She padded into the living room, slipping it on. It smelled like him, and she inhaled deeply. Then, on impulse, she looped his bow tie around her neck.

She folded the wide garment closed around her body and headed out to join him on the balcony.

When she stepped outside, he scanned her body and grinned. "You do know there are robes in the closet."

"I'm happy with this." She helped herself to a steaming cup of coffee, crossing to a padded wicker chair opposite.

A quick glance around the balcony overlooking Lady Bird Lake told her it was completely private. She sat down, leaning back, letting the jacket fall open around her.

Mitch's gaze zeroed in on her nudity, and he stared at her in silence for a long moment. "Nice tie."

She took a casual sip of the coffee. "I stole it from a guy I slept with."

"You know you're not going home today."

She spoke over the rim. "I'm not?"

He slowly shook his head. "I don't think you'll even be leaving this suite."

"I'll be late for work on Monday."

"Ever been late before?"

"Not even once."

"The boss'll forgive you."

She felt her heartbeat deepen and her stomach flutter. She swallowed. "You sure?"

His eyes turned to blue smoke. "I am positive."

They'd finally left the hotel around three o'clock in the afternoon. Mitch had bought Jenny some clothes at the hotel gift shop, and he'd assured her Jeffrey would clue in Cole and Emily. And after a walk through a lakeshore park, they'd come across a gorgeous botanical garden, wandering hand in hand amongst the trees, succulents and colorful flowers. They'd ended up in a downtown club, listening to a local country band and laughing over burgers and colas.

Then they'd spent another night together, stretching out the trip to the last second, before taking a compact private plane back to Royal.

It was nearly noon before Jenny arrived at the TCC offices. The outer door was closed, so she knew she'd beaten Mitch to work. She hustled her way along the short hallway.

"Finally," came an exasperated male voice from behind her.

Jenny glanced over her shoulder to see Brad Price catching up to her.

"Where have you been?" he demanded, taking her by surprise.

She concentrated on inserting her key into the office lock. "Good morning, Brad."

"It's afternoon," came his sharp retort.

Jenny pushed open the heavy door and glanced down at her watch. He was right about that.

Brad followed her inside. "I understood the office opened at nine?" It was more a rebuke than a question.

"I've been in Austin." Mitch's voice joined the conversation, and Jenny turned to see him stride through the open doorway. "Won an award at the Longhorn Banquet," he said to Brad. "Don't know if you heard."

"What about Jenny?" Brad challenged.

"I gave her the day off."

Brad folded his arms across the chest of his business suit. "I think we should be clear on the policy regarding office hours."

Mitch widened his stance. "Win the election in December, and you can write any policy you want."

A tense moment of silence ensued.

"I need to talk to you," said Brad.

Mitch gestured to his office. "Come on in."

Once Mitch's office door closed behind the two men, Jenny breathed a sigh of relief. She tucked away her purse, turned on her computer and pressed the button to listen to her voice mail.

As she moved into her regular routine, uncertainty crowded in. They were back on their home turf again. Would Mitch end things as abruptly as he had last time? Was she ready to have her heart crushed so quickly?

Drawing a breath, she reflexively raised her hands to her chest and pressed them down. She'd gone into this thing with her eyes wide open. She needed to guard her heart, and she needed to be ready to walk away at a moment's notice.

Mitch wasn't long-term. And the new, impulsive, carefree Jenny had to be ready to accept that. What they had at the moment was fun and exciting. She didn't need to quantify, classify and organize every nuance of their relationship.

She blew out her breath. She typed in the answer to a routine email request for information on the TCC. Then she opened a note of complaint about the proposed new clubhouse. She added it to the folder to bring to the attention of the board.

Then the phone rang, and she spent twenty minutes going over the rental options for a bride-to-be, the daughter of one of the long-term TCC members. It was going to be a spring wedding and, luckily, they were able to find a mutually workable date for the main hall and the grounds.

As she hung up the phone, Brad appeared. He bid her a reserved goodbye, and left.

"Jenny?" came Mitch's formal voice from inside his office.

Her stomach clenched with nerves. Was this going to be an abrupt and final kiss-off? Would Mitch once again suggest they forget their lovemaking ever happened and go back to normal?

"Jenny?" he called again.

She swallowed. "On my way." Then she reflexively grabbed a notepad and pen. Maybe it was nothing. Maybe he simply wanted to talk about business.

But when she paused in the doorway of the big, rectangular, dark-paneled room, he was frowning. He moved from behind the huge ebony desk, pushing the high-backed diamond leather chair out of the way.

"Close the door," he told her, and her heart sank.

She pushed back on the door, latching it shut, leaning against it for some kind of defense as he made his way past the round meeting table and the low conversation group of a leather couch and matching armchair.

"Sorry about that," he muttered.

She didn't know what to say.

"Brad's under a lot of stress right now. The election, the feud with Abigail, and now he's really under the gun with those blackmail threats."

"They're getting worse?" Jenny was one of a very small circle of people who knew Brad had received blackmail threats involving the paternity of an illegitimate child.

Mitch nodded, but he kept moving forward, closer, closer still, until he drew her into his arms. "God, I missed you."

"What about Brad?"

"Brad can find his own woman."

She cracked a smile, hugging him back as relief flooded through her.

He cradled her head against his chest.

"You dropped me off an hour ago," she reminded him. At Cole's house, she'd quickly changed into business clothes, jumped into her own car and driven directly to the office.

"Seems like longer." He cupped her face, drawing her back and leaning down to kiss her.

Relief continued to sift its way through every fiber of her body. He wasn't going to break it off, at least not this second. As the kiss went on, longing took the place of relief, until she was molded tightly against him, deepening their kiss.

He pulled back and sucked in a tight breath. "We can't do this."

For a moment, her heart stood still.

"Not in the office," he continued. Then he dropped his arms and took a step back. He raked a hand through his dark hair. "I'm thinking, at least for now, we should be circumspect while we're here."

Jenny gave herself a little shake, then nodded her head. He was saying the fling should continue, right? But they should keep it a secret? Could that work?

Certainly Emily and Cole had figured it out, since she was supposed to have stayed at Cole's rented house in Austin. And Jeffrey knew they'd left the banquet together. How clandestine was Mitch thinking they could be?

She longed to ask him what he meant, but with the relationship so new and tentative, she didn't dare go into specific detail. Besides, that was old Jenny. New Jenny could go with the flow.

Maybe.

"I'm going to try to focus on work," Mitch told her with a sheepish grin. "Can you do the same? For a few hours? Then I'll drop by Cole's later?"

Jenny nodded more vigorously this time. She could do that.

"It's a weird time," he said, suddenly sounding tired, face

pinched in worry. He shook his head, one hand going out to brace against the back of an armchair. "You helped me over the past two days. I'm grateful. But it's starting to sink in, you know?"

She knew. She remembered. Their exhilarating weekend together was one thing. But his career had also ended. She took a step toward him. "Anything I can do?"

"I wish there was." Unexpectedly, a small smile twitched the corners of his mouth. "There is one thing you can do. But your special brand of physical and emotional therapy will have to wait until after business hours."

She was relieved to see the worry ease from his expression. "You know I'm just a temporary stopgap."

"I'll take it anyway." His midnight blue gaze bore into hers.

"Did you think about this possibility at all?" she found herself asking.

"I tried very hard not to."

"You had no kind of a plan?"

He shook his head. "Every single one of my coaches taught me to visualize success, not failure. When the tackles are bearing down on you, and the receiver is out of position, you don't dare, not even for one second, picture that ball missing the hands of the receiver. It's the kiss of death."

She found herself easing closer still.

"So, yeah, I knew this might be a career-ending injury," he admitted. "But I never let my mind go down the pathway to what that meant. I'm running blind here, Jenny."

She longed to reach out to him. But she mustered her self-control. "Can I hug you later?" she asked, voice low and throbbing.

"Hugging is the least of what I was counting on for later."

Jenny was surprised to find Emily sitting at the breakfast bar in Cole's kitchen, munching her way through one of his cook's famous oatmeal almond cookies.

"You just get home?" asked Emily.

"Are you waiting for me?" Jenny slowed to a halt, wondering how much, if anything, Emily had figured out.

Emily glanced a little guiltily toward the back hallway. "I'm visiting Cole."

Well, well, well. This was interesting.

Jenny pulled out one of the breakfast bar stools and climbed up, cornerwise to Emily. She searched her friend's expression for a clue. "*You're* visiting Cole?"

Emily responded with a sly grin, taking a slow bite of her cookie and chewing. "*You* stayed an extra day in Austin."

Jenny returned the smile self-consciously. "I did."

"We couldn't help but notice you didn't come back to the rental house."

"Any more of those cookies left?" asked Jenny, leaning forward and reaching for the brightly colored tin. She eased off the lid and plunged her hand inside, concentrating on selecting one of the round, grainy treats. Then she glanced around the kitchen to confirm they were alone. "Mitch had a nice hotel suite."

"And, so…?" Emily probed.

Jenny shrugged. "So, I saw the hotel suite. Liked it. Decided to stay awhile."

"And?" Emily leaned forward. "Give. He's with you now? What changed his mind?"

Jenny hadn't wanted to examine that question too closely. Her best guess was that Mitch had changed his mind about her being too fragile to risk dating.

"Jenny?" Emily prompted.

"I don't know what to think," Jenny confided. "I guess I'm just taking it one day at a time, you know?"

Emily nodded, reaching out to pat Jenny's hand. "I hear you. Cole and I are just testing the waters. Messing around to see if anything happens."

Jenny took another contemplative bite of the cookie. "Messing around? Literally?"

"Started off a bit rocky at the dance," Emily told her in a low tone.

"Yeah?"

"I asked him if he thought Emilio would be willing to get me pregnant."

Jenny nearly choked on an almond. "You *what?*"

"After some discussion," Emily continued matter-of-factly, "we decided Cole should do the job himself."

"Seriously?"

Emily nodded.

"That must have been some dance."

"Yeah. Well." Emily got a faraway look in her eyes. "Apparently, you don't have to be that tall to be a kicker. I figure my sons can try out for the special teams."

"Or shortstop." Cole appeared from the hallway, crossed the kitchen and helped himself to a cookie from the tin, taking a position beside the patio door and leaning against the wall. "They might want to play baseball."

Jenny glanced from one to the other. They had to be joking. Didn't they? "Are you two seriously thinking about making a baby?"

"Don't misunderstand," Cole continued. "I plan to ask her to marry me just as soon as I find the right rock. But right now I'm kinda busy keeping her in my bed and away from the offensive line."

Again, Emily nodded her agreement.

"Ain't that a bitch?" Mitch's voice joined the conversation.

"Hey, Mitch," Cole greeted amicably, while Mitch took in the cookie fest and apparently decided to join them, helping himself.

"Have a good time in Austin?" asked Cole.

Mitch grinned, settling in next to Jenny. "Had a great time. You?" He bit down on half of the cookie.

"The best," said Cole.

Jenny took in the glow on Emily's and Cole's faces, and found her emotions calming down. They might be joking about getting pregnant, but their true message was that they'd fallen in love.

"You're getting married?" she asked, wanting to confirm the meaning of Cole's offhand remark.

Emily made a show of a heavy sigh. "I guess I will have to marry the guy."

Cole pulled her close against him. "She finally came to her senses."

"He's not that short," she admitted. "And he does have this incredible—"

Cole cut her off with a solid kiss, and Jenny found her gaze straying to Mitch. His answering smile warmed her heart.

"I brought you a present," he whispered, straightening away from Emily and Cole.

Curious, Jenny twisted to watch him cross the kitchen floor. He retrieved a flat gold box from the telephone table just inside the kitchen doorway.

"What is it?" she automatically asked, thoroughly puzzled by the gesture.

"Open it and see." He set it on the island countertop in front of her.

"Is this a joke?" For some reason, she steeled herself. What was this all about?

"I'm dead serious." He pushed it in her direction.

"Should we leave you two alone?" Cole asked.

Mitch gave him a mocking eye-roll. "It's not X-rated."

"Too bad," said Emily, and everyone looked her way. She shrugged. "It could be fun."

"Open it up," Mitch prompted Jenny.

She took a bracing breath and lifted the lid.

Pulling back the mauve tissue paper, she found a gently folded rainbow silk dress. It took her a moment to realize what he'd done, and then another long moment to speak. "You bought a new one?"

"It was a great dress," said Mitch, moving up close behind her, gazing over her shoulder and smoothing his broad palm down her hair to the back of her neck.

"What happened to the last one?" asked Cole, a thread of laughter in his voice.

"You'll never find out," Mitch answered.

Emily reached out and touched Jenny's arm. "You looked fabulous in it."

Jenny didn't know what to say. It was an expensive gift, a very thoughtful gift. She did love the dress, but things like this were going to make it hard for her to keep her relationship with Mitch in perspective.

"Would you have preferred something different?" he asked her in a low voice.

She shook her head. She would have preferred to not feel this tightness in her chest, this rush of soft emotions and the urge to bury herself against him and hold on forever. She felt vulnerable and frightened. The old Jenny would have demanded to know what the gift meant, and where Mitch thought he was going with all this.

But she couldn't do that. And, unfortunately, the new Jenny didn't have a coping mechanism for a guy who was sending out mixed messages.

"Anyone up for dinner?" asked Cole, breaking the silence. "Seafood? Gillian's Landing?"

"Sounds great to me," said Emily, sliding off her high chair.

Cole braced her while she settled her feet on the floor.

"Okay by you?" Mitch asked Jenny. "We can go back to my place and grill something instead."

Jenny shook her head. "No. Gillian's sounds great." Better not to spend too much time alone with Mitch, dreaming of things that might never be.

* * *

Later that night, Mitch reflected on how much he loved being alone with Jenny.

He lay in his bed, propped up on one elbow, the light sheet covering him from the waist down.

Jenny had slipped into one of his faded football jerseys and rolled the long sleeves up to her elbows. It was green and white, with the number twenty-two across the back, and it hung nearly down to her knees.

Her hair was mussed from their lovemaking, and she couldn't have looked more adorable.

"And this one?" she asked, lifting a gold trophy from the shelf beside his dresser.

"High school," he told her. "Junior year."

She held the etched plaque close to her face, squinting. "Player of The Year. All State."

"It was a good year. I had a lot of lucky breaks." He patted the bed beside him. "You must be getting cold out there."

She replaced the trophy, picking up the next one. "You need to dust these."

"If you're going through the entire set, it's going to take all night," he complained.

"The Dallas Devils?"

"College."

"It's heavy." She hefted the tall trophy.

"Careful."

"I won't break it."

Mitch rolled out of bed. "I don't want it to break you."

She giggled, as if his worry was absurd.

He strode across the hardwood floor and lifted the trophy from her hands, setting it safely back on the shelf.

"What are these?" She opened a cherrywood box that his mother had given him when he was about fifteen.

"Come back to bed."

"They're rings," she exclaimed, running her finger through the box. "They're gorgeous. Look at these."

"I've seen them."

"The Lightning Bowl. The Ibex Cup."

He bent to kiss her tender neck. "You can look at those any old time."

"Are these real diamonds?"

"I don't know. Probably."

"How many of these have you won?" She checked through the contents of the box.

"I have no idea." His kisses were making their way toward her lips.

She held a ring up to the light. "Tell me that's not a real emerald."

He didn't bother looking. "That's not a real emerald."

"You're lying. Look at that color and clarity."

"You want the ring? Take the ring."

"I don't think it'll fit." She dropped it and let it fall loosely onto the base of her thumb, spinning it around for a moment before putting it back.

Mitch gave up on kissing, pawing his way through the box and extracting a gold ring with a flat face, a ruby chip and the entwined platinum letters *S* and *C* in relief. "Try this one."

She accepted it in her palm. "It's nice."

"My first." He smiled. "Sixth grade. It might fit." He snagged her hand, slipping it on to the ring finger of her right hand.

Laughing, she tried to pull away.

But he held her still. "See, it fits fine."

"I'm not taking your ring."

"Why not?" Grinning, he kissed her palm. "It's not like I'm going to use it again. You want to go steady?" The words were out of his mouth before he could stop them.

Her smile disappeared. "Don't do that."

"I was just—"

"I know how you feel, Mitch. Don't mess around." She determinedly tugged off the ring.

He opened his mouth to explain. But what could he say? He'd done nothing but make his position on a serious relationship repeatedly and abundantly clear to her for the past few weeks.

"Sorry," he mumbled.

She dropped the ring back into the box. "Nothing to be sorry for." Then she pasted a determined smile on her face, snapped the wooden box shut and set it back on the shelf. "You've had an amazing career," she bravely carried on, but there was a warmth missing from the tone of her voice.

"You're what's amazing," he told her honestly, but she shifted away.

He wanted to kick himself. He'd hurt her feelings again. Hurt her feelings, frightened her and forced a cool distance between them, when all he wanted to do was carry her back to his bed and make love to her, or maybe just hold her in his arms for the next few hours, or days or weeks.

Eleven

After Mitch's stupid slipup about going steady last night, Jenny had left his house. It had been nothing but a joke, but it had obviously rattled her. And now he didn't know how to fix it.

This morning, he was frustrated and in no mood for Cole's interference. He glared at Cole across his office desk. But Cole didn't back down, parroting Mitch's words. "No, this is absolutely *not* rich, successful Cole Maddison, throwing *poor, pathetic* Mitch Hayward a bone."

"Then give me an explanation."

"The explanation is that you should get your head out of your ass."

"You're saying the White House randomly thought of me? A washed-up quarterback from Royal, Texas, who hasn't won a significant sports award in nearly a decade?"

"No. Someone at the White House probably watched your touchdown rush in the Folder Cup, saw your charitable endorsements to Childhood Special Teams, read about your work with underprivileged teenage players, noticed the hundreds of thousands of hits on your fan site and heard about your *Youth Outreach Award from the governor last week!*"

"Keep your voice down." Mitch's office door was closed, but Jenny could arrive at any moment.

"Then listen to me. This is not some fabricated, make-work, patronage position invented out of pity. You'd have a staff, a budget, three regional offices and a mandate that covers the country."

Mitch drew back, trying to wrap his head around the unexpected proposal. "And it's the *President's* council."

"The President's Council on Physical Fitness." Cole's voice was flat, his frustration still evident. "You'd be the Director for Children and Youth."

Mitch tried to picture it, but couldn't.

"Listen," said Cole, backing off and plunking down in one of the two guest chairs at the front of Mitch's desk. "It sucks that you got hurt. It truly does. But you did, and you can't change that. So, you can sit around and cry about it, or you can pick yourself up and dust yourself off, and get going on the rest of your life."

Mitch resented Cole's implication. "Have I, *ever once,* come whining to you in self-pity?"

"You've got a lot of self-discipline. I'll give you that. But actions speak louder than words." Cole glanced around the big office. "In December, this gig's going to end. And then what?"

Mitch had been trying hard not to think about that. But Cole was dead right on that count.

"And it has to be in D.C.?" Mitch forced himself to think through the potential of the unexpected offer.

"You gotta be where the action is. Part of your job will be to schmooze senators and congressmen to make sure the program is well funded."

"I don't schmooze."

Cole barked out a laugh. "After the embezzlement and sabotage here two years ago, you nearly single-handedly brought the TCC back from the brink of disaster to a solid, thriving organization."

Mitch gave a snort of disbelief. "If this paternity thing with Brad blows up..."

"I'm sure you'll deal with that, too. My point is, you do know how to schmooze. You've got the gift for talking anybody into anything."

Mitch knew he could hold his own when it came to persuasion. He'd never thought of it as lobbying, but he supposed that wasn't too much of a stretch.

"And your celebrity doesn't hurt one little bit," Cole continued. "Plus, you've proven your ability to engage young people beyond the realm of sports. I can't imagine anyone more perfect for the job."

"Do you need a soapbox of some kind to stand on?"

"Was that a joke about my height?"

Mitch barked out a laugh at Cole's unexpected response. "Emily really got to you over the short thing, didn't she?"

"Emily...has seen the light."

"Congratulations on that, by the way."

Cole gave a nod of acceptance. Then he waggled his brow. "Take a look." He reached into his jacket pocket and extracted a black velvet box, handing it over to Mitch.

"You're going to ask her?"

"I am."

Mitch snapped open the box to reveal a big square-cut diamond surrounded by miniature sapphires. Something hitched in his stomach, and he found himself thinking about the ring he'd offered Jenny last night. Stupid.

He had nothing in him but a joke, while Cole was ready to take a lifetime plunge.

"You worried?" he asked, genuinely curious about how Cole could be so certain about his decision.

"Not really. I'm sure she'll say yes."

That wasn't what Mitch meant. But he had to admire Cole's confidence. "As long as you're sure."

"What's not to be sure about?"

"It's for the rest of your life."

"Hey, when you know, you know."

Mitch closed the box and handed it back. Would he know? Should he know? Did he know?

"Did you like the ring?" Cole asked.

"It's fine," Mitch answered absently.

Cole grinned. "You couldn't give a damn, could you?"

"Not in my frame of reference," he lied, pretending he wasn't thinking about putting more than just a football ring on Jenny's finger.

He shook away the ridiculous idea. This was a brand-new infatuation, a knee-jerk reaction to his career ending. And if he tried to make more of it, tried to force it, he risked hurting Jenny even more than he already had.

"D.C., you say?" he asked Cole.

"Yeah. Why do you keep asking?"

When he thought about leaving, Mitch's thoughts went straight to Jenny.

There was no good choice in all this.

"Go to D.C.," Cole insisted. "Check it out. See if it fits. If it does, you'll have a great Beltway office. You'll be doing good for the youth of America. It'll keep you out of trouble. And they'll pay mileage on your jet."

Mitch drummed his fingers on the desktop. He supposed there was no harm in talking. And, who knew, maybe they'd be willing to wait a few weeks, or maybe a couple of months. Surely by then his relationship with Jenny would have run its course. She'd probably be itching to be rid of him.

"You'll keep this to yourself?" he asked Cole.

"Won't tell a soul. Not even Emily."

Especially not Emily. If Mitch did this, *if* he did this, he'd have to be very careful about when and how he told Jenny in order to keep from hurting her.

As she stared at the three sets of house plans taped to the wall in the mostly bare, airy room on the second floor of Cole's house, Jenny tried to forget about the debacle two days ago, when Mitch had offered her the ring.

Mitch's joke about going steady had driven home for her just how quickly and how thoroughly she'd fallen under his spell. In the split second it had taken for her to come to her senses, she'd realized how desperately she wanted go steady with him, to have him be an ongoing part of her life.

"Time's up," Emily said from beside her. "They're shaping the foundation tomorrow. Are you going with your heart or your head?"

Emily had been the one to insist that they continue to consider all three sets of plans.

Jenny's heart was leading her toward the whimsical French country house. But she'd trusted her heart last night, and look where it got her.

What started off as a relaxed romantic interlude had ended in awkwardness and embarrassment. She'd all but fled from Mitch's house, and then this morning, he'd abruptly left town with the lamest of excuses, some vague story about paperwork and the football team.

"I'm going with my head." She moved to stand in front of the two-story, three-bedroom, telling herself she'd be happy there.

Emily came up beside her. "Funny. Lately, I'm leaning toward my heart."

Jenny forced herself to smile, not wanting to inflict her mood on Emily's happiness. "Did he ask you yet?"

"Tonight."

"He gave you advance warning?"

"He says he found the right ring. And we have reservations on the rooftop at Chez Jacques. I can fill in the blanks."

"You're going all the way to Houston for dinner?"

Emily waved a dismissive hand. "There's a helicopter involved. Millionaires are crazy."

Jenny leaned into Emily's shoulder, determined to be happy for her good friend. "That's fantastic."

"It is," Emily sighed. "You can't even imagine how smart he is. He gets calls from New York and D.C., Switzerland and Brazil, movers and shakers in the high-tech world, politicians, even movie stars. They want his advice. They want to be his friend. And he's funny, wickedly funny. But he's not geeky. He's not even short."

Jenny couldn't help but smile at that. "He magically stopped being short? Imagine that."

Emily gave her hair a little toss. "Five-eleven's not short. I was giving him grief about it on the dance floor, when I was asking about Emilio." A blush formed on her face. "Man, was Cole ticked off about that. Anyway, he's making a point, and I realized he was towering over me. And then I realized how much sense he was making, and how much I respected his opinion."

She rolled her eyes. "Listen to me. I sound like a dork. Back to your house."

"You're not a dork."

Emily pointed. "So, this one."

"This one." Jenny nodded. "Definitely."

"I would have bet you were going to go the other way." Emily cocked her head at the French country house. "I was beginning to think—"

"Mitch left this morning," Jenny blurted out.

Emily drew back in obvious surprise. "Huh?"

"Not that I didn't expect it. It was bound to happen sooner or later." Jenny had given away her insecurities two nights ago, probably panicked Mitch. Why couldn't she have just joked right back? Why did she have to freeze up like a schoolgirl?

"What do you mean, he left?"

"He went to D.C."

"On business?"

"He said it was football business."

Emily searched Jenny's expression. "And?"

"And, I think he lied." Suddenly dizzy, Jenny braced a hand against the wall.

Emily reached for her. "Jenny?"

"I'm fine."

Emily took her arm and helped her to one of two armchairs in the corner of the large rectangular room.

"What the hell is going on?"

Embarrassed, Jenny eased down into the chair. "Same old, same old. I'm crazy about him, and he's just having a good time. I thought I could handle it. I really did."

"Did he say that?"

Jenny shook her head. "Two nights ago…well, he joked, and I kind of freaked, and this morning he left. And I don't know what that means. And I'm trying not to care. But I do care." Her chest hitched. "I really do."

Emily crouched down next to the armchair, placing her hand over Jenny's. "I'm so sorry I went on about me and Cole."

"I'm sorry to be such a wet blanket." Jenny felt a sting in the back of her eyes. "Honestly, I don't know why I'm so emotional."

"PMS?"

Jenny laughed. Wouldn't it be nice to have such a simple explanation? In fact, now that she thought about it, maybe that was the explanation. She did the math in her head.

She usually got her period on a Saturday. Was it this Saturday? It had been nearly three weeks since the wedding, and before that—

Her stomach crashed into a free fall.

"Jenny? You just turned white as a sheet." Emily tightened her hold.

Jenny struggled not to panic. "Do you have a calendar?"

"Sure. In my phone." Emily produced the phone and pressed a few buttons with her thumb, holding it out for Jenny to see.

"Which weekend did we go to the Albatross Club?"

Emily turned the phone so that she could see the calendar. "That had to be the twelfth. Because it was a pay week for me."

A roar sounded in Jenny's ears. "Oh, no."

"Oh, no, what?"

"Oh, frickin' *no*."

"What?"

"I had my period that weekend."

"And?"

"And, I'm just doing the math."

"But—" Emily's eyes went wide, and her mouth formed a perfect circle.

Jenny stood up from the armchair and took two staggering steps backward. "It can't be. No, no, no."

"The night of the wedding?"

Jenny made an inarticulate exclamation.

"You must have used a condom."

"We did. We *did*."

"Then the mathematical odds are in your favor."

"Right."

Emily was right. Jenny forced herself to calm down. What she needed now was more information.

At the interview in D.C., Mitch had been offered everything Cole predicted and more. It was a significant and meaningful job, with a laundry list of perks and a chance to work with kids all over the nation. If he had to leave professional football, there was no better way to do it than this.

So why was he hesitating?

Why had he asked the White House Senior Advisor for a few days to make up his mind? It wasn't geography. He'd never planned to stay in Royal long-term. And if he wasn't with the team, it didn't matter where he lived. The salary was great, plus he'd built up an almost embarrassing nest egg through appearances and endorsements over the years.

So, it wasn't the money. It was Jenny. It always came back to Jenny. He didn't want to leave her.

He paused in the lobby of the Rathcliffe Hotel, gazing unseeingly through a shop window. First he only saw a reflection of the lights behind him, then slowly his eyes focused on the shiny jewels in the display. Against a backdrop of autumn maple leaves, gold necklaces, platinum bracelets and colored stones of every description were arranged on crystal stands.

He found himself staring at a round diamond solitaire, set in platinum, with tiny emeralds at each side.

"Nobody buys an engagement ring in a hotel gift shop," came a familiar voice.

Mitch shook himself back to life and turned to see Jeffrey. "What are you doing here?"

"We're playing in Baltimore tomorrow night."

"And that brings you to this hotel how?" Mitch resented Jeffrey's sudden appearance. He really wanted to be alone.

"Cole told me you'd be here."

Mitch cursed out loud. "He *swore* he'd keep quiet about the job."

"He didn't tell me *why* you were here. Though you just did. What job?"

"It's nothing."

"You're looking at a job in D.C.?"

"None of your business."

"What about Jenny?"

"*None* of your business."

Jeffrey braced a hand against the wall. "You're zoned out staring at engagement rings here, Mitch."

"I'm not staring at anything. I'm just zoned out." Mitch paused. "I'm thinking about the job."

"So, that's it. You just leave her? Thanks for the memories."

"It was always going to be like that." Just not yet. *Not yet.*

"You're a moron, you know that?"

Mitch clamped his jaw against an angry outburst. What the hell was Jeffrey doing here anyway? "Why are you here?"

Jeffrey's tone abruptly changed. "I heard the verdict came in on your shoulder."

"Twenty to life," said Mitch, knowing he sounded bitter.

"Man, I'm sure sorry about that."

Jeffrey and Mitch's friendship definitely didn't lend itself to talking about their feelings.

"Don't worry about it."

"It sucks."

"I'll live."

"Mitch." There was clear compassion in Jeffrey's tone. He was in a better position than most people to understand what Mitch was going through.

"You know," Mitch gave in. "Half the time, I think, yeah, I've had a good run, better than most, longer than most. I am thirty, and it ain't gonna last forever. Other times, I want to put my fist through a wall."

"Might want to use the left."

Mitch coughed out a cold laugh. "Good advice."

Jeffrey slid his glance away. "You know I'm here for you, right?"

"Thanks." They didn't need to belabor the point. But Mitch appreciated the offer.

Jeffrey cleared his throat. "So, when does the job start?"

"I haven't said yes."

"Are you going to say yes?"

Good question. Mitch shrugged. "I guess it's more about the timing." So, how long did he need? Two weeks? Two months? The TCC Board had made it clear all along they would understand and make arrangements if he needed to make a career change. But how could he possibly pick an end date for the relationship?

"And more about Jenny?" Jeffrey guessed.

"It's complicated," Mitch allowed, tired of pussyfooting around.

"Make it simple."

"I can't."

"You know, man. If you don't want her."

Mitch felt his blood pressure spike, and his hands curled into fists. He struggled not to snarl at Jeffrey. "You can't have her."

"Dude. Did you just see what you did there?"

"Showed some good taste?"

"Your head flies off at the mere thought that some other guy might look at her."

"Not every other guy." Just guys like Jeffrey who would most certainly hurt her. Mostly. And, yeah, okay, all the other guys, too.

"Yes," Jeffrey articulated slowly. "Every other guy. And I've already made my position crystal clear when it comes to Jenny. So you have less reason to worry about me than most guys. But look at you."

Mitch couldn't argue. For a long moment, he found himself imagining her expression if he was to give her that ring in the window. And then what? Marry her?

Part of him wanted to go for it, but a more rational part worried this was all happening too fast. It couldn't be real.

"Let's go grab a beer," Jeffrey suggested.

"Only if we change the subject."

"No problem."

"The lounge is on five."

"Let's leave the hotel. There are some great places down Pennsylvania Ave."

Mitch shrugged. What did it matter? Liquor was probably as good a way as any to switch up his thought patterns. And he didn't really care where he drank it.

A uniformed doorman let them out, and they turned right, going against the majority of pedestrian traffic along the wide sidewalk. It was four in the afternoon, late enough that the business crowd was swelling the streets, while last-minute shoppers rushed through their errands. The street was a maze of cars, minivans, buses and high-end automobiles ferrying VIPs from meetings to dinners to corporate and political functions.

"See, if it was me," said Jeffrey, pulling on a glass shop door. "I'd wow her with something along these lines."

Confused, Mitch glanced at the sign. Too late, he realized Jeffrey had just ushered him into the showroom at Tiffany's.

"Very funny." Mitch gave a mock laugh, while a salesman quickly approached them, obviously appraising the quality of their suits and watches as he did.

"Good afternoon, sir," the man greeted heartily.

"Just looking," Mitch quickly put in.

"Something in a solitaire," said Jeffrey. "The last one he liked had a couple of small emeralds."

The man beamed. "I'm Roger Stromberg. At your service. Please, let me show you our Esteme collection."

He motioned them toward one side of the store, and Jeffrey immediately fell in behind.

"I'm outta here," Mitch declared.

Jeffrey clapped a firm hand on his back. "Wouldn't try it if I was you. You've got a bum shoulder, and I'm a better tackle."

"This joke's gone on long enough."

"He's got cold feet," Jeffrey loudly explained to the salesman, dropping his large frame into one of two padded chairs in front of a display case.

"I understand." The suited salesman gave a sage nod. "Thing to remember in this circumstance is that picking out a ring doesn't commit you to anything. We're happy to keep it on hold for a period of time. Or we'll simply use today to make sure you understand your options. Then if, at a later date, you want to make a quick decision, you're all set.

"These ones here—" he pulled three rings from the display and set them in their cases on top of the glass "—are all flawless, D and E." He glanced up. "Do you mind if I ask your price range?"

"Not an object," said Jeffrey.

Mitch gave up and took a seat. "I sure hope you're the guy popping the question," he said to Jeffrey. "Because I'm just a spectator on this."

Jeffrey and the salesman exchanged a significant glance, but Mitch just chuckled to himself. Jeffrey wasn't going to goad him into anything so rash as choosing a ring.

Twelve

Jenny was going to be a single mother.

She couldn't believe it. She could barely bring herself to acknowledge it, never mind say it out loud. She'd checked the test wand four times this morning. Twice in the bathroom, again halfway down the stairs, then she'd pulled it out of the trash once, just to be sure.

The line was blue.

She was pregnant.

Thank goodness Mitch was out of town. She'd landed right smack-dab in her mother's predicament. Difference was, she wasn't going to repeat her mother's mistake.

She absolutely would not let a man marry her because she was pregnant and then start hating her. Still, in her weaker moments, she'd caught herself thinking about telling Mitch, imagined him breaking into a wide smile, telling her he was happy, assuring her they were going to make it work. But then she'd exit Wonderland and pull herself together.

Reality was hitting her fast and hard. Since arriving at the office, she'd twice had to dash to the bathroom to vomit. And she was facing the stark fact that she was going to have a baby all by herself.

Just like her mother, she'd have to hold down a job, juggle day care and PTA meetings, make budgetary ends meet and try to comfort a lonely little boy or girl who desperately wanted siblings.

Working her way compulsively around the office, she shoved the sparkling clean coffeepot back into the freshly polished machine that sat on a compact, shiny countertop in the corner of the office. Then she centered the wicker basket of assorted teas that she'd lined up alphabetically by variety: blueberry, chamomile, Earl Grey, ginger, Irish breakfast, jasmine green, lemon, mint. They had only one peppermint left, and all the other packets were in even numbers. She briefly considered brewing and drinking it, but her stomach had rebelled.

Again, she said a silent thanks that Mitch was in D.C. If he'd been in the office, today would have been an even bigger disaster.

She rewiped the shelf that held the sugar packets, checked the coffee can to make sure it was at least half-full, centered the stainless steel faucet above the sink and refolded the dishcloth.

The desk phone rang, but she ignored it.

The last three numbers on the readout had been Emily's. Jenny had purposely escaped from the house this morning before Emily and Cole saw her. She knew if she didn't answer the office phone, Emily would show up at lunchtime. But she'd face that in an hour.

She glanced at the clock on the wall, noting it read 11:02. She automatically checked her watch, making sure the times synced up. Then she crossed to her desk and sat down, folding her hands on the pristine wooden top, trying to figure out what on earth to do next.

The red message light was flashing on the face of the phone. She didn't want to listen to Emily's voice and feel the guilt that came with ignoring her best friend. But there was an off chance it was a TCC member who needed something. And she couldn't ignore what might be an important matter. There were three weddings coming up this month.

Her throat closed up, and she was forced to swallow the lump. Three radiant, blissful brides would say their vows under the Leadership, Justice and Peace plaque, something that would never happen for Jenny. True love was obviously not in the cards for her. Fate had single motherhood in mind instead.

Blinking the moisture from her eyes, she determinedly lifted the telephone handset, pressing the button for voice mail. She entered the password and heard the computer-generated voice inform her there were two new messages.

The first one was from Emily, short and to the point, obviously worried and telling her to call back just as soon as possible. The second was from a member. Thankfully, it was for general information, and it could wait a few hours. Then she punched in Mitch's number and his pass-code, learning there was another message on his account.

She tapped her pen on the pad of message paper as a hearty male voice spoke. "It was great to get your message yesterday," it said. "I know you didn't ask me to call, but I didn't want to waste any time in offering my thanks and my congratulations. The entire D.C. office is looking forward to working with you, Mitch. As I said in the interview, we're flexible on timing. But I will courier over the employment documents in the next few days. As I'm sure you can appreciate, working this close to the White House staff, there's a fairly rigorous security procedure, and we should get that started. Call me when you get back to Royal. If I'm not in the office, Melanie will give you my private line. It was really great to meet you. We'll talk soon."

There was a click, and the line went silent. Jenny sat frozen, the phone still at her ear while the computerized voice listed the voice mail options.

"End of new messages," the computer voice said.

Jenny couldn't believe it. Mitch had gone to a job interview? He'd rushed out of town yesterday to find himself a new job?

She gave a slightly hysterical laugh. So much for going steady. He was obviously leaving Royal. And he was definitely leaving her.

Any small, lingering hope that she might have had for their future evaporated in the blink of an eye.

"Press star to disconnect," instructed the computerized voice.

Jenny's stomach rolled. Her gaze flew back to the clock on the wall. Mitch was probably on his way home right now. If he didn't make it to the office this afternoon, he'd definitely be here tomorrow morning.

What was she going to do? How was she going to face him? How could she possibly even hope to pretend everything was normal?

What if she had morning sickness tomorrow? Worse, what if she was sick every morning for the rest of the week, or the rest of the month? She'd never keep the pregnancy a secret.

She came shakily to her feet just as Emily burst through the door.

"Why aren't you answering?" Emily demanded, swinging the door shut and barreling forward. Then she halted midstride.

"Oh, no." Her hands reached out, and she came forward again, rounding the desk and pulling Jenny firmly into her arms. "You are, aren't you?"

Jenny nodded, twin tears leaking out. "The test this morning was positive."

"Oh, honey." Emily smoothed her hands down Jenny's back. "Why did you leave without me? Never mind. It doesn't matter. It's going to be okay. I promise you, it's going to be okay."

But it wasn't going to be okay. It was going to be very, very far from okay for a very long time.

"I have to get out of here," said Jenny, her voice shaking.

"Of course you do." Emily drew back to look at her. "We'll go to Cole's house. Or are you hungry? Should we go to the diner?"

Jenny's stomach lurched at the thought of greasy fries and heavy milkshakes.

"Uh-oh," Emily repeated. "Is it bad?"

"Pretty bad. But, oh." Jenny closed her eyes and waited for the nausea to pass. "I really have to get out of here. Not just out of the office. Out of Royal altogether. I have to leave before Mitch gets back."

Emily nodded. "You're worried about how to tell him. I understand."

"I'm not *telling* him at all."

"Well, no," Emily said gently. "It doesn't even have to be today."

Jenny grasped her friend's upper arms. "Emily. Listen to me. Mitch told me a thousand different ways that he wasn't in this for the long haul. He's nowhere near ready to commit. He went to D.C. for a job interview. And he accepted a position. He's leaving Royal. He's leaving me."

"But—"

"But, nothing. He doesn't want me. He sure doesn't want a baby. And I am not—I am *not* going to have my child raised by an unwilling father."

Emily's eyes narrowed in confusion. "You can't keep it a secret. He has friends in Royal. Cole will—"

"Not forever," Jenny conceded, knowing she'd have to eventually tell Mitch he was a father. "But I can keep it a secret for now." At least, she could if she wasn't around him. If she could figure out how to get away, a plausible excuse to get out of Royal until Mitch left permanently for D.C.

She braced her hand on the edge of the desk. "I need a plan. A good excuse to leave. Then he'll come back, resign from TCC, leave for his new job in D.C., and then I'll decide what to do and when to do it."

Emily bit her bottom lip. "I don't know, Jenny."

"It's the only way." Her throat closed over again, and her voice broke. "I can't trap him. I *won't* trap him, Em."

Emily wrapped a firm arm around Jenny's shoulders. "Then I'll help you. Of course I'll help you. You can go up to the cottage at Lake Angel, for a week, or two, or three. As long as you need. Tell Mitch it was an emergency. Leave him a message."

Jenny was nodding. "I could do that. I could tell him someone is sick." Her hand went to her stomach. "I'm definitely sick. And I can say I'm at a friend's house. I'll be at yours. It's not even a lie."

Emily gave a sad smile. "It's not even a lie."

Jenny sniffed, sitting down. "Are you sure your folks won't mind?"

"Not a bit. They won't be at the lake for months. The cottage is the perfect place for you to regroup."

Jenny turned her chair and started to type. She could barely make her fingers form the words that would take her away from Mitch forever. She was suddenly bone tired. She wanted to crawl into bed and sleep for a month. She didn't want to face Mitch or anyone else.

As Mitch powered his Corvette away from the small airport on the outskirts of Royal, his hand strayed from the gearshift to pat the small square package tucked away in his suit jacket pocket, while his mind settled comfortably into thoughts of Jenny. If someone had told him forty-eight hours ago that he'd be buying an engagement ring, he'd have told them they were out of their mind.

But things changed, people learned. They learned things about themselves, and they figured out things about others that had been staring them in the face for months. What Mitch had learned was that he wanted Jenny, now and forever. He loved her. And he wasn't about to let one more day go by without telling her so.

He swung off the interstate and took the three corners to River Road. He'd driven this route a thousand times, knew every curve, every bump, every blind spot. But he'd never driven it faster, never wished it were shorter. And by the time he pulled into the TCC parking lot, he was having a very stern talk with himself to calm down and curb his enthusiasm.

He couldn't tell Jenny he loved her next to the coffeemaker. And he sure couldn't propose to her at the office. He pushed the shifter into First, set the park brake and turned off the key.

He had to take her out on a date tonight, somewhere exotic and wildly romantic. Maybe they'd go to the beach again. There had to be dozens of fine restaurants overlooking Galveston Bay. He wanted something with candlelight and white linen, a private little alcove where he could say all the things he needed to say.

He took the TCC stairs two at a time, striding through the front foyer, heading directly to the second floor, down the short hallway and into the outer office.

"Jenny?" he breathed, before he realized she wasn't there.

He quickly moved to his own office, entering through the open door, expecting to see her inside, straightening his papers, watering his plants, putting his mail into those neat little piles, like she did every day.

He drew another blank and frowned.

Maybe she was in the conference room, or the ladies' room. He told himself to wait it out, but his feet took him back across the outer office, down the hallway and into the conference room.

It was empty, and he couldn't very well check the ladies' room. So he headed back to the office, cooling his heels, gazing unseeingly at the familiar surroundings.

It was quiet, somehow too quiet. It felt like a weekend, and it took him a moment to realize it was because her computer was shut off. Her chair was neatly pushed into the desk. There wasn't a single paper on her desktop, and the morning's mail was piled haphazardly in her in-basket.

Was Jenny away?

Could she have missed a day's work?

He ventured closer to her desk, spying a crisp white envelope in the center of the desk. His name was scrawled across it in Jenny's handwriting.

Mitch picked it up, staring, getting an unsettled feeling in the pit of his stomach. She'd left him a note? Why didn't she email, or text, or give him a call if she had to miss work?

He tore off the end of the envelope and slid out a single piece of paper.

Dear Mitch, it opened.

He read further through the letter, becoming more confused by the second. Jenny was gone?

He flipped over the sheet of paper, but there was no additional information on the back, no destination, no return date, no explanation of who was sick. Nothing.

He didn't know whether to be mad or worried.

He retrieved his cell phone and dialed her number.

It rang through to voice mail.

"Jenny," he said to the machine, struggling to keep his tone neutral. "It's me. I'm confused. Call me as soon as you can, okay?"

He hung up, waiting a long moment, took a deep breath, then pressed the speed dial for Cole.

Cole answered right away. "Maddison here."

"It's Mitch."

"Oh, hey, Mitch." There was definitely something off in Cole's tone. He knew something.

"I'm looking for Jenny," said Mitch, giving his friend one chance to be straight with him.

"Really?" Cole asked. "She's not at work?"

Mitch ran out of patience. "What the hell is going on?" he barked.

There was a long pause that only served to reinforce Mitch's suspicions.

"What do you mean?" asked Cole, his tone still carefully neutral.

Mitch's voice went to steel. "Where's Jenny?"

"I don't know."

"Bull. Emily has to know."

"She might," Cole replied. "But she didn't tell me."

Okay, this just got weirder by the second. "Where's Emily?"

"She's at work."

"So she's not the one who's sick? And she didn't go to some friend's place with Jenny?"

"No." Cole didn't elaborate.

"What did I miss?" Mitch demanded

"As far as I know, nothing."

"As far as you *know*? What kind of an answer is that?"

Cole's tone went back to normal. "They didn't tell me so I wouldn't have to lie to you. Something's obviously up, but I haven't a clue what it might be. Did you and Jenny fight? Did you do anything?"

"Like what?"

"I don't know, see a girl in D.C.? Maybe somebody saw you and—"

"I did *not* see a girl in D.C." Unless you counted the mental images of Jenny that followed him 24-7.

"Well, she took off for some reason," said Cole.

Mitch paced across the office. "Find out what it is. Talk to Emily."

Cole barked out a cold laugh. "You want me to compromise my relationship with my fiancée to help you?"

"Absolutely."

"You really don't know how these things work, do you?"

Mitch paused for a long second. "I'm learning," he admitted.

Cole went silent. "Elaborate."

Spill his guts? Own up to his feelings to Cole before he even told Jenny? "I don't think so."

"You want my help?"

Mitch punched the heel of his hand against the office wall. "Fine. There's a lecture from Jeffrey on squandering chances echoing inside my head, an engagement ring sitting in my jacket pocket and I'm ready to tear this state apart looking for Jenny."

"You bought an engagement ring?"

"Yes," Mitch hissed.

"You want to marry Jenny?"

"Who *else?*"

"Well, I don't know what the hell you did in D.C."

"I accepted a job and bought a ring."

Cole's tone turned to surprise. "You took the job?"

"Where is she, Cole? Help me find her."

The line was silent for long seconds. "Can I tell Emily you're proposing?"

"*No!* It's bad enough that you know before Jenny. You're not telling her best friend."

"I don't know how else I'm going to—"

"Lie, cheat, steal. I don't care."

"You're not asking much, are you?"

"I'd do it for you."

Cole hesitated a beat. "Fine. I'll talk to her tonight."

"Now."

"Tonight. Summon up a little patience. It's not my fault it took you this long to make up your mind."

"I didn't—" Fine. Mitch would own that mistake. He should have realized he was in love days and days ago. If he had, if he hadn't been such a stubborn idiot, he'd already be engaged to Jenny.

Assuming she'd have said yes.

Of course she'd have said yes.

He was sure of it.

Almost.

Jenny knew deep down inside that coming to Lake Angel had been the right decision. She was still nauseous in the morning, and it took her a good hour to get her stomach calmed down. People were bound to have noticed, especially Mitch.

He would have arrived back from D.C. yesterday. She'd kept her cell phone deliberately turned off. In her more optimistic moments, she was afraid he might try to call. But then pessimism would take over, and she was afraid he wouldn't bother.

She told herself it was better not to know. And, if he did

call, she'd probably break down and cry, confess everything, humiliate herself and back him into a corner where, heaven save them both, he might decide to try and do something noble.

She couldn't live with that.

So the cell phone was staying off.

It was nearly ten in the morning. She'd managed a slice of toast and some orange juice earlier, taking great care to eat slowly. Coffee was definitely out of the question. Just the thought of it made her stomach roil.

Now, she wandered through the compact two-bedroom lakefront cottage, opening up each of the windows and letting the breeze flow through. Emily's family truly did have the most beautiful, picturesque spot on the lake. The cottage was nestled into a small cove, backed by a lush green forest. A dock stretched out from the crescent strip of sandy beach that ended in big piles of jagged boulders on either side.

Other cottages were visible in the distance across the crystal-clear blue lake. When the sun went down, their lights twinkled on the airwaves. The neighbors on either side of the property seemed friendly, but not at all cloying. Mrs. Burroughs kept busy in her massive gardens, while the Claytons said they commuted most days to jobs in the nearby town of Rex Falls.

Jenny eased into the big cushioned wicker chair in the corner of the airy living room. She'd managed to keep down a prenatal vitamin this morning, and now she planned to sip her way through a glass of milk, taking up where she left off reading in a mystery novel. She forced herself to read her way through the words on the page, banishing her speculation on where Mitch was and what he was doing right now, and fighting the memories of their amazing days and nights together.

She could do this.

She focused.

Thirteen

Über-detective Norma Wessil had just broken into a luxury penthouse hotel suite, discovering the body of Terrance Milhouse, ex–hit man and prime suspect in the murder of socialite Bitsy Green. Terrance's body was in the bedroom, halfway out of the bed. The cops were on their way up the elevator. And Norma had foolishly touched the murder weapon, leaving her prints behind.

As Jenny read Norma's internal debate on whether to hide the weapon or wipe it clean, the door to the cottage suddenly burst wide open. Jenny nearly jumped out of her skin. Her head shot up, and her gaze focused on Mitch. *Mitch?* The book dropped to her lap.

She found her voice. "How on earth—"

"It was my fault," Cole confessed as he barreled in behind him.

Jenny jumped to her feet, backing toward the wall.

"What are you doing here?" Mitch demanded without preamble. "Why did you leave Royal?"

"What?" she rasped at Cole, her heart pounding fast, stomach contracting in dread.

"Don't blame Emily," Cole quickly elaborated. "I tricked her into giving you up."

"What?"

Emily had told Cole? Cole had told Mitch? Emily had actually betrayed her confidence?

Mitch was moving toward her. His blue-eyed gaze was compassionate and gentle. "Jenny," he breathed in what sounded like sympathy. She quickly realized he wasn't mad. He was something else entirely. And there was only one explanation. He knew she was pregnant.

No, no, no. This couldn't be happening. What had Emily done?

"Please don't blame Emily," Cole repeated.

Then Emily rushed in, breathing hard. "Jenny, please, I didn't mean to—"

But Jenny's brain was a haze of shock and fear. "Tell him *I was pregnant?*" she finished Emily's sentence.

The entire room went stock-still.

Emily cringed, and Mitch gave a long, slow blink.

"I tried to phone you," Emily put in helplessly.

"You're *pregnant?*" Mitch rasped.

Jenny opened her mouth, but nothing came out.

He hadn't known? Then what was he doing here?

Emily's hand went to her forehead. "I only told him where you were. I didn't…I wouldn't…"

Mitch stepped forward, blocking Jenny's view of Emily. His blue eyes had gone hard, and his mouth was grim. "You're pregnant? And you're hiding from me?"

Her world contracted to him alone. "I didn't—"

"Didn't what? Didn't want to tell me? Didn't think I deserved to know? What the hell is the matter with you?"

Jenny tried to swallow, battling a paper-dry throat. "You had made it abundantly clear," she managed, voice trembling, "that you weren't in this for the long-term. You didn't make a commitment, and I didn't ask you to make—"

"So you decided I was an irresponsible son of a bitch who'd walk out on a woman who was pregnant with my child?" He raked a hand through his hair. "What have I ever done, Jenny? What have I done to make you think so little of me?"

He didn't understand, and she wasn't explaining it right. "Don't you see?" she pleaded, fighting tears. "That's the point. I knew you wouldn't walk out on me. I knew you'd stay. I knew you'd try to be noble, and you'd hate me for it in the end." Her hand went to her stomach. "I can't live my parents' nightmare all over again."

His expression cleared, and his eyes softened, and his shoulders dropped from their tense position. "I'd never hate you, Jenny. I—"

"You can't change your feelings just because I'm having your baby." She gave a watery laugh. If only things worked that way. If only Mitch could feel about her the way she felt about him.

He reached for her hands. "But I don't have to—"

"You'd feel frustrated and trapped." She tried to tug away, but he wouldn't let her. "And you'd get angrier and angrier—"

"I would—"

"—until one day, the fighting would start. And it doesn't end, Mitch. The plates hit the wall one after the other, after the other." She involuntarily cringed at the last memory of her father's harsh voice, and her mother's helpless pleas. "In my house, my father finally started throwing the china cups. And then he walked out the door, and my mother told me it would be all right. We just have to clean it up."

Jenny stopped talking, breathing hard.

Mitch drew her toward him, his voice going soft and gentle. "I'm not your father, Jenny. He didn't love your mother. I love you. That's the difference."

She looked him fully in the eyes, knowing she had to be strong. If ever there was a moment in her life she had to say everything exactly right, this was it. "Words are easy, Mitch. Especially for you."

"You think I'm lying about loving you?"

"I think you want to be a good guy."

"I'm not a good guy."

"You are."

"And you are unbelievably stubborn." He smiled.

"You took a job in D.C.," Jenny accused. "How is that love? How is leaving me love?" Even as she spoke, she steeled herself against the persuasive words he was sure to speak.

"It is," he insisted.

"You don't even know what you're talking about."

"But I do."

Something tightened in Jenny's chest, but she warned herself not to believe him. Mitch was the consummate diplomat, and right now he thought his mission was to sway her. She had to stay strong for both of them.

Then his voice went lower, more intimate. "Love is when you know deep down in your soul that you're never going to look at another woman. It doesn't matter where you go, or what you do, or who propositions you. Your mind is full of one gorgeous, feisty, funny woman back in Royal, Texas, and she's spoiled you for the rest of the world."

He stopped and waited.

"You're *so* good at that," Jenny responded with all the emotional strength she could muster, fighting hard against the desire to buy into his fantasy. "What happens when it's time for you to talk your way out of my life?"

"Feel inside my pocket."

Her brows went up at the bizarre request. "Excuse me?"

He chuckled. "Not that pocket." Then he let go of one of her hands and tapped the breast pocket of his suit jacket. "Feel it."

Her mind still full of suspicion, she reached up. Gingerly, she pressed against the spot he'd indicated. It was a hard lump, and she shrugged her shoulders in incomprehension.

His mouth was curved into a smile as he reached inside and extracted a small box. It was pale green leather, almost silver in its sheen. He tilted it toward her, and she read the embossed words, "Marry Me."

Something the consistency of concrete slid through to the bottom of her stomach. It wasn't possible. There was no way.

Mitch lifted the lid to reveal a stunning diamond solitaire against a tiny satin pillow.

She blinked, while goose bumps tingled to life across her skin. "I don't understand?" she managed.

"Guys who aren't in love and who, by the way, have no earthly clue their girlfriends are pregnant, do not buy engagement rings and wander around with them in their pockets waiting for exactly the right moment."

"He's right about that," Cole put in, and Jenny saw Emily press an elbow into his ribs.

Mitch gave Jenny's hand a squeeze. "Will you marry me, Jenny? Please."

She gazed up at him. How could this be happening? He hadn't known she was pregnant. He'd had no idea there was any reason for him to be noble.

"I don't understand," she repeated.

His smile was tender, and his eyes shone blue-silver. "I love you, and I want you to marry me. And it has absolutely nothing to do with you being pregnant. Though, I'm thrilled about that. And I am going to be a fantastic father. And I am never, ever, *ever* leaving you, Jenny."

Tears formed in her eyes, and she glanced at Emily.

Emily was grinning ear to ear. "I believe the word you're looking for is *yes*."

Jenny shifted her incredulous gaze to Mitch. These weren't just words. He wasn't being diplomatic. He wasn't trying to make her feel good. He honestly—

She drew a shaky breath. "Yes."

He kissed her fast and hard and deep, and then scooped her up into his arms, glancing around. "Which one is your room?"

Jenny laughed in surprise, nodding to a door beside the kitchen.

"Excuse us," Mitch said over his shoulder to Cole and Emily.

"You might want to put the ring on her finger," Cole called from behind, laughter threading through his voice.

"Later," Mitch growled in Jenny's ear. "With flowers and champagne and me on one knee."

Lying in her cottage bed, Jenny gazed up at the diamond that sparkled on her finger. They hadn't bothered waiting for the flowers and champagne, hadn't even made it out of bed all afternoon. Emily and Cole had headed back to Royal, obviously seeing no reason to stick around and say goodbye.

Mitch's body was warm against Jenny's, a light sheet covering them both while the breeze from the ceiling fan wafted its way down.

His hand trailed over her stomach, cupping it with his warm palm. "So, I'm going to be a daddy."

She put her hand on top of his. "Yes, you are."

He kissed her temple. "You okay with all this?"

"I am now." She tipped her head to look at him. "You?"

"I'm not going to be like my father."

"And I'm not going to be like my mother."

His free arm went around her, and he gave her a squeeze. "We're going to do this right."

"And, apparently, we're going to do it in D.C.?"

"That was part of my plan. But only if you agree."

"It's a good job?" she asked, thinking she'd live anywhere in the world with Mitch. Sure, she had good friends in Royal, but Emily meant the most to her, and it looked like Emily's life was about to get very mobile. Cole had houses all over America, and in at least four other countries.

"It's a very good job," Mitch replied. "But you and the baby are my priority. We can stay in Royal if you want. I'll find something to do."

"Can we come back to visit?"

"As often as you want. We'll keep your house. Hell, we can keep mine if you'd rather. Two might be overkill."

"I do like my lot on the lakeshore," Jenny admitted. "And we'll have to teach the baby to swim somewhere."

"And there are those great French country house plans on your short list."

"I picked the other one."

"Not anymore you didn't."

Jenny couldn't help but smile at the conviction in his tone.

Mitch's hand flexed convulsively against her bare stomach. "A baby. It boggles the mind," he admitted in a whisper.

"Well, I'm excited."

"Yeah?" There was a salacious edge to his tone.

"Not that kind of excited."

He gave an exaggerated sigh. "Too bad."

"But I am hungry. I'm eating for two." She paused. "Well, one and a very little bit at the moment."

He drew her more comfortably into his arms. "It happened that very first night?"

"That very first night."

"It must have been fate."

"I think it was Emily's burgundy dress."

"That was Emily's dress?"

"Yes."

"You should buy it from her."

Jenny laughed. "You know, she's probably not going to want to wear it again."

"I'll make her an offer." Mitch glanced around. "I sure wish you had room service here."

"You better get up and cook me something. I'm in a delicate condition." For some reason, her stomach felt much stronger now.

He propped himself up on one elbow. "You need to eat?" Then he sat up and swung his legs over the edge of the bed. "What do you want? I'll make something right now."

She laughed. "Wow. This delicate condition thing is really going to work for me."

He turned and flicked his index finger across her nose. "No. This having Mitch Hayward in love with you is going to work for you."

"I'll take a cheeseburger, please."

He stood. "I'm bringing you a salad and a glass of milk with that."

His cell phone chimed from the pocket of his pants that had been discarded on the floor, and he bent to retrieve it.

He checked the display. "Cole."

"Tell them they didn't have to leave."

"Oh, yes, they did." He pressed a button. "Yeah?"

Mitch paused to listen for a moment, then he shifted the phone out of the way. "Cole wants to know if he can spill the beans. The temporary admin person heard that message on the office voice mail from D.C., and people are wondering where you've gone."

Jenny shrugged. She was over the moon with happiness. Cole could shout the news from the rooftops. In fact, if he didn't, she just might.

Mitch went back to the phone and said, "Go for it." Then he laughed. "Are you serious? Why?"

"What?" asked Jenny, but Mitch held up his index finger.

"It'll be up to Jenny," he said. He shook his head. "People are strange. Okay. Call you when we get back to town."

"What?" she asked after he'd signed off.

"Apparently, Brad is talking to Cole about making the Tigers' home city Royal and giving me a job in management."

"Wouldn't they have to build a stadium?"

"I suspect this had more to do with Brad distracting the

electorate from the blackmail issue than any serious bid for the team."

"Would you do it?" Jenny pulled back the covers and got out of bed herself. Burgers on the deck watching the sunset with Mitch would be fabulous.

"Up to you." Mitch stuffed one leg into his slacks.

"Do I have to decide now?"

"You absolutely do not have to decide now. I told the people in D.C. that I need a couple more months in Royal." He moved around the bed to where she was retrieving new underwear and pulled her into his arms. "I was hoping to spend it with you."

"Before you broke my heart?" She settled against his bare chest and the cool fabric of his slacks, reveling in the feel of his strong arms around her, wondering if dinner could wait.

"By that time, I'd come to the conclusion you'd be the one breaking mine."

"Never," she whispered, stretching up for a kiss that somehow went on and on.

Mitch was the one to pull back. "I *am* going to feed you," he vowed.

"It can wait."

"No, it can't. Our baby is hungry."

Jenny's heart melted into a pool of joy. "I love you, Mitch."

His expression sobered, and he gently cupped her cheek with his palm. "I love you so much, Jenny." Then he sighed. "Took me a long time to work that out, didn't it?"

The tenderness in his expression went straight through to her soul. "It doesn't matter. Not anymore. We have the rest of our lives together."

* * * * *